THE PROMISED PRINCESS

THE PROMISED PRINCESS

BRITTANY L CARR

Contents

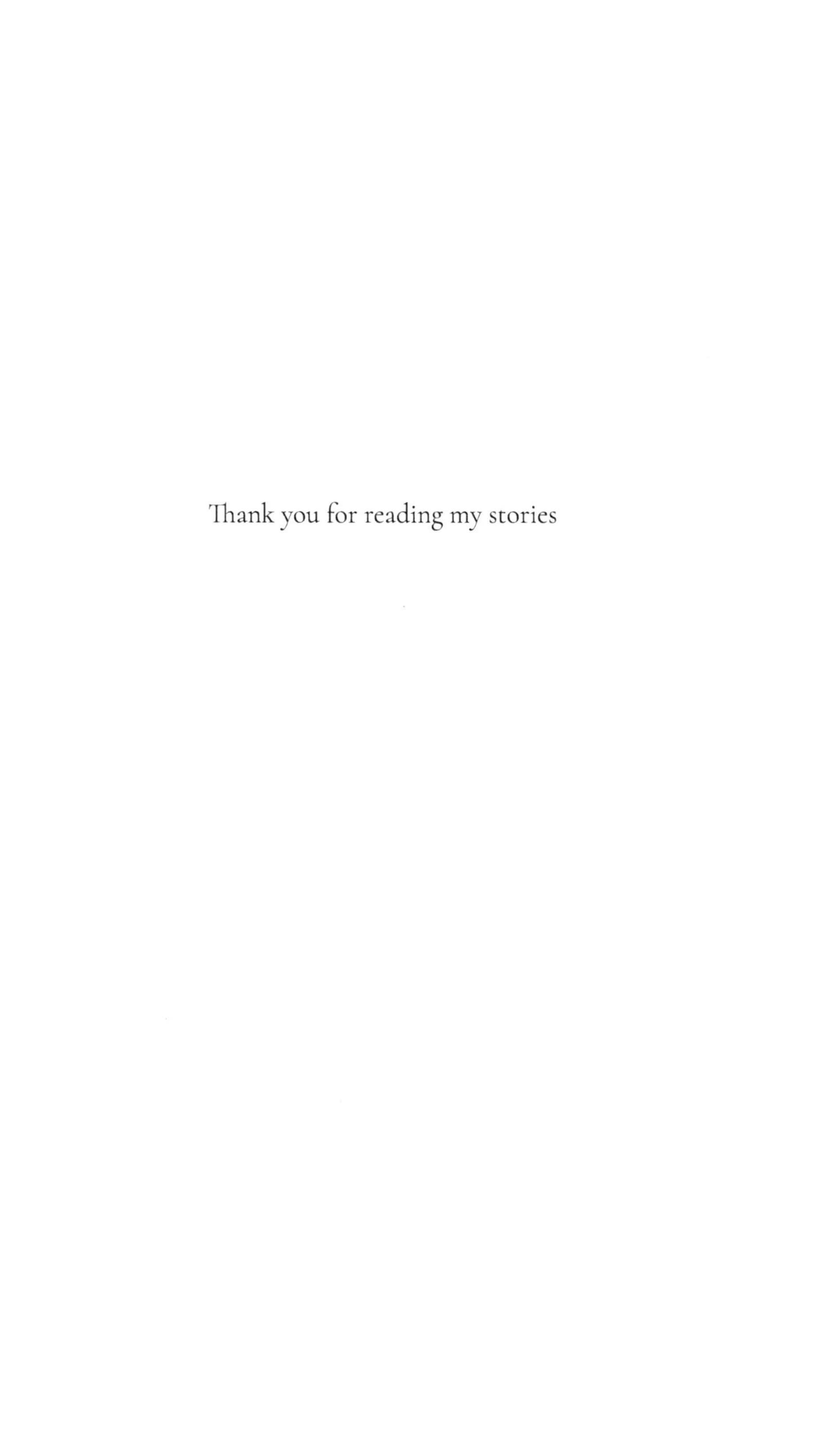

Thank you for reading my stories

One

Tandy

Tandy stared at the woman in front of her without emotion, her face completely blank. Even as the woman continued to spew ridiculous and baseless lies, Tandy remained still. She had been released from the reform school and handed over to the family nearest the castle only hours ago and had maintained a neutral expression the entire time she had been there. Since her arrival, her childhood friend had tried everything she could to get Tandy to react. However, Tandy knew that what Mariana said wasn't true and had no reason to contradict her. Any contradiction she made would have been met with resistance, anyway. She sat there unresponsive to the nasty words being thrown in her face, masterfully hiding her own feelings. No one would be able to tell what she was thinking, least of all Mariana, just as the Fine Etiquette and Reform School had trained her.

"He told me that he'd be disgusted to share a bed with someone that looks like you," Mariana sneered as she grew more and more frustrated at Tandy's lack of reaction. The old Tandy would have rolled her eyes at the comment as Prince Davian had taken Tandy as his lover years before the betrothal was even announced. Sex started young in the Royal Circle, something Mariana was thoroughly aware.

"You're hardly what anyone would call Princess material, and you're certainly not woman enough to have a Prince in your bed," she insisted as Tandy only blinked at her. Mariana narrowed her eyes and leaned towards her, nearly knocking the teapot over in her desperation to upset Tandy. "At least if you looked like me, you'd have a real chance with him. I don't have to do anything to get him into *my* bed."

The lies were half assed at best, Tandy knew. Davian had always been unable to keep his hands to himself, and she hadn't had the self control all those years ago to deny him what they both wanted. Fucking in the dark corners of the palace was how they spent her early teenage years, and she was sure Mariana remembered the details that Tandy had shared.

"It's a pity I'm the one betrothed to the Prince and not you, seeing as how in love you both are," she sipped her tea, forcing her lips to curve into a polite smile.

"You're a brainless whore with nothing to show for it," Mariana said through gritted teeth but Tandy only blinked at the insult. She was not only very highly educated, but she was a Duchess betrothed to the future King as Mariana well knew. Her title and betrothal status spoke for itself, though she did wish Mariana would take her place.

As she continued to speak, Tandy could hear Mariana's mother through her stream of poisonous words. Martina had always encouraged Mariana to use her feminine wiles to her advantage, but it did not go the way Mariana had believed it would. The entire kingdom began to only see her as a woman that was easy to bed and not as wife material. Tandy knew she would have a hard time marrying due to her past, and she suspected Mariana knew, too.

Despite the years she had been away, Tandy knew that the reputation Martina had created for her daughter had kept her from marrying someone suitable. She would have flaunted a wedding ring the moment she saw Tandy if that were not the case.

As she reflected on Martina's ways as a mother in their younger years, Tandy couldn't help but think back on her own. Tandy's mother wasn't like Martina in any way. In fact, she hardly knew her mother at all. Simone was a polite and confident woman when it came to socializing in her vast circle of Royal acquaintances but Tandy saw little of her outside of those moments. She hadn't seen Simone in years and rarely received letters from her, either.

Despite having many siblings from her father's first marriage and more born during the years she spent in the reform school, she felt as though she was an orphan. She lacked the presence of a mother or father throughout her entire life, and was robbed of sisterhood as well. She wasn't sure who to blame for her lack of family life, but wasted no breath over the loss as it was all she knew.

Tandy was drawn back to reality as she stared into Mariana's eyes. It was a tragedy in itself that Mariana had been led astray by her own mother because even in her anger, Mariana was strikingly beautiful. With straight black hair, lovely brown eyes and alluring curves, she had everything Tandy didn't. Tandy was tall and lean with light hair and eyes, but lacked the curves Mariana had. Martina had been jealous of Tandy's blonde curls and steely grey eyes and made a point to bring attention to their contrasting features whenever they were in the same room, as if she wanted the girls to be in conflict. For years they had sidestepped Martina's cruelty but in Tandy's absence it seemed the rivalry was blooming under her vile hands.

"He'll never want you like he wants me," Mariana continued. "He told me yellow hair is hideous on a girl." Tandy forced another polite smile onto her face. Mariana's rich brown eyes glared from across the table as her hands gripped the tea cup so tight her fingers turned white.

"Prince Davian is very familiar with what I have to offer," she reminded her.

A maid brushed into the room quietly as Mariana visibly tried to swallow her anger, slamming her cup onto the table. Tea sloshed over the side, spilling onto her skirts. She stood rigidly and walked from the room without another word. The maid quietly collected the dishes onto the tea cart and left as quietly as she entered. Tandy stood when the maid left and returned to the guest room where her bags were being stored. She could only wait to be delivered to her next keeper, the Prince.

She didn't want to return to the castle or to ever see Davian again, and she certainly did not want to marry him. She had written to her mother and father from the reform school and told them that she had no desire to follow this through, offering that Mariana could take her place instead. Her mother answered her letter with a firm no and told her the contract was binding. If either party scorned the betrothal, she'd be nothing more than a spinster in a few more years while her family was left bereft. She told Tandy to be grateful that Davian was a friend and not a stranger.

As she gazed out the window, her thoughts collected over the last time she had seen Prince Davian. The day of the ball thrown in honor of their betrothal had begun like any other day, but her excitement ended quickly. She had worn silver, the color that made her eyes shine bright and was thrilled to see her fiance and share the evening with him as a proper couple. However, when she arrived, she was only greeted by sneers and ire from her peers in the Circle as the adults continued to dance none the wiser.

In a moment, she had lost her girlhood and innocence amidst the slew of horrific rumors that poured from everyone's lips. Her entire reputation was ruined, and she had no understanding of who could slander her in such a way. Accused of being nothing more than a common whore, impregnated by a member of the Royal Circle and too incompetent to know who sired it, she was cast to the side upon entry of the ball. Each time she tried to speak to her fiance, she was denied. She was shunned from her friends entirely as she watched her fiance flirt and dance with other girls instead.

"No one would marry a girl like you, least of all love you," Davian had said after the last time she had tried to gain his attention. She had smiled with confusion as he spoke, dismayed by his words and unsure of how to react. But he pushed past her as he sneered, joining the other eligible young ladies across the room. Mariana had stood beside him as she looked down her nose at Tandy.

There had been a time when she had believed herself in love with Prince Davian, but that moment was short lived and long past. He had revealed his cruelty and the pain he left behind was something Tandy had never recovered from. She was unable to understand what had happened in the short time between the ball and the brunch they had shared earlier in the day. The Prince's words echoed through her mind as the days passed, locked away. His sneer as he spat at her was forever stained behind her eyelids. His cruel voice when he said that he could never love her again, that he would never marry someone like her, whispered through her ears each night as she tried to sleep.

It was clear that the only two people she ever loved, the two children she had grown up with, were never actually her friends. Nor had they ever loved her after all, if they were so swayed by a rumor.

She shook her head of those thoughts, trying to clear his voice from her mind. It had been years since she had been back in the Realm, having been sent away the very next morning to the Fine Etiquette and Reform School. At the time, she hadn't been sure what she'd done wrong to scorn her friends but learned that she'd never find peace and happiness, and that love and friendship had no place in her life.

Over and over she wondered why they could believe a rumor and deny her the right to prove herself pure. She had only ever been intimate with the Prince and had never so much as glanced at a man aside from her betrothed, but it was too late. The Royal Circle had made its claims, and Tandy was nothing but a whore. She sent countless letters to Davian and Mariana pleading for them to rescue her, but she had never received a response. Letter after letter was ignored and every attempt to explain herself and prove her innocence was denied. She couldn't stop writing to them, though, despite how hopeless it felt.

The only letters she received were a sparing few from her mother, and only ever reminders that she was still betrothed to the Prince. Though it made little sense that the betrothal remained despite her fiance believing heinous lies spread by the gossips who fabricated their own drama, Tandy could only wait for a response. She never received an answer from Davian to know if he had refuted the betrothal, and only had her mother's words to go by. She lived in a state of uncertainty for years as she waited at the reform school, hoping each day there would be her last.

For years she had tried to fight against the reform school breaking her down despite the consequences rebellion led to. It only made her suffering worse as they increased the punishments, but nothing was strong enough to wear her down.

Her spirit finally broke only a few months before her release when the Headmistress revealed the one who had requested her enrollment into the reform school. She told Tandy her *betrothed* had been the one to send her there to learn her place, but Tandy knew it was really a punishment for the rumors he had believed. The news both shocked and enraged her until she finally sealed her heart away for good. After the reveal, there was simply nothing left of Tandy. She stopped sending letters, she stopped fighting the lessons. She was the perfect student.

The title of Duchess that she was born into was a curse she could not break. She could only accept the world as it was, a place where no one could love her. She no longer believed in kindness or mercy as she had long lived without it and she prepared herself for a marriage filled with the same.

Two

Davian

Davian was set to take the throne when he turned thirty-five years old. However, there was no doubt that he had already been running the kingdom from his father's shadow for the last seven years. As the King's love for wine and women grew, his ability to perform even the most basic of tasks as ruler became nonexistent. Davian had no choice but to rise to meet the needs of his people and entertained every subject that called on the King, taking on meetings day after day without a break to compensate for his father's inadequacy.

For his last meeting of the day, a merchant led a discussion on Magic use along the borders where trading posts had less enforcement of the Royal laws. They were seeing a rise in unlicensed Magic sales and sickness from improper marketing of the ingredients. The lord had come from the north Port where his Province was affected by the rise in an Elixir of Oblivion. He requested a more strict patrol unit along the areas where Magic potions were being distributed illegally to protect the Realm. The meeting was well led but Davian could only grind his teeth. He had been fighting for the merchants like this man for years, but the numbers were increasing faster than he could send additional aid.

"As we have seen a rise in the making of this new elixir on the market, we are losing not only customers to this drink but also *lives*," the merchant said, aggrieved in his speech. "It is bringing down long standing families in the Ports and the Provinces within the Realm. Healthy sailors are succumbing to the elixir within the year when imbibing large doses, poverty is on the rise because there are no able bodied men and women to carry the communities. We need the help of the Crown desperately, Your Highness," the man begged. "We had believed that it would be eradicated from our homes *years* ago. Something needs to be done to save us all."

The merchant's words were cut off by the sound of snoring cutting through the room as the King nearly slipped off of his chair. Wordlessly, the King's advisors helped him to leave and all Davian could do was roll his eyes and grind his teeth. His father was a shameful King and he resented the man for it.

"Continue, my Lord," Davian told him, intending to hear the man's proposition through to the end despite the disruption.

Magic was not common in the inner regions of the kingdom as humans primarily lived in the Royal circle. It was illegal within the palace's province in order to protect the human Royals who could not entirely protect themselves from such power. A merchant had to provide records to the throne of all Magic items sold to ensure safety measures were met, but it was unfortunately becoming an epidemic as more and more people ignored the laws.

"I will arrange for more soldiers to be brought to the affected regions," he told the man before dismissing the meeting. "Our Kingdom will be protected, I will make sure of it." He made a note for himself to send for more recruitments in those areas, as well, to keep a flow of aide available for the rise in need.

After the remaining advisors and servants left the room, Davian's stomach churned as he realized the time. His fiance would arrive shortly and he had no choice but to go to his rooms and get ready for her.

The last time he had seen her, he had been excited to learn of his betrothal and couldn't wait to tell the world that the girl he loved would soon be his wife. The happiness soured during that afternoon as he drank wine and stood with the guests, a horrible sense of dread filling him as he waited for Tandy to arrive. Even still, the same sensation filled him any time he thought of his fiance and their future together. Dread seemed permanently etched into his soul from the moment the wine had touched his tongue, bitter and lacking any sweetness.

Part of him still didn't believe that Tandy, the sweet girl he loved, was capable of being a cheater. In fact, all of their memories together were passionate and full of love. He had known her for their whole lives and never *once* did she reveal such characteristics. He had always been unable to keep his hands off of Tandy when she had reciprocated his desire as teenagers, and nothing could stop them from fucking in each dark corner of every hall. But each time he received a letter addressed from Tandy after that day at the ball, the feelings of dread and anxiety were all consuming and as bitter as the memory of that wine.

He sat in silence after his servants helped him to dress for the arrival of the guests and tried to quell the worries from his mind, though it seemed impossible. The sound of horses on the stone met his ears, though he couldn't see it from his room. He headed to the throne room to greet them appropriately, his heart racing with each step. He made his way solemnly and attempted to school his expression into one of apathy, though a scowl was permanently etched onto his face. Davian sat on his throne beside the King, his mother sitting on the other side.

After what seemed like hours, the doors finally opened. His heart raced as he listened to the herald's announcement of names as people filed into the room one by one. He noticed Mariana first, in a light blue gown that exposed her chest. Her parents followed behind Mariana before Tandanea finally swept through the doors.

At first there wasn't much of a difference from the last time he had seen her. But as she continued walking towards the throne he realized how much she had changed. She dropped a curtsy at the base of the stairs where he saw her in her entirety for the first time in years. His brows raised, shocked at the beautiful woman before him. He somehow had expected her to still be a giggling teenager but the woman before him was striking, her curves modest yet unmistakable under her plain white gown. From her travels, her skin was sun kissed and freckles lined her nose. She was gorgeous, and his heart raced once again. Longing and dread warred within him at the sight of her. To be held in her arms again, to scream at her for her betrayal - he could hardly understand his own thoughts as she curtsied delicately.

Davian realized after a moment that the King had not greeted the group and stood to address them with a booming voice. Tandanea's eyes met his as he straightened, icy grey and stone cold. He couldn't tell what she was thinking which alarmed him and sent a flutter of dread and desire through his bones. Her expression lacked any inflection at all and he had no idea what to make of her, the woman he had spent the last seven years pretending didn't exist.

He quickly addressed them and dismissed the group after the short introductions and ordered the maids to lead their guests to the rooms they'd stay in until after the wedding. When the room was empty again, the King walked down the steps and headed out of the room without a word, followed by the Queen.

Davian led himself to the banquet hall and tried to steady his nerves. The table had been shortened down to a modest size for the small party and after going over the seating arrangements, he gazed out the window and stared over the garden as the flowers swayed in the breeze.

As he waited for Tandy and Mariana to arrive, he found the beat of his heart had steadied and the disquiet of his mind had settled. Seeing her again after all these years had been as though a festered wound was finally healing, her face soothing the ache in his chest that had long ailed him. He was at a loss as to where the bouts of dread had gone but was unable to explain it. He briefly glanced at a glass of wine on the table and the memory of his fear tasting of its dry bitter blend suddenly intensified.

Seeing Tandy had made him feel almost *good*, as though something was missing. He thought of her letters that he had ignored and the way they made him feel ill with bitter rage and despair and compared it to the memories of their childhood, how their romance only gave him a sense of peace. He found that was able to reflect on their memories before the ball without feeling sick, but the moment he switched to the memories made *after,* a swell of violent rage flowed through him. He thought of the letters once more and the taste of a dry and bitter wine seemed to ghost across his senses. He ground his teeth as he began to question *why* he had become so angry and distrusting and *when* it had initially begun. Why did some of his memories taste of wine lodged in his throat?

For a moment, he thought maybe the wine he'd had with lunch was upsetting his stomach. However, with a full schedule and constant meetings that week, he hadn't had even one glass in days. He felt calm and rational, and only a small sense of anger bubbled in his chest leftover from the tension he held in the conference room. Could his emotional disturbances have been so easily explained? The lack of drink made him feel clear headed after seeing Tandy again. After so many years of anguish at the mere suggestion of Tandy's name, he didn't know what to think.

Was the wine to blame? He asked himself. His memories of Tandy had only turned poisonous *after* his first sip of wine the day of their betrothal ball. Was it really so simple? Had he thrown away a happy future with his love over being unable to handle his booze? He was turning into his *father*. He growled under his breath at the thought, silently vowing to abstain from any form of liquor until he knew why he experienced the pain he had suffered over the years.

He shook his head and pinched the bridge of his nose. He was a damned fool. He needed the truth from Tandy and closure over the betrayal no matter what the truth turned out to be. He needed to know if she had fucked his friends and gave birth to one of their children while she was on tour of the Realm or if the whole thing was a made up rumor spread by someone who had wanted their marriage to fall through. He clenched his jaw at the thought, closing his eyes.

"Gods *fucking* damn it *all*," he spat.

Seven years was a long time to avoid finding out the truth. Even worse, Davian knew he could have found out sooner if he hadn't acted like his father, drinking to avoid the discomfort of his emotions and had actually *read* her letters. He knocked a glass from the table as his anger bloomed, sending it shattering to the floor. Illuminated by the sunset, the red wine staining the ground cast a sinister glow as Davian fought the rage boiling in his chest.

Three

Tandy

The place Tandy was exiled to was cold and hardly saw the sun, depriving Tandy of the warmth on her skin. When she finally made it out of the reform school, she had vowed to cherish the outdoors each time she was able to. She would spend as much time in the gardens that she possibly could to make up for the days spent in the cold and headed outside where she used to spend her time chasing Davian and Mariana around.

As she sniffed the honeysuckles, she heard a sound and turned to find the source. Mariana stood behind her with a surprised expression but Tandy said nothing. She only turned away and looked back out at the garden, steeling herself for another round of Mariana's cruel words. Mariana stepped closer to her as they stood there quietly in the cool breeze but said nothing. They stood there for a while before one of the maids called them to the carriages.

The women were led to the carriages where Mariana's parents climbed separately into the first two and left them to clamber into the third with each other. Tandy felt more alone at that moment than she had during the entirety of her schooling and travels. She hadn't made any friends at the reform school and received no letters from the ones she had grown up with.

While they sat in silence in the tight space, her stomach turned at the thought of the upcoming wedding. To be fucked by the man that accused you of awful things to produce an heir made her sick to even *think*. She had never seen him in such a state of anger before that night. He didn't seem like Davian, but like another being in his skin. His harsh and violent words felt like knives, his breath heavy with the bitter scent of wine, so unlike the man she loved.

She had been forced to endure countless lessons both physical and emotional at the reform school. She had practiced removing all traces of emotions in her face from the lessons that made her a shadow of who she once was. Despite the abuse, small pieces of who she used to be remained even if they were just remnants.

Her eyes grew tired and strained in the bright sun, making her turn away. She glanced at Mariana as she turned and noticed the woman gazing sadly out the window. As she looked at her, she noticed marks on Mariana's neck that hadn't been there during tea. The closer she looked, she also saw bruises on Mariana's wrists. Tandy turned to look back out the window and wondered what the marks were.

As the hours passed in the warm carriage, Mariana dozed across from her until the palace came into view. It was beautiful, just as it had always been, with flowers blooming and fountains spraying water into the sky. The white and gold of the palace walls amplified the light, making it hard to look at directly despite the sunset. They all climbed the stairs into the castle as Martina led the group, barely hiding her giddiness.

Tandy's dress and slippers kept her from moving as quickly as the rest, leaving quite a few paces between herself and Mariana. Just as they were about to be announced into the throne room,

Martina quickly grabbed her daughter's upper arm tightly and hissed loudly into her ear.

"You better be on your best behavior, no fucking around. This is the *palace*," she all but spat in Mariana's face.

"*Excuse you*," Tandy said in a low voice, forcing her brows into an angry glare. Martina let go of Mariana quickly as her eyes widened, surprised by Tandy's interruption as though she had forgotten she was there. She glared until Martina looked away, pushing past her daughter and husband with a huff. Mariana kept her eyes on her feet and glanced at Tandy, but she had already resumed her blank expression by the time she looked her way.

The herald called them into the room and Tandy strode in behind the others, curtsying before the King. She forced herself not to look at anyone in particular, even though she could feel Davian's eyes on her. She had no choice but to look at him as he rose to greet them in lieu of the King and met his eyes directly. Her stomach felt like lead as she maintained a neutral expression, giving away none of the pain and anxiety she was feeling. Davian gave them an introduction and sent them off with the promise that a servant would guide them to their rooms.

Mariana and Tandy's rooms were next to each other in the west wing, while Mariana's parents were kept in the east wing with all the guest rooms. Tandy was still unaware of the whereabouts of her own mother and father, but knew it didn't really matter as they wouldn't call on her anyway. Tandy did not care where Dav's room was but one of the maids pointed it out in the corner of the west wing, overlooking the rear of the castle. Tandy's bedroom overlooked the side gardens and Mariana's overlooked the front of the castle. With a large bathroom connected to her bedroom and an antechamber for hosting guests, it was quite spacious in her rooms though plain of any real decorations. The blankets and furniture were extravagant but aside from that, not much else was there. The sunset fell through the windows and reflected off the lake in a dazzling display of color that Tandy forgot was possible.

She gazed out the window as the maids emptied her bags into the drawers around the room. She could see the birds swimming in the gentle water from where she stood, glowing from the hues of the sun. She hoped she would be allowed to walk the path along the lake for the first time in years once again.

All too soon, the maids ushered her and Mariana back downstairs and into the banquet hall. She could see servants standing by the doors with trays of food laid out, and knew they were only waiting for the King's word to place them on the table. Tandy kept her eyes down like she was taught, docile and demure, and stood in front of the chair that had her name card on it. She waited for the King to call for them but Davian rose instead, announcing the meal to begin. She sat gently in her seat as a servant pulled the chair out for her.

Her eyes met Davian's as she straightened in her chair. His striking brown eyes stared unwaveringly at her, though a small scowl rested on his lips. As she noticed the tensing of his jaw, she knew he was still angry with her. Her stomach coiled tight as a wave of nausea filled her. She maintained her cool expression as she had been trained and would maintain it under any circumstance, even at the unpleasant swirl in her belly. If it made her lose her dinner later tonight, no one would know but her.

The meal was delicious but Tandy could only force down a mouthful or two. She pretended to chew exceedingly slowly and waited for the servants to come and clear everything away. Sitting beneath Davian's angry gaze made her feel intensely ill, unable to hide under his stare.

As they had eaten dinner, the King and Queen were drinking wine with Martina. Mariana's father was nearly catatonic during the entire meal and said not a word the entire time they sat there despite the boisterous laughter from his wife. *What is wrong with him?* Tandy wondered.

Mariana flinched suddenly when her mother slammed a glass down a little too hard. Unconsciously, she glanced at Davian when it happened. They shared a look for only a moment, before Dav scowled again. She was concerned for Mariana's safety and hoped Davian would see it as well. Thankfully, Davian stood up and offered the King a bow.

"I will be showing the ladies around the castle now, and refamiliarizing them with the estate," he announced. There was no room for disagreement in his tone but his words were unnecessary. The King didn't turn their way and continued drinking and laughing over the table.

The girls stood from their chairs, and accepted Davian's outstretched arms. They both looped their hands through his and made their way to the gardens. The sun had set completely as they had dinner and it was dark, but the moon looked over the land and left them with plenty of light. None of them said a word, and as soon as they were out of sight of the servants and maids, Davian dropped their arms. A lightning bug flew around Tandy's face, making her pause. They hadn't been in the north where she'd gone to school, but the sight of them filled her with a childlike wonder just as the gardens had.

Tandy looked around to find Davian and Mariana after the lightning bug flew away, but noticed them far ahead with their arms linked back together. Their heads were bowed together, and Tandy could faintly hear them whispering. She let them take the lead with no intention of chasing them down, knowing they did not want her in their way. She had memorized the blueprint of the palace long ago and could easily find her way back to her room without them, but waited. She knew they would have words for her first and stayed within their view to get it over with. Finally, they turned around when Tandy was closer, still looking at the flowers.

"Your lies will catch up to you, Tandy," Mariana spat, though Davian squeezed her arm and looked at her with a frown, shushing her as he tugged her back.

"I have never lied," Tandy said. Her light hair reflected the moon and gave her an ethereal glow as she spoke with no emotion. Mariana rolled her eyes and clutched Davian's arm tighter.

"It should be *me* here and you know it," Mariana said.

"As I wrote in my letters, I attempted to have you take my place as betrothed," she said evenly, stroking a white rose. "Despite my best efforts, the wedding will occur in one month. If this displeases Your Highness," she looked at Davian for a moment who looked shocked at her admission before looking back at the rose, "you have the ability to refute the betrothal at any point until then and I shall return to my schooling." She turned to them for a brief curtsy and walked away at an even pace.

When she made it back to her room, she was undressed by her maids and left in her nightclothes. At one point in her life, a conversation like that would have left her in tears. Though it was painful to lock each emotion tightly inside of her, she knew there would be no other way for her to survive in the Royal Circle. She laid in the large bed after locking her doors and fell into a fitful sleep.

Four

Davian

Davian had chewed on his tongue during the entire dinner. He thought over the nights where that bitter red wine was served with dinner and how a letter arrived *each time* he'd drank from the glass. The pungent taste overwhelming his senses as he gazed upon Tandy's perfect penmanship of his name on the front of the envelope. His brow furrowed for the entirety of the meal despite trying to maintain a neutral gaze as he tried to make sense of what it could all mean.

After so many years of discomfort when thinking of Tandy's return, his mind was somehow soothed by her presence across from him. When Davian and Tandy shared a look as Mariana flinched under her mother's crude behavior, he could only see his young love before him. Why would she care to react to Mariana's obvious fear if she wasn't genuine in her kindness? *You are a fool, Dav,* his mind supplied over and over as suspicion and doubt filled his mind.

When they left dinner, he had pulled Mariana ahead of Tandy to tell her of his suspicions. Mariana was not receptive to his words, only jittery and sporadic and would not listen to what Davian said. He whispered as loud as he could without Tandy hearing them, but she was resistant. She was entirely keyed up and intent on an altercation, pulling away from Davian's grasp.

"Did you drink wine today?" He asked her, needing to know if there was a reason for her sudden irritable behavior. If she hadn't had any, he would assume it was stress caused by the loud noises at dinner, but her response was immediate.

"Of course I did, but it was the shitty bitter blend I hate that keeps making its rounds through the Circle," she rolled her eyes. Davian bit his lip in thought, certain that the wine was the culprit. They turned toward Tandy after a moment and he hoped to be at least civil with a mild conversation, if for the sake of his marriage. Before he could stop her, Mariana began to shout harsh words at Tandy. Though he grabbed her arm and shushed her, she continued and he worried Tandy would think he agreed with Mariana. Before he could clarify himself, she spoke.

"I have never lied. As I wrote in my letters, I attempted to have you take my place as betrothed. Despite my best efforts, the wedding will occur in one month. If this displeases Your Highness, you have the ability to refute the betrothal at any point until then and I shall return to my schooling."

As she revealed her attempts to end their betrothal, Davian's throat felt tight. It hurt to hear the words, though he supposed he had brought it upon himself. The last seven years narrowed into a point as the reality of the abandonment Tandy faced made him ill, knowing he had ruined any chance he had with Tandy and reconciliation. Tandy walked quickly away and he groaned when the sound of a door shutting in the distance reached his ears.

"Mar, could you refrain from speaking in such a way to my betrothed?" Davian snapped, putting a hand to his head.

"*What?*" Mariana asked, confused. "After all this time, have you forgotten what she did to you?"

"All I know right now is that we *never* gave her the chance to explain or to apologize and I am still destined to marry her," he sighed heavily.

"I don't understand what's changed for you. Has she already seduced you and gained your trust once again? You know how it's going to end, Dav," she said angrily. "You're thinking with your dick."

"Shut the fuck *up*, Mar. Something is *wrong* here. Listen to me," he said, leaning into her. "Do not drink any wine until I say you can. You need to do this without a question, Mar. I need to find out why we both have a problem with that bitter red wine, why it's making us pissed and paranoid. It could be more potent, or it could be rancid and upsetting our constitutions. Either way, do *not* drink anything unless it's water, no matter *who* offers it to you."

"That wine is definitely rancid, now that you mention it," she agreed, looking up at him with wide brown eyes as they walked back to her room.

"Did you read the letters she sent?" Davian whispered as they neared their doors. Mariana tensed at the mention of the word which made Davian even more suspicious. Surely she felt the same way when it came to Tandy which made no sense at all.

"No, I didn't," she whispered back. "I *couldn't,*" she added.

"Did you read *any* of them?" He asked.

"No, my mother burned them in front of me," she admitted, her voice barely making a sound. "I really couldn't read them if I wanted to." Davian frowned at the admission and narrowed his eyes at the mention of Martina.

"Do we actually know where she's been all these years?" Davian asked as they reached Mariana's room.

"She's been gallivanting around the world on her parent's dime," Mariana said with a huff, repeating the same phrase that had been echoing through the Royal Circle for years.

"If she was traveling, there'd be a record of the Leighten family's carriage around the provinces and borders and receipts on their account, both of which do not exist. Besides, there is no proof in rumors, Mar," he said, running his hand through his hair. "Trust me, I was looking for signs of her all these years. She's been *gone.*"

"That's hypocritical of you to say when *you* are the one that told *me* about the rumors of her fucking everyone we know," she hissed.

"*You* told *me* that she was fucking everyone we know," he said, exasperated. His hands tugged on his hair as he groaned, frustrated by everything he was hearing. "Obviously something is wrong, here, Mar. Not only did your mother burn your letters from the *Prince's* betrothed, but something is wrong with the wine. Why am I feeling this way about letters and red wine?" He huffed. She moved to open her mouth but he shushed her. "We're not discussing this here. Just stay vigilant." He bid her goodnight and turned to go to his room.

When he made it to his rooms, his servants changed him into his night clothes. He wandered to his office and pulled open a drawer that was nearly hidden in the corner of the room and opened it, pulling out the box of letters he'd saved over the years. He glared at the box, angry with himself. While he had his ways of checking in with the Leighton family's treasury to find the areas they had spent money outside of their usual trading, there had been minimal changes on their books. The Leightons were on paper entirely missing from the Circle, but Davian had told himself over the years that it meant nothing and never pursued it further. He had relied on the word of the Circle to speculate on Tandy's location over the years, completely dismissing any information he learned in order to protect himself from the pain caused by hearing her name.

He reached for the box of letters, ready to face the anxiety they gave him. The amount of letters was astounding, the small square envelopes completely filling the box. She had sent the letters weekly despite their lack of response but finally, Tandanea had stopped altogether earlier that year. He wasn't sure why he kept all of them since even touching them filled him with dread, but he was unable to throw them away. It hurt worse to think about removing her existence from his life permanently and so kept them in the box. He had tried to open the letters and read them plenty of times, but whenever his hands reached for the small envelopes, another wave of anxiety made it impossible to think straight and his hands would tremble.

Just as before, they were still impossible to read. Even looking at the box where they sat for so long was painful and disorienting. He was breathless with the flood of fury that filled his chest and he fought the urge to throw the letters into the fire, to destroy the cause of his despair. He brought the letters to the window and headed back to his bed. He would read them, just not yet, and hoped a good night's rest would help.

***

He woke early and had his servants help him dress into exercise clothes. He went for a run most mornings as it was the only solitude he was able to get before being pulled into meetings, paperwork, and other duties and craved the small freedom it gave him. With the wedding just a few weeks away, his calendar consisted of preparations for each part of the celebration and offered no reprieve from his usual routine.

Davian headed to the parlour down the hall for brunch after changing from his run. At the table were Mariana and Tandanea sitting eerily quiet and Davian could only imagine the worst. Before he could speak, Tandanea stood and with a curtsy, left the room.

"I told her she makes me sick, gallivanting the world after fucking her fiances friends," Mariana told him.

"Gods damn it, Mar," he snapped, slamming his hand onto the table. "She will be the Queen no matter what anyone thinks about it and if anyone heard you say that, you would be found in a *lot* of trouble." Mariana frowned but nodded. "What did I just say to you last night about this?"

"I am sorry," she stuttered, looking at him with wide eyes. He quickly ate the breakfast he was offered by the servants and glared into the table.

"You need to remember your place, Mariana, or I can't help you when the wrong people hear you say such things about the soon to be Princess," he sighed. Mariana nodded with a frown. He stood and offered her his arm and led her back to her room without a word.

When he headed to his room, he nearly bumped into Tandanea as she stood in front of her doors. She looked at him as he approached unconsciously, but only blinked at him and curtsied before walking past him in the same direction he was heading.

"Take my arm," he told her his voice colder than he intended, still frustrated with Mariana.

"Yes, Your Highness," she said, taking his elbow with a blank expression. He didn't like the plain expression she had worn since her arrival and didn't know what to make of it. Her arm felt warm and soft in his and for a minute his emotions ran wild, shifting between anger and happiness rapidly. He knew he needed to talk to her one way or another considering the rapid approach of the wedding, but it didn't make his thoughts less overwhelming. They needed to discuss logistics just as well as they needed to discuss their past and their future, but Davian was certain she would be resistant to his attempts at reconciling and he couldn't blame her.

Though his jaw clenched shut for the entirety of the walk, he guided Tandy to the parlour where they'd spent their rainy days as children. He directed her to the plush couches in the room, still bright with the morning sun filtering through the windows that lined the entirety of the walls. A maid trailed into the room behind them and he quietly ordered for tea to be brought to them.

"I wanted to go over some things," Davian began while Tandanea sat perfectly still as she looked at him. "Firstly, our duty will be to provide an heir as swiftly as possible," he told her. Tandanea nodded and looked out the window, eyes turned to the birds flying around the lake. "Do you have anything to say about that?" He asked, unable to read her face.

"Whatever pleases you, Your Highness," she said, still looking away.

"You look well," he said stiffly, frustrated by her lack of emotion but desperate for a response.

"As do you, Your Highness," she said hollowly without even sparing a glance his way. He sighed at her response but realized that Tandanea didn't speak unless he spoke to her first. Davian stared at her and watched her face closely, noting that there wasn't even a flicker of emotion on her face. He didn't understand how someone could be so apathetic, so unlike the girl he had been raised with. He swallowed hard before continuing, knowing it was a hard discussion he would be opening.

"The second thing we need to discuss is what happened at the ball," he said slowly. "*And* what happened before the ball." Tandy slowly turned toward him but he could not tell what she was thinking at *all* and it was driving him mad.

Servants suddenly swept into the room and wordlessly poured them each a cup of tea. They placed a large tray of food on the table and left quietly. Davian grazed on the sandwiches but Tandanea didn't touch any of the food offered, only stirring the tea.

"You didn't eat last night, either," he frowned. She looked at him with her icy stare but said nothing. He sighed heavily, rubbing his face. He couldn't keep his emotions hidden the way she could, it was painfully obvious. "Tandy, it can't be like this," he said. "We have a lot we need to talk about. Just tell me the truth, did you do those things with the boys in the Circle?" For a moment, Tandy only looked at him. Her stone grey eyes bore into him and he had to force himself to maintain eye contact under her intense gaze. He suddenly felt stupid for asking that question and wished he could take it back, because surely she had told him in the letters she had sent over the years. She looked through him as if she realized he had not read them and though her face remained emotionless, he could not help but wonder if she was upset by his words.

"Last night you noticed the way Mariana acted with the loud noises," she said finally, evading his question. He remembered the look they shared and nodded. "I noticed bruises on her, as well, Prince Davian."

"Where?" He asked.

"Her neck and wrists," she told him, looking back out the window. His brows furrowed as he took in her words.

Something isn't right, he thought to himself. They sat quietly for a moment longer before he looked at her. He took in her grey eyes, her blonde curls. He shook his head and stood, reaching for Tandy's arm to lead her back to her room. She went with him obediently and once again his emotions flitted between anger and desperation. The warmth of her felt like safety and he truly didn't know what anything meant anymore.

His father had told him scandalous things the day of the betrothal ball. He had said that Tandy was a wolf in sheep skin. He said that money talks and women no matter their age would use their wiles on *anyone*. His words made Davian believe that his future wife had attempted to seduce the King, but he had brushed it off simply because Tandy would have been too young to know of such things when the betrothal originally began. When he met with some of his peers who told him of their flings with Tandy, though, his growing dread had hit an all time high and his sudden bout of distrust grew. He had no idea what was true, but the pain was *real* and so intense, he could only fight against it by lashing out at Tandy.

Why did they continue the betrothal if the King insisted she was not to be trusted, and *the Royal Circle thought her a whore?* Davian couldn't help but think.

His grip tightened on Tandy unintentionally as his thoughts swirled, but she remained unphased. He needed to talk to her for real *and* learn of what happened all those years ago. It was the only way there would be closure. No matter what happened in the past, they needed to reconcile for the sake of the crown. He needed to read the damn letters. He was going to have to work past the sick feeling in his stomach to find out the truth. He had left things to rot for too long and his future was in danger, simply because he was angry with Tandy for too long.

Five

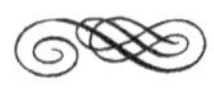

Tandy

His questions had been a sharp stab in her heart as she realized what he was saying. *He didn't read my letters at all, did he?* She hadn't shed a tear in years but her eyes burned at his admission all the same. Her stomach ached and would not allow her to eat with Davian, something she hadn't expected him to notice. When he did, all she could say to avoid addressing his questions was to mention the marks she had seen on Mariana the day before. Considering that they thought so little of her she wasn't sure if Davian would even believe her, but it didn't matter anyway. Her words did what they needed to do, relieve her of his questioning. It would no longer concern her, Davian would handle it from there.

She fought the stomach ache rolling through her belly as she laid in her bed still clothed, antechamber doors wide open. The nausea had been a near constant in her life since she began at the reform school, but it hadn't been so intense in years. She could hardly stand to call for a maid to help her out of her dress, let alone stand to change in the first place. She laid there fighting her stomach lost in thought.

The school was clean and empty, devoid of life. The brick walls and floor were always cold, the Headmistress colder. In the lessons she was forced to take, she learned extensively of the histories of the Realm, of the arts and sciences. She knew how to do everything for her future husband, how to be a leading lady and how to be obedient. She knew how to play several instruments with the utmost perfection, a repertoire of memorized songs to perform always at the ready. Those lessons were easy, though. The *other* lessons made it difficult to sleep at night for months on end.

Under the direction of the Headmistress, she had to learn how best to please her husband by learning the ways to seduce him with extensive training and demonstrations. Tandy eventually passed those lessons, but not without the tears and lashings to show for it. The insomnia had nearly killed her from exhaustion alone and paired with the intense emotional training lessons and abuse, Tandy was tired. She could only handle so much and finally made a plan to escape, to disappear into the Realm. To hell with the Crown and her parents that had abandoned her in that god forsaken place.

It was only when she'd made it onto the grounds surrounding the school that she realized a harsh truth.

There was no way to leave.

Surrounded by nothing but frozen wasteland, mountains, and frigid ocean water, she was completely trapped. The guards had found her and she was disciplined heavily by the Headmistress and more intense desensitization tactics were used from then on. She learned in the most excruciating ways on how to mind her emotions at *any* cost. Any tear, any smile, any brow furrow. The tiniest of emotions would bring on heinous punishments.

She'd sent letter after letter begging her friends for company during those days. Even though Davian had said cruel things to her the last time they'd seen each other, she had hoped it was all a misunderstanding. For a while, she'd thought maybe the school wasn't sending her letters out as they had said they were. But the other girls had all gotten mail returned to them, weekly, from everyone they cared about. Aside from her mothers scarce letters, Tandy didn't receive even one.

The months turned into years and Tandy stayed alone in the cold and cruel reform school. She'd had no hobbies and no friends for the entirety of her stay. She wore the same boring uniform everyday, an old brown dress with buttons and an apron. She was forced to learn only what was on the syllabus and nothing more. Though her education was extensive, the boredom was immense.

When she had learned of Davian's betrayal, she had sent one last letter. It was short, only a sentence long and she knew that if Davian had read the letter he would have seen the tear tracks littering the page.

How could you do this to me?

Like the other letters, that one too had received no response.

A knock rang through the room and Tandy stood to answer it, closing the bedchamber doors behind her. Her head swam and she swayed on her feet but she ignored it as she reached for the door.

"Your Grace," a servant curtsied. "It is time for your wedding dress fitting." Tandy nodded and let them in. A woman with her hair wound tightly in a bun guided a servant to place a pedestal on the ground. They stripped her down to her undergarments before the woman spoke.

"Has your Grace decided on a specific style of gown for the wedding?" The seamstress smiled at her.

"No," Tandy said. She didn't even know what current fashion *looked* like, let alone seen a wedding gown before. "I have no preference, choose as you see fit." The seamstress nodded with a smile and was quiet for a few moments before speaking again.

"Is Lady Mariana Ligotus to be a part of the bridal party?" The seamstress asked. Mariana was the only person she knew of that was there in the palace and available for the wedding and it was traditional for the bride and groom to each have one person in the bridal party. Mariana was the only other soul she knew in the Realm that *wasn't* Davian, so there were no other choices.

"Yes," Tandy said.

"Excellent, I'll send for her now to be done with this in one sitting," the woman told her, gesturing to her servant to retrieve Mariana. It was only a few moments before Mariana was brought to the room.

"You'll be next after Duchess Tandanea, my Lady," she told Mariana. After the measurements were taken, she stepped from the pedestal and was dressed into a new gown. The maid then helped Mariana onto the pedestal.

"You're quite curvy, dear, there are a lot of dress styles that would suit you very well. Do you have a preference?" The seamstress asked Mariana. Mariana looked confused for a moment and only shook her head. The seamstress grinned with hardly contained excitement, her eyes flicking between Tandy and Mariana.

"*Excellent*, I will bring several style options to you in the next few days. After meeting with the Prince, we will be able to see what style we prefer before moving onto the color of the fabric," the seamstress said. She gathered her belongings and hastily made her way from the room with her servant in tow, the pedestal clutched in her hands.

"Will you be needing anything else, your Grace?" The last servant asked after stepping away from Mariana.

"We need tea and lunch," she said despite not feeling hungry. She knew she needed to keep up appearances and maintain a polite facade despite feeling nausea and fatigue. The maid nodded before leaving the room as Mariana stood still and eyed Tandy suspiciously. When the door closed, Tandy sat at the table by the window.

"What are you doing?" Mariana asked.

"Lunch will be here soon," she said blankly before looking back out the window. Mariana sat down slowly across from Tandy with an expression that looked like she was waiting for Tandy to take a swing at her. Tandy said nothing to avoid her words being misconstrued. As they watched the goslings across the field, the quiet of the room was startled by the sound of Martina yelling in the hallway.

Tandy could hear Mariana's mother looking for her daughter, the sound of her banging on the door next to her room reverberating through the walls was unmistakable. Tandy spared a glance at Mariana and found her gripping the table, knuckles going white. Her face was equally pale as the shouts grew louder.

It was obvious Martina was the reason for Mar's bruises and discomfort. Between the marks and the scolding before entering the throne room, there was no doubt in Tandy's mind. She only hoped that Davian saw it, as well.

A maid entered the room with a tray of food followed by another carrying the tea. Tandy kept her eyes on the hallway as Mariana clutched the table, nearly shaking with fear. She braced herself for Martina to peek inside as she walked away and wasn't disappointed when she met her angry gaze.

The woman marched into the room when she saw Mariana, mouth open with what Tandy was sure nobody wanted to hear.

Tandy stood fluidly and stepped forward, blocking Martina in her path.

"I don't recall inviting you to this meeting," Tandy said in a lofty voice, lips drawn into a dramaticized frown. "How inappropriate to enter a private room without first being called on," she turned her nose up in a haughty manner, glaring into her eyes. She wanted Martina and the maids to bristle at her words to draw attention to the impropriety she displayed. It worked, of course. Despite the empty feeling inside of her, the perfectly manipulated expression on her face paired with her words highlighted Martina's bawdy actions of barging into her rooms. The maids turned their noses up at the woman at the slight, leaving Martina red cheeked.

"We're busy discussing wedding plans," Tandy told her with a false smile, grotesquely pulled across her cheeks. She tilted her head and swept her hand toward the door. "Don't worry, the maids will direct you to where you belong," she said in an artificially sweet voice as the maids complied, ushering Martina from the room. Martina could say nothing as Tandanea was above her in social status but Tandy knew she was only temporarily cowed.

As the room cleared, Tandy sat at the table again before pouring the tea into two mugs. She offered one to a pale and trembling Mariana. Tandy waited for the venom Mariana was sure to send her way after she calmed down and braced for it with a blank face so different from the display of emotion she'd had only seconds before.

"Why did you do that?" Mariana whispered as she gingerly reached for her tea. "And yesterday, you yelled at her too."

"We're going over wedding plans," Tandy said.

"That's not true and you know it," Mariana said, sipping her tea. Tandy said nothing, though. "Come *on*," Mariana huffed.

"She was rude," Tandy said after a minute. "You should talk to Prince Davian about it," she added, looking at Mariana. She frowned, sighing at Tandy's words. Even if Mariana didn't mention it to him, Tandy was well within her rights to demand the woman be barred from entering the west wing of the castle ever again.

They sat quietly as she begged the nausea to stay away this time for the sake of being absolutely famished from the lack of appetite she'd had the last few days.

"If you want to use my room as a quiet place, you're free to do so, Lady Mariana," Tandy said after she finished her tea.

"I don't need you to do that," Mariana frowned.

"Should you *want* a safe place to be away from people, please let this be your formal invitation for my quarters." Tandy insisted as she picked up a small sandwich on the tray, taking miniscule bites in the hopes of keeping it down.

"What should we discuss for the wedding?" Mariana sighed as she picked at more of the food on the tray.

"What color do you want to wear?" Tandy asked her. Mariana blinked at her confused.

"It's your wedding, you tell me," she countered.

"It's *your* dress, Mar, you have to pick it out."

"You didn't find any new fashion trends while traveling the world?" Mariana asked, making Tandy look at her with confusion though her face gave nothing away. The fact that she had worn the same brown dress for the last near decade as a school uniform made Mariana's accusation laughable. All the gowns she was sent over the years laid in storage, only returned once she finally left the reform school. She ignored the minefield of a question and offered her color preference.

"I'd prefer pink," she said as she poured more tea.

"My mother says pink makes me look like a slut," Mariana muttered with a frown before covering her mouth and looking away, eyes wide. Tandy blinked at her, unsurprised by her words. She feared the worst of Martina was only just beginning to bubble through.

"A color is a color, and it's *my* wedding. She has no say," Tandy said reasonably. "Pick what you like." Tandy stared out the window and prayed that Davian would be able to solve this problem for Mariana, before anything bad happened.

Six

Davian

Even though Davian was still wary of the wine, he was unsure if its existence was environmental or intentional and couldn't point his fingers in any direction without more information to go off of. His advisors seemed apathetic at the worst and though he monitored anyone he was in direct contact with for deceit or treachery, no one drew his attention. However, he *was* sure that his advisors were attempting to kill him through sheer boredom with the amount of meetings he was scheduled for. He could hardly stand even *one* additional meeting added to his already full schedule let alone the dozens that called on him first thing in the morning. He sent the florists and chefs to find Tandanea for her input instead, washing his hands of them.

A few days after he had spoken to her, she called for him to join the lounge for one of the final consultations. He was relieved to be free from the conference room but wasn't thrilled for the wedding details he knew awaited him, or the tension he'd face with Tandy. He supposed he was relieved he had managed to limit most of his input for the wedding altogether, though.

When he entered the room, he found Tandy and Mariana at the table. They were looking closely at a pile of what looked like handkerchiefs, heads bowed together as they studied each one. They didn't see him at first, talking quietly as they pointed between the colors. The seamstress greeted him with a smile, making the girls turn to him. Mariana smiled as she straightened while Tandy's face remained blank. They all curtsied before the seamstress spoke.

"Your Highness, thank you for joining us," she said warmly with a bow. "Your fiancé would like your input on what you'll be wearing so the rest of the color selections can be made," she told him. He nodded, stepping toward the table to peek at what the girls had been focused on. Mariana slid him some of the fabric squares with a smile.

"We decided on what Tandy will wear, but we also need to decide on the colors we will decorate with to coordinate your formal wear as well as mine," Mariana pulled more swatches from the pile and Tandanea gestured to the selections.

"We were leaning towards this palette for the wedding theme, but it's rather feminine. What is your preference?" She asked him before locking eyes with him. For a moment, Davian's breath froze in his chest. Her unflinching gaze was strong, her voice delicate. He hadn't remembered just how icy grey her eyes were. He hadn't remembered how stunning she was, how much more beautiful she'd become. Her pale blue dress brought the depth of her eyes to his focus, her curves hard to ignore. He remembered the feel of her on his lips, the softness of her skin against his. His heart raced for a moment as a swell of anxiety and longing filled him, but he breathed through it and glanced at the rest of the swatches. There were five squares of fabric with blues, purples, and pinks. He took them from the different piles they'd made and created a new one with three swatches. He pursed his lips as he looked over the new color selection.

"Lets see this darker blue with those colors," Mariana suggested and added another square to the pile. "The ballroom is large enough that this many colors will be easy to coordinate and keep them from overwhelming the guests with too high of a saturation of only one color. Blue, burgundy, champagne and pink will look great with the decor of the palace, as well." Tandy nodded at the suggestion.

"What color would you want your gown to be out of those, Mariana?" Tandanea asked as she sat down, drinking the tea she'd left on the table.

"I suppose blue," Mariana said sadly as she ran her hand along the swatch of pink fabric. Tandy glanced at her with an unreadable expression while Davian wondered why Mariana sighed so long-ingly at the pink fabric she stroked with her fingers. Tandy turned her gaze to Davian and pointedly looked at Mariana as she held the pink square. She raised one brow and nodded slowly until he understood what she meant.

"Blue is too dreary for someone in the bridal party, Mar. The pink would be best out of all the choices," Davian said. Mariana scoffed and rolled her eyes before sitting down, too.

"Too dreary for a wedding, but you want to cover the walls and tables with it," Mariana rolled her eyes.

"Fine, then we can take out *all* the blue -" he said with a grin, but Mariana stopped him.

"*No,*" she said emphatically while Tandy slid the squares out of his reach. He laughed as Tandy waved the seamstress over.

"These are our selections for the wedding theme. For Mariana's gown, we want it in this shade of pink to match," Tandy told her.

"Pink is a lovely choice," the seamstress agreed as she noted the colors down in her notebook.

"Why are you color coordinating Mariana for the wedding?" He asked finally after a cup of tea was placed in front of him. The girls looked at him at the same time before Tandy answered.

"She's my maid of honor," Tandy said as Mariana rolled her eyes playfully.

"Obviously, Dav," Mariana teased. He couldn't believe the camaraderie between them, so different than only a few days ago. *It had to be the wine, then,* he told himself, hoping Mariana had listened to him about it. He let himself smile widely at their interaction and was met by an equal grin from Mariana, dimples much like his own punctuating her small laugh. He glanced at Tandy as she looked away, seemingly lost in thought before she met his gaze again. Her head tilted to the side as if she were analyzing him deeply.

"Who will your best man be?" Mariana asked him. "What color will they match me in? And what color are you wearing?" She asked in rapid succession. Davian sighed heavily and pinched his nose.

"Gods damnit," he grumbled. Mariana laughed, throwing her head back completely unabashed at Dav's reaction. He couldn't help the laugh that slipped from his mouth, before Tandy looked at them both back and forth as she looked lost in thought once again. He wasn't sure what she saw before they were interrupted by Mariana's mother. The laughter died in Mariana's throat immediately when she noticed Martina standing in the doorway, her body going rigid. She glanced at Dav and made an almost imperceptible gesture with her finger, pointing toward Martina. Dav followed her pointing hand and turned to watch the woman staring at them in an extremely disconcerting way.

Despite the smile on her face, Martina looked anything but happy to be there. She looked almost feral as she crossed the room and made a grimacing face at her daughter.

"You're needed elsewhere, dear," she said in a sickeningly sweet voice. Mariana looked down and stood, not looking at anyone as she did. Martina then curtsied tursely and finally acknowledged Davian and Tandanea. He didn't bother to stand in greeting as she had so boldly ignored him upon entering the room. As Martina smiled at him in an unsettling way, he couldn't help but feel there was something she was hiding that he wouldn't like to find out. When they left the room, Mariana being all but pulled along by her mother, he looked at Tandy as she watched them walk down the hall. They'd left the door open, leaving them in full view of Martina whispering furiously into Mariana's ears.

"How disrespectful to Your Highness," the maid said with a click to her tongue. They turned to look at her, making the woman's cheeks flame. "I mean, it's none of my business," she said hastily, "but after stomping into Duchess Tandanea's private quarters without invitation, and now *this*," she tutted. Davian bristled at the statement, glaring at the doorway where Martina had dragged Mariana through.

"That was *very* disrespectful to Your Highness," Tandy agreed as she looked at Dav with a face that said *I told you to watch out for her*. Dav bit his lip in thought, wondering what the woman's uncharacteristic behavior meant. His thoughts were drawn back to the wine being the answer, but he wasn't sure how he'd prohibit drinking during the upcoming balls on such a large scale. He may not have seen the Ligotus family in a long time but he'd certainly never seen an interaction like *that* between the mother and daughter before.

"Please do keep your ear out for anything like this should it happen again," Davian ordered, not pleased at all by the fact he even had to experience it. They nodded in agreement easily.

"Your Highness, your Grace, there is one more color you need to select," she glanced at Davian pointedly. He sighed, but Tandy responded for him.

"Have him match my gown's base color, with lace accents and appliques. Add beadwork into the stitching wherever you can," she said. Ms Ralliegh practically vibrated with glee as she ran from the room, murmuring to herself feverishly. He smiled at her reaction, glad that somebody was having fun with wedding planning.

He sighed before looking at Tandy who met his gaze. He wasn't sure what to say, but the room felt tense as they looked at eachother. He stared at her freckled nose, her soft features on her delicate and beautiful face, taking in the details of her body in a way he hadn't in a long time. She'd always been pretty, but as a grown woman now it was undeniable that she was gorgeous. Her hair was pulled back into an elaborate updo, with decorative barrettes and loose curls framing her cheeks. Her grey eyes were hard to look away from, but he couldn't help but lower his gaze to her breasts, full and nearly spilling out of her gown. He wasn't sure how long he looked before meeting her eyes again, her expression unreadable.

"Why is it impossible to tell what you're thinking?" He asked, surprising himself.

"To best suit the crown, I underwent extensive training and schooling, " she answered as if reciting the words.

"*What* does that mean?" He asked, confused as he leaned back in his chair.

"As you requested, I was sent to Mistress Alice Vaine's Fine Etiquette and Reform School for proper Royalty lessons," Tandy said hollowly. "To be the *proper* wife I was supposed to be, I did what was commanded by you and completed my schooling there."

The name of the school sent a wave of dread into his stomach as he thought about that horrid place. His brows furrowed in thought, unable to believe her words. *She had no record of an existence,* he reminded himself. Her family had been all but missing for years with no financial record to pinpoint their location. *Tandy* had been *exiled.* His stomach recoiled at the thought.

It had been well known amongst the Royal Circles that girls that were sent there were never the same nor were they ever seen again, only ushered to their betrothed's home and married off without a spare thought. Davian looked at her for what felt like the first time, taking in her slight frame and the dark undereyes she wore. He hadn't noticed at first, but she looked as though she'd skipped several meals and had several restless nights of sleep. He couldn't help the pang he felt in his chest at this discovery. His heart broke as his father's words unraveled at Tandy's admission.

"My father said you were traveling the world," he said, though doubt filled his expression. She looked at him without blinking before her words registered in his mind, a frown creasing his brows. "What do you mean *I* had you sent there?"

"I was told after... the ball, that you expected me to be trained properly before returning to the castle and continuing the betrothal," she mentioned the night he'd accused her of something wicked and he felt even more sick than before. "I was told I needed to be put in my place after the rumors traveled through the Circle and brought you shame." Her empty lilt and blank expression made sense to him then and he wanted to punch himself for being such a fool. *Rumors* rang through his mind like a curse.

"I would never have sent you anywhere near that place no matter the circumstance," he said honestly. He couldn't tell what she thought, though, and he could only wonder what she was think-ing before she stood up and moved away from the table. He moved to follow her, offering his arm unconsciously. "I was angry, but I would *never* have sent you there."

"Whether it was you or your parents, it does little to know who sent me there," Tandy stated with an empty tone, walking past his outstretched arm. "Banishment was an efficient teacher and the throne will not suffer for having a well trained Queen."

"Tandy," Davian sighed heavily, unsure how to respond. It was horrible that she was sent there and he knew there wasn't much he could say to make it right. She ignored him, stepping to the door before turning around and leaning into him.

"Before we leave the room, there's something else you should know," Tandy whispered, close to his ear, tall enough that her lips barely grazed his skin. Chills crawled over his body as he felt her breath close to his neck, a sudden flame in his belly at the feeling. He remembered how she sounded when he was inside her and he had to fight the urge to kiss her neck, to breathe in her scent. He leaned his ear closer toward her as she told him what she saw a few days prior, the reaction Mariana had to her own mother. He was not happy to hear what she told him, and felt a sense of worry over the situation.

"I think it has something to do with the wine," he murmured.

"What's wrong with it?" She whispered.

"I think it's why Mariana was acting erratic in the gardens that night, and why I -" *never answered your letters,* he thought. "It was causing me distress, as well," he said into the curve of her neck, pulling her closer. They looked to be in a loving embrace as they shared secrets together. She remained still in his arms and he wasn't sure if she would ever feel the same.

"Are you well now?" She asked him.

"I haven't had any of it in over a week, and I'm feeling much better now," he told her honestly. "I told Mariana not to have any either after the night in the gardens. Did she tell you anything more about the bruises?"

"No, but I offered her my room as sanctuary to avoid Martina after she barged into my room," she whispered. "She has also been notably more calm the last few days, if that answers your question about the wine. I know my standing is low with you both currently, but even still her presence had seemed..." her words trailed off.

"Crazed and erratic?" He supplied. She agreed softly before pulling away from him. She held onto his arm as they walked back to their rooms.

"More guests will be arriving this week," Davian told her as they came to her door. She turned to face him, listening to what he had to say, hand on the door knob. "My mother is insisting on a ball to be held for everyone before the wedding, a masquerade," he sighed. Tandy nodded, he was sure she remembered his mother's obsession with those masks and elaborate gowns. "I'm going to have Knights at our doorways, and block any guests from this wing of the castle. There's plenty of rooms on the lower levels of the palace for any of the guests we have, so there should really be no reason to be up in this wing at any point in time. Knights on each of the stairwells and outside the balconies on the ground level, as well as the towers. Martina won't be allowed in this wing without explicit invitation, so see that she doesn't bully her way through to Mariana." Tandy nodded, eyes unwavering.

"Yes, Your Highness," she told him. He wanted to roll his eyes but he remembered her words as she had told him of her education and knew she had been ingrained with the protocol for addressing Royalty, to an inhumane level.

"I didn't send you away, Tandy," he told her gently. She didn't even blink at his admission, and it made him want to shake her for a response, to force her to acknowledge his apology.

"Don't forget to select a groomsman," she said as she closed her door behind her. Davian sighed as she ignored him and headed to his room.

In his office, he sat at his desk and ran his hands through his hair. He was devastated to hear that Tandy had been suffering in isolation all along. He couldn't believe his arrogance and obstinate behavior had cost her nearly a decade of her life to train her into someone that would please the crown. He felt sick, that bad feeling permeating through each pore in his body. He was left feeling heavy and defeated as he sat there, rubbing his forehead against the permanent migraine that settled itself behind his eyes. *I should have read her letters,* he thought with regret. He sighed before reaching for a pen, shaking his head in frustration.

He wrote a letter to Bryson, his only real friend as of late and invited him to the wedding as his groomsman. Bryson had recently been Knighted and he'd been one of his closest confidants during their years at the academy. Bryson wasn't one to settle down, instead taking flight across the Realm and roaming between different positions for the Royal Guard.

After sending the letter off with a maid, he notified the Knights of their new positions and expectations as the rest of the guests arrived. He made sure to tell them that only himself or Tandanea were able to accept calls in this wing, no one else without permission from himself or the future Princess would be welcome. An extra Knight would be present at all times to escort guests to visit in his quarters or Tandanea's, and also to find either of them to verify the guest is actually allowed to be in the west wing. He also sent a

Knight to find Mariana and make sure she was alright, still wary of Martina's behavior.

The only thing he could think about as he readied himself for dinner was why exactly his father was lying about Tandanea and where did the rumors originate in the first place.

Seven

Tandy

Wedding preparations were held in the lounge room where person after person prompted Tandy on details she didn't care for. She was for once grateful for the ability to completely erase her emotions as she was faced with an endless flow of rapid fire questions. It all seemed to be a web of trick questions that she was answering incorrectly, but she told herself it was hardly her fault for not being up to date on her fashion.

When Mariana had walked into the room for breakfast, she immediately took the lead on answering the questions. She directed the meetings almost instinctively as different merchants prompted them with the fabric, floral, and food choices that would be needed for the biggest wedding the Kingdom had seen in years. Mariana had a knack for event coordination and an eye for color and details that Tandy simply didn't have experience with.

By the time Davian found them, they had nearly completed everything besides selecting the fabrics for their attire. With a pointed look she hoped Davian would understand, they were able to place Mariana in the color of her choosing and not the color her mother had insisted on. When Davian and Mariana laughed, it all seemed like a memory she had nearly forgotten. When their smiles revealed matching dimples, Tandy looked away as she tried to recall something she couldn't quite place.

When they were children, Martina had made Mariana laugh with her hand over her mouth so as to minimize her presence. Of course, Tandy could tell by the practiced way Mariana's lips rose and fell politely that she had undergone rigorous training as she herself had. Mariana likely hadn't shown a real smile in *years.* Because of her demure and hidden smiles, she hadn't remembered that Mariana had dimples on her cheeks that matched the ones on Davian's. Besides the Prince, the only other person she knew that had dimples was the King.

The wolfish grin on Martina's face as she dragged Mariana away left a sour taste in her mouth. Even the seamstress and maids saw her behavior as abhorrent. With Dav pushing more Knights into their wing, she felt a little better that there would at least be more safety precautions that would keep that woman away from her and Mariana's bedrooms.

After Davian left her to her rooms, the maids changed her into an evening gown and readied her for dinner. Tandy wasn't sure if dinner would be served in her room, in the lounge, or if the King would call for a last minute formal meal in the banquet hall and could only wait. She had to keep her thoughts from racing until then because she was certain her body would fail if she continued skipping meals from the nausea of her anxiety. She wasn't sure how she managed to even survive the boarding school considering the amount of times they withheld meals or antagonized her until she had no appetite.

Finally, a maid came to her door and told her dinner would be served in the lounge room tonight. A Knight guided them to the room and she sat at the table by the window as the maid placed a plate of food in front of her. Her mouth watered and she begged her stomach not to ache after only a few bites, desperate for nourishment. As she was staring out the window, she heard someone enter the room and turned to see who it was.

Davian joined her at the table and a plate was quickly brought to him. They began to eat together quietly as they waited for Mariana to join them. After Tandy took a few bites, Mariana finally swept into the room with an angry expression on her face. She stumbled as she sat in her chair and stared at the plate that was placed in front of her. Tandy and Dav shared another glance, his brow raised in an unspoken question.

"How was your mother?" Davian asked before sipping his water. Mariana glared harder before turning to look at Tandy. Her face was full of absolute fury, the angriest she'd ever seen her before. It was hard to deny the stench of wine on her breath as she glared. Immediately, Tandy's stomach clenched and she nearly gagged on the bite of food still in her mouth. She swallowed it with a gulp of water as she met Mariana's gaze, dreading the words that would come from her mouth just as she had before.

"You ruin everything," Mariana spat. "You just had to put your nose where it doesn't belong." She pointed a finger at Tandy. "I could've had it *all* if you were never born, and now I'm stuck playing dress up with you instead of planning my own wedding," she fumed. Tandy didn't say anything, it wouldn't have done any good. She wondered what Martina must have said in order to upset Mariana this much.

With wine on Mariana's breath, Tandy considered Davian's concerns about the beverage and if he was rightfully concerned. She couldn't meet Davian's eye, afraid he'd only take Mariana's side despite what he said before. She didn't want to hear him scold her again, though she knew it would be coming.

"If you hadn't gotten your way when we were kids, doing gods knows what with gods knows who, I would be sitting *there* and you *here!*" She shouted before standing, her hands smacking the table.

The reverberations knocked Tandy's glass over, spilling it on her lap. She didn't blink or even glance at it, just kept her eyes locked with Mariana's. Even with her having told Davian she had gone to the Fine Etiquette and Reform School there was still a chance that he would change his mind about believing her. Why wouldn't he, with Mariana screaming in her face about the transgressions Tandy supposedly took part in. *Is she really claiming I, as a child, seduced my way to the throne? What little they think of me.*

Delicately, Tandy put the glass back onto the table after it landed on her and let Mariana keep yelling. There wasn't much to be done and she couldn't leave until she at least excused herself. Her training held true, not a single tear or muscle twitch crossed over her face as Mariana continued screaming.

"You couldn't let *me* win anything as kids and you're still spending your days rubbing my nose in your achievements! Why don't you go and fuck the King again and just *leave*," Mariana's chest heaved. Tandy looked down at her hands and rose from her chair with a small curtsy before striding from the room. Knights were in the hall blocking the way but they nodded when they saw her and let her pass.

"No one is to call on me, no exceptions," she told them. They nodded at her in understanding and she continued walking to her room with one Knight falling into step behind her. She locked her door tight and stripped off the wet gown.

She sat at her vanity and picked each hair pin from her head until her curls rolled down her back. She'd never liked the color of her hair, nor the color of her eyes. She hated the circles under them that punctuated the dull grey color. The freckles upset her, too. The girls in the boarding school told her she looked like she was a commoner with sun spots on her face, telling everyone that it meant she had poor breeding and worked in the fields. Eventually, their words adhered themselves onto her, forever changing the way she looked at her reflection. Whenever she looked into the mirror, all she could do was obsess over the unruly way her hair laid, the lack of breasts she had, the knobby knees she had, the slightly too broad shoulders.

She had a glass of water from the pitcher on her bedside table and laid in her bed. There was nothing to pray for, she already knew what they would say about her after she'd left the room. Davian would comfort Mariana, holding her close to his chest. She'd comfort him in return and before long would end up in Davian's bed as Mariana had said he'd been before. They'd weep and mourn over the fact that Davian was bound to marry a wicked and unfeeling woman and she'd be a joke of a wife as her betrothed's mistress carried his children. Tandy had been able to push the vile words Mariana had spat at her when she first arrived, long past caring if Davian would ever love her again.

She begged her mind to turn off, but sleep eluded her. She tossed back and forth, trying to get comfortable but unable to. For a moment, she thought she heard knocking on her door but ignored it. She knew no one cared about her and rolled over in her bed, unable to feel comfortable. She stared at the ceiling on her back as the room grew darker and darker, before fading completely leaving her to lie in the pitch black room. Not even the moon shone through the windows. It wasn't until she heard birds chirping with the sky turning a deep blue that she realized she'd been awake all night long. Her eyes felt heavy then, and sleep finally, gratefully, pulled her in.

She sat on a picnic blanket, weaving flowers into a crown like her nanny had taught her. She was getting better at it, her small chubby hands braided dutifully. She accidentally snapped the bud from the stem, and began anew with another flower from the pile.

Mariana sat wearing a full set of flower jewelry, her gifted hands making quick work of the necklace, bracelet, and ring she adorned on her body before beginning on her own crown.

"You're so good at this!" Tandy squealed in delight. Mariana smiled shyly before posing with her flowers as though she were awaiting a painter to catch sight of her, making Tandy laugh before Tandy placed her flower crown on her best friend's head. "Perfect!" She grinned. They heard grumbling from the other side of the blanket and turned to see Davian holding a pile of grass, struggling to braid them together.

"Dav, you can't braid grass," Tandy said with a giggle. "It's not long enough, silly." He weakly held up a ball of grass, making a face at it.

"This was supposed to be for you, Tandy," he muttered before dropping it onto the blanket. Tandy picked it up tentatively and tried placing it on her head. She didn't want him to feel bad so she wanted to wear it anyway.

"Er, it looks amazing! Thank you," she told him with a smile. He looked at her with pink cheeks, before the wad of grass slipped off her head and landed in her lap with a wet plop. The sound sent Mariana into a fit of laughter, making Dav and Tandy giggle, too. Before long the trio were laughing loudly, bringing the gaze of their nannies. Though her mother and father were sitting with Mariana's and Davian's, they were busy drinking from the large glasses with long stems, the strong smelling juice filling them to the brim. They didn't look over, but Tandy quieted as she heard the whisper of the nannies behind her. Mariana and Davian laughed harder and harder, the only sound was of their wheezing as hysterical tears fell from their eyes. They gripped their bellies at the same time, and Tandy tilted her head to look at them.

They laughed harder, eyes squinting. They both had the same shade of brown hair, the same delighted giggle. They clutched their bellies in much the same way as the King laughing boisterously behind them, dimples on both sides of their cheeks. Mariana, Davian, and the king, though not sitting together, continued to laugh for a minute longer before the whisper of the nannies caught up to Tandy's ears.

"Oh my, they're truly twins," they murmured, scandalized. Their lips were hidden by the fans they held for the summer heat, but the way they breathed gave Tandy pause. Though she was still young, she knew something was strange about the way Mariana and Davian looked so much like each other, though they had different parents. But Tandy laughed when Mariana held up the lump of grass, staining her hands green as she held it up for the world to see.

The moment passed, and they continued to braid more of the flowers together, the girls guiding Davian until he made a crown of his own.

Tandy jolted awake to the sound of knocking on her door. The sun was high in the sky, and she wasn't sure the exact time. Her whole body felt heavy, her head foggy and confused. The knocking continued at her door until she heard a voice call out her name. She stumbled out of bed nearly toppling to the ground as her legs shook from exhaustion. When she made it into the anteroom, a maid was on the other side. She let her into the room and watched dizzily as she placed the food on her table and handed her the note.

"Your Grace, Miss Ralleigh requests your presence in the sun room for the first fitting. The fabric is easier to work with in the bright sunlight, so we'll be back to find you this afternoon when the room is brightest," with that, they turned to leave and Tandy was left alone once again. She stared at the tea and brunch on the tray and found she wasn't even slightly hungry. She staggered back through her bedroom door and took a sip of the water still next to her bed. She laid back down and closed her eyes, waiting to be called on again by the maids.

As she dozed, her thoughts circled around the dream she had. She was confused by what it meant, if it was a memory or just a strange dream brought on by stress. It seemed as though the nannies spoke of Mariana and Davian looking like twins. She could very faintly remember that day and she thought the nannies spoke of Davian and the King. The more she thought about it, the more confused she became. She knew that Martina and her husband did *not* have dimples, and that Mariana and Davian did seem to have a lot of similar features in common with the King.

Not much time had passed before the maids came for Tandy. She called for them to open the door and they found her in much the same state as she had been left in. They helped her from the bed and pulled her into a dress before walking her to Miss Ralleigh. She met the woman's happy smile with only a blank look, and the maids began to help her undress without a word. She was stripped down to her underwear quickly and she ignored the chilled and exposed feeling it gave her. She hardly blinked in the bright light though it stung her eyes. Ms Ralleigh helped her step into the gown before she began pinning and adding lace and brocades.

"We'll add more beading and gems more toward the end, just to make sure the fabric is hemmed properly and we don't make more work for ourselves with any unnecessary adjustments," Ms Ralleigh murmured as she carefully made notes and continued pinning. After nearly an hour, Tandy felt dizzy but ignored it and was grateful when the maids helped her from the dress. She stood in her undergarments as the maids helped Ms Ralleigh collect the seamstress' belongings before they turned to Tandy.

A maid began to help her into her dress but before she could step into it, she heard a maid exclaim at the doorway.

"Your Highness, Duchess Tandanea is not ready for a guest at the moment, she's in the midst of a wardrobe change," the woman said with alarm. The door opened despite the woman's protests.

"You're excused," Davian told the maid. Tandy stood there in her under garments, legs and breasts nearly on full display wearing only her bloomers and corset. She ignored him, leaning over to straighten her gown before attempting to step into it without a maid. Her breasts felt as though they'd fall out of her corset as she leaned forward, but she ignored the pangs of embarrassment as he watched her. Davian sat in the chair in front of her and she met his eyes unintentionally. He wasn't looking at her face, though. His eyes were focused on her chest, her fair skin nearly as light as the corset from the lack of sun on her skin. Freckles lined her shoulders, and his unwavering gaze filled her belly with heat, almost making her legs tremble. She remembered how he felt between her thighs, though she willed the memories to fade.

His intense gaze roved over her body, taking in her form slowly as he sat back lazily in his chair with a raised brow and a smirk. He trailed his eyes over her lips before meeting her own, golden brown meeting grey. She made no expression, only pulled her dress up and over her body and slid her hands back through the sleeves. Davian stood suddenly but she didn't react. She only adjusted her bodice as Davian moved behind her, lacing her gown and buttoning the collar. Tandy felt bitter as he helped her redress, though the feeling was secondary to the dizziness she was experiencing. She didn't thank him as his hands fell back to his sides, and she moved to walk out the door.

A hand reached for her and she stumbled back against Davian's chest as he held her tight. His hands gripped her hips, before they slid slowly up her sides, trailing softly over her breasts before he rested them on her shoulders. He leaned in close, breathing into her ear with his nose. She made no move to struggle away from the feeling even though it tickled. She wasn't sure what he was trying to do, but she wasn't going to say a word. If he thought she was whoring herself out to any man she met, there wasn't much to do that would convince him otherwise. Reacting to his touch would be all he needed to verify those rumors, and she refused to give him any more reason to think of her in that way. She felt her cheeks heating as one of his hands slid down her breasts, slowly caressing, until it rested against her belly. He moved his other hand to grip her chin, before breathing deep into her neck. He pressed his nose against her skin just below her jaw, his lips grazing her flesh as he whispered.

"You didn't answer the door last night," he said softly. When she didn't answer, he pulled her even closer to his chest.

"I didn't hear you," she said. He tutted against her cheek and it sent butterflies through her belly.

"I had wanted to tell you that Mariana was instructed by her mother to drink the wine I had told her not to touch. I was right that it seems to be altering our mental states in some strange way, and dinner last night was *not* how the evening was supposed to go." He told her, voice low enough to make her legs weak. Davian laughed against her neck and her hands reached out to grip his wrists as he tightened his hold around her. She pressed his hands away from her but he ignored her motion. "I tried to explain it to you last night, but you didn't answer the door. Next time make sure you let me in." He kissed her cheek, nuzzling against her. "You'll dine with me in my quarters tonight so I can tell you more." A shudder ran through Tandy as he spoke.

"I want to feel you again," he whispered after a moment of silence before kissing her cheek again. His hands lingered on her for a moment longer before he let go of her, leaving the room as quickly as he entered. Tandy stared after him in a daze. She blinked and tried to clear her head, confused as to what just happened.

She sat in her chair and watched the birds fluttering around her balcony until a maid knocked on her door and summoned her to Davian's room for dinner.

Eight

Davian

Davian had stared at Mariana in surprise as she screamed insults at Tandanea. He didn't know what happened with Martina but knew it wouldn't be good. It certainly wasn't an excuse to lash out at Tandy when she had done nothing to warrant such anger.

Before he could stop Mariana, she accused Tandy of bedding his father. He could only stare at her in shock. Tandanea stood after she said that, eyes cast downward before swiftly leaving the room. He stood and walked after her but she was fast and Mariana began to wail behind him, impossible to ignore. He waved the maids from the room, not wanting them to have a front row seat to whatever else Mariana said.

"Shut the fuck up, Mariana," he shouted after the maids left. Her cries stopped abruptly in shock. He looked at Tandy's still full plate and shook his head angrily.

"My mother said she's making a fool of me, that's why she's putting me in the wedding. She's been using everyone around her for *years* and no one has caught on," she tried to explain. Dav took a deep breath before rubbing his hands through his hair, jaw clenched as he smelled wine on Mariana's breath.

"Gods damnit, Mar! You weren't supposed to drink anything but water. Your breath *reeks* of that fucking wine," he groaned. "Do you even know where Tandy has been these last seven years?" Davian asked her.

"She's been sight seeing with her parent's coinpurse, no doubt fucking every man that looks her way," she glared at him, crossing her arms.

"She's been studying at the Fine Etiquette And Reform School since she was sent away," he said levelly, waiting for Mariana's reaction. He didn't have to wait long as she tensed at the name, looking at him with wide eyes.

"There's no way that's true, Dav, she's just saying that to make you feel bad for her. It's just another way for her to gain control over you," she insisted, wiping her eyes. "Her letters said she was going on a trip. *That's* the truth."

"How many letters did you read?" He asked her.

"Well, I didn't read any but my mom said -" she started.

"Your mother is a fucking liar, Mariana. She burned all the letters Tandy sent you. She probably sent the secrets of the Kingdom and we will never know," he yelled, knocking one of the chairs over.

"She was only fifteen when she was sent to the reform school. I don't think she knew where she was being sent until she'd already arrived," he said. "I don't even know if she knew why we were angry with her in the first place." Mariana frowned before looking at him, wringing her hands.

"My mother said she had been demanding to be Princess her whole life and antagonized her parents and the King until he complied. She said she had used her body to get what she wanted," she muttered.

"Martina is a *liar*. She's manipulating you into using *your* body on men, by telling you Tandy did it too." He said bluntly. She flinched at his words before looking down at her hands and rubbing the light bruises on her wrists.

"Where'd you get those?" He asked her. She quickly tucked her hands under her, hiding them.

"I don't have anything," she turned her nose up and looked away.

"Tandy told me she saw the bruises days ago. The girl we swore hated us was the one to warn me of the abuse you're facing," he sighed. "Why would she do that, Mar? Tandy, who we've never actually seen act cruelly, compared to your mother. Not only did she disrespect me today by waltzing into this room without addressing me properly, but she also damn near dragged you from the room, too. *And* she barged into Tandy's room this week without an invitation." He met Mariana's eyes as they filled with tears. "She is *one step* from crossing another line and I'll have no choice but to punish her. Is that the hill you want to die on? That Tandy has been fucking my father since she was at least *three* years old? Since we've been betrothed since she was a toddler, she had to have started bedding him prior to that by your logic. So Mariana, what do you think? A toddler was bedding a grown man to become a Princess, something she even told us she *never* wanted to become?" His hands smacked down on the table and Mariana held her face and wept.

"I - I don't know Davian, she's been telling me this forever. I don't know what is true," she cried.

"You and I both know the stories aren't adding up. Do you think Tandanea would actually have done that as a child? Unless her parents arranged it, which I highly doubt, as a woman's virtue is nearly the only thing she has to offer in a marriage agreement, there's no way any of them would have wasted that. Not the King, not Tandanea's mother, and I'm certain Tandy would also have disagreed." He said, voice still harsh in the empty room.

"I don't believe it, my mother wouldn't *lie*," she tried to reason. He laughed humorlessly and sat back in his chair.

"My father told me something very similar to what your mother told you, as we are well aware. And yet I'm still able to see the holes in the logic without hurling accusations again," he crossed his arms.

"Oh please, how fast did she change your mind? Did you find her in your bed this morning or something?" Mariana rolled her eyes.

"Go to hell, Mar," he spat.

"And let's not forget what you said at the ball all those years ago, why she was sent away in the first place," her face twisted as she snarled back at him. Davian froze in his seat, remembering the ball that night. It had been an excuse for his mother to have a masquerade, their engagement, and he'd told Tandanea horrible things. His father had just insinuated the same things Mariana was claiming now, but now Davian wasn't a stupid, angry, hormonal teenager. There was more to the story and they both knew it.

It was Tandy that had suffered from it most, having been isolated from her friends and family while at least Mariana and Dav had stayed in each other's company. He understood why Tandanea had just left the room instead of acknowledging Mariana's words. He had no doubt that she felt as though anything she said in defense of her character would be misconstrued and wouldn't waste her breath. He sighed as he leaned his hands onto the table. Mariana met his eyes tearfully, leaning her head onto her hands. Tandy had no hope in them, and it broke his heart.

"Do you really think she lied?" She said softly.

"Well, my father had been ass over elbows intoxicated with his peers at the time he told me, so I'm not holding much light to that supposed truth. As far as I'm concerned, we were both manipulated into believing something horrid about a friend. Why were we ready to accept those words as real when it went against everything we *knew?*" He asked. "You were acting fine all week and suddenly you're acting insane, screaming at Tandy out of nowhere. You had the wine, right?"

"Yeah, but not on purpose. It was in a metal chalice instead of a wine glass. I expected it to be water, but my mom had given me wine instead," she admitted as tears trailed down her cheeks.

"*Martina* gave you the wine that makes us lose our minds?" He asked through gritted teeth. Mariana's mouth hung open as she realized the implications of her mother supplying the drink.

"Well, what does it mean? That she doesn't know how to brew a good wine?" Mariana asked, frustrated.

"It means that if she meddles with anything, I will be punishing her," Davian told her. "If I find she has *any* connection to the wine that makes me feel sick in my fucking head, I will be taking *hers.*" Mariana was solemn as she listened, her eyes downcast and fearful.

"She's made me drink it before, whenever Tandy would send a letter. Or if I tried to send my own," she whispered.

"I was served that wine with every letter, too," he said slowly. They looked at each other with unease, unsure of what it would mean for them and the Kingdom. They stood after a while and headed down the hall, lost in their thoughts.

"I *wanted* to believe she wanted me there, but then my mother said - well, she said what she said and it *hurt*, and I was so angry at

Tandanea because why *would* she still be my friend? Of course my mother was right," she said but her voice wavered, unsure.

"Nothing is as it seems has never been a truer statement," Davian murmured. As they approached their rooms, they came to a stop at Tandy's door and knocked. When there was no answer, Davian tried again.

"Duchess Tandanea told us that she won't be accepting any calls for the evening," the Knight behind them said. Mariana looked at Davian, both of them raising their brows before Davian knocked once more, harder than the last time.

"I guess we should give her time to calm down," Mariana offered in a sad voice after the room remained quiet.

"We'll talk to her tomorrow," Davian told her. "We should read the letters, too."

"Yeah," Mariana agreed softly.

He led her into her room and bid her goodnight before returning to his own. He stared at the box of letters for a minute before carrying it to his bedchambers, leaving it on the ottoman by his chair with the intent to read them in the morning.

***

Davian rose early the next morning as was his routine. He liked to run before the sun rose as there were fewer people to interrupt him and demand his attention for things he cared little about. It was the only relaxing moment he had at any point in the workload of his duties. He felt antsy if he didn't have the time to dedicate to running at least once a day, and so made sure to make room for it even if it was still dark.

As he made his way back to his room for a bath, he stopped to send a message to one of his advisors to find out more about Tandy's stay at the boarding school, and told him to find him as soon as he had the information he wanted. Right after he sent the note to be delivered by a maid, he was met almost immediately by his assistant and was pulled into meetings as soon as he was dried and dressed.

After a day full of meetings, a note was delivered from a maid. He eagerly took the large stack of papers in her hands and brought them into his personal office. He scanned the papers, his heart dropping as he saw in plain script that Tandanea, in fact, *was* enrolled in Mistress Alice Vaine's Fine Etiquette and Reform School for girls for the last seven years. She hadn't even been sent home for *one* single family occasion. She'd been essentially trapped in a prison for the last seven years, devoid of even her family. He was going to be *sick*.

He stood, pacing his office as he fought down the urge to vomit. He slammed his hands on the table and groaned loudly as anger boiled in his chest. *How could I be so stupid?* He thought. He slammed his office door shut behind him as he walked through his antechamber and into his bedroom where he'd left the letters Tandy sent. He grabbed the box and placed it next to his bed, desperate to read them and yet still unable to fight the sick feeling whenever he beheld them.

He left his rooms and brought the papers to show Mariana. He went to Tandanea's room and knocked but received no answer.

"Your Highness, Duchess Tandanea isn't taking callers," a Knight reminded him. Davian nodded before continuing and found Mariana in her rooms having a late breakfast. She at least looked well rested and less pale since he had banned anyone entry to their wing.

"Did you talk to her yet?" She asked when she saw him.

"She's still not letting anyone inside her room," he sighed before sipping the tea. He handed the letter to Mariana and she nearly choked on her breakfast when she realized what it said.

"Oh gods," she murmured, going over the same details Davian had just read.

"She wasn't lying," Davian said sadly.

"We fucked up, Dav," Mariana dropped the papers to the table and held her hand to the bridge of her nose, shaking her head.

"Beyond fucked up, Mar," he agreed.

"I have to meet with the seamstress today to be fitted for my dress. She had sent someone to tell me, she'll be here any minute for me to see how I like it so far," she told him. He nodded in understanding knowing he'd need to take his leave as soon as she arrived. "She's supposed to have Tandy's dress, too, but since she won't open the door I'm not sure how she'll be able to."

"We'll make sure they pull her out of there. She has appearances to keep, so she won't stay hidden for long," he said.

"You don't think the pink is a mistake, right?" She asked after a moment of silence, picking her fingers without looking at him.

"If I know Miss Ralleigh as well as I think I do, which I do, your gown *and* Tandy's will be breathtaking. She does nothing in halves, she will make sure you and Tandy look like a part of a set and not as if you're in competition with each other. I know it will be a sight to behold, especially with myself and Bryson by your sides," he told her with a smile.

"Bryson will be your groomsman?" She asked with a small smile. He wasn't sure why, but he always felt an almost brotherly bond to Mariana that helped him find the words to speak to her plainly, and in some cases with profanity, but always with the uttermost honesty. It was no different now than it was when they were five years old, though the stakes had certainly changed.

"That's all you heard out of that," he rolled his eyes.

"Shut up," Mariana laughed as she finished her meal.

"I'm not sure how to get through to Tandy," he admitted as he leaned back in his chair, stretching his feet out. "She was there a *long* time, with no one to support her."

"I'm not sure much *would* get through to her. One of my cousins had a friend that was sent there and she never smiled again," she said sadly. He knew a lot of people who had girls in their families shipped off to that hell. Either they disappeared or returned only a shell of a person. "It would take a lot to get her to feel anything again, if it's as bad as they say," she stirred her tea with more honey, lips pursed. Davian raised his brows at the way she worded her last thought. *Get her to feel again*, he thought. *I'd like to feel her again, too.*

"Well, we're all creatures of carnal desire," he said pointedly. Mariana looked at him with a scandalized face before laughing in surprise.

"Davian, do *not* use your wiles on her," she warned. "She isn't in the right place to deal with that kind of attention, especially since she most likely hasn't even been touched in *years*, not to mention the shit we said to her before she left."

"We were always so physical," he reasoned. "We were like animals, constantly finding empty rooms to fuck in." Mariana only shook her head, pursing her lips.

"It's been too long, " she said. "She's been alone too long, in *that* place. There's no guarantee she will take to you so easily."

"I missed her," he said sadly. Mariana put her hand over his, sighing softly.

"Just tell her the truth about *why* we couldn't answer her. She might take pity on us," she suggested.

A knock at the door signaled Miss Ralleigh had come, and Davian stood to greet her entourage.

"Good morning, Your Highness! Having a peek at your bridal party's outfits?" Ms Ralleigh exclaimed as she and the maids carried in several large garment bags. One of the maids placed a pedestal on the floor and laid the bags on the table. "Let me know how you think it turned out," the seamstress breathed as she delicately pulled a gown from the bag she laid on the top of the pile. Mariana gasped and he raised his brows, impressed. It was covered in accoutrements, with lace designs and small beaded decorations lining the gown.

"Oh my," Mariana breathed.

"It's not finished, of course, my Lady. There will be quite more sparkle once I'm completely finished, but for the sake of your fitting I wanted to have it ready as close to the final product as possible so you could decide if it's too much," she explained as she fanned the skirts out to see them in their full beauty.

"How did you make this so quickly?" Davian couldn't help but ask. Ms Ralleigh laughed and turned to him.

"I had help, naturally, but it was very fun for me to try something this special," she told them.

"Enjoy your fitting, Mariana," he said as he left the room.

"Don't do anything stupid, Davian," Mariana called after him. He waved his hand at her, dismissing her words.

On his way out a maid was trying to open Tandy's door, but it was locked. The maid straightened when she saw Davian and bowed quietly.

"She hasn't taken in any food?" He frowned as the maid nodded.

"No, Your Highness, she hasn't opened the door yet," she told him. He sighed but nodded, worried that she was hungry.

"Check with Ms Ralleigh and Mariana, and see what time Tandanea's fitting will be. You have permission to bang on this door as long as it takes to get her to open it. She *will* be going to this fitting," he said evenly, before walking to his quarters. There wasn't much to do beyond that, and went to his room to savor the silence of a day without meetings before he went for his afternoon tea in the sunroom. He liked to take a small break for downtime to go over the notes he had taken from the meetings of the day, to make sure he was still up to date on any minor changes. He glanced at the letters now placed by his bed and walked over to the box.

He took the oldest dated unopened letter from the box and placed it on his end table, before lowering the box to the floor and tucking it under the bed as best as he could to keep it out of sight. He held the letter in his hands for a minute before placing it back onto the table. As he held the little envelope in his hand, he felt the urge to run away,

Finally, though, it was time for his tea. He headed to the sun room and was glad to see a maid already waiting at the door, but he realized he also saw Ms Ralleigh and her gaggle of maids collecting the seamstress' items and garment bags, as well. It seemed they had used the sunroom for Tandy's fitting, and vaguely heard them addressing her. He picked up his pace and began to head through the doors when he was stopped by a maid.

"Your Highness, Duchess Tandanea is not ready for a guest at the moment, she's in the midst of a wardrobe change," the maid said.

"You're excused," he said abruptly and opened the door anyway. He nearly gasped at what he saw when he entered the room. Tandy stood in nearly nothing, her bloomers and corset the only thing covering her. Her breasts spilled over the top of the corset, her fair legs exposed all the way up to her thighs. The sheerness of her undershirt was enough to make out her nipples through the fabric, and he nearly fell over himself as he made his way into the room. Delicate bows decorated the simple undergarments making her look innocent and alluring in a way he couldn't wrap his head around, his entire body aflame with need. She looked amazing and he felt an overwhelming desire to touch her. He took a seat directly in front of her as he watched her leaning to pull her dress over her legs, leaving her breasts to be eye level with him. He licked his lips at the sight, enjoying the view. She continued to ignore him, but he felt her eyes on him as she straightened and raised the dress to cover her body, sliding her hands through the sleeves.

Davian had never been able to keep his hands off Tandy. When they began their relationship, there wasn't anything that would stop him from having her. As he watched her, the hunger he had for her all those years ago burned in his chest. He *needed* her like he needed air to breathe and he wasn't sure how he was able to survive so long without her. He needed to feel her again, to taste her. The longing was so intense, he couldn't sit there any longer.

He stood suddenly and moved behind her when her dress was on her body completely, and began tightening the ribbon and buttons. She didn't react, and moved to walk out the door before he pulled her back to him. He ran his hands over her hips, sliding them up her body, a caress over her skin as he felt her breasts. He leaned into her neck and breathed deep, making her tense at the sensation. He couldn't help but smile, her body soft under his touch. He stroked his hands over her body again, sliding one hand to her lower belly, while the other held her chin. He felt her swallow and shift her legs.

"You didn't answer the door last night," he whispered into her ear.

"I didn't hear you," she breathed. He tutted against her cheek before he continued.

"I had wanted to tell you that Mariana was instructed by her mother to drink the wine I had told her not to touch. I was right that it seems to be altering our mental states in some strange way, and dinner last night was *not* how the evening was supposed to go," he told her, chuckling against her neck as her body reacted to her touch. "I tried to explain it to you last night, but you didn't answer the door. Next time make sure you let me in." He kissed her cheek, unable to fight the urge, her skin soft beneath his lips. "You'll dine with me in my quarters tonight so I can tell you more."

"I want to feel you again, Tandy," he murmured as her grip on his wrists tightened. Her breath came out in pants and her legs squeezed together. He kissed her cheek again slowly before letting go of her and walking quickly from the room. From the corner of his eye, he watched as she stared after him.

Walking away from her was agony. He knew her touch would heal his heart and he prayed she would be able to forgive him.

Nine

Tandy

Tandy was led to Davian's room and was seated at the table in the corner of his antechamber. It looked like a meeting room with couches on the opposite end of the table, dark but inviting with the sconces lit and the fireplace crackling. She watched as the maids placed dinner on the table and waited for Davian to arrive.

When Davian entered the room, he dismissed the maids. As they left, he began to pour water into their glasses. His hand outstretched and reached for her cheek, gently resting against her cool skin while he filled her cup. He raised her chin to make her look at him. Her eyes met his as he trailed his thumb over her lips. The heat from the fire overwhelmed her as butterflies filled her belly at his touch. The want she still had for him was unbearable. She knew intimately how he felt when he was inside her and despite the years she spent resenting him, she had *always* been putty in his hands. She knew that no matter her anger and resentment, Davian had always been her weakness. She took a deep breath and waited for Davian to pull away. When he did, she felt only loss. All those years couldn't snuff out the flame he filled her with.

Davian lifted the cover of her plate, revealing her dinner.

"Eat, Tandy. I mean it," he said with a smile when her stomach growled audibly. Though she couldn't eat very fast or her stomach would end up in knots, she made sure to take her time. They ate quietly together, the silence comfortable. Though she wasn't able to clear her plate, she ate more than she had in days. She hoped she would be able to keep it down for once and prayed that nothing would unsettle her while she was so full.

"How was it?" Davian asked, his chair suddenly much closer to where she sat. Davian reached a hand out to her again, his hand sliding over her cheek and cupped the back of her neck. His thumb grazed over her ear lobe and she let out an involuntary shudder at the sensation. Davian grinned before standing, pulling her up to him. He pressed her against his chest and slid his other hand down her back, gripping her ass. She stifled a gasp as he pulled her body tight to his.

"Would you like to play, Tandy?" He looked at her with a glint in his eyes. He'd said those same words long ago when he wanted to fuck her creatively. A shiver ran up her spine at the memories.

"No, thank you, Your Highness. I'm quite tired," she said before turning her head away, though she wanted him desperately. It was as if the last seven years caught up to her and she felt years worth of lust all at once. He put both of his hands around her waist before hoisting her up, sitting her on the table where there was nothing to hinder their movements. She glanced at the table and realized he must have planned for this. The table was suspiciously devoid of any place settings while the side they sat on was still cluttered with the remnants of their meal. She turned back to face him, watching his face as he smirked and raised a brow at her suggestively. She blinked at him before attempting to slide off the table.

He stepped closer, her knees spreading as he pushed himself against her. She gasped as he dragged his hands over her back, sliding one over her waist as the other wrapped around the back of her neck. His nose touched hers as they breathed the same air, close enough that their lips grazed.

"Didn't you miss me?" He whispered. His hips nudged her where he was nestled between her legs. She bit her tongue at the sensation as warmth filled her again. Davian leaned back to stare at her, his grin wolfish and hungry as she reacted to his touch. He slid his fingers into her hair, tightly wound in a simple bun, and fanned his fingers through the curls until he was able to use his hold on her to guide her eyes back to his.

"What do you want," she breathed, not sure what to do as a part of Davian made its presence known where he rested his body against the heat between her legs. Hot and hard, she felt his erection from beyond the layers of her dress. She wanted to look away from his eyes, but couldn't despite the flush on her cheeks.

"You," he told her simply before pressing against her.

"You want me to prove how much of a slut I am, is that it?" Tandy asked, turning her head so her cheek was pressed to his lips.

"Only for me, right?" He asked before trailing his lips down her neck. She breathed through her nose at the feeling, her hands unconsciously gripping his shirt. *Of course, only for you,* she thought. He opened his lips and left a wet kiss on her clavicle, sending a thrill through her. She was sure her panties were soaked, but clenched her jaw so as not to make a sound. He ran his tongue over her neck all the way to her earlobe. Her hands grabbed him around the back of his neck as her thighs tightened around him. He placed another kiss on her jaw, right under her ear. She took a deep breath and steadied herself, leaning away from his touch.

As she pulled away, her hands let go of the grip she had on his shirt around his collar. She wasn't even certain when she had grabbed him in the first place. She met his eyes as she pulled away, but he held her waist tight.

"I need you," he told her, licking his lips. She couldn't help but stare at his mouth as his tongue danced along his lip, her cheeks burning bright though she held fast to her expression.

"I need to leave," she told him.

"But I missed you," he breathed. She almost believed him, she *wanted* to believe him.

"You haven't spoken to me in years," Tandy said, shaking her head. "You sent me away because of a rumor, ruined our engagement ball and I never received one letter in the years that I was gone." She leaned away from him and he stepped back slightly, his hands still wrapped around her. "You forgot I existed, and now that I've returned you expect me to warm you in the same bed that's been warming Mariana for years," she continued.

"That isn't true," Davian stopped her. "Most of the shit Mariana said was a lie."

"The rumors were also lies, and yet everyone believed them. How is this different?" She asked. Davian stared at her with a sad expression. He sighed before rubbing his eyes.

"I'm trying to explain," he told her. That was *not* what she expected him to say, but she maintained a cold demeanor.

"You had seven years and dozens of letters to do that."

"I know it was my fault that you were punished for no reason, and my fault for not reaching out during those years," he started after a moment. His brown eyes were soft and it took all of her training to not pull him closer. "Something was affecting me physically and I couldn't touch the letters without feeling discomfort."

"I don't understand," she said finally. Davian cupped her cheeks before turning her gaze to meet his. His thumbs rubbed gently against her skin, overwhelming her with his touch.

"I don't either, but I am *trying*. I missed you, Tandy, and I would like to fix this," he told her.

"Surely there will be another rumor in the not so distant future where you'll change your mind about me again," Tandy said as she crossed her arms over her chest. As he held onto her, she felt her careful construction of apathy begin to crumble. If he would let her leave, she could mask her feelings in her rooms. If he kept pushing her, she'd inevitably break. It was too much for her to bear, looking into his eyes and feeling his touch after so long.

He pulled her closer, hugging her tightly. He ran his hands from her hair to her ass as she sat on the table. He lifted her suddenly before kicking open the doors to his bedroom and marched her to his bed.

"What better way to blow off steam than to angry fuck the man that abandoned you?" He asked cheekily. Gods, she wanted him to fuck her.

He climbed over her on the bed until he nestled close, pressing her knees apart with his own. He leaned over her as he rested between her legs and raked his eyes down her body, before looking her in the eyes. He reached one hand out and ran it along her belly to her breast, sliding it achingly slowly until it cupped her cheek. His thumb grazed her bottom lip, pulling it down and exposing her tongue. He licked his lips before looking back into her eyes and raised his brows. He pressed his hips against hers. Her skirts were in the way but the heat and weight of him as he rolled himself against her made her gasp and clutch the blanket she laid on. She turned her head to the side as he leaned down, trailing soft kisses down her cheek to her neck.

"I'm sorry for hurting you, Tandy. Please let me fix this and start from where we left off," he said gently. One of his hands found the end of her skirt and slowly ran his hand along her calf, her thigh, before stopping against her belly. She squirmed under his touch as he kept kissing along the exposed skin around her neckline as his fingers danced around her body everywhere except where she wanted him to be.

She let out a frustrated whimper when his fingers teased her sex before quickly dancing along her thigh. She opened her eyes as he tickled her cheek with his rough stubble. As she was about to melt into his touch, her eyes caught sight of something familiar on his bedside table.

"What is that?" She asked, almost to herself before pushing against Davian's chest. He moved out of her way easily, confused at what she was looking at. She ignored his expression as she reached for the small envelope on the end of the table, a delicate pink that she remembered vividly, her handwriting still perfect on the envelope.

"You," she said softly, "you never opened them." Her lips trembled, her throat felt tight. She wasn't sure he'd even gotten them. But there the letter was, as fresh as the day she had sent it. She struggled to crawl to the end of the bed, only to find an entire box of letters sitting on the floor nearly hidden under the mattress. She stood only to crumple to the floor in front of the box, nearly bumping her head. Davian jumped down behind her and held her back against his chest.

"I'm sorry, I was going to read them soon," he started to say but she pushed him away from her, elbowing him hard. He fell back on his ass as her vision spun. She pulled the box from where it was hidden and brought it close to her. Davian sat back behind her, and pulled her back against him again. "No, you're not leaving," he told her gently. She felt like a trapped animal, desperately wanting to escape as she held the pink square in her trembling hands.

"You *abandoned* me," her voice sounded like a little girl, a tremor in her words. She pushed him off of her again as she grabbed some of the letters. She stood on her knees as Davian sat back on the floor, legs straight. He moved to kneel in front of her, but she stood shakily, still clutching the envelopes. They were dated from the days she had experienced some of the worst of the abuse, her pleas for someone to rescue her discarded and left to gather dust.

"Tandy, I'm sorry," he said softly, hands raised in apology. She realized she was crying only after her vision blurred as the tears fell. *There goes all my training,* she thought bitterly. She threw all but one of the letters at him, watching them hit him and bounce to the ground. She tore the envelope open and began to read out loud a moment suspended in time.

"Dear Davian,

The other girls warned me that these lessons would start soon. I hadn't believed them, I thought they were only trying to scare me. But my class of five were led to the stage in the auditorium and it happened. We were made to "perform" for our husbands to be. Di'Liean and I were expected to go first but we both were too confused to understand the lesson. We were struck with reeds and made to complete the lesson. I was unable to complete it as was expected and was punished again, and again. Lashes and no food or sleep until it was perfect. After a considerate amount of punishment and reeducation, I was able to finally perform a lascivious and carnal performance of fellatio and coitus that made Headmistress proud, and I hope you as well."

Tandy paused as her eyes blurred with tears before continuing.

"To please you, I made sure to complete the lesson to the best of my ability. You will be glad to know your future wife scored perfectly due to my diligence and always striving for excellence. Even the guards watching the lesson commented on how lucky my husband would be to see me

on my knees this way when I graduate. I hope to be released sooner, to show you how well I was trained for you.

I swear to make it up to you for allowing my character to be doubted in such a way that disrespected you. The rumors are unfounded, but I can find you without fault for believing them. I am sorry to have caused you to doubt me, and hope my efforts here prove my dedication to you and only you. I should have done more to prove to you my innocence and I am sorry. I hope you read this letter with pride and rest well knowing how hard I work and will continue to work to make you happy.

Yours always,

Tandy"

She stopped reading and dropped the paper as she moved to walk around him. He stopped her, grabbing her hand and pulled her down hard. He sat her on his lap, making her straddle him. She was desperate to escape, though, and tried pushing him to get free, but he held tight to her hands and kept them at her sides.

"You wanted to see the ice Princess finally break character?" She weeped. "You were going to run into Mariana's bed as soon as you made a fool of me, taking me and bragging about how much of a whore I am to give in to you," she said, groaning as she struggled to get her wrists free. "The worst days of my life I had to spend *alone* while you had your share of women and parties and opulence, while I *begged* for *death* since escape was impossible. And *all this time*, every single moment I've been alone thinking the Headmistress was withholding my return correspondence, it was *you* all along," she cried, tears pouring down her face.

"I cried for you and Mariana, I cried for my mother and father. I never saw *anyone* the whole time I suffered in that prison and you're here now, trying to fuck me like no time has passed at all." Her chest heaved with her sobs, she could do nothing to control the sounds she was making. "It almost worked too, because I am a weak and sinful girl that never learns." All her training was *ruined* as she exploded at Davian years of pent up rage. She vaguely knew she was screaming in Davian's face, but she couldn't stop. The voice inside of her begged her to stop and just allow him to fuck her, to take her and use her just to please him. What did it matter after all. She couldn't stop, though, as tears leaked from her eyes steadily.

"How could you do this to me?" She weeped. Davian only held her tightly in his hands. "Let me go!" She pulled against him with no avail. She dropped her head and cried. Ugly, shaking, screaming tears. Davian pulled her down, tucking her against his chest again. He rocked them back and forth as she cried.

"It's okay," he said softly, stroking her hair. "I'm so sorry." With another sob, she pushed herself away from him and stood, trying to run to the door. Davian scooped her up without a thought and placed her back onto his bed. She only cried louder, unable to escape, and held her face in her hands.

"What did I ever do to you, for you to abandon me?"

Ten

Davian

"What did I ever do to you, for you to abandon me?" Tandy cried, holding her face in her hands. *Oh no,* he thought. That was *not* what he thought would happen tonight. Mariana was going to *kill* him. He stepped toward her again, knowing she would probably only push him away again. He deserved it, though. Her heartbreak was *his* fault. He felt sick as she had read the letter to him.

What exactly had they made her *do* there? His skin crawled as he thought of all of those girls being bred into nothing more than docile bed warmers. He could have saved her from the hell of the reform school if he had read *any* of the letters.

"I'm sorry, Tandy, I didn't know -" he started. She looked at him with icy eyes, though her lips quivered with emotion.

"You *would* have known if you had opened up a single fucking letter!" She yelled. He nodded, that was also well deserved.

"I read some of them," he said slowly, a clear lie. She glared at him, a sight he hadn't seen in forever. She had always been able to see through his bullshit.

"*No,* you did not or you'd *know* those rumors were a lie *and* that I was *imprisoned!*" A sob punctuated her words. He wasn't sure what to say, but knew the truth was the only way out of this. "I am going back to my room now. I'll even send Mariana in here for you to laugh about me and my emotional outburst and for letting you touch me like that. I'm *so* stupid," she muttered. "Why *would* you want me when you could have her," she slid off the bed, but Davian grabbed her and sat her back down.

She screamed in frustration and cried harder. The sound broke his heart, he really didn't know what to do. He sighed before stepping closer to her, gently brushing back loose curls that had fallen from her bun. He pressed his lips to her head, before wrapping his arms around her and pulling her to his chest in a big hug.

"Mariana and I were never together, Tandy," he sighed, clutching her close. "We never have nor will we *ever,* despite what may have been said before."

"You're lying," she sobbed against his chest.

"No, I'm really not. I was a real son of a bitch, but I could never think of Mar like that," he said honestly, the mere thought disgusting him. "Whatever was said before was a lie. I had no hand in Mariana saying it the other day," he paused, "and what I suspect she said when you arrived in her care."

Her tears soaked his shirt as she clawed and pulled at him, unable to decide if she wanted his comfort or if she wanted to push him away again. His words did little to soothe her and all he could do was hold her tight while she cried. The emotions clearly had no way to regulate or escape her as she had been conditioned to ignore it. With Davian pushing Tandy past her limit, he knew her reaction would be explosive. He kissed her hair and her forehead, softly whispering that he was sorry for everything. She tried to push herself out of his arms but he held her tight.

"No, you and I need to talk. You can't leave yet," he told her.

"What do you need to say?" She sighed, resigning herself to be pressed against him.

"I'm sorry, Tandy," he told her honestly. Tandy looked at him with wide eyes, bottom lip pouting as she tried to control the flow of tears.

"I'm *so* sorry," he continued, nearly begging her to accept his apology. "I had missed you and what we had before," he admitted. She wiped her eyes, looking away from him. "My beautiful bride," he whispered, placing his thumb on her chin.

"You didn't miss me," she shook her head as she glared at him, swatting his hand away.

"Yes, I did," he urged. "I may have been the asshole that ignored you for years, but there was more going on than you think," he told her. More tears fell from his eyes as he pulled her close. He pressed his face to her cheek and kissed her neck, breathing in the smell of her floral perfume.

"What more could there have been? All this time you've believed the *same* rumor that had me sent across the world. What *else* happened?" She demanded. Davian could only shake his head and sigh. There was no good way to answer that and he knew it. He groaned, running his hand through his hair before meeting Tandy's eyes. "Why did you *believe* those rumors in the first place? Did taking my virginity mean *nothing* to you?"

"Tandy, it meant everything to me. Please, I'm trying to explain," he pleaded. "Just hear me out before you decide you don't want me anymore."

"Why should I hear anybody out? Where have I *been* all this time while *my* pleas were ignored? When I begged for your understanding, where were you?" Her voice was like venom to his ears, burning him with each word.

"You need to hear me out because what else can you do?" He said finally. She closed her eyes and sighed heavily.

"Fine," she said, her face nearly as empty of emotion as it had been since her arrival. "Say what you need to say."

"In all honesty, there are many layers to this that I am only recently uncovering," he said slowly, gathering his words. He was worried he would lose her before he even started.

"Just get it over with," Tandy said dejectedly. He frowned at her words but nodded and pulled her back to the bed.

"Relax, Tandy. I'm not going to fuck you tonight. Just lay down with me so we can talk." She stood there rigidly, refusing to move with a shake to her head. The extravagant window overlooking the lake cast the light from the sunset into the room and bathed Tandy in a seductive light, though he felt guilty for wanting her even as she cried.

"I fucking *missed* you and need to feel you, Tandanea. Get over here, *please*," he said, voice gravelly with emotion. She closed her eyes for a moment as if bracing herself before allowing him to pull her in after him.

"Explain," she sighed as he pulled her to his chest.

"On the night of the betrothal, my father had told me you performed a rather enthusiastic seduction attempt to earn your right to be my wife. At the time, I was only seventeen, and the words quite literally felt like a dagger to my gut. When you showed up at the ball looking stunning, all I felt was betrayal," he explained. "How could someone as beautiful as you find *me* worthy? I wanted to hurt you, so I said some awful things." He ran his hands over Tandy's arms and kissed her hair. "Then each boy in our Circle told me they'd gotten with you, though they never specified when or where. Considering we'd been inseparable for years by then, I should've seen through their lies immediately."

"I fucked the *King* in another rumor?" Tandy scoffed. "*When?* When could that have happened when I could hardly walk the gardens alone without being ravaged by *you*, Davian?" She shook her head. "And all of our friends said they fucked me, too? How could I have managed that when we traveled together exclusively and majority of our Circle were only spoken to through letters?"

"I was a moronic dumb ass, obviously," Davian shrugged before sighing and continuing in a more serious tone. "It sounds bad no matter how you look at it, Tandy. It was as if when I drank that night, *every* single horrible fear I've had was amplified physically," Davian said empathically. "I could hardly swallow without despair and rage filling my throat, choking me with its intensity."

"From the *wine?*" Tandy muttered, clearly not convinced. He sighed but continued, there was nothing else for him to do.

"As the weeks passed, I thought about you constantly. But it seemed whenever I thought of you or a letter arrived, the same red wine that I tasted at the ball found its way to my glass. And every time I tasted it, a confusing mix of emotions filled me. Anger, love, despair. I became volatile and angry, lashing out much like I did at the ball when I spoke to you last," his voice trailed off, lost in thought.

"Even now it's hard to explain the way memories of our past would make me happy, but thoughts of our future spurred on *hours* of anxiety and despair. The sadness made me angrier, and I lost my temper over small things *a lot* over the years because of it," he said.

"Whenever I tried to read the letters, the wine burned my throat and I'd see rage by the time I swallowed it down. I was unable to touch them even when I wanted to know the truth," he tried to explain. "I would react violently at the sight of them, and then I began to resent the letters themselves for the emotions I was losing the war to." He paused to collect his thoughts. He sounded insane and he was sure Tandy wouldn't believe him. "My mind made a connection like a bull in the ring. The letters caused pain and therefore were not safe, though I wanted to read them desperately. I saved them even when it hurt me to touch them. I hid them somewhere safe for the day I was stronger than whatever had suddenly come over me."

"I am sure that I was affected by something, I am not that kind of man to act in such a way. You know me better than anyone and I would never act that way of my own free will," he said finally. "It sounds like an excuse, but I promise you it's true. You saw how Mariana acted after drinking just yesterday," he held her tighter. "You saw me on the day of the betrothal. I was loving and attentive that morning and yet by the time you arrived at the ballroom I was a different man, out of control and vicious."

"Wine wouldn't make you resent me so easily," she said, though she hesitated. "The rumor was ridiculous, Davian. For it to have even been considered as truth is even more ridiculous."

"No, my seduction attempt that failed catastrophically is ridiculous," he sighed. "This, however, is *treasonous*," he looked into her eyes for a moment, intense with emotion. "From what I remember of that day, everything was fine *until* I had the red wine and then every day since then, I've been haunted by the taste of it stuck in my throat. Since I stopped consuming anything but water, I haven't had explosive outbursts or depressive episodes that left me immobile."

"I suppose it is possible you were poisoned," Tandy said after a moment. "It seems...unlikely, though."

"I wouldn't lie to you," he told her.

"Wouldn't lie to me?" She asked, pushing against his chest. "How could I know that? We aren't the same people we used to be."

"Every day I spent without you was empty," he looked down at her. "I've been in agony without you here. You know the kind of man I really am, Tandy. I know I fucked up but I'll prove to you its the truth. I didn't abandon you on purpose, my love," he told her, cupping her cheek.

"Your abandonment hurt more than I could ever express," she admitted, fresh tears spilling over.

"Please forgive me, Tandy," he wrapped his arms tighter around her as he pressed his face into her hair. He hoped she could feel his honesty as he clutched at her.

"Saying please gets you nothing, as Headmistress would say," she whispered.

"Don't talk like that, Tandy, it doesn't sound like you," he said with a frown.

"How would you even know what I sound like anymore?" She countered.

"Please let me make it up to you," he said with a broken sigh. "I'll prove to you I'm telling the truth when we figure out who fucked up the wine."

"If you and Mariana were both poisoned, I'd find it hard to believe," Tandy shook her head. Davian opened his mouth to object but Tandy pressed a finger to his lips. "It wouldn't have *only* been you two. It would also mean someone connected to the both of you had someone within the palace *and* Mariana's home with access to the letters and the wine. You're asking a lot from me to even consider all of this." She withdrew her hand from his mouth as his brows furrowed in thought. "If your words are true, a *huge* attempt on the crown is being made and you are sitting idly by while it happens."

"I am trying to keep the Kingdom afloat while my father watches idly by," Davian tried to explain. "I've been doing my best for the last decade to be the King my subjects need, but it hasn't been easy."

"You've been acting as King?" Tandy asked after a moment.

"Yes, essentially. I hardly had time to sort through my own feelings let alone dedicate my time to anything but the Kingdom's needs," he frowned, rubbing his head. "Listen, I understand how it sounds. There are a lot of answers we need to find," he said. "Will you be there for me while we find them?"

"Like the way you were there for me when I asked for answers on my exile?" She asked, her eyes taking on the same unreadable expression she had used since her arrival. "After all these years, you have the nerve to ask for *my* help when I was punished for a crime I never committed?"

"I was unwell and struggling, Tandy," he started.

"I was battered and abused, Davian. You'll have to give me more proof of this treasonous attempt on your life. A poison that *only* affected your ability to communicate with your fiance sounds awfully convenient for you. Goodnight, Prince Davian." She pulled the blankets off her and stepped off the bed.

"Tandy, *please*," Davian called after her, scrambling to his feet.

Tandy pulled away from him and left the room, the doors closing behind her. Davian sighed in disappointment and rubbed his eyes. His Princess would need more to forgive him and he would set out to do it come morning.

As he climbed back into his bed exhausted from their conversation, he couldn't help but think over her words. It *was* oddly specific that his communications with Tandy were so affected by whatever was wrong with the wine. What could possibly do that to a man's body? More importantly, *who* would do that to the Prince and soon to be Princess?

Who would benefit the most from ending their engagement?

Eleven

Tandy

Tandy entered her room and locked the antechamber doors before closing each of the curtains in her bedroom. She stumbled over the chairs and furniture as the room became darker and darker around her, but managed to slide into her bed without injury. Her stomach was overly full and she willed herself to remain calm, she couldn't afford to lose another meal when she was already so malnourished. She ignored the nausea rolling through her, rolling onto her side and clutching her arms around her. Much like her bouts of forced isolation at the reform school, Tandy laid in the quiet room as her heart raced.

Though she was certain any chance she had of reconciliation was completely destroyed by her outburst, she didn't know how else she was supposed to react to his words. To blame his abandonment on *wine* was ridiculous. To have wine be the reason he had left her to rot for the better part of a decade hurt to think about. She tried to push his words from her mind but no matter how hard she tried, she couldn't help but repeat what he had said.

I was a different man.

Though it seemed unlikely, Davian *had* been a different person at the ball. Someone she had never seen before with anger changing his face and warping it into a stranger. *Could he have been poisoned with that wine?* She didn't know for sure, but doubt slowly filled her mind as the night crept on.

She hadn't been in the Realm for so long, she had no way of knowing what lurked the corridors of the palace anymore. If someone had been stalking the Prince and a Lady across the Kingdom of minimal Royal connection, surely that would mean a greater threat lay just in the shadows.

"The Royal Court is madness," she whispered to herself as tears streamed steadily down her cheeks as thoughts of doubt and anger swirled through her.

***

Tandy woke up curled into a ball, blankets on the floor. Her fingers and toes were so cold they felt numb, making it difficult to stand up. She vaguely heard someone knocking on her bedroom door but ignored it. She picked up the covers and laid back down, pulling them over her head. She fell back to sleep quickly, so tired she could hardly open her eyes.

Hours passed Tandy before the doors were rattled enough for her to rouse from a deep but restless sleep. Her head felt tight as a headache settled into her brow, blurring her vision. Her eyes blinked heavily as she unlatched the door, wobbling on her feet. She made it back into bed before the maids even realized the door was unlocked.

"Your Grace," the maid cried as she pushed open the door. Bright light streaked through the room, but Tandy only pulled the blanket over her eyes.

"You need to be getting to lunch, Duchess. You were called on by the Prince. He said you can't miss another meal," the maid said gently as she raised Tandy, sitting her up from under the blanket. They dressed her as quickly as they could, but Tandy felt so tired and drained that she could hardly help them as they guided her legs into a gown. The girls tutted around Tandy, pulling and tugging her until she was upright and in the hallway, hair done and dressed.

Tandy blinked and suddenly she was guided into the room where they'd gone over wedding swatches, having zoned out during the walk there. The maids held the door open for her before curtsying and walking away while the Knights remained in the hall. She could hardly see through the bright sun shining in from the window, her eyes still sensitive from having been in the dark for so long.

Davian and Mariana stared at her as she took a shaky step to her chair, their eyes wide as they took her in. Tandy ignored it and sat as calmly as she could, staring at her plate with her hands on her lap. She made no expression, but the food gave her pause. It was some of her favorites as a child - sticky buns, a fruit bowl and small sandwich rolls.

"What the fuck did you *do* to her, Dav?" Mariana asked, concern in her voice. He shrugged, eyes wide.

"I don't *know*," he admitted as he rubbed his hands through his hair. "You have to eat something, Tandy," Davian told her gently. Tandy could think of dozens of things she'd rather do than eat when she felt this ill, but reached for a strawberry anyway.

"I had dinner with you last night," she said as she nibbled the berry, annoyed at how critical he sounded.

"Tandy, it's been *days* since we had dinner. Have you not eaten anything this whole fucking time?" Davian nearly yelled. She paused chewing as she heard his words, not realizing it had been so long.

"Who cares? I've gone longer between meals before," she answered after swallowing the fruit. It was sweet but her taste buds burned at the flavor.

Davian sighed before standing up and gesturing to Mariana. They stood and pulled their chairs next to Tandy. She immediately felt trapped and anxious between them, her hunger making her reactions slower though she kept her emotions in check all the same. She would not break her training protocols this time, she *couldn't*.

"Here, Tandy. The pastries are still warm," Mariana said in a delicate voice as she placed a raspberry cream danish on her plate next to the fruit. Tandy didn't move, though her stomach growled loudly as she smelled everything.

"Please eat, Tandy," Davian urged her, his hand brushing her cheek. She flinched and leaned her head down, a knot forming in her throat.

"It was the school that made you this way, wasn't it?" Mariana asked sadly. Tandy didn't answer but she knew despite her best efforts, she would cry soon if she didn't leave immediately. She tried to push her chair away from the table.

"No, Tandy. You *have* to eat now," Davian said. He put his arm around her shoulders and pressed his chair as close to Tandy's as he could. *Please don't break, please don't break,* she willed herself over and over. But Tandy couldn't fight back the tears any longer and kept her head bowed as they flowed freely down her face. Her face remained neutral, the flow of tears were the only thing to signify her sorrow. Davian brushed her hair from her brow before using his thumb to wipe away a tear as it made its way down her cheek.

"I'll get her to eat, you start talking," Mariana murmured to Davian as she began cutting the food on her plate into bite sized pieces.

"I'm not hungry," Tandy whispered, though her stomach growled again.

"You may not feel hungry because you've starved yourself for *three* days now. Have you even had any water?" Mariana's voice was stern but not unkind, making Tandy's tears flow harder.

"Tandy, I wanted to tell you that we read your letters. That night when you left, I tried to follow you but you didn't answer the door. So I found Mariana, and we read each letter," he said directly into her ear, curving himself against her side. Mariana placed a small bite of food at her lips, urging her to eat as Davian spoke.

"We even wrote you some letters back, even though they're long past due. We're very sorry, Tandy," Mariana offered as Davian fell silent. "The truth is, things weren't much better for us over here. Davian has been running the country since about the time you were sent away, and I -" her voice broke off for a moment before continuing. "Well, I've been dealing with Martina. And you've seen how that's going," she admitted in a whisper. Tandy finally looked up and saw Mariana's face full of tears of her own.

Tandy couldn't stand it another moment, sitting pressed between them like that. She pushed her chair out from the table harder than before, the harsh shriek of the legs against the floor rattling through the room. Tandy turned out of her seat quickly, and made it to the door before sweeping out into the hallway. Her body revolted against her as her movements caught up to her, though. She was simply too faint from hunger to move so quickly. Her vision tunneled into a bright white haze as her ears rang. The darkness swallowed her up as she lost consciousness before she even hit the ground.

***

Tandy groaned as she woke up. Her head felt stuffed with cotton and she didn't know where she was.

"Thank the *gods*, Tandy," Davian said as he hurried to her side with a glass of water. She was confused for a minute before she remembered where they had been and what they were doing.

"Stop trying to get me into your bed, Davian," she sighed as she pinched the bridge of her nose. Mariana laughed from the recliner, no doubt waiting for Tandy to wake up.

"I told you that you're not as smooth as you think you are," she snickered at Davian before walking over to Tandy. She handed Tandy a glass of something that looked yellow while Davian stood to the side, still holding the water glass.

"Drink this, Tandy. The doctor brought it when you fainted. It's really just lemons and vitamins, but it will help you gain your strength back," Mariana told her. Tandy hesitated to take it, but when Davian huffed out a frustrated breath she grabbed it quickly.

"You went too far, Tandy. Withholding food and water from yourself is *not* okay," he admonished gently. "Drink the damn cocktail, or I'll *make* you drink it." Mariana scoffed at his words.

"Dav, would you just shut the fuck up?" Mariana asked, exasperated.

"She could have *died*, Mar, *no* I can't," he grumbled.

"I wasn't going to die, Davian. I've dealt with worse at the reform school," she said before taking a sip of the yellow liquid. And very nearly choked to death on it when she did.

"What *is* this?" Tandy coughed and sputtered on the sour yet surprisingly sweet concoction.

"The doctor said it was a blend of lemon, sugar, salt, and some types of fruit oils," Mariana giggled. Davian took the jar from Tandy's hands and took a small taste of it, before spitting it out immediately.

"Oh no, Tandy, that is all for you," he handed it back to her. She wiped the tears from her eyes as she cleared her throat from coughing. She braced herself before drinking the vial in one big sip, and then grabbed the water from Davian to chase it down.

"We brought lunch back into Davian's room, I think you should eat something while we talk," Mariana said as she took the empty glasses from Tandy. Davian brought a plate of food to her and handed it to her on the bed.

"Eat until you feel sick, Tandanea," he urged her before bringing a chair to the side of the bed and sitting down.

"I always feel sick," she muttered as Mariana sat on the edge of Davian's bed on the other side of Tandy. Davian sighed before he spoke again, shaking his head sadly at her.

"I'm sorry," Davian told her sadly. "I'm *so* sorry Tandy, you're right that I abandoned you. I'm grateful you heard me out the other day, though," he said in a soft voice. "I know what I said sounded like an excuse but it's not. I hope you can forgive me," Davian told her, his eyes focused on her. Mariana moved forward and began breaking Tandy's food into smaller pieces and gesturing for her to eat while Davian talked. She sighed but slowly ate small bites of food.

"With a clear head now, I'm able to see a pattern in the behavior of the Circle. The letters appeared right away and with them, so did the wine. The wine started at the ball, of that I'm sure. I'd never tasted that blend before," Davian explained.

"I won't lie, the wine made me become paranoid and angry. I think you witnessed my last wine induced outburst," Mariana sighed. "There's definitely a connection."

"You want me to believe that you were both not only poisoned from the same wine in different provinces of the realm, but that the entire Kingdom said that the Prince's bride was a whore and the betrothal remains anyway," Tandy put her fork down for a moment, thinking over her words. "Do you understand what you are asking me right now?"

"Okay, yeah," Davian said sheepishly as he ran his hand through his hair. "It does sound really stupid, but I promise you it's true. You should know, though, that I never considered ending our betrothal. Ever. Even at my worst and even if the rumors *had* been true, I would not have ended our betrothal," he admitted. "The bouts of rage and paranoia were also exacerbated at times, like when my father told me that women would *never* be friends with me and anyone that pretended would get me and the kingdom into trouble."

"If the public sees me as an unloyal slut, how could the Royal family keep our betrothal at all? Surely my reputation is ruined and would damage your name," Tandy wondered.

"At this point, it wouldn't matter to me if your name *was* damaged," he said honestly. "I feel like I've woken up after a really long nightmare, Tandy." Davian looked at her with his brown eyes glistening with unshed tears. Tandy sighed and rubbed her head, a headache finding itself between her brows again.

"It's too late for that now," she grumbled. "Just tell me what other rumors you heard."

"One of the rumors was that you were traveling to get rid of a bastard child from one of the random gentlemen in attendance at the last ball, the one held for my seventeenth birthday party," his voice was nothing beyond a whisper. "Some also said you were nothing more than a bitch in heat, carrying gods knows what kind of illnesses with your indecencies."

"They said I was with *child?*" Her voice was calm despite the anger simmering within her. "Carrying a bastard and *still* your fiancé," she shook her head.

"A lot of the other boys in the court had said they'd been in intimate relationships with nearly all of the girls in their circles, including me," Mariana said quietly. "Since they weren't lying about fucking *me*, surely that meant they weren't lying about you," Mariana admitted.

"You should've just asked me," she told them.

"I'm sorry," Davian said earnestly.

"I'm sorry, too," Mariana told her.

"If you were worried about what your father said, you should've ended it. Why would your parents keep the arrangement if that was his opinion of me in the first place, especially if my name was tarnished in the Kingdom?"

"At this point, you know as much as we know," Davian told her with a shrug. "I didn't end our betrothal and neither did our parents attempt to. It has remained unchanged since it was documented and announced."

"Well, who would benefit the most from our betrothal being canceled?" She asked. "Do you think there are advisors working with whoever may be trying to negate the betrothal?" Tandy asked, though another idea emerged before Davian spoke.

"It *must* be more insidious than it looks to be on the surface. My father has been completely disengaged from ruling for the last six years. His last cohesive thought was most likely before you were even sent away. I've been running the country for *years*, Tandy," he admitted. "I was too young to take the throne and most of the last few years are a blur to me because of the anger and resentment I carried with me."

"Could the King have been drinking the same wine that you and Mariana were given?" Tandy asked. Mariana and Davian shared an uneasy look.

"It would explain his emotional decline," Davian said finally. "If the Prince was targeted, surely the King and Queen would be as well."

"There is another thing to consider," Tandy told them with a sigh as the facts all added up into one point.

"What is it?" Davian asked as he pulled his chair closer to her.

"When you and Mariana laughed together the other day, I noticed something strange right before Martina came in," she paused again, her stomach churning as she thought of Martina's untimely arrival. "You both have the same dimples as the King," she said finally. "I'm afraid Martina must have seen it, too, because of the timing and her reaction. You both look an *awful* lot like the King and honestly, quite like each other," Tandy said, pausing as she glanced between their similar faces.

"A lot of people have dimples and brown hair, though," Davian shrugged.

"You are undoubtedly, brother and sister. I mean, *look* at you," Tandy said. They glanced between each other with narrowed eyes. "Smile," Tandy instructed. They sighed but grinned at each other, revealing their dimples.

"Well," Davian started.

"Fuck," Mariana huffed. It was undeniable as they stared at each other.

"I had a memory of our nannies saying "*They could be twins*" and for a while, I had thought they meant Davian and the King," Tandy mused.

"Mariana looks just like her mother, though," Davian argued, glancing back at Tandy with a serious expression. "If there *is* somehow a connection there, that is worrisome since Mariana is older than I am."

"What she said the other day finally makes sense," Mariana shook her head slowly, her eyes full of concern.

"What did she say?" Davian urged, leaning forward.

"She kept telling me that it was my turn, it should've been me all along. She was crazed, I thought she had finally lost her mind. She just kept shaking me and screaming at me, and then ranting and pacing, forcing wine down my throat. The only thing that I understood entirely was that she knew all along I didn't belong to Easton, but never had proof because of how much I look like her. I thought it had always angered her that I didn't look like Tandy, but it was really about how much I look like *her*. She couldn't have known who the father of her child was, because there were no differences between her and I," she said, words bubbling out of her mouth rapid fire as she tried to explain herself.

"Do you think she thinks this will be the way to get you to where Tandy is?" Davian asked.

"Dav, I don't think she would want you to marry your sister," Tandy said.

"I think she wants me where *you* are, Dav," Mariana finished. They all shared an uneasy look with each other. "At least you know that I absolutely would *not* want the position. I would rather bite off my own toes," Mariana said with a grimace.

"And if Mariana is older than me, even by a few weeks, it poses a risk to the birth order of the Crown," Davian sighed. "I just don't believe dimples would be enough of a reason to identify your bloodline."

"It's more than that, I assure you. You have the same eyes as Mariana, the same shape and color. Your dimples are identical, your smiles are a mirrored image," Tandy said. "And frankly, you're both infuriating." Mariana laughed when Davian rolled his eyes at Tandy's words.

"But how is it possible she hadn't seen your dimples *years* ago?" Davian asked, waving his hands.

"She had no use for me until I was of an age in which she could use me for her gain. She instructed the nannies to keep me quiet, which meant *no* giggling in Mother's presence. She was always strict about me being the perfect lady. There was to be no smiling, slouching, or sedition, as she always told me. I learned how to smile without smiling," Mariana demonstrated the different smiles she used. "I was punished for anything other than perfection. Martina *never* saw me smile because she is a soulless woman and couldn't care less for anyone that's not her. She is jealous that I wear her face." Tandy and Davian sighed as Mariana spoke. Tandy grieved for her friend who fared much the same as she had for all those years.

"I think a proper investigation should be held before things continue any further, in case our theories are wrong. After being nearly ruined by a rumor, I wouldn't want to do the same to another," Tandy said, rubbing her eyes. "It is just quite suspicious to me that not only was our betrothal targeted, but the face Martina made when she saw your shared smile *and* the wine that was possibly poisoned and altered your perceptions..." She trailed off, a chill on her skin. "All I can think is that *if* you were truly poisoned to sever our betrothal, you were likely not the only victims and another plan must be underway. A plan that most likely doesn't include me *or* Davian anymore." Tandy could see Davian bristle at her words, his brow furrowing in thought.

"I swear, I know nothing about any of my mother's plans. She keeps me in the dark most of the time unless she needs something from me," Mariana said, voice wavering. "I would tell you if I knew anything, and I'll listen to more of her ramblings to make sure I don't miss anything important again."

"Stop, Mar," Davian said, shaking his hand. "I'm the least bit suspicious of you in anything, least of all aiding that woman for any reason other than for your self preservation. Tandy's right, I need to investigate this further." Davian rubbed his eyes and groaned. "I've been acting like my father this whole time, blinded by a stupid drink and now our lives are in danger."

"I'm sorry," Mariana said, rubbing his arm.

"Stop," he said, rolling his eyes. "I'm not Martina, I don't need to be placated. I'm telling you, if it was affecting you nearly as much as it did me, you had no ability to fight it. Tandy was probably the safest at the reform school, unfortunately. Gods know what could have happened if you remained in the Court," Davian shook his head as he met her eyes. She wondered for a moment if she would have been executed or shamed her family into losing their titles. She wasn't sure which fate would have been worse.

"Eat some more food, Tandy, and then you need to have another potion. The doctor said you need three by dinner, and then another three each day until you're well again," Davian said as he stood up to get her more food.

"I'm going to burst if I eat anymore," Tandy protested. She really didn't want to eat, she felt stuffed.

"Tandy, I also wanted to apologize for screaming at you the other day," Mariana told her.

"Thank you," Tandy told her. Mariana smiled at her before she stole a bite of fruit from the tray that Davian placed back onto the bed.

"What has Martina been doing to you, Mar?" Davian asked after looking her over. Though she wore a modest gown that covered her neck and arms, the bruises she had were still peeking from under her clothes.

"I don't want to talk about it," she said, bristling at the turn of the conversation.

"I think you *have* to talk about it," Tandy agreed.

"I think we need to talk about the letters," she countered. Davian sighed audibly and nodded, though he rolled his eyes anyway.

"We will finish tonight with the letters, and then it's your turn to talk, Mariana," he warned her. She nodded quickly, clearly grateful to be free of the direct questioning.

"If we talk about this, I cannot physically eat another bite of food. I will be sick if I do," she warned them.

"I understand," Mariana told her. Davian didn't argue, but she knew he was scanning her plate as he carried it to the table to see if she'd eaten enough.

"You'll eat dinner and a *lot* of dessert later, then," he said. He carried the box of letters to the bed, newly organized with additional letters in between the ones she'd sent to Davian all those years ago. Her stomach rolled at the sight of them.

"We read the letters, Tandy. We tried to write a letter back for each but we didn't finish those yet," Mariana told her.

"You don't have to write any more," Tandy told them. She shivered as Davian handed her the first response letter. "There's more important things to worry about."

"You don't have to read it out loud," he offered as she opened the envelope, ignoring what she said. She took a deep breath as she began to read Davian's message.

Dear Tandy,

I need to know if it's true, all of the things my father told me. Even the friends I have from the academy are insisting these rumors are true. I know I was cruel during the ball, but I deserve to know the truth. It is one thing to have an affair, but another thing to run off with another man's child. A man I most likely called 'friend' at one point. I need to know if it is true, Tandy, I can hardly sleep.

I just don't know how you could hurt me in this way, and then go sightseeing without me as if nothing happened. Don't I matter to you at all? I miss you desperately but I am hurt by what was said and done. Please respond with the truth, and hold nothing back.

Yours,

Davian

Tandy blinked as she read the letter. It felt as if seventeen year old Davian had written the letter. For so long she had waited for those words, though they weren't kind or gentle in any way. A piece of her fifteen year old self felt almost a sort of relief to read it, though seven years late. Davian wordlessly handed her another one.

Dear Tandy,

I don't understand why you were sent to the reform school, especially if the rumors were unfounded and bold faced lies.

Who sent you there?

I'll do whatever I can to return you home to your family. Maybe even move our wedding date so you may return home sooner. I'm sorry you're there but I will do what I can to ease your discomfort.

I love you and beg your forgiveness for ever doubting you. I will see you safely home soon, please hold tight for me a little longer.

Yours,

Davian

He handed her another letter. The tears in her eyes began to flow freely again as she read on.

Dear Tandy,

I'm appalled to hear about the 'lessons' they are putting you through. As soon as I learned of these sexual performances, I felt ill. You need not partake in these activities. I assure you, there is nothing you need to *"learn" that we couldn't learn together. Knowing you were made to pantomime these private acts in order to please your future husband only makes me feel sorrow for you and the trauma that you must be holding onto.*

I promise you, I will not allow them to treat another girl in this way. The school will be reopened under the crown with personally handpicked staffing devoid of any malice or corruption. You will not have suffered in their care with nothing to show for it, I will make sure of that.

The Head Mistress that forced you to perform these acts will be charged for multiple accounts of assault. There will be no girl forgotten or left behind as we clean out the faculty and maintain punishments for the crimes and atrocities they afflicted onto young and defenseless girls, along with the families that were aware of the treatment.

I will continue to investigate the Royal Circle and find any clues or reasons as to why you were sent there. No stone will be left unturned.

You will be home with me soon enough, and I will miss you until you return. Stay strong, Tandy.

Always yours,

Davian

Tandy dropped the letters to the bed and held her face in her hands. She wept freely, her shoulders quaking. She felt like she was a teenager again somehow. The letters made her feel as though she were given the missing pieces she was looking for during her imprisonment, that small ray of light between the clouds. She blinked her eyes open and grabbed the letters again and held them to her chest. Davian and Mariana moved to sit next to her, gently holding her as she cried.

Twelve

Davian

Davian held Tandy as she cried, the sun setting through the windows.

"I'll call for dinner and a sleeping gown for Tandy," Davian murmured to Mariana. "Hold her while I'm gone," he told her. Mariana wordlessly sat next to Tandy, holding her as Davian had. He left the room to call for a servant and returned a few minutes later.

Tandy had thankfully begun to calm down by the time Davian returned. Though he hadn't taken long, the seconds had passed like hours. Davian reached for Tandy as soon as he entered the room and wiped her cheeks free of tears before kissing her forehead. They waited in silence, sitting closely together until the servants brought dinner and pajamas for Tandy. She changed quickly in the bathroom while Davian cut her food into tiny pieces. Mariana arranged the last of the potions on the table for her to drink to finish with their meal.

"Do I really need to drink more of these?" She said, looking at the yellow juice as she joined them back at the table.

"Yes," Mariana and Davian said simultaneously. Tandy sighed but nodded before taking one of the jars, drinking it down quickly without any more protest.

"You need to eat at least half of that plate, Tandy," Davian warned her. She said nothing, only ate bite after bite. Davian watched her as she ate, worried about the small amount she always consumed. When she had eaten a small portion of her food, he saw Tandy's eyes fill with unshed tears.

"Are you okay?" He asked as he pushed his now empty plate away. Tandy nodded but the tears fell down her cheeks as she tried to eat another bite.

"If you're full, you don't have to eat anymore," Mariana said gently, reaching her hand to Tandy's.

"I don't know how to tell," Tandy admitted in a whisper. Davian's heart broke all over again, and he couldn't stop himself from pulling Tandy into a hug. He held onto her before pulling her up from the chair so he could sit down with her on his lap.

"You didn't talk about this in your letters," Mariana said.

"They always used food as a means of control," she explained. "When you're hungry enough, or tired enough, you eventually are unable to fight. The perfect docile wife is born." She paused for a moment, hands twiddling together as she thought. "I noticed later on that I wasn't hungry after the punishments and that I was physically ill whenever I ate. It was easier to be hungry than sick," her voice trailed off.

"Were all of the girls like this?" Davian asked as he held her.

"No, some of the younger girls seemed to fall into it easier. There were certainly favorites, and despite my standing as your betrothed I was really not offered much in that department. I was too oppositional and defiant, unruly and not easily controlled. The other girls would always get in trouble for associating with me and so I was avoided like the plague. They found me at fault every day, I was punished nearly constantly until I was either too starved or sleep deprived to do anything other than follow through with their expectations," Tandy explained as she was tucked under Davian's chin. "I wished I were empty headed the whole time I was there, that I could succumb to their lessons and be who they tried to make me. I feel like I was emptied of all that I was and only the shell of a girl called Tandanea remains. I think I'm broken," she told them quietly. Her words crushed Davian, pain blooming in his chest as she revealed the reality she was forced to live in for all those years.

"I think you've eaten enough for today, Tandy," Mariana leaned closer and ran her hand through Tandy's curls. "You should get some rest now."

"Do you want to sleep in here, or your rooms?" Davian asked her.

"I don't know," she said. He shared a glance with Mariana and she nodded softly as she leaned her head toward Dav's bed. He wanted to keep a closer eye on Tandy and it seemed Mariana felt the same. Davian rose with Tandy in his arms, her small frame suddenly alarming as he took in just how underweight she was. He'd get her to gain an appropriate amount of weight in order to be healthy, even if it killed him. She was skin and bones and hardly looked her age for it.

"You'll stay with me so I can keep my eye on you," Davian told her.

"You just want to seduce me," Tandy said through a yawn as Davian tucked her in. Mariana laughed before kissing their cheeks and headed to the door.

"Be nice to her, Dav. I'll see you in the morning," she said with a smile. She left the room and the maids came in to clear the table.

Davian locked the door and got ready for bed, making his way under the blankets long after the maids left the room. When he was comfortable, Tandy slid out from under the covers and went to the bathroom. Davian was worried after a few minutes while she was in there, silent behind the door. But he waited as patiently as he could for her to come back. Finally, though, Tandy left the bathroom and put herself back where Davian had originally placed her. She rolled over and Davian couldn't help but pull himself to lay behind her, holding her around her waist as he pressed a kiss to her head. She didn't say anything, but he felt her body melt against his.

"I missed you, Tandy," he told her with another kiss. She sighed in a pleasant way before readjusting herself slightly, her ass pressing into him unintentionally. Davian immediately clenched his jaw with restraint, the feel of her against him hard to resist. He didn't want to push too far like he had only days before, but her soft curves tucked against him felt like home. He didn't want Tandy to worry about being alone with him, and tried his best to control himself.

"I missed you, too," she said quietly before she laid a hand on Davian's where it rested. His memories ran through every intimate moment he'd had with Tandy in their younger years. He realized then that they had only ever had quick and quiet romps when they were left alone for long enough - which wasn't often, in all honesty. Having her pressed against him in nothing but a sleeping gown was agony.

"I want to make it up to you," Davian whispered after a moment as all rational thought left his mind, breaking the silence. Tandy's head tilted toward him in question. He wanted her so badly he wasn't sure he'd be able to hold it in. He thought of all the ways they had not yet made love, and the ideas he had as a grown man now were astounding. He kissed her neck just under her jaw with a feathery light touch, pulling a gasp from Tandy. He would just *ask* her and see if there was a chance they could rekindle what they had so many years ago. If she said no, he would be the man she deserved and roll over. He wouldn't hurt her again, he couldn't bear to see her tears anymore.

"Why are you so insistent?" Tandy said breathlessly as she turned around to face him. He leaned in closer in the dark and pressed his lips to hers. He poured as much feeling into her that he could, kissing slowly but hungrily as she laid so close. He pulled away after a moment, but Tandy's lips followed after him before she gasped again and leaned back.

"You like it," he said with a smirk. He pulled her into a deeper kiss, his tongue meeting hers. She moaned softly into his mouth, hands pulling him closer. His cock throbbed at the sound, painfully hard between them as his tongue traced every part of her mouth.

Davian pulled Tandy closer before hitching her leg over his hip, grinding against her pussy through the layers of their clothes. It wasn't nearly enough and he wanted to feel her bare against him, but he knew that would be a step too far for him to take. She deserved to feel safe in his arms and he just wasn't sure if he had earned that yet. It had been a *long* time.

"Gods, Tandy, I want you so badly," he breathed into her as he kissed from her lips to her neck. He nipped small bites against her throat as he reached his hand to her ass, squeezing it hard and grinding against her. She whimpered as her head tossed back at the feel of him. She moaned and squirmed against him as he kissed every bit of her neck. "I'll stop if you tell me no," he murmured as he kissed her neck. "I want to make you come," he sighed. Her breath stuttered at his words and he felt her nod against his lips.

"I -" she gasped, "I don't know, Davian. It's been so long," she told him.

"I know, and I'll stop if you want me to," he assured her. *Please,* he thought. She moaned as he ground against her again and again.

"You always made it so hard to think about anything other than your cock," she huffed as she shifted her hips.

"Nothing really changed, then, did it?" He asked between kisses. "Do you want me to stop, or can I *please* make you come?" She sighed as he ran his hands through her hair, and through the moonlight he saw a coy smile grow over her cheeks as she tapped a finger against her chin. She looked like she used to, as if nothing changed in the last seven years. She'd made that face at him countless times when she teased him, playing cat and mouse before they even learned of the betrothal in the first place. He had missed her *so* much.

"I want to come, please, Your Highness." *Thank the gods,* he thought before plunging his tongue into her mouth, swallowing her moan. He leaned onto his knees and hitched her dress up before pulling her panties down.

His fingers slid through her wetness with no hesitation. He moaned into her mouth as her hips stuttered against his touch and he ran his tongue from her lips to her throat, tracing the path he'd only just made. He kissed each breast before tugging her nightgown up and over her breasts, exposing them to him completely. He sucked a nipple into his mouth until she was writhing, thighs tightening around him. He sank lower over her body until her pussy was in front of his eager lips. He kissed her thighs as they trembled, before sweeping his tongue over her center, her head falling back into the mattress as she groaned.

"We never explored this particular activity," he said against her core.

"We never had enough alone time to explore," she agreed breathlessly.

He licked feverishly against her clit, making her keen. He pressed a finger at her entrance before sliding it inside of her slowly, drawing a low moan from Tandy's lips. He stroked his finger inside of her, making her tremble as his tongue matched each curling motion of his finger. Her fingers desperately clutched at the sheets before pulling his hair hard, pressing him against her pussy. He moaned against her as he swirled circles with his tongue. He felt her tensing against him, body coiling tight as her thighs tightened around his face.

"Missed you," she said between moans.

"Come for me," he told her before adding another finger, curling it against the nerve inside of her that would send her over the edge as he sucked her clit hard.

"*Dav, please,*" she cried out before her body tensed, pussy clenching around his fingers. She moaned, back arching off the bed. He stroked his fingers inside of her until she pulled him away, oversensitized to his touch. Davian kissed her thighs and belly, before raising himself over her. He pulled her into a heated kiss, the taste of her still on his tongue. She met his lips with a languid and drowsy kiss of her own, body still limp underneath him. He desperately wanted to bury himself inside her, but it was too soon. He didn't want to take more than she freely gave, no matter how enticing the tight, wet heat of her pussy was and how much he missed it. He pulled her to lay next to him, running his hands over her as she settled, her breathing slowly returning to normal.

"How was that, your Grace?" He asked.

"It was alright, I suppose," she said, turning away from him. She propped her head on her hands as she laid on her side, but Davian immediately crawled behind her, wrapping his body along hers.

His hand slid across her belly before he quickly pulled her top off over her head and threw it to the floor.

"What the -" Tandy exclaimed before his tongue filled her mouth. She moaned against him and he moved her back down onto her side before resuming his position behind her.

"It's my turn," he told her, voice deep. He pulled her hand behind her back and placed it on his cock. She gasped at the feel of it in her hand, tightening her grip on him instinctively.

"Mmm," he groaned into her ear, drawing a pant from her lips. She stroked her hand slowly along his length, though it wasn't enough to alleviate the need he felt.

"Let me try something," he told her after a minute. He removed his hand from where it was holding hers and put his fingers in her mouth, coating them with saliva before running the liquid over his cock. Then he used his fingers, entering her slowly, making her shudder and moan before he wiped her juices on himself, lubricating his cock from her arousal. He lifted her thigh as she lay in front of him and slid his erection between her legs. He pressed her thigh back down and pumped his cock through the slit he'd made of her thighs, groaning against her throat as he pumped in, and out.

Her breath left her in a loud moan, body trembling as he rolled against her. His cock brushed through her wet folds, just shy of her clit. She shifted her hips desperately, seeking the friction he was making with each movement. He felt her squirm and reached his hand to hers, guiding it to the head of his cock. She was soaked, her wetness enough to make him glide easily over her soft skin, and she eagerly held her fist around him with each thrust.

"Tighter, love," he murmured, making her squeeze her thighs around him. He moaned, sucking a mark against her neck. She could only tremble and moan as his fingers danced over her flesh, until his thrusts grew more and more erratic. He kissed her hard before his hips stuttered and he let out a deep moan against her mouth, coating her thighs and hand in come. She squirmed desperately before using her fingers to rub her clit in fast circles, moaning as he still laid between her thighs. She tightened her thighs around him, fingers massaging her pussy and moaned as she brought herself to orgasm.

"Oh my gods," his voice rasped. He watched her for a moment as she came hard, moaning his name. He leaned down to kiss her and licked into her mouth, desperate to taste her. "*Fuck,*" he hissed, kissing her once more before sliding out of bed for a cloth to clean them up. Once they were dry he pulled Tandy to him and laid back against the pillows and pulled the blankets over them.

"Good night, Dav," Tandy said with a yawn as she curled against his side. Davian kissed her forehead as he settled against the pillow.

"Sleep well, Tandy," he told her. They were asleep within moments, tucked into each other's arms.

***

Davian woke as the sky lightened to a hazy blue. He stretched, but was trapped within the blanket he laid under by a warm figure next to him. When he shifted, the figure mumbled and turned toward him, making him smile. He leaned over and kissed her head until she blearily looked at him in the morning light.

"Wha-" she said as she looked at him, brows pinched in sleepy confusion. He couldn't help the laugh that bubbled up from his belly as he pulled her to his chest.

"Wake up, love," he said as he ran his hands along her back until she roused completely.

"Dav, the *fuck,* the sun's not even up," Tandy groaned as she lifted her head, eyes squinting, gold curls flying. Davian laughed at her response as she smacked him away, pulling the blankets from him and tucking herself angrily against his pillow. He pressed his body against her back as she lay there squirming under his weight.

"Oh, my wife is certainly not a morning person," he crowed as he pressed a finger to her waist, tickling her. She squirmed against his touch but let out a small laugh, unable to fight against the sensation.

"I'm not your wife, you cretin," she huffed. He finally pulled her free from the blankets she was wrapped up in and pulled her to his chest.

"Mmm, soon enough," he breathed as he groped her ass.

"How are you functioning," she grumbled.

"I always get up this early," he said easily, grinning. "It's the only time I have to myself," he admitted. She just hummed thoughtfully as she rested against his chest, his hands letting go of his hold on her only to run them through her hair. She yawned again before nestling against his chest. A moment passed before he spoke again, rousing her more.

"I was thinking," he started.

"Hmm, must've been hard on you," she said dryly, making him laugh.

"I think we should pretend there is still animosity between us in our public displays with each other. I think we need to hide what we know in order to protect ourselves from whatever is going on in the Royal courts, and by continuing the relationship as perceived enemies we might be able to hear the whisper of the manipulators a little more clearly than if we act like *this*," he punctuated his words with another squeeze to her ass.

"That sounds wise," she agreed through a snort. "I guess I shouldn't be seen leaving your room in my clothes from yesterday, then," she sighed and started to stretch.

"I'll find you a robe to wear and bring you to your room," he laughed before standing and changing into his own clothes. He turned around to see Tandy standing there, stretching in absolutely nothing at all. A sudden wave of lust rolled through his body and he crossed the room, pulling her into a heated kiss. She gasped against his mouth as he licked against her lips before she invited him in with equal heat.

"You have to let me go back to my room if you want this rivalry to be convincing," she moaned when he slid his hands through her hair, gently tugging on her curls. He huffed but pulled away before turning around to find her gown and his robe. He quickly covered her with it before stuffing her clothes into her hands, and tugged the robe closed.

"Let's go," he sighed, not wanting to let her leave without another taste first. As if she read his mind, she spoke.

"Don't worry, there will be plenty of time another day," she said before following him to the door. He peered out and instructed the Knights to move out of their hall for the next fifteen minutes before resuming their positions, staying in the corridor with the other Knights. He was sure they already knew Tandy was in here, but he at least wanted her to have privacy upon entering her own room. After the Knights left, Tandy and Davian ran to her chambers where he kissed her goodbye.

"Call on Mariana when you can, I'm sure she'll want to talk more about everything. We really don't know what we're dealing with yet, so be mindful."

"I'm well trained, Your Highness," she agreed. "No one will know what I'm thinking unless I want them to. I can feign any emotion, should the need arise." Davian frowned, sad at her expense.

"I'm sorry," he said softly, kissing her head before he backed away.

"It'll be invaluable soon enough, I'm sure," she whispered before the doors were finally closed, separating them once again.

***

As the day continued and he entertained meeting after meeting, more questions came to his mind. The only real solution he had was to go directly to his father's chamber and speak to him there, though the idea made him uneasy. His father had forbidden him entry into his quarters when he was a child, punishing him with a heavy hand for it the one time he disobeyed. After that, Davian hardly saw them outside of formal events. He couldn't remember when he hadn't felt lonely.

Not since before Tandy left, his mind supplied. He slammed his fist on the table in frustration at the thought and sighed heavily, trying to stifle his reaction at the intrusive words bubbling up from somewhere hidden in his subconscious. He would be grateful that Tandy at least was making steps towards forgiving him of his fuck up, though he was sure the guilt would last forever.

In the hall, he saw his Head Housekeeper and stopped her for a moment. He asked her quietly what was going on in the King's and Queen's rooms, hoping for more information before entering.

"Mrs Hollahue," he nodded at her. "Is the King in his study?"

"Your Highness, I am unsure of his location though I can certainly fetch a maid to assist you," she offered gently. She had soft blue eyes and dark hair, a trait she gave her own children. She had been a pivotal part in his life through the years, often acting as a second mother to him when he found himself aimless under his crown. He had survived as long as he had because of her support and he was grateful for her in many ways.

"That won't be necessary, but I thank you for the offer," he told her. "I'll head to his rooms, then." Mrs Hollahue made a motion to stop him but she quickly put her hand down with a worried gaze and said nothing, only biting her lip. Davian stood quietly, waiting for her to explain.

"I don't think you should go to his rooms." She said with finality.

"Why?" He asked. She paused again as she thought over her words.

"I was told no one is allowed in there," she said hesitantly.

"They don't have Guards stationed there, or else I would believe that," he said pointedly. She deflated, sighing. She closed her eyes and then nodded, quietly explaining her hesitance.

"I promise you, you don't want to go in there. I was advised to not clean, straighten up, or do anything within their main bedroom. The only rooms I am allowed to enter are the private study, and the antechambers. Trust me, Your Highness," she shook her head slowly.

"What was in there?" He stepped closer to her and kept his voice low. Her eyes suddenly looked misty. "I'm only asking because I suspect there may be something amiss," he said softly. "Just tell me what is in the room." She sighed again, eyes scanning the halls. She reached for his hands and held them in her own.

"I have never seen anything quite like it. It was nearly destroyed, and I've done my time in tenement housing and slums. I know squalor, Your Highness, I'd seen it first hand as a girl." She shuddered at the memory.

"Why haven't I been made aware of their habits?" He frowned as he thought aloud.

"For your protection, Your Highness. I wouldn't want you to see your own mother and father in such a light," she told him gently. "I was also obeying the King's command as he told me to leave it alone, and so I did," she said evenly though she glanced around him, eyes seeking out a safe place away from conflict. "There was no other choice." He nodded and agreed, there was not much that could be done.

"I need to see for myself," he told her, feeling heavy under the weight of her words.

"Please be warned, Prince Davian. I do not know what has become of them." She kissed his hand with a small smile.

"Please let me know if another guest falls into their habits, Mrs Hollahue," he told her as she turned away.

"Of course, Your Highness," she agreed, letting go of his hand and turning away.

Davian continued for the King's quarters as quietly as he could. Though Knights guarded every hall and he would be seen no matter what, he didn't want his parents to see him.

He opened the King's door slowly and peered in. Nothing seemed amiss in the study, but the housekeeper had said that this would be the case. She was only allowed in the rooms that held guests or small parties, as she'd told him.

He stepped further into the room and quietly but quickly made his way to the bedroom doors. He noticed before making it across the room there was a strange odor permeating around him, but he wasn't sure what it was. He stepped closer and opened the office door that led to the main bedroom, and very nearly gagged at the smell.

The room was filthy. The floor was covered in refuse and unknown garbage. The stench was so thick, Davian's eyes watered uncontrollably. The curtains were drawn except for one, which hung off a broken rod. A single stream of light fell into the room, shining through the filth and illuminating the still forms of his mother and father.

He froze where he stood, shocked to see them sitting so lifelessly in the midst of the filth. They sat at the small table with a bottle of a strange viscous liquid, radiating in the sun as it sat between them.

It looked entirely like a bottle of poison.

The liquid was bright and otherworldly, a color he had never seen in the natural world before. Its shocking pink and purple hue was intensely magnified by the light of the sun. They each had a small glass in front of them with minimal traces of the liquid still in them. Their eyes were half closed, and yet they snored in a deep sleep. Davian felt panicked as the filth of the room overwhelmed him, and he quickly made his retreat and ran to his bedroom without finding any of the answers he had been searching for.

There was one thing that he knew for certain, though.

His parents were all consumed by the elixir making its rounds in the inner cities of the Kingdom. It had made its way to the Royal courts, endangering them all. Lethe, Elixir of Oblivion, would eat away at his parents until they were nothing more than flesh and bone. Those that tasted it would be compelled to have more and more, unable to fight the constant ache for it. Some succumbed quickly to it, and some very slowly, but it was not something that could be undone. Once you were deep in the throes of Lethe, your mind would thus stay. It ate away at the brain of the consumer, changing not only their minds but of their bodies as well. Personalities would be lost to the elixir, once healthy bodies would bend and break beneath the weight of the turmoil Lethe caused.

"It can take out entire communities, completely insidious and slow acting. People can change before your very eyes and yet it could be years before the hold is all consuming, leaving nothing of the person they used

to be. Even just one experience under Lethe is enough for you to crave it, painfully," Davian remembered Bryson's words only last year, telling him of the consequences they faced if Lethe weren't contained swiftly. He thought of the warnings given to him by the many merchants that pleaded for his action in the eradication of the Magic brew. Though he had sent as many soldiers that could be spared and increased the recruitment of new cadets, it had not been enough. He shook his head, fearing it was already too late to change the Kingdom's fate.

As he stared at the painting, he remembered something about his bedroom. There was a *reason* Tandy's quarters were next to his. There was a reason the large painting was there.

It *wasn't* a painting. It was a tapestry, a thin woven fabric. He stood quickly and ran to investigate the door hidden behind it, long forgotten now. He wasn't even sure anyone was aware it was still here, the last Prince had been his father and he certainly wouldn't remember considering how he fared. Traditionally, the bride's suite was next door to the groom's room, to be unlocked when they married for appearance's sake. It was so the husband and wife could host their own guests without interference. If he were able to get the door to open, it would help keep the trio from being seen as they talked about what was going on, and they'd be able to lock their doors and pretend they're in absolute no contact with each other according to the outside world's view on it.

He lifted the edge of the tapestry, rolling it up until the door was exposed. It had been made to look as though it were part of the wall, with the crown molding and nearly hidden door knob. After patting the door down to feel for the lock, he finally found it. Almost near the base of the door, there was a small groove. He pressed it down, a click echoing through his room. A wave of excitement cut through the worry he felt as he pulled the small knob.

It gently swung open, not very heavy at all. The door on Tandy's side was still locked, so he closed the door quietly and lowered the tapestry down. He didn't want anyone to notice, so he decided to slide the small table over as a decoy.

After he pushed the lounge chair and table over, he stepped back to see if it looked believable. With the books, and Tandy's old letters placed there, it appeared to be a calm reading nook. He was satisfied and immediately went to Tandy's room to check in.

"Your Highness, I've just received dinner," she told him as she answered the door.

"Thank you," he said though he wasn't hungry in the slightest. The stench of that room had upset his stomach. "A tea would be nice," he said before dropping into a chair and running his hands through his hair. Tandy made him a cup of tea, placing it in front of him gently before sitting next to him.

"Tandy was telling me about the time she tried to escape the reform school," Mariana said to Davian.

"I was punished quite severely for that," she said.

"They held her in solitary confinement for *days*, with only one meal per day," Mariana whispered.

"I don't know the actual length of time I was in there, I thought it felt like months," she said softly. "Not to mention the other punishments that came with it, too."

"She doesn't want to talk about those yet, though," Mariana said to Dav. He could only nod as a weight filled him, a heavy and overwhelming sense of guilt.

"Don't make that face, Dav, I survived," Tandy said.

"I'm sorry I didn't check on you," he told her. They sat quietly for a moment before Davian remembered why he was there. He stood up and headed to Tandy's bedroom, searching for the large tapestry in an almost mirrored place to the one in his room. He found it easily, though it was more narrow than the one he had. It was only a few inches wider than the door and a lot easier to roll up. Mariana had exclaimed at his sudden entry to Tandy's bedroom, but he ignored her. Their footsteps followed just behind him and he knew they'd see soon enough.

"Mariana, lock the door. I don't want anyone to notice us right now," he told her quietly as he rolled the tapestry. She quickly ran to lock the main entrance to the rooms. He pressed around the woodwork until he felt the small groove again, and clicked it. With a small *clink*, the door unlocked and he pulled the small knob back, until the door swung open weightlessly without a sound. Mariana gasped and peered behind him as he pushed through to his room, the tapestry blocking the way. He slid underneath before rolling it up and opening the door completely. He ran to lock his own door before anyone tried to enter, and Mariana and Tandy came tiptoeing in behind him.

"Oh wow, you two are going to fuck like animals now," Mariana giggled. Tandy swatted at her making Mariana dance away with a prim expression. Dav rolled his eyes but couldn't help but laugh, too.

"I was considering this for more along the lines of being able to hide and sneak away from the public eye, specifically for whatever is going on in the palace as of late. But sure, having a secret fuck door is good, too," he said dryly. Mariana squealed with laughter as his words caught up to their ears. Tandy's mouth held in a firm line at his humor, while Mariana grabbed onto Tandy's shoulder to stay upright from laughing so hard.

"*Davian,* how unPrincely of you to say such things," Tandy said, though there was a glint to her eyes he hadn't seen in a long time.

"In front of your own betrothed, too," Mariana said breathlessly, wiping her eyes. "How indecent!"

"*You* started it, Mar," he huffed, trying not to smile. He ushered them back through the doorway before unlocking his room and climbing in after them, the tapestry back in its place. He shut Tandy's door and rolled down the tapestry there, too, and sat back at the table with them.

"There's something you need to know," Davian began as they sat quietly. The girls looked at him, waiting for him to continue. He sighed before recounting his experience in his parent's room, and of what he had found with them.

"They had Lethe?" Mariana gasped. "It's so prevalent in the poor areas, well inside the inner cities. What could it be doing all the way in here?"

"Who could have brought it into the castle?" Tandy asked.

"The last few years we have been struggling to clean the inner cities and rid them of the highly addictive substance, but there have been an immeasurable amount of accounts of the people that can brew it. We squash one, another begins brewing the elixir within the week. The only ones who ever venture to the areas with the most prevalent addictions are the ambassadors we send to those areas. Unfortunately, that doesn't narrow it down in the least as we always have a healthy rotation of ambassadors. On top of that," he took a deep breath as he was winded from his flow of words, "Many ambassadors *and* anyone with a highborn title have multiple properties with access to both the castle, neighboring cities, and everywhere in between."

"What exactly does Lethe do?" Tandy asked.

"It's brewed with Magic ingredients, some of which we have been completely unable to regulate the sales of for a few years now," Davian told her.

"If drunk in high enough quantities, the person will succumb to it essentially. It changes you from the inside out until you are naught but recognizable," Mariana explained. "I saw it once, what it did to a friend in the city. She was well-off enough, but come the following summer she was skin and bones, angry, and unable to move her body in a natural way," Mariana shuddered at the memory.

"How does it work in small doses?" Tandy asked, brow raised.

"Smaller doses would mean addiction is less likely, but the emotional outbursts and an overall sense of doom would still occur," Mariana explained. "Some victims of the Lethe were able to prevent the dependency by only sampling it occasionally, but the mood swings and irrational thinking was still recorded as a symptom."

"And you both agree that the *wine* was off and it was the cause of your emotional disturbances?" Tandy said with a pointed look.

"Gods *dammit*," Davian yelled. "We were fucking *poisoned!*"

Thirteen

Tandy

Tandy waited in her room for Mariana to join her for breakfast. She nearly rolled her eyes when Mariana walked in wearing a smug smile.

"So did he fuck you after all or did you hold strong?" She had asked immediately before the door even closed.

"*Gods*, Mar," Tandy said.

"I remember you used to walk funny after a rendezvous with his Highness. Take a strut around the room for me," she giggled as she sat down, pouring a cup of tea the maids had left with breakfast only moments before Mariana had entered. "I always wondered out of all the males in the court, who did it best," she added. Tandy swallowed her tea too quickly and sputtered at Mar's words. Mariana cackled at the minute reaction. "I guess that's my answer," she said, flipping her hair.

"We should have known you and Davian were siblings *long* before today," Tandy said coolly, only making Mariana laugh harder. She quieted after a moment, a somber look drawing over her face.

"I'm sorry I didn't answer your letters," Mariana said sadly. "I should've known something wasn't right," she said. "I should've tried to listen to what you said when Dav and I attacked you at the party like that."

"We were young and there was something at play we had no power over. But we've talked enough about the letters, I think. Do you want to talk about Martina today?" Tandy asked.

"I -" Mariana started but paused, finishing her breakfast before pushing it away. She sipped her tea and breathed in deep before looking at Tandy. "It started getting worse around the time you and Davian were announced as betrothed. As soon as it met the public's eye, everything drastically changed for me. I tried to hold on to our childhood, but no matter what I did it wasn't enough. She told me she was only helping me find a good husband, but each man she introduced me to was anything but a gentleman," she whispered, looking away. "I was told it was the only way to secure a husband - by seducing the bachelors and gaining their favor. 'Make them sweet on you,' she told me," Mariana frowned as she sipped her tea.

"I'm sorry," Tandy said. There was nothing more she could do except offer her comfort through her words and wait for her to share her story.

"I've never really said it out loud, and I don't want to be seen as dirty," she whispered.

"You don't have to say anything unless you want to," she said. She sighed and breathed deep for a minute, before nodding as though she was encouraging herself to finally let the words out.

"Martina uses me," she said emptily. "She sends me to meet men. At first I believed they were marriage suitors, at the villa and in the palace. But she told me to do *anything* they said to do, if we wanted to keep our lives in the Royal Circles. She said if I didn't do *everything* I was told to do, then I may as well personally cast my mother and father into poverty and debt," there was an edge to her words. "The demands those men made of me increased in depravity, in violence, but she never cared to see my tears. I had to clean myself up and drink a bitter blend of tea each morning, to make sure I didn't end up with their spawn," her voice rasped as her words grew angrier. Tandy rested her hand on Mariana's shoulder. All she could do was offer her support by holding onto her until she quieted down, leaning heavily on Tandy.

"Let's go lay down, Mar," Tandy offered her quietly. Mariana stood willingly and Tandy helped lay her down, covering her up with blankets. She wiped a tear still on her cheek before sitting on the bed next to her.

"What was it like at the Fine Etiquette and Reform School?" Mariana wondered through a yawn. "I know we read the letters, and Dav wrote some back, but I still think there's more to it than you told us."

"To put it plainly, I thought I'd die there. I thought they would surely kill me," Tandy told her honestly. "One of the worst days, I tried to run away. But it's a wasteland up there, hardly anything at all. Even if I'd made it out of their hands, I would have died in the elements. I considered doing just that, too," Tandy said, looking away and taking a sip of tea. "They'd have us learn and memorize extensively all of the school work we would have had here. We were versed in the laws of the kingdom, memorized any decrees that pertained to the laws. We were punished for showing any emotion, and punished harder if we reacted to their abuse. Food and sleep were used as the most effective forms of obedience. I'd been in a solitary room for I *thought* months at a time, rarely eating. When my bloods stopped coming, I lost track of time altogether," she continued in a haunting voice. Mariana weeped next to her as she took in her words.

"At least you weren't made to seduce random men," Mariana offered eventually with a bland smile.

"Well, we *did* have lessons on how to please our husbands in bed, too," Tandy sighed.

"Do I even want to know what that looked like?" Mariana asked warily.

"It's as uncomfortable as it sounds. I never said anything more in that letter to Davian about it in case he was not pleased by it. After all, he had assumed I was a slut in the first place, and didn't want to rub salt in his wounds," Tandy trailed off for a minute, lost in thought. She blinked before continuing. "We were made to *perform* as though we were bedding our future husbands, while the Headmistress shouted instructions at us from the side. It was always done in an auditorium, with each girl having her chance to show everyone just how good she was," Tandy made a disgusted face. "After they'd taken our freedom, and our emotions, and used sleep and food as a means to control us on top of the floggings for disobedience, we just did as we were told. For some reason, I put up more of a fight than the others and was punished more severely for my inadequacies. I told myself to just *listen* but I couldn't, and after being forgotten in an empty room with only a meal a day, I wanted to give up. I finally did, not long ago. I didn't think I would ever leave," Tandy admitted.

"What made you give up?" Mariana asked.

"Headmistress told me that it was Davian who had sent me there," Tandy sighed.

"Davian would have *died* before sending you there, it couldn't have been him," Mariana looked at her through teary eyes.

"I know that now," Tandy said, offering her a handkerchief.

"It must not have helped when I said those things when you first arrived," Mariana said shamefully.

"No, it didn't, but I wasn't all that surprised," Tandy agreed. "But I'd been trained in how to erase my own feelings and put forth a facade, so it didn't matter anyway."

"It's all quite fucked," she snuggled into the blankets, grumbling.

"It certainly is," Tandy sighed.

***

"Gods dammit, we were fucking poisoned!"

Davian's words circled Tandy's mind on repeat as the hours passed. The girls shared worried glances with each other throughout the day but said nothing, knowing not much else could be done as the Royal Circle disintegrated before their eyes. The fear was palpable in the room and voicing it was too much after everything else they had talked about that day.

They sat quietly together while Tandy embroidered a small handkerchief to pass the time, with Mariana leaning on Tandy's shoulder as she watched. Everything that Davian had shared with them about Lethe and its arrival in the castle sat heavy with them and all they could do was wait for Davian to join them for dinner. What more could be said, if the Royals were poisoned?

For once, the quiet was soothing to Tandy despite the charged energy in the air. There hadn't been a time in recent years that she had a friend to lean on, quite literally, and soaked it in as Mariana pressed her cheek against her. The sun began to fall low in the sky while she embroidered before a maid came to her room with dinner, quietly setting the table before taking her leave.

A knock sounded at the door and Tandy put her embroidery down to open it, finding Davian frowning. She stepped aside to let him in, wondering what else could have him looking so cross.

"Some of the guests arrived early," he said, stomping to the table before sitting heavily into a chair. "Apparently, my mother had planned the masquerade for next week, but this morning decided it wasn't soon enough, and demanded it be held tomorrow instead." Tandy was not happy in the least to learn that.

"What do you think we should do?" Mariana asked.

"Nothing, it's already decided. I'm just now concerned if that means she'll demand the wedding be moved up, too," Davian admitted. "Tandy, you better eat what's on your plate," he sighed as she pushed food around with her fork without eating any. She stifled a grimace but began slowly taking small bites while he looked at her pointedly.

"I'm afraid that if the wedding is moved up, our lives may very well be in danger more so than before," Davian looked at Tandy and Mariana pointedly and frowned, sighing. His brows were pinched tight as if he were considering something grave. "You helped some of the families in the inner cities, Mar. Do you know what the early symptoms of Lethe are?" Davian asked, looking down at his plate.

"Most people who partake in Lethe began with small and controlled doses because they paced themselves to avoid a full blown addiction. It pulls negative emotions out of you when given in low doses, increasing rage and irritation gradually as the dose is increased. Then there is a *very* short window of elation and pleasure before it begins to eat away at your mind. Typically, those that only *taste* it feel unsettled and that's enough to steer them away from it. But the ones who start off with a higher dose generally form an immediate addiction to it." Mariana explained, eyes cast to the side as if lost in memories, running through her experiences.

"What does it look like when small doses are paired with external triggers?" Davian said after a long moment, holding his chin.

"Even without a trigger, negative emotions are pulled from you. Bouts of irrationality, destructive rage, paranoia and a feeling of sudden doom. I've heard some describe it as feeling like everyone hates you, wants the worst for you, and an overwhelming sensation of betrayal and loss amplifying within your whole body." she told him. Tandy bristled at his questions, suspicious of what it would mean. Mariana seemed to feel it too before she leaned forward with worry clear on her face.

"Do you think small doses of a poison were the method used to sabotage the betrothal?" Tandy asked. "It seems strange it would be so localized to the Royal Circle if it is tearing through the cities and ports at such devastating rates."

"Only my mother would have an ulterior motive like that," Mariana said coldly, though her body trembled as she spoke.

"We don't know for sure, yet," Davian rubbed the hair from his forehead, brushing it back behind his ear. "We need to be certain that we're not being drugged or poisoned."

"You mean, poisoned *anymore*," Mariana supplied.

"It will be hard to monitor so I'll start with just placing more Guards in the kitchens and supply rooms. But I am afraid that we experienced the same underdosage because of the bouts of intense anger, explosive and violent rage, and overwhelming feelings of fear and loss. It's the only thing that makes sense, those are the exact feelings I had to fight every day for *years*. The amount of fights I've started, the destruction I've caused when the outbursts cannot be contained inside of my chest for any longer, " Davian dropped his head into his hands, sighing heavily.

"Put Guards at the wine cellar, too," Mariana said. "Martina is always holding a wine glass, but never smells like wine. I would monitor anything that is remotely connected to food and drink," she advised. " I can get more information from her as best as I can, but she will *not* expose herself when she believes anyone is listening. So even if I were able to gather more information for you to prove beyond any doubt that she is guilty, it would be my word against hers. She is no fool, though she is a fool all the same," Mariana said. "Will you trust me when I gather that information?"

"I will trust your word," Davian agreed.

"We can assume everyone is guilty," Mariana said.

"I worry that we may be pointing fingers too soon without much information to go off of," Tandy said after a moment. "It seems extremely unlikely that she was the one to spread Lethe through the Royal Circle, considering it was in the towns and ports first."

"She probably just took it from someone and brought it back here," Mariana suggested. "We had access to a lot of the areas that were found to be in production of the elixir."

"I suppose she isn't capable of anything more wide-scaled," Tandy thought aloud. "However, if you have both been drugged since our betrothal was originally announced, it seems really unlikely she would have gone through all the trouble to slowly alter your minds over the course of seven years. Why would she wait so long if she was the one behind it? What could her motivations be for taking such a long time to pull off the game she's playing?"

"There have to be other factors at play," Davian said.

"What was she waiting for?" Tandy asked, lips pursed. "Why did she drug the King and Queen over it if she only wanted to break our betrothal?"

"Maybe she was waiting for the King to announce the birth order was changed," Davian said after a minute. "Maybe she thought she had enough time since I won't be officially crowned until I turn thirty-five. The drug was probably used in order to make him accept suggestions more easily."

"But that wouldn't explain why she drugged you for so long," Tandy frowned. "Why would there be a need for that, if it didn't matter until you were thirty five years old anyway?"

"Because she hadn't been certain of my lineage until now. Originally, she would have had me in *your* place. But because she now knows the King sired me, she will be attempting to put my name on the birth registrar and title me a Princess," Mariana told them as she ate her last bite of dinner. "She's going to be telling the King the truth soon, if he doesn't already know."

"She won't be able to get through to him," Davian sighed. "He's been in nearly a vegetative state for years and only knows how to laugh at this point."

"I worry she will have a damaged reputation if we are wrong," Tandy said softly. "I know I said some negative things before about her, but I know what it feels like to be a victim of a rumor."

"We have more evidence now than we did with you, Tandy. You *saw* her eyes when she saw my dimples. You *saw* that predatory gaze. You saw the marks she left on my skin, of what her *suitors* left on my skin..." her voice halted slowly, losing volume as her words caught up to her lips. Mariana looked pale as she pleaded with Tandy, begging her to see it differently.

"I just don't want to accuse your mother of anything unless there is no doubt, Mariana. Treason is a real crime, and the damage of a hearing cannot easily be undone should our theories prove incorrect," Tandy said in a softer tone than before. Mariana was right, she knew. But the feeling that she was reliving her own betrayal by talking about someone's alleged crimes only made her feel sick.

"I agree with you, Tandy. It *is* a real crime. One of which I think she is not only capable of, but also ambitious and insane enough to follow through with it. You haven't *seen* what I've seen or experienced what I did by *her* hands," Mariana told Tandy earnestly. "Trust me on this, Tandy. She is not to be trusted and you may very well be in the most danger out of us all, alongside Davian. But even if it isn't my mother, it is *someone.*"

Tandy couldn't disagree with that and silently wrung her hands under the table where no one could see them as everyone finished eating. Mariana was clear in her depiction of her mother, there was just no mistaking it. Martina was a cruel woman, there was no doubt. But how could she poison a mother, a father, a child?

Easily, she supposed, considering she had fed her own baby girl to the very wolves that lurked the castle halls.

Fourteen

Davian

While Davian had no other leads for who brought Lethe into his home, he intended to issue a full blown investigation after discussing it with Bryson first. As soon as he left Tandy and Mariana, he ran to find his Housekeeper.

"Do you know of anyone that has access to both my personal wine, my quarters, and my mail?" Davian asked her furiously. She blinked at him in surprise but thought it over.

"There are only two people, aside from me, that have the clearance necessary to be able to do all of those tasks without another staff member's help," she whispered, stepping closer to him. Her eyes glanced around them as though worried for Davian's safety. "There are maids and servants that would have an overlap of those tasks, too. I keep a strict ledger of the whereabouts of everyone and their assignments every day and can verify exact names and dates. Most of the staff are doubled for each task, so anyone working with them would witness their meddling if it had occurred. Is there something wrong, Your Highness?"

"I will be needing the logs on specific dates, which I will bring you tomorrow," Davian said. "There's a lot, but it may help to narrow down the staff. I'm sorry, I won't say more than that. I need names, Mrs Hollahue."

"Of course, Your Highness. I will be ready for you when you find me tomorrow. Good night, Your Highness," she curtsied and turned away, a frown lining her face.

"I would advise you to avoid the wine for the foreseeable future, my Lady," he warned her. "Goodnight and be careful." She nodded worriedly as she hurried away.

He wanted to fire them all and send them to the dungeon, but he worried that it would alert the rest of the guilty party. It may make them run away, or it could worsen the current state of the castle. He needed more information before he could punish any-one, though, and headed back to his room.

Before he had left Tandy's room, he had told them that they should consider a room change; Mariana in Tandy's room, and Tandy should stay in Davian's. It would be easier to keep track of them if they were able to access each other without the need for announcing their company, and he'd feel safer with them closer anyway.

After laying in the dark with a handful of candles to light his room, he heard a rustling in the hidden door. He grinned as he re-alized Tandy had agreed with the room switch. Of course, that was not how he'd seen it when he'd floated the idea in the first place, but as Mariana laughed and wiggled her brows at them sugges-tively, he couldn't help but smile cheekily before strutting out of the room. Playing with Tandy while also keeping them safe didn't seem that bad of a plan.

He sat up when he saw her, and waved her over to him on the bed. He smiled and waited for to come to him, his arms out-stretched. It was quite late, and she'd changed into a light sleep-ing gown. Her soft form was illuminated by the moon through the window, and his mouth watered at the memory of the taste of her. He leaned forward, pulling her against his chest and placed a kiss at the base of her neck. He ran his fingers through her loosened hair, the blonde curls hanging low down her back.

"I wonder if you would be open to some more activities," Davian asked, turning her around as he swept her hair to the side and draped it over her shoulder. He kissed along her back, pulling her tighter against his chest, sliding his hands around to the front of her. He molded his hands around her breasts, kneading them as he held her against him, her ass pressed against his erection. She pressed against him without a sound, her head leaning to the side and exposing a large expanse of her soft skin. He kissed her neck softly before biting her, a gasp leaving her lips. He turned her around and kissed her, lips parting as he delved his tongue into her mouth. She whimpered against him, arms sliding around his neck as she tugged against him, tighter and tighter. He bit her bottom lip, making her gasp.

"What kind of activities, Your Highness?" She asked.

"I can show you," he said softly before sliding back onto the bed, pulling her with him. She laid over his chest, legs straddling his waist as he waited for her to respond. She wiggled to adjust herself, and moaned as she felt him hard against her core.

"I'm not opposed," she gasped as she braced herself against his shoulders, hands holding her up. He ran his fingers over her cheeks, cupping them as her hair fanned out around them, a soft tent of curls. He smiled before pulling her lips to his and kissed her softly, before deepening the kiss and making her moan against him. He slid one hand down and held her ass, pulling her against his cock through his pants.

He flipped them over suddenly, sending a gasp through her as he sucked a nipple into his mouth, gently biting until she moaned.

He switched sides and ran his tongue along her other breast until only her heavy and panting breath could be heard.

"I hope the doors are sound proofed," he murmured against her skin, "because I won't let you be quiet in my bed." He pulled her panties off and tossed them to the floor, kissing up and up her legs slowly before reaching her pussy. He ran his tongue through her wetness before finding her clit, tracing shapes against her until she moaned pitifully at his touch. She writhed in his hands, hands fisting at the sheets as he tasted her. He pulled away from her before meeting her lips as she whined, hands finding his hair.

"Tandy," he said softly as her breath slowed down.

"Hmm," she hummed, trailing her fingers through his hair.

"If you want to come, you'll need to earn it," his voice came out in a rumble, lower than he'd realized. Tandy tensed at the sound before her legs tightened around his waist and she nodded, mouth open. "Good girl," he told her with a kiss. She whimpered at the praise and kissed him back feverishly. He rolled over and sat up, peeling his clothes off. Tandy helped him drag his pants down and sent them flying much like her panties. He pulled her to his lips for another kiss, holding her with a deep grasp of her hair.

"You'll use your mouth on me like I did for you, and if you do a good job I'll give you a reward," he told her in a rough voice, making her gasp. He guided her to sit between his thighs where he spread them slightly, giving her enough room to comfortably fit.

"Spit on it," he told her. He nearly moaned when she did, but he held himself in check as he guided her hand to stroke him with her saliva as it lubricated his cock, the feel of her fingers a sweet heaven. He guided her hands and just as he was about to tell her to spit on him again, she did it without him saying a word. He moaned, laying his head back at the slide of her hand. He felt her tentatively lean forward, her breath a ghost against his straining flesh. He wanted to be inside of her, to feel her wet heat on him, and hoped she tasted him soon.

Her tongue licked up from the base of his cock before she pulled the head of him into her mouth. Her tongue laved around the sensitive skin there, hot and wet. The heat of her mouth and the movements of her tongue sent lightning through his blood, and he vaguely felt himself bury his fingers into her hair roughly the harder she sucked. She bobbed her head against him, never lifting away from his cock as her tongue swirled around the head. Suddenly, she sucked him down to the base, licking there, before sliding back up and doing it again.

"Holy *fuck*, Tandy," he groaned as he tried desperately to keep his hips from fucking into her mouth. She didn't slow, instead quickened her pace and used her hands to grip him around the base of his cock, spit coating her hands as she stroked him in time with her mouth. Davian couldn't hold back anymore and used his grip on her curls to pull her down against his hips as he rutted into her. She sputtered against him as he hit the back of her throat but made no move to push him away. He frantically bucked into her and moaned, fingers tight in her hair. She moved her tongue on the underside of his cock and moaned into his flesh, the sensation sending a wave of pleasure through him.

"Tandy, I'm gonna - " he moaned as he plunged deep into her mouth with one last frantic motion before filling her with his come. A delicious, all consuming heat enveloped him as he came inside her mouth, everything blurring around him at the intensity of his orgasm. She slowly let him fall from her lips, leaving small kisses against his skin as the tremors rolled through his body until the sensations came to be too much and he dragged her off of him. He kissed her languidly, body still trembling as she melted against him. After a moment he finally gained movement in his limbs again and pulled her up to him. He kissed her softly before sitting her up as he laid down on the bed. He could almost hear her internal questions, but used his strength to sit her directly over his mouth.

He delved his tongue into her pussy, her juices dripping over his face. He moaned into her heat, tongue deep inside of her. She writhed against him, knees straddling his head as he held her ass tighter to him, keeping her pussy locked where he could reach it. He wanted to make her come with just his tongue but the urge to fill her up as much as he could made him heavy with want, and so he slid two fingers from behind into her pussy as he sucked on her clit. A sharp keening noise left her lips as she desperately grabbed at the head board for balance. She ground her core against his face as she moved to the strokes of his fingers and tongue, and soon enough after only a minute of angling his fingers, he found the spot deep within her that made her wail with pleasure. With his free hand he pulled her hard against his tongue and curled his fingers just so, making her cry out in desperation.

"Oh *please*," she begged him over and over, legs trembling. He deepened his strokes and sucked harder on her clit before her breath was nothing more than whimpering and gasping, music to his ears. Her breath stopped as she arched her back, pussy clamping around his fingers as she came hard against him. Praise and gasps filled her mouth as she came, hands clutching the head board as her thighs tightened around him. When she stopped, he pulled his fingers from her before pulling her back down to lay next him, her sated form as weak as a wilted flower. He nearly laughed but knew he had fared much the same when she'd made him come.

"Good girl," he told her as he kissed her gently. She only hummed against him with a faint smile as her breathing slowed to normal once again. They lay together for a while, not saying anything as Davian ran his hands over her back, down her arms, through her hair. After a few minutes, Tandy yawned and stretched.

"That was a lot," she murmured sleepily, making him laugh.

"You're a natural," he shook his head stunned.

"I learned some things at the reform school," she hesitated to say. He looked down at her, the words not registering in his mind right away. "I know a lot in regards to finding your pleasure." Davian was quiet as he slowly came to realize once again the horrors of Tandy's experience at the Fine Etiquette and Reform School for girls. She had mentioned it in her letter, but he hadn't completely wrapped his head around how those lessons would have gone.

"I didn't realize it was like *that*, Tandy. I'm sorry," he told her.

"Our education was quite extensive," she said. Davian pulled her tighter to his chest, sighing softly, unsure of what to say. He worried any form of sex would cause her distress if she had been exposed to such abuse. The guilt weighed heavy on him for a moment until Tandy ran her hand over his cheek. He turned to rest his face in the crease of her neck, kissing her clavicle softly.

"I can't unlearn what they taught me, Dav. While it was a traumatizing experience altogether, intimacy with you has never and I suspect *will never* cause me distress," she told him. "I don't think I'd have ever been able to resist you, truly. Whether I had been exposed to more abuse or less, I don't think it would have affected you and I in any way."

"I wish that made me feel better about what you experienced," Davian sighed.

"It should help, though," she kissed his brow.

"You don't even *eat* properly, and I'm taking advantage of you now," he ran a hand over his face. "Gods dammit, I'm a pig." Tandy let out a sharp laugh, startling him to look at her.

"You are, but it's not like I'm incapable of consenting to our playtime," she laughed. "I can leave whenever I want to, Dav. I always had that choice, and where did my choices always lead me?"

"I don't know," he grumbled.

"To *you*, stupid," she rolled her eyes. "Now hush."

"Bryson will be here tomorrow," he sighed after he frowned for a few minutes. "I know that the seamstress will want to measure him as soon as he arrives."

"That should hopefully be the last fitting until nearer the wedding," Tandy said gratefully. Davian found himself lost in the questions he had and knew he wouldn't last until morning without saying them.

"I'm wondering though, if Martina didn't bring Lethe into the castle, it poses another question. Who else could possibly have a reason to tamper with the betrothal?"

"I didn't want to make assumptions and cause a rumor to ruin someone else, but I can't think of another likely reason that someone would have to change the wedding in any way," Tandy said, hesitating over her words as though guilty for feeling that way. "That person would have had to have a spy in the castle that had access not only to parcels and to the wine cellar, but also your presence. To alter your perception on your fiance and warp the Circle into amplifying the rumors that troubled you is *extremely* calculated, Davian. *Extremely*. And not only that, either. They would need a motive to do any and all of that. The only motive that would make sense is for someone to want *their* heir on the throne, and unfortunately Martina is the only one I know of that has the greed and the means to do it."

"I don't think we are wrong to make this assumption about Martina. You are entirely right about all of that," he agreed. "I haven't met any more people with dimples and an overall anger problem."

"Let's really hope we don't," Tandy shook her head, making Davian chuckle.

"I'll keep Bryson with you and Mariana throughout the day," he said with a yawn.

"No, I'll stay with you and Sir Bryson can stay with Mariana. Besides, heaven knows she deserves a kind man like him," she said. "I hope he's still the same as the last time I've seen him," she added warily. Dav laughed, nodding.

"He's the same, only much taller," he said. "The man has inches on me, now."

***

In the morning, Davian woke Tandy early and sent her back to her room to change. After going for a run, he called for the House-keeper to join him in his quarters and went over the dates on the letters that Tandy had sent him.

"These dates in particular are important, I need to know who brought me that bitter red wine or who had seen the wine poured," Davian told her as she wrote down the dates on the envelopes.

"I will bring the log details to you after I go through them. There are a lot here, but I will do my best to do this quickly," she told him.

"Thank you," Davian said gratefully, standing by her side until she was done. After a while, she put down her pen and gathered her notebook.

"Is there anything specific I should know about this search?"

"Only that the wine may have been tampered with," Davian sighed.

"I will be very thorough, then," she said gravely before following Davian out the door. As they separated, he bid her goodbye and headed to the conference room.

By midday, Davian had met with several advisors and subjects that had requested his presence. He was already exhausted when the seamstress popped in to tell him that his suit and Sir Bryson's were nearly ready, and that the final measurements were underway. He told her to inform Tandy and Mariana of the news and had a maid find Sir Bryson to have lunch with them in the lounge room when he was settled. He knew his friend would at least understand their hesitation and careful wording to see that there was something gravely wrong with the palace, and that they needed to be discreet. He'd have to find a way to inform him of what was going on, and hope that Bryson took it in stride but was nearly certain he'd immediately launch into a discussion on strategy.

Whatever it may be, and wherever they may go, the next few weeks would certainly not be easy on any of them. Davian listened to the last of his advisors as they driveled on about what the inner cities and farm lands have been cultivating, and ideas for numerous festivals to be held during the holidays. He found he just didn't care, his whole consciousness focused on the fact that someone may or may not be plotting his demise, or Tandy's. Nothing was sitting well with him, but he listened to the advisors dutifully and noted their recommendations with the farmers in the north requiring additional support on the harvest, and the suggestions for how to maintain a crowd during the parades. He was so grateful when the meeting was finally over that he nearly ran to the lounge, hoping to find Bryson to greet him at last.

He was not prepared for what he would find.

Fifteen

Tandy

Mariana and Tandy shared breakfast in Tandy's antechamber while they waited for the seamstress. With everything that they had discussed the last few days, Tandy couldn't help but feel that there was still so much that needed to be done. Between the wedding, the ball, and the investigation, she hardly felt prepared to start the day at all.

"Today will be agonizing," Mariana groaned as she finished her third coffee for the morning.

"I'm sure caffeine will help pass the time," Tandy said wryly. Mariana stuck her tongue out at her as she poured herself another cup. "Let's sit on the balcony while we wait," Tandy suggested. Mariana brightened at the idea and they headed through Tandy's bedroom doors to sit outside.

"I haven't been able to enjoy this place in years," Mariana sighed as they gazed out at the lake.

"It's still as beautiful as I remembered it being," Tandy murmured.

A few hours passed before Ms Ralleigh called on them for the final fittings. Having dozed and sunbathed all morning, Tandy and

Mariana were ready to stretch their legs and headed to the lounge. Sir Bryson and Davian would meet them there when they were ready, and all four fittings would be complete for the time being.

"You are going to love the final looks," Ms Ralleigh grinned after they'd been guided into the room by the Guards. "My Lady, if you would come with me to try your gown first," she told Mariana. She eagerly stepped behind the privacy screen in the corner to be changed.

After a few minutes of helping Mar into her dress, they stepped out from behind the partition and stood in front of the windows where the mirror stood. Tandy's mouth almost dropped in astonishment, the gown absolutely phenomenal in its design. It was covered in pink lace fabric with pink gems and embellishments of floral designs over the whole gown. The pink fabric in a slightly darker shade underneath the lace made it look as though there was an overall ethereal energy over the gown. The sleeves stopped before her elbow, and the bodice was sleek with a high neckline outlined with sparkling stones. It was modest, but anything but quaint. Mariana turned to her with a look of pure childlike delight, nearly vibrating with joy as she wore the a-line gown. There were spare traces of gold and silver gems and silver thread that framed the bodice and skirts in a delicate yet extravagant way.

"I made it a bit fuller than a typical gown in this style, it seemed it needed more volume to match its glamorous style. I'm quite pleased with how it turned out, especially for a wedding within our gardens or the chapel should weather prevent us from being under the sun," Ms Ralleigh said, the smile still plastered to her face.

"This is a perfect color on you," she smiled, making Mariana smile harder. She twirled to showcase the layers, and Tandy could only gape as the pink lace and jewels glittered in the light.

"I hope I'm not interrupting," a man coughed behind them, making Mariana freeze. Tandy turned around to see Sir Bryson standing in the doorway nearly a head taller than Davian. They curtsied and greeted each other warmly, Mariana moving to get changed.

"I'm so sorry, Sir Bryson," she said hurriedly. He only grinned and raised his hand.

"No, keep it on. I've been told that I also need to try mine on and it's best to see them together," he said gently. Ms Ralleigh nodded in agreement, nearly dragging him to the partition to change.

Sir Bryson only took a few minutes to change into his suit, though it was still covered in pins as it awaited his adjustments. The pair were dazzling as they stood together in front of the large window in perfectly matching attire.

"Your turn, your Grace," she told Tandy before leading her away. Ms Ralleigh and her entourage helped Tandy get into the dress, and nearly half an hour passed before she was finally inside, with every button and ribbon in place. She emerged from behind the partition and approached the window, waiting to see her reflection in the mirror propped up in the window sill. Her mind went blank when she met her own gaze in the mirror, the gown more than she could ever truly imagine.

The gown was a bright white, with matching lace flowers coating the entire gown. Swirls of sparkling gemstones and pearls made the perfect, clear, white gown positively shine in the direct sunlight. Tandy almost felt the need to squint at the brightness, but couldn't look away from the sight of herself in the mirror.

The thread used to sew each piece to the dress was made of silver, with silver embellishments and lace flowers that were lined with gems along the bodice and spiraled down to the skirts, where it delicately floated just above the ground. It was extravagant, completely opulent, and absolutely stunning. Tandy looked at herself and slowly swished the fabric side to side, the ball gown somehow light despite it all. It was so beautiful she could hardly look away, and as Bryson and Mariana stood to the side behind her, she couldn't help but feel as though they'd appeared out of a fairy tale. She saw Mariana grinning in the reflection and turned around to glance at the back of the dress. The corset bodice laced in the back, fitting her frame perfectly. The sleeves were long and most of her chest was covered in a very modest way, though the lace along her arms was almost translucent.

As she grinned back at Mariana, a true and unbidden smile lighting up her eyes, the door to the lounge opened and revealed Davian. He blinked at Tandy when he entered, stunned silent as he saw her in her gown. Mariana couldn't help but jump where she stood as she saw his reaction. His eyes were wide, his mouth hanging open.

"You'll catch flies like that, Your Highness," Mariana laughed before twirling in her gown, linking her arm through Tandy's. "What do you think, Davian?" Mariana's cheeks dimpled. He finally seemed to come to, and blinked dramatically for a moment.

"Holy *shit*," he said at last.

"Well said, brother," Sir Bryson chuckled. Ms Ralleigh pulled him to the partition to change.

"I will never have a moment as perfect as this for the rest of my days," Ms Ralleigh murmured as she led Davian toward the mirror. Just like Bryson's matched Mariana's perfectly, Davian's matched Tandy's nearly identically. White and silver brought out the honey brown of his eyes. He smiled as he walked up to Tandy before linking their arms together and swatting Mariana away. She giggled before reaching her hand out for Bryson as they all looked into the mirror together.

"Stunning," Ms Ralleigh murmured, hands clasped under her chin. Tandy could swear there were tears in her eyes as she watched them admiring her work.

"You have, as usual, outdone yourself," Davian smiled at her through the reflection.

"Thank you," she said softly, voice wavering. It was true, she had blown them away with her skill. Tandy should have known that the gowns and suits would have been nothing other than spectacular, just by Davian's trust in her alone. They stared at the gowns for a moment longer before Ms Ralleigh directed them to change back into their day clothes, and told them their masquerade gowns would be sent to their rooms when the alterations were complete.

"You've been very busy," commented Bryson. Ms Ralleigh laughed and nodded, pleased with herself.

"Oh yes, very busy," she agreed. The seamstress and her entourage made quick work of the clothes, and placed them carefully back into their linen bags before collecting the mirror, partition, and pedestal they used for the fitting. They headed out the door with all the supplies and Tandy and everyone else sat at the table, slightly exhausted.

"So, I'm imagining something weird is going on," Bryson began, stretching in his chair.

"What makes you say that?" Davian asked him, brows raised.

"The lack of parental supervision, and the *scary* lack of Royals present upon arrival. The servants and stable boys were strange, whispering and hesitant. And not to mention, I haven't seen your parents, or Tandanea's, *or* Mariana's. Usually Martina is nearly the first person to call on me whenever I have been at an event to tell me to scram, and she is suspiciously absent," he said before glancing at Mariana. Dav chuckled, leaning forward. He put his elbows on the table and sighed.

"You've always had a keen eye," he said. "Let's wait until lunch is here before we talk about any of that," he added.

"They'll be here shortly, I told the maids to bring it around an hour after we started the fitting," Tandy told them. Sure enough, within a few minutes two girls arrived with food and served the four. Davian told them to stand outside the door and wait to be called on, and to alert them of any visitors. As soon as the maids waited outside the door, Davian began explaining to Bryson quietly about the goings on. Mariana and Tandy added information as needed, and they waited for Bryson to respond.

"Well, that's certainly worse than I expected," he said finally.

"What were you expecting?" Mariana asked curiously.

"I thought Davian had gotten Tandy pregnant before the wedding ceremony," he said, making Dav spit water out of his mouth in surprise. Mariana giggled at his reaction.

"By the gods, Bry," Tandy huffed. He grinned with a wry laugh, shaking his head.

"Just kidding," he said. He'd left for Knight training before Tandy had been sent away, and though he was larger than she had last seen him, he still was the same Bryson.

"All of the guests are here for the masquerade ball tonight," Davian said as they ate. "With everything going on, it is definitely strange that guests were able to arrive so quickly."

"Run me through more of the details," Bryson told them, his face serious.

"Well, first off, I think we may have been dosed with Lethe," Davian said, making Bryson frown. "We also believe Mariana and I are siblings."

"Because of your dimples, complexion, and overall dispositions," Bryson nodded in agreement.

"Wait, how did you know?" Mariana asked. He turned to her with a gentle smile.

"Of course I knew," he said. "I pay attention to everything. I do recall warning his Highness about the problem with Lethe, years ago at this point. What makes you think you were poisoned with it and not given it as a recreational beverage?"

"That specific wine was served with the letters Tandy would send, and it brought up debilitating emotions that triggered a physical reaction when paired together," Davian explained.

"Sweaty, angry, tunnel vision and an overall sense of despair?"

"Yes, exactly," Davian agreed.

"Why would you be poisoned with Tandy's letters?" Bryson asked.

"We believe that someone was attempting to dissolve the betrothal between Tandy and I in order to place someone else in her place," he said.

"Does Martina know Mariana is of the King's lineage?" Bryson questioned, voice serious.

"She does *now*," Mariana murmured.

"I would be hard pressed to find anyone else with such a motive," Bryson sighed. "I would say her plan changed from marrying into the family, to be crowned as Princess quite quickly once the information was uncovered."

"That's exactly what we believe," Mariana agreed with a frown, her body drooping.

"Well, it will be alright now that there is an expectation for a formal investigation. I suppose you'll want my help with that," Bryson glanced at Davian who nodded in agreement. "I had a feeling when I got here that I'd need to be discreet. I changed my room from what was assigned in the guest book to the one just across the hall from Tandy's room."

"There's no bedrooms on this side of the castle wing," Davian said with a frown.

"There aren't," Bryson smiled. "But there *is* a servant's quarters there hidden in the hall. I want to be as close to Davian's room as possible in case something goes wrong."

"What can you do from behind the hidden doorway, Bry?" Davian laughed.

"It's the servant's quarters, Dav. It has a bell system connected to all three of your bedrooms," he responded. "No one knows I changed the room, not even the Housekeeper."

"How did you even know the room was there? *I'd* forgotten it existed," Davian asked.

"I memorized the blueprint of the palace when I was ten, Dav," Bryson laughed, making Dav roll his eyes. "*And* I know about that bridal suite door that I'm sure has been coming in handy, eh Tandy?" Mariana snorted as Tandy held an impenetrable gaze.

"A lady never tells," she said primly, to which Mariana burst into laughter.

***

The girls got ready together quietly, unsure of what to expect. The dresses were formal but plain, an exaggerated level of girlish femininity. It was very over the top in bows and lace, with frills around each sleeve. Tandy wore a light pink dress, and Mariana wore a fair blue one, the gowns nearly identical aside from color. They looked as though they were children, despite their full breasts and curves. They could hardly look at one another as they wore them, the ridiculousness of the dresses was enough to send them into fits of laughter. It was worse when Mariana pulled matching hair bows for them to wear over their pulled back hair.

"Who picked these atrocities out?" Mariana finally gasped as she looked in the mirror, checking the large bow that now adorned her head. Tandy shook her head, making her bow's loose ribbons smack her in the face when she turned too quickly.

"At least you get to be the whore," Mariana nudged Tandy's shoulder.

"Did she say anything about what blue is for?" Tandy wondered.

"She said blue is for prissy old prudes," she rolled her eyes comically.

They left the room to see Davian and Bryson standing there waiting for them, both wearing their formal regalia. Bryson was in his Knight's adornment, aside from the armor. They both wore their swords at their hip, and offered them each a hand to walk down to the throne room.

"Make sure you two stay close, but not too close. We need you to hear as much as you can. Rumors, drunk passing comments, anything at all. We are only to be greeting the guests and I'm sure there will be nothing to gather until later, but please stay alert all the same." he told them.

As Tandy held Davian's arm, she couldn't help but feel a sense of dread. His grip was tight on her's, their arms clutching one another. The feeling grew heavier and heavier with each stair they climbed down, but she couldn't figure out just what she was feeling. There was no way to know, really, and as Davian and Tandy walked closer and closer to the throne room, she could only brace herself for the inevitable.

Sixteen

Davian

"I welcome you all with open arms as we celebrate the engagement of my lovely soon to be bride, Duchess Tandanea and myself. We cannot wait to share with our closest friends and family the coming nuptials and celebrations. I hope you all find yourselves at home and want for nothing while you are in our care. Let our night be one of joy and entertainment, and we shall see you all quite soon. Don't forget your masquerade masks!" Davian projected his voice down the throne room hall, with a fake grin plastered on his face. His crown sat heavily on his head, uncomfortable where it sat. Tandy held his arm politely with a small and very pretend smile on her face as Bryson and Mariana stood to the left of them. As the four stood in front of the thrones, he hoped no one noticed that the King and Queen were absent as the seats remained empty behind him.

The room was emptied and the guests were led to their rooms. When the doors were closed with a sharp *clank*, he finally dropped his smile and groaned. He put a hand to his face as he leaned against Tandy, exhausted beyond reason. She placed her forehead against his bicep with a sigh, accepting his weight on her shoulder.

Under the skylight of the throne room, the heat stole what little energy they had left.

"Come on," Dav said weakly, before they made their way back upstairs.

"All that for a tiny hello, and we have to go right back up to change again," Mariana huffed.

"Where are our parents?" Tandy asked, her voice perplexed.

"It's really concerning that the King and Queen weren't here to accept the guests," Bryson said, brows drawn tight in thought. "What could they possibly be doing?"

"I imagine they are still sitting in that filthy room, unaware of even themselves," he said. "I am so sick of having to do this for them. It makes the kingdom look bad when they just fuck off like this," he grumbled. "It's like we don't have an actual present ruler."

"I'm sure they would be here if they weren't under the influence of something as strong as Lethe," Mariana said softly.

"You're doing your best, Dav," Tandy offered.

As they walked to Tandy's rooms for lunch, his mind swirled with thoughts of the looming uncertainty wrapped around Martina and the mysterious Elixir of Oblivion that had been brought into his home. He didn't know where any of their parents were, or if Tandy and himself were safe from whatever was at play. Lethe was more insidious than he could have ever believed possible, and with his parents simply locked within a room of their own filth and wasting away, he just wasn't sure what this would mean.

"Stop thinking so hard, you'll hurt yourself," Mariana scolded him as they reached Tandy's rooms.

"There's a lot we don't know, I feel like we're walking into a battle for which I will be completely unprepared for," he told her as he ran his hands through his hair.

"We have a few hours until they serve dinner, at least," Mariana sighed before sitting next to him on the chaise. She leaned on him as Tandy sat on his other side, their cheeks pressing into his arms. Their warmth against him was soothing, somehow. It reminded him of a time when they were children, snuggling side by side in the garden as they rested during tea. Bryson smiled at them from the chair he was leaning back in, engulfed in the plush cushions.

"I always noticed how similar you two look," he commented. "I just never considered what it meant."

"You've been away from the castle for so long, we were only children when you would have noticed," Davian told him.

"I'm older than you by a few years, Dav," Bryson laughed. "My father was in the King's Guard and the only reason we even met."

"I forgot about that," Davian said with a frown.

"I should've mentioned it when I noticed back then," he sighed. "I don't think it would have helped to comment on the philandering nature of the King I was sworn to protect," Bryson continued. "I was young, but I wasn't wise yet. There are many in the castle that could say the same."

"I'm sure the rumor existed when we were children," Tandy said. "The staff will always talk. If conversations were able to be manipulated by the elixir over the last seven years, I imagine the same thing happened when we were children as well."

"The only one that didn't notice our similarities was my mother," Mariana mused. "The fear she put into me kept me from smiling in any kind of way that was real, only those small and practiced smiles. If she had truly loved me, she would have known who sired me a lot sooner."

"I'm sorry you experienced what you did, someone should have helped you," Tandy told her. "You deserve to be loved, Mar." Mariana sniffed, not saying anything for a moment. "We all seemed to fare quite the same."

"As I always do when I arrive somewhere, I listened to the murmurings of the guests and staff as I made my way to the fitting today. Since there was such a strange energy within everyone, I thought it best to listen closely," Bryson told them.

"Did you hear anything about Lethe?" Davian asked.

"No, nothing about that, though I will be listening for that tonight at the ball now that I know it's in the castle. Mostly I heard that everyone believed this engagement party of sorts was a means to cover an unplanned baby," Bryson said, making Tandy roll her eyes.

"How many children must I have already," she said before picking at the strawberries. "Isn't that the old rumor, anyway?" His lip quirked as he tried not to laugh at her statement, though Mariana giggled into her tea.

"The other thing I heard the most from several different people, guests and staff alike, were the comments on the absence of the Royals. Some of them even agreed with others that they hadn't *actually* seen nor heard from the King or Queen in months, except through correspondence. They seem to think you have them locked away so you can rule before your time," Bryson continued as Mariana scoffed loudly.

"Oh, *please*, I bet I know who started *that* rumor," she said angrily, "I've been to every single party the King and Queen have thrown for the last decade, and I can assure you, they have been at *every single one*. That is just mindless blather, spread around for the sake of demonizing the future King so the foundation in which he rules can come crumbling down *long* before he even accepts the crown. We've seen this before, it is the most effective way to bring down anyone from the Royal Circles that aren't favored well enough. By inciting mass rumors while feigning worry, you can get anyone to believe anything. Have we learned anything from Tandy's treatment?" She bit into a square of cheese hard, brows furrowed as she stared at the table.

"Mariana, how much about the other gentlemen and their family situations would you say you're privy to?" Davian asked her carefully, his brow quirked. Mariana met his gaze, a slow smile creeping over her face.

"Oh, I know much more than they'd like, *and* I know how to put fear in their hearts," Mariana told him. "If they were to start a rumor, or spread one, I would know exactly what to say to get them to rescind it, post haste."

"Well, I need to know what your death blow looks like," Bryson said as he leaned forward, curiosity on his face.

"Well, Tandy isn't the only one that could have a, shall we say, *surprise,*" she grinned. Bryson frowned before he laughed, finally understanding.

"If you tell them you are with child, and it's theirs, they would *never* repeat the lie to anyone for fear of consequence. It would be absolutely diabolical, and even if it has been a while longer than a baby would take, I can assure you a married man would still be in an absolute panic. He'd simply lose his ability to do the math on it as terror filled his heart," he said as Mariana cackled with delight, nodding happily as Bryson explained what her intentions were.

"I wouldn't even have to say it to a man I'd ever bedded. If I feign dramatics and act hurt that he doesn't remember our night of passion at the last party, he would simply assume he'd drank too much that night and doesn't remember. Which would certainly be fun to try," Mariana added. Tandy nodded and sipped her tea.

"It is one of the things they taught us in the Fine Etiquette and Reform School, to use your reactions to entice the other party into reacting the way you want them to. By withholding affection, or adding emotion where there should be none, you can manipulate the party into a behavior you design. It's quite manipulative, but it is effective," Tandy shrugged as she picked up another strawberry. Davian was both impressed and disturbed by the two women before him.

"You know I'm in favor of using any and all means that we have to protect ourselves in a battle, and it would seem to me that our next few months may in fact *be* a battle," Bryson told him as he chewed. For a moment, he felt no better than Martina for wanting Mariana to use her wiles for his own sake. He chewed his lip as he thought of the morals of such a situation despite knowing he was the one that brought it up.

"I can *hear* you thinking, Dav," Tandy said as she held her tea delicately. "If it eases your heart, here is something to consider. Our weapon is our femininity and everything that goes with it. This is essentially the only thing we are taught, Your Highness. Mariana and I, we were raised differently than you. Down to our teachers, our parents. We are cattle, brood mares, with only one purpose and everyone knows it. It's the only skill we were encouraged to heighten, aside from the other skills we were taught to ensure a good marriage. It all leads back to the same thing, the goal we all were raised for. It's okay to let us use that gift to help our current situation. It won't change our upbringing, but it may aid our current dilemma without endangering anyone needlessly," she said. She was being gentle, while also being extremely blunt. It helped assuage his guilt but made him somehow feel worse at the same time.

"Fuck, Tandy, that is absolutely miserable," Bryson grumbled.

"They taught you that at that fucking reform school?" Davian asked.

"You've been at the Fine Ettiquete and Reform School this whole time?" Bryson looked stricken when he realized. "I should've checked in with you all more," he said, shaking his head.

"Not just the school taught me that. I was taught the same things here. The only differences were the punishments I received for failure to comply with that standard. I am only to exist to please my future husband, by any means necessary. If Davian had expected a docile and timid wife that spoke only when spoken to, I know how to be that perfect girl. If he wanted me to be a firm, direct leader with a large and spirited voice, I can do that, too. There isn't a role I couldn't play," she finished as Mariana nodded sadly.

"It's true, just 'be a vessel they breathe life into,' is what my governess always said. I won't say what my mother told me, but it's more or less the same," Mariana murmured.

"I need something stronger than tea, if I have to hear of the suffering of women as they suffocate their entire being in order to be forced into the role of wife and mother," Bryson said as he ran his hands over his face, groaning. Davian nodded earnestly, wishing for his own large tankard of the strongest ale he'd ever had in his life.

"I asked for the Housekeeper to give me the names of anyone who had contact with my mail, my wine and food, and me all in the same day," Davian sighed, changing the subject.

"What did she say?" Bryson asked curiously. "That would have been the next thing I looked into."

"She said she would return with the information I need from the dates on Tandy's letters. She takes detailed notes on staff positions within the castle so I imagine she will have what we need," Davian explained. "If we can narrow down the list of suspects that may have poisoned me, we may be able to gather information on who they work for or what their goals behind the plot were."

"Can she be trusted?" Mariana asked.

"Mrs Hollahue can be trusted," Davian said emphatically. "Of everyone in the castle, I would trust her the most."

"That's a very strong statement to make," Bryson commented.

"It's true," Davian shrugged. "She was a mother to me in many ways and I trust her to find out what she can. But the next time we see a Knight, have a few assigned to her for protection. Helping me is dangerous, as far as I am concerned. She should have extra eyes on her," Davian told Bryson.

"Consider it done, I'll assign them immediately," he said easily.

After they ate, they sent for maids to clean the table. During the clean up, there was a knock on the door that Bryson answered quickly, trotting to see who it was. A maid handed him two garment bags and quickly left. He laid them on the back of the chair he had been sitting in, making sure not to wrinkle the gowns inside.

"We'll see you tonight," Davian told them as he and Bryson made their way to the doors. "We'll be taking a look around before the ball begins and see if we're able to find our parents without much of an issue."

"Until we meet again," Bryson smiled before taking a small bow and leaving the room with Davian following behind. They sighed before heading to Davian's room, first, and greeted a maid that stood there seemingly waiting for him.

"Your Highness," she said before raising the garment bag in her hands, bringing their attention to it.

"Leave it on the bed and bring Sir Bryson's as well," he said before sitting in his chair, holding a pink envelope in his hands. The maid left quickly with the promise to bring back Bryson's suit. When the door closed, the two men sagged in their seats and sighed heavily.

"This is definitely *not* good," Bryson commented dully as his head found his hands. "How did you get me to come here just as I'm Knighted, before I've even been home for long, just to come right back into the viper pen." Davian laughed, rolling his eyes. He put the letter down and joined him at the table.

"It's been well over six months since you were Knighted, and if I recall correctly, you were *bored* on your vacation," he laughed again, not believing Bryson in the slightest. "You *thrive* on mystery and drama, sir, don't pretend otherwise." Bryson peered up at him before smirking, unable to hide it.

"You do have me there," he told him before standing. "The Housekeeper has an assigned team, Dav."

"Thank you," Davian said as he watched Bryson pace around the large room with his hands behind his back with his brows furrowed. Davian waited while he was thinking, letting him formulate his own plans and ideas. Bryson was always thorough, and he always had a plan. He would concentrate for as long as he needed and would eventually tell Davian every scenario he imagined, with options on how to handle them. He was an odd man, but he had a very analytical mind and Davian appreciated his steadfast honesty and dedication to his role as a Knight of the kingdom, even since he was a boy.

"Alright," Bryson finally said, sitting across from Davian. The sun was lowering in the sky, almost dinner time, and Davian had moved back to his comfortable writing chair to avoid the harsh glare. He looked up and waited for his friend to continue. "I think when we go downstairs, we should look as formal and decadent as possible. You will constantly have a glass of wine in your hand as you greet guests, and pretend to be as friendly and social as you possibly can. Don't drink it, just flourish it a bit too much and let it spill over the sides when people are distracted. We want people to come up to you on their own, the more social you are, the more you smile, the more this will happen."

"Why do I need to carry wine and smile?" Davian asked with a frown. It didn't seem very appealing in the slightest.

"I'm going to be watching and listening from a distance, and I want to see if anyone tries to tamper with your cup. Do not drink it, Dav. I only want to incite commentary on your behavior, and listen for the hum. It will rile everyone up, both good and bad, and we *want* them to approach you and whisper about you. The more we know of their intentions, and the depth of their lies, we will better be able to understand where the information stems from and keep us safe. Specifically, *you* safe," Bryson crossed his arms as he looked at Davian, waiting for a response.

"I'm more concerned Tandy will be hurt, she's only a gust of wind away from injuring herself as it is," Davian frowned. Bryson snorted, shaking his head.

"Tandy would be at risk by *you* being a target. The fact remains that we don't have enough information to know what is going on. We can *think* everything points to Martina, we can *feel* that everything points to Martina, but that's just not enough. How could one single woman be manipulating this many pieces?" Bryson's brows rose as he looked at Davian pointedly.

"There is something we are missing, something important and we cannot put anyone at risk if we focus on one component, and not the big picture." Bryson sat across from Davian, looking at him seriously. "Davian, we are about to face uncovering a life threatening scheme if the King and Queen have been deposed internally. You may very well have been slowly poisoned along with your parents, by the *gods* you have all the signs and symptoms for it. If something has been going on and *no one* has noticed, not even *you while being drugged,* it most likely means this is literal *decades* worth of deceit."

"We are in over our heads. You have a Knight, a Prince, a Duchess, and a Lady on your team. We don't have what we need to understand what we're facing, let alone implement a plan to eliminate the issue. It clearly has webs, and goes deep, and we *need* to see for ourselves just how far it goes. This is *real* and it is happening *now.* You need to play the game with me, just for tonight, just for a few hours, and then you and Tandy can use your little sneaky door to do whatever you're going to do later on. But right now, I need womanizing, arrogant, party Davian to socialize and act the part of a spoiled Prince. Can you do that?" For a moment, Davian was stunned and only stared at Bryson. He hadn't realized just how confident and controlled Bryson was, as a man and as a Knight. He knew objectively, of course, but never had he been given such a stern and passionate speech from his friend before. His lips quirked, impressed with Bryson's sound mind.

"You're right," he finally said with a nod. "It doesn't mean I like it, though. I hate drinking during the balls. Nearly every time, it gets knocked out of my hand, or people bring me glass after glass and expect me to chug it. The more cups I hold, the more women that flock to me. It's suffocating," he sighed.

"We will be going into battle, Davian," Bryson said as he stretched out in his chair. "We will do what must be done and come morning, we will start again."

"By the gods," Davian prayed.

Seventeen

Tandy

Tandy had the maids set up a privacy partition for her room so that she and Mariana could get ready together. Neither of them said it, but Tandy knew they were both afraid of what would happen if they were left alone, even for a moment. They checked over their shoulders any time there was noise outside or in the hall, and shared uneasy glances while they waited for the maids to return. Tandy also had a feeling that if she were to let Mariana into her room by herself, Martina would intercept her. It wasn't worth the risk.

After the partition was set up, the girls were helped into their gowns. As the corset was tightened, Tandy couldn't help but stare at herself from across the mirror and ogle at her own reflection.

"What is the theme of this masquerade, *sex?*" Mariana shouted from behind her partition. Tandy let out a huff, nearly laughing before Mariana emerged in an emerald gown. Their dresses were the same shape, though Mariana's curves filled it out quite more than Tandy's. The deep cut of the bodice gave them both an indecent and provocative appearance. Mariana raised her brows, impressed with the dress before turning around and looking over her curves appreciatively.

"Holy *shit*," she laughed, sounding both confused and delighted.

"Who approved these gowns?" Tandy couldn't help but ask. The maids only shook their heads with a shrug, also stunned by the sheer amount of skin showing. "If I breathe too deeply, I'll expose myself to the entire kingdom," she stood next to Mariana in the mirror.

"I think the Queen insisted it would be an immersive experience," one of the maids offered. "The theme is titled Decadent Desire."

"I heard it would be entirely anonymous. We have to wear masks *all* night, even through the buffet dinner. They'll have food waiting for everyone. The Housekeeper told us to tell you that the Queen and King wanted everyone to 'move and be' as one," the other maid added, though she made a distasteful face at the thought. "She seemed a little worried about it, especially since she has the Knights with her everywhere now."

"Tell her thank you for the warning," Mariana said.

"Thank you, ladies. Would you bring us a late lunch, as well?" Tandy asked them. "Enough for His Highness and Sir Bryson, too."

"Of course," the maids curtsied with a nod, shutting the door behind them.

"I wouldn't eat anything served tonight. It sounds quite suspicious to me," she said warily.

"Do you think the food may have been poisoned as well?" Mariana asked. "I have no idea what to expect, this is just too much to deal with. Do you think the housekeeper was able to stop the spread of Lethe? If she was aware, maybe the food and wine *will* be safe." They sat silently in the lounge chairs by the windows, looking out over the low hanging sun.

"I don't honestly know, Mar. Don't you think with the influx of guests and the staff they brought with them, that they would have more opportunities to slip something into the safely prepared food from our kitchen once it's moved into the ballroom?" Tandy reasoned. "It seems like there are too many factors to be worried about. If we keep the fresh food prepared by Mrs Hollahue and have it sent directly to us, we may be in safe hands."

"I suppose that makes sense. Once it's in the main ballroom, there would be no stopping someone from mixing in the elixir when no one is looking," Mariana sighed.

"It's been quite a while since I held court, though I was trained excessively in the traditions and remember a lot from our youth," Tandy said after a moment. "This doesn't sound like any ball or gathering I have ever been a part of before. Has the culture changed that much?"

"It certainly isn't typical of the Court held balls. I'm not sure the King and Queen have ever held a ball that didn't first serve dinner. But I *have* been to a few balls with a more revealing gown selection before where the styles have ranged from modest to risque, especially in the last few years. These won't be out of the ordinary," Mariana gestured at her breasts, nearly spilling out of the gown as she sat there. Tandy couldn't stare as she looked down at her own chest, shaking her head in wonder that her normally small chest looked as full as it did in the silvery blue fabric.

"The green looks nice on you," Tandy told Mariana as they sat there quietly. Mariana grinned, as she raised her chin trying to see the mirror from where she sat. Her hair pinned up elegantly and curls framed her face much like Tandy's hair.

"Blue is nice on you, too," she responded easily as she looked back at her friend. A knock rang out from the door before Brsyon walked in wearing his formal wear. He'd changed into something more modest, though it was sleek and enticing in a way that made the girls raise their brows and glance at each other. They stood to greet him and were stunned as the man stared, mouth open, as he took in their gowns.

"The *fuck*," Bryson breathed, gaping at them. Tandy noticed his eyes focus on Mariana, her womanly form nearly making his eyes turn black.

"Close your mouth," Tandy told him delicately while Mariana blushed and looked down.

"My Lord, take a seat," she said quietly, bringing a matching blush to Bryson's cheeks. He tried not to look at Mariana as she sat down. Tandy followed behind and sat next to them, glancing at the door to see if Davian was following behind.

"Davian is changing now, he said we would have to meet him in the banquet hall. I hadn't wanted to let him out of my sight, but a frustrated advisor had been seeking out the King and Queen all day so he needed to handle that before coming back here. He brought several Knights, though, so he will be fine," Bryson told them seriously, though the pink of his cheeks made him look anything but. As they sat there quietly for a few moments, a knock on the door sounded through the room as a maid entered with a large tray of food.

"That was fast," Mariana said in surprise.

"Many of the maids and servants were dismissed from their positions, my Lady," the maid said quietly. "There are extra hands in the kitchen today."

"Why were you dismissed?" Bryson leaned forward, curious.

"Most of the guests are already in the ballroom enjoying their evening and didn't need assistance," she told him.

"Thank you," Tandy said as the maid left the room. "We think the food may have been tampered with. Mrs Hollahue warned us that the Queen had said something that was highly suspicious, and the food will be buffet style," she explained to Bryson.

"She specifically told the Housekeeper that the theme of Decadent Desire would have us 'be as one,'" Mariana clarified. Bryson finally met her gaze, though his expression was sharp and analytical as opposed to the embarrassment that had framed his face only moments before.

"It's a good thing I advised him not to indulge in anything, but I suppose it is time to head toward the ballroom," Bryson said as he stood up. "Let's just eat something quickly and go."

After eating a light meal, Tandy collected the matching masks covered in soft pearls and gemstones lining the sides as feathers framed the top, and handed Mariana the one that matched her gown. They placed them carefully on their faces, and looked in the mirror to admire the beauty of the designs. Bryson pulled his own mask from his pocket and placed it on as well and finally, they began their walk to the ballroom.

As Tandy braced herself for a formal introduction upon entering the banquet hall, she breathed deep and set her chin high. However, no herald stood at the door to greet them. Bryson pushed open the doors himself and Tandy could only stare in shock at what she saw. Mariana gasped next to her as they were met with a throng of people, moving as if suspended in time.

Tandy wasn't sure what she was seeing and blinked to clear her eyes. Everyone was swaying on their feet, an ocean of bodies. Music played gently in the background of the cacophony of voices but the tune was distorted and slightly off pace, ominous and unsettling as they stepped through the threshold. The banquet hall was hardly decorated, with only lanterns and candles placed around the room seemingly at random. The room was haunting as they were cast in the shadows of the flickering lights with the bodies of the Royal court stumbling and swaying around them.

"They must have started partaking as soon as they entered the castle," Bryson commented as they sidestepped a couple leaning on each other for support. In the dimly lit room, they looked nearly as though they were embracing but as they looked closer it was clear they could hardly hold themselves upright. They continued to move through the crowd, everyone wobbling and slurring around them. Mariana gripped Tandy's hand and pulled herself closer, mouth tight in a grim line as she clutched her arm. It was disturbing, to say the least, and the girls continued to hold hands as people spoke all too slowly around them. Tandy looked around but didn't see Davian, and she shared a worried glance with Mariana.

"We should move slowly like everyone else," Mariana whispered into Tandy's ear, and she nodded slowly. Tandy stepped closer to Mariana, clutching her arm. Bryson turned to look at them, brow raised before he understood and moved to stand behind them. He draped his hands across their shoulders, his tall frame looming over them from behind to ward off anyone who approached them.

Bryson continued to scan the banquet hall as the smell of food and perfume made Tandy nauseous. She hated the feeling of being packed into the room, with so many people pushing and pulling around them. She felt as though someone was watching them as they stood in the center of the large room, a prickling feeling on the back of her neck.

"I don't see your parents anywhere," Bryson murmured into their ears, the girls' turning their heads toward his mouth to hear him over the discomforting and bizarre music.

"I don't see Davian, either," Mariana whispered back.

"Do you think he could still be with the advisors?" Tandy asked, still holding Mariana's arm in her own.

"He could very well be anywhere in the castle right now, there's no way to know," Bryson murmured before straightening to his full height. He scanned the room again, his head turning to each corner of the room. It was just too big between the sheer size of the hall and the amount of people swarming around them, they couldn't make out anyone other than themselves.

"Everyone is wearing such revealing clothes," Tandy muttered. "I can't tell who they are with the masks on, either." She was beginning to feel worried that they hadn't sighted him yet, or that he was blending in well enough because he'd already imbibed in the Lethe. Bryson sighed behind them before lowering his head to their ears once more.

"We're bringing too much attention to ourselves in a group like this," Bryson nodded toward the eyes watching them. Though they were all glazed over, many of the guests were peering at them in a dazed but intrigued way, wondering what the three of them were doing.

"You two go ahead, I'll look for Davian," Tandy said as she let go of Mariana's arms and stepped away.

"No, Tandy," Mariana hissed, pulling her back.

"Bryson is right, Mar, we're bringing too much attention to ourselves like this. We need to keep you safe from Martina and find more information from the other guests," Tandy held her hand and squeezed it tightly. "I'll use my training and I will be fine. Go with Bryson, where I know you'll be safe," she urged.

"Be safe," Bryson whispered to her before linking arms with Mariana. She glanced at them one last time before diving into the crowd.

Sweaty bodies pushed against her, the smell of alcohol mixing with their perfumes. She wanted to gag as she led herself through the jumble, feeling suffocated and desperate to be anywhere but here. She kept her eyes on the crowd, looking slowly through the mass of people. She kept moving until she found herself next to the musicians, standing in the center of the dance floor. Couples surrounded her, draping themselves over one another in a faux dance. Bodies languid and slow, writhing and stumbling over each other.

Tandy wanted nothing more than to run straight back out of the ball, right back to her bed. She didn't care where she ended up, either back in her parent's home or even back to the reform school. She felt trapped here in this room, and wanted to be far from everyone around her. Hands kept finding her shoulders, some brushing against her waist as she slowly moved out of their reach. She knew if she moved away from the musicians, the people trying to dance as they fell over themselves would stop reaching for her.

Another song began on the harp, the violin joining the melody. The song was stronger than the others, and Tandy looked at the musicians as they played. It seemed as though the elixir was wearing off on them already, as they couldn't eat or drink anything while playing their music. She was relieved at least to see that the effects wouldn't last very long, so Davian would be alright if he had accidentally ingested any of it. Another body fell against her and she nudged it away, pressing against another by accident. Hands roamed over her and she broke away slowly, trying to avoid any notice.

Suddenly, an arm wrapped around her waist as another ran fingers down her chest along her exposed breast. She gasped, pushing herself away instinctively, her breath catching in a panic. Lips met her throat as a dark chuckle filled her ears.

"Found you," the voice was heavy, growling into her skin. She felt her cheeks heat as she gripped the hands holding her tight, trying to pry them off. "Oh, darling, you're not going anywhere just yet. I've only just caught you, after all," the man holding her kissed her neck before nuzzling against her cheek. Tandy let out a shaky breath as she realized who was holding her, relief washing over her.

"Davian," she breathed, "how did you know it was me?"

"I'd know those tits anywhere," he laughed as he kissed her shoulder, her skin bare to him as he held her tight to his chest. "You should really be more modest, wife," he said as he slid both hands over her exposed breasts, the amount of skin on display still shocking her as she looked down to watch his hands dance along her body. She rolled her eyes, elbowing him and stepping away. He grunted at the impact but only grinned, stepping forward to catch her again with a playful glint in his eyes.

"We're not married, yet, Your Highness," she said, side stepping his reach. A thrill filled her as he stalked after her, but she continued to evade him. She wasn't sure if she was being sneaky, or if he was just biding his time but she couldn't deny the rush she felt from his predatory gaze. His voice seemed clear, his movements sure and steady which gave her hope that he hadn't had any of the elixir. "Besides, it's my turn for a fling or two, after all, wouldn't you say? I think I deserve a bit of fun," she said before turning away from him and walking back toward the music. She wanted to hide their words from the ears of anyone nearby, but as she turned around, he spun her back around. Holding tight to her curves, he pressed in close before placing his lips on her shoulder. She hadn't seen his face yet having been held away from him, but she caught a glimpse of silver feathers as his breath tickled her throat.

"Oh, it certainly is your turn for a fling, I'd say," he whispered into her skin, sending goosebumps over her whole body. His hands ran over her hips, meeting over her belly with a warm heat. She could hardly breathe, afraid she would moan under his touch. She remembered how those fingers felt on her body. She was certain the desperation to feel him again would overcome her if she didn't escape his touch soon. She felt her desire creeping up, settling a fire into her belly. She leaned her head back against his as he rested on her shoulder.

"I'll be going then, to find a fling of my own," she said as he kissed her neck. She pushed away from him again, spinning to see his face for the first time since he'd caught her. He grinned at her, his silver mask similar to her own, a single feather looming over his hair. It lined his face enticingly as his lips and eyes were the only features she could see. His tongue ran along his lips, moistening them, and she could only stare at him with her mouth parted. He moved in closer to her, pulling her against him with a hand wrapped around her lower back. She placed her palms against his open and sparsely buttoned tunic, hands meeting his bare skin as she took in the sight of him.

"Well, wife," he said quietly against her ear, lowering himself until his lips pressed against her soft skin, "in that case, I'll give you a head start." She shivered, his deep voice sending a ripple of desire through her.

"A head start?" She asked him, breathless but confused. "There's something we need to talk about, and we have to find -" her words were cut off by his lips as he pressed a languid kiss to her mouth. She moaned against him, grabbing his shirt collar to bring him closer. He bit her bottom lip before pulling away, leaving her panting and desperate for more.

"The *only* thing you need to concern yourself with, is doing as you're told," he said. Though he was quiet, there was a force behind his voice that sent another shiver through her. "I'll give you a head start. See that door? You're going to take it and find your way to the garden," he told her. She frowned, still confused.

"What on earth for?" She asked, unable to deny herself the need to ask.

"You're going to run from me, and when I find you, I'll claim my victory and take my prize," he said with a grin. Her belly flipped at his dangerous smile making her heart race at the mere idea of being claimed in such a primal way.

"You may just be insane, Davian," she breathed, fighting a smile. "We have to at least find Bryson and Mariana, to tell them you're okay." Davian laughed, a deep belly rumble as he threw his head back. The sound gave her butterflies, but she was still confused as she looked up at him.

"Oh, Bryson knows I'm fine. *And* he knows I'll be busy for the rest of the night," he told her, still grinning like a cat that got the cream. Before she could ask *how* he would know anything, Davian continued. "I saw you the moment you walked in, but these laggard fools were impossible to move through. I haven't seen any of our parents here, much less anyone I recognize between the lighting and the masks. But Bryson is hard to miss with his head nearly touching the chandelier, so I found you quite fast," he explained. She almost laughed at his comment on Bryson's height, the man was certainly tall but the light fixtures were still a dozen feet above them. "I made it to them first and followed you over here. I'm ready to have fun at a ball for once and would like to earn my prize now, should it suit you." He pulled her into another kiss before turning her around and pointing her to the door.

"We have to figure out a plan for dealing with the Lethe -" Tandy tried to say, stumbling under his hands. He scoffed in her ear, pulling her closer.

"Tandanea, darling, there is *nothing* any of us can do with all of these people under the influence of an elixir. They have to sleep it off, it's the only option we have. Do you think their drooling, slurring bodies would even understand that they'd been drugged right now?" He pressed his lips to her neck, pulling a small laugh from her at the sensation. "The only thing we can do now is have fun of our own while they sober up. *I* know what I want, Tandy, do *you?*" His voice was like a purr in his throat. A flood of warmth filled her as she nodded. "Good girl, now here's your chance to escape me. Better make the best of this head start, because I *will* catch you."

"How much time will you give me?" She asked, suddenly nervous. He laughed again, kissing the top of her head gently.

"Better run fast, my love," he snickered, not answering her. By his laughter, she knew he had no intentions of making this easy for her. "Ready, set, *go,*" he said with a gentle nudge.

Tandy immediately took off, running to the door she recognized dimly from the last time they'd used it so many years ago. The candles were dimmer along the edges of the room and she found that no eyes followed her there. She had simply moved too fast for their intoxicated minds to follow her movement, though she hadn't run very quickly at all. When she made it to the door, she noticed her legs felt shaky with adrenaline. The excitement was surprising, and not the least bit confusing. She had no idea what it meant, but she couldn't deny the giddiness that she felt as she pushed through the door and found herself running through a corridor. She followed the moonlight to the exterior garden doorway.

She wasn't out of breath from running, but the excitement certainly made her feel breathless as she glanced around her, orienting herself in the dark garden. She was on the back end of the castle, spit out right by the roses. She began to run toward the left, trying to put distance between her and Davian. Her dress was certainly not good for all this activity, and her hem kept dragging over the grass and stones lining the ground. She hoisted her skirts as high as she could in her small hands, exposing her calves nearly entirely. She figured with the amount of her breasts she had revealed in the ballroom, showing some of her legs was the least of her problems.

As she made it to the large gazebo, she ran around to the trellis that lined the back side of the raised platform, hidden under the honeysuckles that lined the diamond hatched frames. The scent of the flowers made her blush as she remembered the last time she'd been there with Davian under the cover of night, making out in a full ball gown, pressed against the flowers and nearly fainting from the urgency of their kisses.

She heard footsteps around the patio as Davian followed after her, taking a much more direct route than through the side door as he'd instructed her to take. *How typical,* she thought as she rolled her eyes, before pausing and gently walking toward the hedge beyond the gazebo. She found herself behind a tree that lined the path along the cobblestone, leading away to the lake on the other end of the palace. She held her breath as she tiptoed around the bushes, trying to avoid the open air as Davian's voice rang out into the moonlit night.

"Come out, little mouse," he called into the crisp night air. It was warm, the humidity from the summer heat all but gone under the moon's rays. A chill ran over her skin as he called out for her, the thrill making her feel the urge to laugh. "I'll find you, darling," he called out again, but his voice was further away. He'd gone toward the gazebo and further along the palace. Glancing behind her to see where he was, she saw his shadowy frame peering around the vines around the side of the walls, running his hands along it. She couldn't tell by his movements if he was facing her direction or away, but she took a deep breath and made a run for the other end of the garden. She ran through the hedges and past the roses, running along the darkest part of the garden path. As she skittered across the cobblestones, she heard Davian curse as he turned around to follow after her.

She laughed despite herself and pushed herself to run faster, holding onto her hem for dear life. If she were to fall over herself, she wasn't sure she'd be able to put any distance between them and their strange game would surely be over before it started. Davian cursed again as he tripped over a stone, a shrill giggle erupting from her lips at the sound.

"Your time will come, my love!" He called after her, but she kept running. The lake in the far distance was glittering under the night sky, and she chased after the moonbeams as fast as her slippered feet could go. Davian's heavy steps behind her made her squeal in delight, though he was gaining on her. She remembered then that he said he had been running each morning, and was certainly going to catch her sooner rather than later. She wasn't sure how long she'd be able to keep this speed up, but she pushed her body as hard as she could before quickly changing directions.

"Fuck," Davian yelled as he slid along the grass, dew drops making it slippery. Tandy laughed again before running after a small pathway, a raised wooden bridge that crossed over a small creek that ran off the main lake. She made it behind the framework of the bridge, a small alcove nestled in a crescent shaped seating area before a heavy weight nearly knocked her off her feet.

"Got you," Davian growled as he hoisted her up and over his shoulder, her ass pointing straight into the air as her arms dangled and feet kicked in surprise. She kicked at him, trying to loosen his grip but he only lifted her higher with a grunt, hardly affected by her attempt at freedom. From where she rested on his shoulder, her breasts were nearly popping out of her bodice and she squeaked in fear. She pushed against his shoulder urgently, but he ignored her, walking them back to the palace at a leisurely pace. After a particularly rough kick, Davian slapped her on the ass.

She gasped in surprise, her whole body freezing at the sensation. She felt her cheeks flaming, but wasn't sure if it was from embarrassment or desire. Davian seemed to notice her hesitation and he laughed before smacking her again, this time focusing on one pert cheek. She moaned, completely unbidden, at the new sensation and squirmed under his touch once more.

"Oh, little mouse, we'll have quite the fun tonight," he said as he rubbed the cheek he'd just abused, patting her gently. When they neared the roses, Tandy attempted to break free of his clutch once more. She let herself roll from his shoulder suddenly, and caught herself as she met the ground. Davian looked at her in surprise, but she only grinned and ran straight into the palace through the long corridor she'd used earlier. Davian chased after her, tight on her heels, but they both laughed as they ran, not caring in the slightest about anything other than the fun they were having.

They ran through the hallways and corridors around the ballroom, avoiding the crowd as Tandy led them further and further through the castle. She let herself play the game of cat and mouse, giddy with excitement. They ran and ran until they once again found themselves at Davian's bedroom door.

Eighteen

Davian

Davian chased after Tandy as she led him to his quarters. He hadn't run nearly as fast as he could, but he was exhilarated at the chase all the same. He wasn't sure what had brought on the idea of chasing her and claiming her, but he would be lying to himself if he said it was anything other than absolutely indecently sexy to hear her giggling as she ran from him.

Tandy nearly slammed open his bedroom door, closing it behind her with a *click* as she locked it before he could follow after her. He heard her laughter from the other side of the doorway and immediately ran into her bedroom, running to the hidden doorway and pushing through to the other side. He glanced around the unlit room, but couldn't see anything in the dark and began to light the hanging torches on the walls as he looked for her. For a moment, he wondered if she was hiding under the bed but heard a scuffling sound by the window. He reached his hands out for her but she evaded him, the touch of her skin ghosting over his fingers as she made it around him. He cursed under his breath, laughing despite himself as she dodged him so effectively.

"Little mouse, give up now and you'll be rewarded," he called out to her. Her only response was a laugh. He sped up after her, chasing the noises she made. She stood at the door, unlatching the lock she'd fixed when she made it through without him. He sped up again, slamming a hand on the door to keep her from opening it. She squealed in surprise, not expecting him to be so close. She laughed breathlessly as he spun her around and latched the lock back over the door. He pulled her mask from her face and threw it to the floor, staring at her flushed cheeks split with a grin. Her breasts heaved under her dress, barely held within the non existent fabric as she gasped in breaths.

"Got you," he told her, taking his own mask off and breathing deep before pulling her in for a kiss. She moaned when his tongue slipped through her lips, hands pulling at his collar. He bit her bottom lip before picking her up and bringing her to the bed. He laid her on her belly, her ass on display for him, and held a hand over the space between her shoulders. She was trapped there, and wouldn't move until he decided it was time. He wanted to hear her call out again like he had when he'd spanked her before, only this time he wanted to see what her fair skin looked like when bare and exposed against his palm. He pulled her dress up and over her body, and pulled her panties down around her ankles.

"What are you doing," she gasped, squirming against his hands. Her hands slid along the blanket for traction as she tried to sit up. He held her tight, and leaned forward to kiss her lower back. She shivered as she settled and he kissed her again in response to her gentle acquiescence to his movements. His hand that wasn't holding her to the mattress traced the curve of her ass slowly, until he saw goosebumps trail over her skin.

"Good girl," he told her as he raised his hand and let out a sharp smack over the right cheek, the sound a shock in the quiet room. Tandy went rigid in surprise before gasping and crying out at the stinging pain. She pressed her hands to the mattress and squirmed harder, and he let his hand fall back down on the left cheek. Tandy's hips jerked as she cried out again, gripping the blanket and pulling it to her face. He soothed the pink skin before letting another smack land once more, and then again in quick succession.

"Oh, *oh*," she moaned as he massaged the abused flesh. He leaned up and kissed her cheek as she panted into the blanket, face red and hair falling out of her bun.

"Just a little more, my love," he said as he smacked the center of her ass, nearing her pussy. She groaned and rubbed her thighs together, and Davian couldn't help but run his fingers through the wetness he found there. His fingers slid through her folds, absolutely dripping with need as she panted under his hands. "It seems you like this, Tandy, how absolutely indecent of you," he teased. She huffed before casting a look over her shoulder, a glint in her eye. "You'll be given a reward so long as you're a good girl," he warned her. If she had any ideas, he would make her legs nothing more than wobbly and useless weights on her body. She was already trembling with desire, he wanted to see how far he could push their game to go.

"I'll be good," she preened at him, wiggling her ass enticingly. His cock wanted nothing more than to fuck her just like this, pinned down and ass in the air. He'd make her come before he took her, since she was being so good for him.

"That's what a brat would say, Tandy," he said with a grin. She pouted and squirmed again, her breath coming in short puffs. He slid the hand holding her shoulders over her back, bringing both hands to massage her ass. He noticed his hand prints were bright pink, staring back at him and he couldn't help but feel a sick sense of pride over them. He rubbed the red skin before using both hands to smack her ass simultaneously on both sides in rapid succession. The sharp clap of his flesh meeting hers was tantalizing, and after two more blows on each side he ran his fingers along her slit before easing one inside of her. He smacked her ass hard as he curled his fingers, a shock of pain and pleasure leaving Tandy wanton and frantic under his touch.

He laid a softer blow to her reddened skin and added another finger. He could hardly stand another minute without fucking her, but held himself in check. He wanted to play, and Tandy was being *so* good for him and he didn't want to squander it. He smacked her ass another time, another, and another before he finally decided she had enough. She flinched against his hand as if anticipating another blow, but he only rubbed the sore skin and left a kiss where his hand prints had left marks. As he laid kisses along her skin, she was nothing more than pliant and moaning on the bed, her hands still clutching the blanket as her eyes squeezed shut. Her legs dangled over the edge of the bed, boneless, and he slid to his knees behind her before kissing the underside of her ass on each side.

From where he sat on his knees, he had the most amazing view of her perfect, pink pussy. She was dripping wet with want, and he couldn't fight the urge any longer to taste her. He kissed up her thighs until he found her core and licked flat along the sensitive folds. Tandy jolted in surprise, but he continued and used his hand to spread her lips apart. He licked and sucked until he found her clit, pressing two fingers deep inside of her. He held them there, keeping them curled as he licked the skin around where his fingers held her open. He twisted his wrist until her clit was exposed to him again, pressing his fingers as deep as he could before gently wiggling them against the bundle of nerves inside her.

"Oh gods, Davian, *please*," Tandy cried into the blankets, legs trembling. She could do little else except accept his tongue on her clit as his fingers continued to wiggle in a *come hither* motion. He licked along her pussy before diving back to her clit, putting all of his attention on finding the spot that would make her come *hard* on his face. She keened when he added a third finger and began thrusting them into her much like he would his cock. He could feel her pressing back against his face and knew she was close by her desperate pleas, begging him for more. He pressed his fingers as deep as he could from the awkward angle before sucking hard on her clit, putting every ounce of control he had into the motions.

"Come for me," he told her as he filled her with his tongue and fingers, urging her to reach her climax so he could feel it for himself. Her body went rigid when his fingers found the soft button inside of her that sent prayers flying out of her mouth.

"Oh yes please, right there, Dav, *please, right there, oh my gods, I'm coming,*" she cried into the bed, body arching as she came around his fingers. He didn't slow his motions and kept fucking her with his hands until every last spasm had left her body, the delicious feeling of her pussy clenching around him sending all the blood in his body straight to his cock. Her body trembled with after shocks as he pulled his fingers out of her. He licked his hand clean before gently laying her onto the bed more comfortably, pulling the blanket down so he could cover her with it. She blinked at him in a daze as he tucked her into the bed and moved to turn out the lanterns. He lit the candles next to his bed before stripping to his underwear and climbing in next to her, pulling her to his chest.

"When do you claim your prize?" Tandy asked cheekily, though her voice was tired and sated.

"I quite enjoyed my victory, thank you," he told her with a smile, kissing her deeply as she gazed up at him. He knew she could taste herself on his tongue and was surprised with the heat she responded to his kiss with. Suddenly, her small hand wrapped around his cock through his underwear, making him gasp.

"What shall we do about this?" She asked him, brow raised.

"Nothing you wouldn't want to do," he said sincerely. She had the nerve to laugh at him as she sat up, moving to pull his underwear down. She tossed it to the floor and looked at him with a smile before turning her head down to gaze at his cock, bare to the world. She pulled her dress off of herself, and threw it on top of the rest of the clothes. His mouth watered at the sight of her bare breasts before him, but before he could reach for one she pulled his cock into her mouth as deep as she could go.

"Oh *fuck, Tandy,*" he cried out in sheer surprise. She only hummed as she pulled him deeper into her mouth, his hips rutting into her unconsciously. She took him with precision and used her hands to stroke what she couldn't fit inside her mouth, making him moan. He pulled at her hair until the bun came tumbling down and her blonde curls fanned around them. She sucked his cock for a minute longer before pulling off of him with a long swipe of her tongue along the underside of the head, making him see stars. She blinked at him innocently but all he could do was stare at her in awe, wondering what she was going to do next.

"Do you want your prize, Your Highness?" She asked him with a feral smile. He was almost afraid of how turned on he was at her words and almost asked her what she could mean, before she moved her legs around his hips to straddle him. She stood on her knees, hovering over his cock as she held it in one of her hands. His mouth watered at the mere idea of her riding him, and he knew his jaw must be hanging open as he drooled.

"Please," was all he could say as he trailed his hands over her hips as she gently pressed the head of his cock against her wet pussy, the barest of pressure. Tandy huffed a moan out as she took a deep breath, relaxing her body of tension as she sank down on him, so painfully slowly that he thought he would surely die. "Go slow," he warned her, but she only met his eye with her lips parted, rolling her hips gently in small circles until she was flush against his hips, sitting on his cock entirely.

"Oh, fuck," she said in a low voice, trembling. Davian almost pulled her off of him in fear she'd hurt herself but she pressed her hands to his shoulders and raised her hips up before grinding back down onto him. "Oh *fuck*," she said as she met his gaze, unwavering, and repeated the motion. "Oh my gods," her voice was wrecked, an absolutely tantalizing sound. He groaned when she rolled her hips around him and used his hands to guide her back up slowly so he could meet her downward thrust in the middle.

"Oh *yes*, like that," she clawed at his shoulders as she moaned. She raised up and met his thrust again and again, thighs trembling with pleasure. He pressed up and into her, the sound of their bodies meeting between them a wicked and voracious slapping sound. She bounced on his cock before slowly grinding on him, only to pick the pace back up, and then slow down, over and over. He pulled her lips down to him, kissing her with a ferocity he'd never felt before. With the new angle, he held her hips tight and fucked into her hard and fast, making her scream out against his lips.

"That good, baby?" He asked her breathlessly as he slammed into her, not quite hard enough to be rough.

"Mmm," she moaned against his throat, "I won't break, Dav, I can take more," she told him as she nearly sobbed with pleasure. He was sure she'd regret being rough for her first time in so many years, but at her urging he was helpless to deny her. She felt so good around him, so hot and tight on his cock. He wasn't sure if their trysts when they were teenagers were as hot as this, or if their separation and age had anything to do with it. He had missed her, but the taste of her and the feel of her soothed the loss just a little.

He could feel each flutter of her pleasure as she squeezed around him, unconsciously tightening her hold on him. He flipped them over suddenly, surprising her for a moment, but as he pulled her knee high over his hip and thrusted deep inside of her pussy, she screamed out praise.

"You feel so good," he told her, pressing kisses over her face as she arched her back at a particularly deep thrust.

"I missed having you inside me," she pleaded in his ears as she clawed at him desperately. "Oh, do that again," she begged. "Just like that, *please*," she gasped as she scratched his back. She held her own knee higher and wrapped the other around his waist, trying to get him to reach the exact spot that surely sent stars to her eyes.

"Gods, you are perfect, holding yourself open for me," he kissed her throat, rolling his hips into her exactly as she'd begged him to. She let out a sob, desperate and so sweet, gasping at his words.

"Just for you," she told him urgently as her hips rolled against his own. "Gods, Dav, I'm so close," she cried, pulling him down for a kiss.

"Good girl," he told her. "Not just yet though, love. I missed being inside of you." She threw her head back in frustration as he slowed his hips, rolling them just enough to torment her as she neared orgasm.

"Please, *please*," she begged, hips squirming to find his rhythm once more. He couldn't help but laugh at her pleas, completely overwhelmed with his cock deep inside her. She felt perfect, *so* perfect, and he wanted to make it last just a little longer. She pressed against his chest, urging him to sit back. He nearly slipped from her pussy as he moved, but she ground against him as she sat herself on his lap to keep him deep inside her. She clutched his shoulders and kissed deep into his mouth, tongue meeting his own. He gripped her hair with one hand as he held her ass with the other, pressing her down onto his cock as deep as she could go. With a frustrated grunt, she pushed him back until he was in the same position they'd started in.

"Fuck," he moaned as she slammed her hips over him, using her legs to find a rhythm that kept her chest pressed flush to his own. She bit him all around his throat and chest, keening as she ground herself onto his cock. He raised his hands to her hips and held tight to them, thrusting up and into her core in quick succession.

"Yes, please, *yes*," she cried, tears filling her eyes as she neared her climax. "I need to come, *please*," she begged in a desperate whisper, shaking with need.

"Yes, baby, come on my cock," he told her, slamming her onto him over and over, her moans turning to screams with each direct hit to her innermost sensitive nerves, until she coiled around him and arched with a gasp.

"Oh, *yes*," she wailed, tears on her cheeks as she came hard around his cock. He didn't stop pumping into her until she was nothing but a sobbing mess, trembling with overstimulation. He rolled her over and slowed his thrusts, filling her still as he sought out his own release. He watched as her eyes glazed over as he ground into her, her hips still matching his pace. He was close, he only needed a little more, when she planted her feet to the mattress and used them as a counterweight to his fucking. Despite the exhaustion and glazed over look, she stared at him completely determined to make him come. She laughed breathlessly as he smiled at her, kissing her lips before quickening his pace. He watched as she licked her fingers and brought them to her clit, staring intently into his eyes as she rubbed herself while he was buried inside her.

"*Fuck*," he said at the sight, sending him straight over the edge with the most intense orgasm he'd ever had in his life. "Oh *fuck*," he moaned into her throat as she played with herself as he gently thrusted into her through his orgasm. She went rigid suddenly, hips rolling against his as she moaned. A warm flush of liquid pooled out of her as she came, soaking them both. "Holy shit, Tandy," he moaned with another series of thrusts as she moaned through the aftershocks of her messy orgasm.

They laid there for a minute, too sated to separate from one another. Davian could hardly lift a finger as his cock still rested inside Tandy, though he knew he should roll out from under her. Tandy's body trembled as they calmed down, Davian's hands soothing her soft skin gently until they both gained lucidity once more. He rolled her gently to the side, pulling out of her before placing her over the pillows. He collapsed next to her, sighing deeply with a hand over his face, a tired grin on his lips. Tandy giggled next to him, and he spared a glance at her only to meet her flushed face grinning back at him.

"Are you alright, Your Highness?" She raised her brow at him, though her flushed cheeks and sweaty brow took away from the mischievous look she gave him.

"Better than," he told her honestly, laughing back at her. He felt lighter than he had in years, but supposed mind blowing sex would do that to a man. "I don't know how I survived without you for so long."

"Me neither," she agreed before climbing out of bed and headed to the bathroom. She climbed back into bed after a few minutes and tucked herself back under the covers, nearly nose to nose with Davian. They fell asleep curled up and facing each other, sated and sleepy.

Nineteen

Tandy

Tandy woke slowly, pleasantly warm as she rested underneath the blankets. An arm draped over her waist, and she pulled it tighter against her as she stretched. Her muscles ached, though in a delicious kind of way that brought heat to her cheeks as she remembered the night before. The sun was only just rising, the sky a deep blue. Davian snored lightly against her neck, pulling her tighter unconsciously. She smiled to herself as she enjoyed the feel of him as he wrapped himself around her naked body. She let herself doze, the comfort of his weight making her feel sleepy in the morning light. She could feel when he woke up, his hand wrapping low over her belly and pulling her flush against his hips. He rutted against her in a teasing motion as he kissed her cheek.

"Morning," he told her, voice still full of sleep. He trailed kisses down her neck before she rolled over, accepting his lips on hers. He kissed her lazily, cupping her breasts one at a time.

"Morning," she said with a smile, watching him stretch. He turned to her with a serious expression suddenly, making her raise a brow.

"How do you feel?" He asked her seriously. She frowned, not understanding what he meant. "Are you sore?" He added when he noticed her expression.

"Very," she told him honestly, stretching her arms and legs out with a wide yawn.

"So no round two, then, I suppose," he sighed dramatically, flopping back onto the pillows.

"I wouldn't say I'm *that* sore," she told him. He snorted at her, pushing her shoulder until she rolled over so he could press himself along her back once again. He wrapped his hands around her, pressing a messy kiss against her neck.

Heat spread through her as she leaned back against his touch, pressing her ass against his cock. Her body ached, but she wanted to feel him inside of her again. Davian laughed against her cheek, kindling the flame in her belly as his deep voice filled her ears. His hands trailed down her belly slowly, sliding over her thighs enticingly. She parted her legs for him, only to have him roll her onto her back. He pressed himself between her sore thighs and kissed her gently, trailing from her lips to her neck. She felt his hardened cock against her thighs and she squirmed, reaching for it before pulling it toward her pussy.

I don't care how sore I will be, I need him inside me, she told herself. It had been a long, *long,* time since she'd felt that kind of pleasure and she couldn't miss any opportunities to feel his cock again for as long as she lived.

She lined him up until he pressed inside of her, kissing her deeply as he filled her. She was still sensitive from the night before and nearly immediately needed to come. His slow, deep strokes brought her quickly to the edge. His tongue filled her mouth, biting her lip, whispering praise with each pump of his cock.

"So good for me," he told her, kissing her slow and deep in much the same way he was grounding into her. She raised her knees, pulling them up and used her hand to raise her ass for a deeper angle, her legs too sore to do much beyond clutch Davian's waist. He understood, though, and ran his hand under her hips and began fucking into her as he raised onto his knees. Her legs trembled with exhaustion before he spit on her pussy, rubbing her clit hard. White hot heat laced through her as she came *hard,* suddenly and with no build up. She wasn't sure if she screamed, or even breathed, but his cock and his fingers kept going until she regained her senses. She was still coming in waves as her pussy tightened around his cock, moaning and pleading desperately for more despite being past the point of exhaustion. She briefly noticed a wetness spill from within her, much like her orgasm the night before. Davian's eyes were entirely black as he dropped her hips back to the bed and bit and licked into her mouth.

"Fuck," Davian said as he plunged his cock into her hard, before groaning as he came inside of her. He leisurely stroked his cock within her twice more, savoring his orgasm before he collapsed next to Tandy breathlessly. Tandy laid there in a daze, still feeling the walls of her pussy spasming as the aftershocks still traveled through her. She couldn't believe she had come so hard. She reached out for him, pulling him into a soft kiss before laying back onto the pillows under the covers where they dozed for a while.

***

Tandy and Davian were awoken suddenly when there was an urgent knock at the door. They gasped and sat up, blankets tangling around them.

"Your Highness!" A voice called through the door, continuing to knock. Tandy stumbled off the bed, scrambling to the hidden door with the sheet off the bed wrapped around her before Davian stopped her with a wave of his hand. He pulled his pants on and ran to the door as Tandy leaned against the wall. She was too far to the side that she would go unnoticed, and whatever they told Davian she would be privy to. A heavy sense of dread filled her as Davian unlocked the door, propping his foot behind it so it didn't swing open beyond how far he wanted it to.

"Your Highness," a Knight said when Davian opened the door, his hair still a mess from sleep. His voice was grave, and from what Tandy could hear, out of breath. She felt chills creep up her limbs, an icy trail that made her feel small and frozen to the spot she stood.

"What is going on?" Davian demanded, voice commanding despite the state of his undress.

"It's the King, Your Highness," answered the Knight, still winded. Davian stared at them blankly, silently urging them to continue speaking. His eyes narrowed as he watched the Knights, and after what felt like forever the second Knight spoke up.

"The King is dead, Your Highness," he managed between gasps. Davian froze where he stood, eyes wide as Tandy covered her mouth in shock. Time seemed to freeze around them, not a sound heard between the labored breathing of the Knights and Tandy's heart beat in her chest. Davian looked over at her, eyes unblinking and wide. He gripped the doorway for support as Tandy saw the words finally reach his heart. For a moment, he looked like a boy again. A boy, all alone and scared. The moment vanished as Davian's brows furrowed, an angry expression blooming over his cheeks before he made a minute motion with his hand, urging her back to her room. She nodded, mouthing *I'm sorry*, before stumbling through the small door. She closed it tightly behind her, startling Mariana as she slept in Tandy's bed.

"Oh Tandy, you scared me," she sputtered as she sat up urgently. She looked at Tandy in surprise and noticed the state of her, hair rumpled with only a blanket around her. Mariana grinned before sliding out of the bed with a laugh. "I *knew* you two would waste no time," she crowed with delight, throwing her a robe that hung on the chair. As she handed it to Tandy, she noticed how pale Tandy looked and paused in alarm.

"Thanks," Tandy managed to whisper as she took the robe from her.

"Tandy, are you okay?" she asked, helping her arms through the sleeves. "Davian, that son of a bitch, I'll tear his dick off. What did he do?" Mariana's hands were firm on her shoulders as she stared right into Tandy's eyes. Tandy felt frozen still, and looked at Mariana with fear.

"The King is dead, Mariana," she whispered. Mariana stared at her, blinking just the same as Davian had as he heard those words only moments ago. "They just notified him at his quarters, they woke us up." The blood drained from Mariana's face as she still clutched Tandy's shoulders. Another moment passed and Tandy finally felt awake again, and nudged Mariana into a chair. She was trembling, hands clutching her nightgown. She looked at Tandy with fearful, watery eyes.

"You don't think it was -" she whispered before a tear made its way down her cheek. Tandy shook her head and waved her hands.

"We can't know that yet," she said.

"What do we do?" Mariana shuddered, wrapping her arms around her shoulders. A knock rattled at the door making them nearly jump out of the skin. Mariana let out a frightened yelp as they jumped together, holding each other's arms. As the knock continued, Tandy steadied herself and went to open the door. She was afraid to know who was waiting for her but breathed a sigh of relief when she saw Bryson and the maids. They brought in breakfast and tea before departing from the room and Bryson quickly locked the door behind them.

"We can't take enough precautions," he told Tandy before he sat heavily in the chair next to Mariana. She laid a trembling hand over his shoulder before looking at Tandy with a question in her eyes. Tandy could only raise her shoulders in a faint shrug, not sure what to say.

"Bryson, do you know anything?" Tandy asked softly, clutching the light robe tight to her body. It was all she wore, and though it reached the floor in length she still felt terribly bare before them.

"I know that the guests are going to wake up to find their King dead," he said with no inflection as he ran his hand over his face. His clothes were rumpled as though he dressed in a hurry, his hair much like Davian's in its disarray. Mariana whimpered next to him as the words left his mouth, and she recoiled from them as though burned. She looked at Tandy helplessly, her thoughts clear across her face. She was petrified that she'd be linked to whatever happened, the fear in her eyes unmistakable. Tandy sighed and walked over to her, reaching for her hand and taking it into her own.

"How did they find him?" Tandy asked, knowing it was important. They needed to understand what happened to be able to figure out if he died of natural causes or if he was murdered.

"They found him in the throne room, pants down, covered in both wine and some strange purple substance," he told them as he crossed his arms. "He also had lipstick stains all over his face and body."

"What color was the lipstick?" Mariana whispered.

"It was red, but may have been another color before the wine and that purple substance mixed with it. There was something else, too," he added as they frowned at the mention of the lipstick shade. Red was a very generic color for the ladies of the Royal court, so didn't really lead to much, Tandy knew.

"I'll be taking Davian to the scene now," he told them, shaking his head slowly.

"He's not going by himself," Tandy was relieved. It wasn't a good idea for him to go alone, especially if his father's body was still there.

"He's changing in his room now, I wanted to let him gather himself before heading down," he explained with a sigh. He glanced at Mariana who sat in her nightgown, still trembling in fear. Tandy saw his cheeks redden as he took in what she was wearing, quickly glancing away to avoid her unbound breasts.

"We should send for a maid to get us some clothes from Mariana's room," Tandy told Bryson. He agreed quickly and peered out the door to a maid waiting for her orders. He told her to get something from Mariana's room that was appropriate for morning tea, and she was on her way.

As Bryson turned back to Tandy and Mariana, a shriek filled the air. They all ran into the hallway to find the maid pale and shaking uncontrollably,

"What happened?" Bryson demanded. She pointed to Mariana's room. Despite not wearing much beyond pajamas, they couldn't help but follow Bryson as he led the way to the room. The maid stood there, tears streaming down her face, and made no move to follow them. Mariana and Tandy held hands without a thought, gripping tight enough to hurt. Bryson pushed open the door slowly and gasped as the girls peered around him to get a glimpse of what was in there.

"Do not go any further. Mariana, Tandy, go back to the other room. I will have maids attend you. No one is to leave the room until Davian and I come to find you," he ordered them, turning abruptly from the door. He told the maid to stand with the Guards posted in the hall and wait for him there before he gently nudged them back into the room, though Tandy desperately wanted to see what was on the other side. Bryson's tall frame had blocked it out of their sight, and she had no idea what must have happened in there except that it was bad enough to terrify a maid that way. "Lock the *doors* behind you," he told Tandy. His eyes urged her to understand what he wasn't saying and she immediately nodded, knowing what she needed to do.

"Of course, my Lord," she told him softly. He sighed before exhaling slowly, expression dark.

"There is much more at play here than we think, I just know it. We cannot leave any stone unturned," he said as he guided them back to Tandy's doors. He nudged them into the room and dipped into a soft bow before closing the door firmly behind him. Tandy debated following after him to make sure Davian was okay, but she was afraid of disobeying Bryson's orders. Whatever was inside of Mariana's rooms must have been *bad*.

"Bryson will help Davian for now, let's just try to have something to eat," Mariana offered in a trembling voice.

"I feel the right thing to do would be to comfort him, but I only skittered away like a rat in the barn as soon as the Knights said the King is *dead*," Tandy admitted quietly.

"You had no choice but to go to your rooms, engaged or not. It would have been improper to stay despite the way you left," Mariana said kindly.

"I wouldn't be the most empathetic person for him to grieve with, anyway," Tandy sighed quietly.

"We all struggled these last few years, especially emotionally. I think Davian will take a while to be able to completely open himself to this kind of grief, much like you and I will. He, like us, has been manipulated in a way that changed him for the worst. We must be more forgiving of ourselves for everything we've gone through," she squeezed Tandy's hand.

"I suppose," Tandy frowned. "I should have offered some kind of comfort, though."

"When Davian gets to a point of overwhelm, he can't take in any more information and shuts down. Bryson will be able to bring him back to reality, and until then we have to wait and see," Mariana explained. "Before with the Lethe, he'd become explosive and angry. Who's to know how he will respond to something of this caliber?"

"I don't think he will be violent," Tandy said finally. "He seems more level headed and self aware than he had been at the ball seven years ago."

"I feel the same about myself, honestly," Mariana agreed. "Whatever is in that elixir, it is surely potent."

Tandy locked the main door to her room and then the small hidden door before finding herself a dress to wear. She offered Mariana a gown that was close to her size and led her to the partition in her bedroom to change. As reality caught up to them, Mariana's skin grew pale and her hands shook as she held the ivory fabric. The trembling made it hard for her to unbutton the back and she struggled for a few moments before Tandy moved to help her. Mariana flinched at the sudden movement but Tandy only hummed gently and ran a hand over her cheek before turning her around to unlace her nightgown. She helped Mariana step into the clean dress, buttoning her slowly into it before she turned her back around to make sure the bodice fit her well enough in the breast. Mariana's cheeks were wet with lightly shed tears as Tandy pulled the fabric into place.

"I know it wasn't your fault, Mar, and Davian does, too," she told her gently. A soft sob exhaled from Mariana's breath before she tucked her face into her hands and wept. Tandy guided her to the small couch on the opposite side of the room where the hidden door was and made her sit down. Though she still wore only a robe, she felt unreasonably sweaty and overheated.

"I'm going to draw myself a bath," she told Mariana. Her thighs felt sticky from the activities she'd partaken in the night before and felt a blush on her cheeks that she'd only just realized how unbecoming she looked.

"This isn't your fault and not only Davian knows that, but also Bryson, " she said before walking slowly towards the bathroom.

"Like he knew the truth about you, all those years?" Mariana whispered as she looked at Tandy dejectedly.

"This is different," Tandy said. "He was drugged, and you were, too." Mariana looked out the window sadly, but nodded at Tandy's words.

She went to the bathroom and waited for the tub to fill up. She scrubbed herself clean, soaking her aching muscles and sore body. She wondered if the King's death had been of natural causes despite still being young. She could speculate as much as she wished, but in the end they would still have to wait until Bryson or Davian came back to learn of anything more.

Tandy finished washing her long hair and finally stepped out of the tub. She dried off and brushed her hair before pulling her clean undergarments and gown on slowly, taking her time. She braided her hair as she sat back down with Mariana, who had at least brightened in pallor since Tandy had gotten a bath, and immediately reached over to braid the rest of her hair, falling into an old routine from long ago.

A knock at the door sounded and Tandy immediately rose to greet whoever it was. Gratefully, it was a maid with a plate of food.

"The tea will be here shortly," she told them as she placed everything on the table and left for the tea. At the sight of food, Mariana smiled as they sat together picking at the fruit and biscuits. Tandy wasn't very hungry, yet, though she knew she should eat soon before she felt sick with nerves. She made herself eat a scone before another knock sounded at the door. Tandy opened the door for the tea and took the tray from the maid. She locked the door before bringing the tea to the table.

"Thank you," Mariana said. They were quiet for a minute as they picked at the food tray, before Mariana broke the silence.

"When do you think Bryson will be back?" Mariana wondered as she bit into a sliced peach.

"I wonder how Davian is feeling," Tandy added. They could only shrug and glance at one another, and finish the breakfast tray. The fear settled within them, so much so that the mere idea of leaving the bedroom sounded daunting.

"I wonder if we could find a way to get more information without waiting," Mariana mused. "If Bryson is the one directing staff, there's no doubt in my mind he already memorized the schedules and room assignments. He likely knows where everyone in the castle has been for the last two days," Mariana said.

"He must have gone over the plans on the way here, has he even been here long enough to attain that much information?" Tandy shook her head.

"His room is in quite the state, there were plans and diagrams strewn about his desk, the floor, *and* the bed," Mariana laughed. Tandy narrowed her eyes as she looked at Mariana, making her blush. She covered her cheeks with her hands as she hid a smile behind them.

"How do you know what his *bed* looks like?" Tandy asked

"I'll have you know Sir Bryson is a gentleman, and I'd never dishonor him in such a way," Mariana said, fluffing her hair in a mockingly haughty way.

"He's a good choice, Mar," Tandy finally said softly. Mariana only blushed harder and looked down as she lowered her hands, dimples alight in the rising sun's rays.

After they finished eating, another bath was drawn for Mariana. They spent most of the day waiting anxiously, before deciding to spend the afternoon under the sun on the balcony. They sighed under the warmth, hiking their skirts to shine the light on their legs. They sighed as the breeze soothed some of the worry and continued waiting for the lunch hour to come around. Or for the men to return to them with more information, whichever came first. Every few minutes would pass and one of them would cast a wary glance at the door, only to turn back around and slump in their seat.

Tandy yawned after a while and sat forward to suggest they send for lunch, when a knock sounded on the door once again. They immediately clambered back into the room to answer it.

"Duchess Tandanea is being called on by Prince Davian," a maid said. They shared a concerned glance with one another as they took in the maid before them. Mar suddenly slammed the door shut and locked it.

"You're not going with her," Mariana said, voice angry and shaken. "You can't leave this room unless the Prince himself claims you, *that* was a very concerning attempt at retrieving you by *someone* in this castle. I do not trust it at all." Tandy nodded in agreement, trembling as she gripped her hands together.

"Who was she, then?" Tandy whispered, concerned there was someone hiding in the castle somehow.

"She might be one of my mother's servant girls," Mariana said, "I could only hear her voice but it sounded very similar. Another knock sounded through the room. Tandy rolled her eyes before stepping to the door and calling through it.

"Who is knocking on my door?" Tandy used a commanding voice, one she had perfected years ago. A gasp could be heard on the other side, followed by the voice of the maid from before, still standing there to be let inside.

"Duchess, the Prince has called upon you and requests your presence," Tandy unlocked the door quickly before snatching the girl's wrist and pulled her through the doorway. Just as quickly, Tandy locked the door as the girl let out a yelp of surprise.

"You'll sit in this room until I know who sent you here," she said coldly as she led the girl to the couch. Her eyes were wide and she was much too young to be spoken to this way, but Tandy knew she needed to get this child to understand who exactly was in control here, in this castle, and it certainly wasn't whoever was causing the drama within the kingdom. No matter how it looked from where they sat now, with everything in chaos around them, whoever brought Lethe to the palace was *not* in control. "You can tell me now who actually sent you to me, and I'll send you back under the guise of I don't feel well from drinking too much last night. Will you accept that?" The girl stared up at her, shaking like a leaf. Her eyes were watery and she glanced around the room before bursting into tears.

"I'm sorry, my family needs the money and I was told I have no choice but to do this, and they'd be out of debt if I did," she weeped pitifully. Tandy sighed and looked at Mariana, wanting to know if it was actually one of Martina's girls. She nodded sadly, before Tandy sighed again, louder. Everything continued to point at Martina as the root of the kingdom's chaos. She was simply not to be trusted, especially as more information was revealed. There would be no way for Martina to clear her name after all of this, with even her daughter against her. To lure the future Princess and Queen right out of her own bedroom with the use of a poor little girl was the final straw. The woman was deranged. Tandy fumed for a moment before going to her desk drawer. She pulled out a silk coin purse and walked over to the girl.

"Where is your family?" She asked gently.

"They're at the farmhouse, they live on the grounds. We were made to move there only recently to pay off the debts, but no matter what we do we can't escape. She said I'd set them free if I did as I was told, and I didn't ask questions," she looked up at Tandy with a trembling lip, "I'm sorry, I just want to go home!" She sobbed into her hands, body quaking.

"What's her name?" Tandy whispered to Mariana.

"Leesa," she answered.

"Leesa," Tandy said in a stern but not unkind voice. The girl flinched before looking up at her as though ready for her last rights to be read. Tandy sat on the chaise across from her to keep her from looking so afraid. As Mariana sat next to Tandy, she pulled open the satchel before asking another question.

"How much does your family owe?" Tandy asked. The girl looked at her confused, before frowning in thought.

"I don't know exactly, but I think we need five hundred copper pieces," she said after a few minutes. Mariana huffed angrily, crossing her arms together as she heard the words leave Leesa's mouth.

"That's all you owe, and she's holding your family hostage?" She nearly yelled before Tandy laid a hand on her leg to calm her. Tandy pulled through the bag and found the smaller bag she used to hold the gold pieces she'd been saving for years. She'd never needed the money, but she had kept it hidden just in case.

"I'll give you these twenty gold pieces for you to take to your family, and I will give you more if you get them out of the farmhouse and bring them *here* to work for me. As the soon to be crown Princess, I have full authority on my staff and such. You will not be hungry here, and you will be treated fairly," Tandy said, holding out the stack of coins. The girl gasped when she saw them, eyes wide. "I, of course, will settle the balance your family owes in full to ensure their safe arrival. However, this will come at a price, Leesa," Tandy's voice grew harder as she spoke. The girl looked at her with tear streaks dripping down over her face.

"What do I have to do?" The girl asked, wiping her face on her sleeves.

"You need to tell me who sent you here, and anything you've been able to overhear. You also need to write a letter for your parents, right now. I will send it to the farmhouse immediately and call for your family. There will be no way your current mistress can stop this from happening once I make this decision. Any attempt at preventing me from completing this transaction will be considered larceny which is a punishable crime." Tandy told her. She stood to find paper and a pen, before bringing it over to the girl.

"What do I need to say?" She asked, confused.

"Write down that the debt has been absolved by the Duchess, and that there will be a carriage to receive them along with this letter. Make sure they leave the transaction receipt with the housekeeper of the grounds, and I'll have my Guards take the housekeeper's signature to ensure their word is secured on a secondary document. I wouldn't want your current mistress to manipulate the records in order to find fault in your family in any way. There will be no way to deny what happened, we will leave a paper trail behind us, and your family may begin a new life here immediately. Make sure they pack what they *need* and nothing more. You'll have it here. Anything sentimental, anything important, that is all," Tandy told her as she scribbled across the paper. After she finished writing, she signed the bottom and Tandy took it before adding another line, informing the family of their new caretaker. She rolled it up and folded it before placing it into an envelope and writing along the front. "After everything settles, I'm sure you will be able to venture to your old home. For now, this is what we can do."

"Sign your family name on the front, please," she told Leesa, who obliged immediately. Her eyes still glistened with tears, but Tandy calmly took the paper and sighed. "I need to find Bryson or Davian so that Guards they trust can be sent to the chateau for Leesa's family. You are not to speak to anyone at all, look down and look busy," she advised. "I'm going to ring the call bell for the Housekeeper," Tandy said. She didn't want to, but the bell system would ensure someone of the appropriate means came to the door.

They waited silently for Mrs Hollahue to knock, but when she did they all nearly jumped out of their skin.

"We need Sir Bryson and Prince Davian," Tandy told her. "And we need several Knights and lunch. There is something imperative the Prince and his Knight must know, as soon as possible." Mrs Hollahue nodded, though she looked exhausted but turned back to the hallway diligently.

"Get comfortable, Leesa, you have to go over everything you have heard for the last several days," Tandy said before sitting on the couch, stretching her arms before relaxing against the plush cushions.

"Not very much, I'm afraid. I only arrived a few days ago and I've mostly been sent to find wine and the seamstress. Lady Martina is quite demanding, and wants things very quickly or she'll be angry. I made sure to make fast work of every task, just so she wouldn't be cross at me if I made a mistake. I didn't over hear anything because I've simply been sent on so many errands and haven't listened at all to anything around me. I've been worried about my family," she admitted.

"What were they doing, that my mother had to all but kidnap you to pay off a debt?" Mariana asked with a huff as she laid down on the chaise, stretching and groaning.

"They had a loan under her but they didn't pay it back as fast as she wanted them to," Leesa said with a frown. "I'm not sure why she agreed to a loan if she was that desperate for the money to come back. We had been living in a homestead on the farmland for years without any help. When my siblings caught an illness last summer, they needed money to treat them. Medicine is so expensive, and we had a very fixed budget. We needed help, and she offered the support we needed. But not five months later, she began threatening us and charging us interest on funds. It wasn't a lot, we'd managed to pay it down nearly entirely. But no matter what we do, she keeps adding more and more fees to the loan. We have been *drowning* in the money she desires, until she finally had us removed from the land altogether a few months ago to begin working on your family home. My little siblings have never lived anywhere but the farm, and now they're scared to death of what will become of us," she sniffed. "Now that I've been sent here, I'm afraid of what's happening that I can't see," she told them. Tandy couldn't help but feel bad for the poor girl as she was being used to further someone else's political aspirations.

"Do you know what she was planning to do to Tandy?" Mariana asked.

"No, but she was acting very erratically. She was both slurring, and yet moving too quickly for her body. It was quite alarming, actually," Leesa said. "I could only understand that she wanted me to bring Tandy to another location. She *did* say that the Prince would be there but the way she kept laughing to herself worried me, though I couldn't do much to stop her request. I'm sorry," she said as she looked at Tandy, eyes still slowly dripping tears.

"We understand what it's like to be manipulated and pulled into what feels like a predesigned and scripted event," Tandy told her. Though she smiled gently, she was anything but happy about this new development. As Leesa smiled back at her, dimples appeared on her cheeks. Mariana and Tandy shared a stricken look as they realized *why* Martina had originally taken in the girl's family.

Twenty

Davian

Davian stood at the closed door to his rooms after the Knights left, completely frozen. He stood until he couldn't feel his toes on the floor any longer, and barely heard the rough knock at the door. Unconsciously, he raised his hand to open the door only after he heard a familiar voice behind it.

Bryson waited for him there, before pushing into the room and locking the door after himself. He guided Davian to the bed and sat him down, going easily and without fuss. He had no words, no thoughts. Just a feeling as though the world around him weren't real, everything disjointed and far away. Bryson brought him clothes and helped him to change into them with only gentle encouragement and nary a negative word. After he was dressed, Bryson guided him to the door.

"I'm sorry, Dav," he told him. Though Davian couldn't answer with his thoughts still in a haze, the words stayed with him. He wasn't sure what he was doing with himself until his mind caught up to his body as they marched down the hallway to see his father. He didn't want to see him, he didn't want to know how he'd be found. He couldn't even think the words themselves, that his father was *gone* in a way that couldn't be undone. He wondered vaguely how his mother was faring in light of the news, but knew she most likely was so tainted by Lethe that her grip on reality may not even be strong enough to understand anything at all.

His parents hadn't been very present in his life, or his upbringing, for years. Even longer than Tandy was away, his parents were apathetic at best and neglectful at worst. It didn't really matter what they did, as his nannies and teachers were always there. His parents were able to lavish themselves as the Royalty they were, and progressively over the years he added more and more onto his own plate. Slowly taking on their responsibilities as they could care less for the petty squabbles of the market in the innermost cities of the kingdom. He'd taken on so much of the King's own duties that he was essentially the sole ruler of the Kingdom already.

He couldn't have known that they were rotting their brains on a powerful elixir, slowly, over the course of the last several years. It was impossible to know just how long, really. It was something no one could have predicted, or seen coming. There had been a rise in the more populated trading areas, yes, but not in the castle. Not in the Royal Circle. Not in his reality. He had been drugged and manipulated for the better part of a decade, and yet he *still* couldn't believe his father could be gone.

His father had been an old fool to gamble away his life. He still felt numb and detached from the world around him but the nagging feeling in the back of his mind said this could have been avoided had the King and Queen been better people with good intentions. If they hadn't been so swept up in the Royal court, the glamour, the gossip, the opulence, his father would most likely still be here and the Kingdom would be stronger for it. A King that rules with intent and compassion is a strong kingdom indeed, and yet Davian found himself at only seventeen, eighteen, running the kingdom on his own with a pack of advisors.

They had been drugged as he had been.

He reminded himself painfully. If they were unwilling victims of the Lethe as he had been, how could he be so cruel to judge their behavior?

Bryson made it to the throne room's door first. Davian's stomach flipped as they entered the room from the main entrance. For a moment, he froze as he beheld the King sitting upon the throne. It looked as though he were taking a nap. His father, the King, was barely covered by a blanket over his lap. Davian paused in his steps and put a hand over his eyes, shaking his head unable to see this for himself. Bryson put a hand on his shoulder without saying a word, only lending his quiet comfort.

The King sat on the throne wearing a shirt much like the one Davian wore to the ball the night before. A long slit in the chest, leaving it bare to the world. The King leaned back on the chair with a faint smile on his lips, his eyes closed as if in a state of bliss. His eyes ran down along the King's body and he noticed lipstick marks all along his skin, bright red, with a purple or maybe pink substance smeared nearly everywhere. Between the chair and the King's body, the jelly-like substance covered him in a similar way to the kiss marks. He continued scanning over his body and noticed then that his pants were around his ankles, and the blanket was covering his private area. He wondered if the Guards covered him for modesty sake.

"Your Highness, the blanket was here when we found him. He's been undisturbed, we wanted to make sure someone saw this in its entirety before moving him away from the room," one of the Knights said. Davian noted that nothing around the crime scene was tampered with, which meant that whoever left his father in this state had covered him up for modesty sake before leaving him there. It must have been a woman with all of the lipstick and kiss marks covering the king's body - there was little else those marks could mean. Someone in the palace undoubtedly knew what happened. If he had to interview each guest, he would. He knew he would start with Martina for obvious reasons, but he was more concerned about the fact that the King's Guard had allowed this to happen. Why hadn't they found him the night before? The thought ate at him as he stood there, his blood pounding in his ears until it was all he could hear.

Whether it was an accident or murder, they would need to comb through the whole palace to be able to understand what exactly occurred in the throne room. They needed to know what led up to the King lying there on his throne, a pleased smile on his lips and only a blanket to cover him. The only setback they faced trying to uncover the mystery was the fact that there were *so* many guests and many of them most likely had a good reason to end the life of the King, whether Davian understood it or not. Bryson tried to stop him as he moved closer, but he shrugged the hand from his arm. He felt both unreal and as if hyperfocused on seeing the scene in full.

Sweat beaded along Davian's forehead as he scanned the room for anything that would hint toward where they could find the last person the King interacted with. He most likely had been intimate with someone that left promptly after the King "fell asleep" and either they didn't realize he had died, or intended for him to pass in such an emasculating way. He hoped it was something simple enough, but he knew in his heart that things seemed to be pointing in only one direction. He'd have to interrogate his mother, too, of all people on top of the trusted King's Guards. He wasn't sure he had it in him, the task seemed too daunting to consider.

Davian wiped the sweat off his brow, a wave of nausea rolling through his stomach and settling into a heavy ball. He tried to move closer to where the body of his father sat, but the closer he moved and the more stairs he climbed, the more the urge to vomit was harder and harder to fight. As his eyes stung with tears, he turned around and left the throne room to stand against the doors. He gasped for a moment, clutching his chest as he fought against the sudden sickness overwhelming him. He rubbed his hands over his face, breathing deep, when a voice interrupted him and made him nearly jump out of his skin.

"You'll be okay, Dav," Bryson said softly. "You overdid it. I can handle it from here if you officially hire me on as your personal Knight." Davian nodded as he squeezed his eyes shut, trying valiantly not to be sick.

"Let me take a look at the throne room and then we can move to a private area to talk. I'll be thorough which will take time, unfortunately, and I'd like to keep an eye on you simultaneously. Do you mind sitting in the corner of the room, perhaps, so I can assure your safety?"

"Alright," Davian rasped. "Bryson," he managed to croak.

"Yes?" His friend looked at him worriedly.

"Why weren't the Guards with him last night?" He asked out loud, letting out the thought that had been ruminating in his mind.

"I will find that out, Dav. Wait for me here, please."

All he wanted to do was to go back and find Tandy and pull her into a hug, never letting her go until the end of time. Life never worked the way you expected it to, so he held his tongue and followed after Bryson. He immediately set to work, leaving Davian sitting on top of a side table. He took off the flowers in a vase and sat it on the floor before taking a seat.

Knowing his father had met his end in that chair made him feel that there was no way he'd *ever* sit on it again. A bad omen for his own rule. He felt clammy and ill as he waited for Bryson to gather all of the information he needed before informing Davian of any leads on what had happened.

"Turn around, Your Highness," Bryson told him, helping him move and face away from the body. "We'll have him moved to prepare him for burial."

Davian turned away wordlessly. It was all too much to bear, and he nearly started screaming when he heard the sounds of the Knights grunting under the weight of the King as they lifted him from the throne.

He sat there with his head on his knees. He swallowed hard, his mouth uncontrollably watering as his stomach urged him to release the contents of everything he'd eaten the day before. He held onto his knees and breathed slowly, willing himself to calm down. He flinched as Bryson startled him once again as he rested a hand on his shoulder. Bryson gently helped him stand, his body wobbling as he straightened to his full length.

"Don't turn around, just let me lead you," he said softly, gently, linking his arm in Davian's. Davian sniffed as his eyes felt blurry. Distantly, he realized he was crying. Davian was led along by Bryson, he truly had no idea where they were going. He couldn't focus long enough on anything, he wasn't even sure what time it was after the morning they had.

"Is it morning?" He heard himself mumble as Bryson opened a door and led him through.

"It's nearly lunch, Dav," he said in the soft voice.

"Tandy," he mumbled. He just wanted Tandy. Tandy was safe, she would be a safe place to be. Bryson agreed as they kept walking. They stopped abruptly as Bryson spoke next to him, but he wasn't sure what he heard. He could tell there was a feminine voice mixed in with Bryson's. He glanced up to see if maybe Tandy had found him first but saw the Housekeeper instead. She looked to be in a rush, breathing heavily as they spoke before they continued on. Bryson pushed through another door and guided Davian to the bed, pulling the blankets down first before moving to Davian.

"Take off your over clothes, Davian, and I'll unlace your shoes," he told him. Davian obeyed the command, simply running on autopilot and accepting the directions he was given. He couldn't form anything in his mind, words eluding him, and he found comfort in knowing that at least he was with someone he trusted in his current state. After his shoes were unlaced, he kicked them off and stepped out of his pants and tossed his clothes to the ground. He was nudged back gently onto the bed and he easily rolled into the pillows as Bryson covered him back up once again. His arms stretched out as he reached for something, someone, but they came up empty. He raised his head, looking for it, before getting frustrated.

"Where's Tandy?" He said, trying to sit up. Bryson pressed him back against the bed and shushed him softly.

"I'm getting her now, Dav, you be patient and wait here. Okay?" Bryson said, making Davian relax and lay back on the pillows. He yawned and nestled into the covers, waiting for Tandy to join him. He dozed, not quite asleep but drained enough to feel the pull of exhaustion behind his eyelids. He laid there in a state of in between when he felt the bed dip behind him and a cool hand slide over his back before resting over his belly. Warm lips met his cheek, pressing against his skin in a soft and reassuring pressure. He sniffed, suddenly overwhelmed with emotions. He wasn't even sure *what* he was thinking, or feeling, but as Tandy pressed her lips to his face, over and over, he couldn't hold back the tears as they fell from his eyes.

Tandy gently moved around him until she was sitting by his head, and pulled him to rest against her thighs. He cried against her belly, wrapping his arms around her waist. He pressed his forehead against her, his cheek resting on her thigh. He couldn't find a position that felt comfortable, the emotions flooded him continuously and he couldn't *breathe*. He started babbling as Tandy ran a hand through his hair, while the other one ran soothingly over his shoulders.

"I don't know why I'm crying," he said into her belly, another sob wracking through his body.

"You lost your father, my love, you can cry," she said softly before sliding her legs further apart, nestling Davian within her slotted thighs. He could feel her whole body along his in this position, and the warmth of her soothed him despite the tears still flowing from his eyes.

"I haven't spoken to my father in years," he told her as he squeezed his eyes shut. She only hummed in response, waiting for him to continue. He wasn't sure what to say, but after his initial admittance, he found there was really nothing to hold him back from telling Tandy *everything*.

"He hadn't been very present when I was a child, I'm sure you remember a lot of the early years," he said through tears. He was about to wipe his cheeks when Tandy pulled the fabric of her dress forward and cleaned him off, her thumb running along his cheek after she'd cleared away his tears. The gentle touch sent more tears to his face and it was a few more moments before he was able to speak again.

"The truth is that they both hadn't treated me like a son in easily a decade, and even before that there was a complete lack of affection, in every way. The most I received were gifts on holidays from the advisors in my parent's name," he said through a stuffy nose. He sniffed, trying to breathe clearer but found that he couldn't. "The nannies were my only comfort, aside from you, Bryson and Mariana for a long time. Eventually, my father began to *entertain* me as his heir," he admitted.

"He began to only acknowledge me during moments he hadn't wanted to deal with the advisors, which was fine. I'd been taught and trained well, and I could handle the very young acquisition of responsibilities as a leader. What I couldn't handle were his hot and cold tendencies. It was a game to him, always desiring an emotional response to anything he said to me. Always followed by either laughter or a scathing round of venomous words. He knew what to say to rile me up, and my mother always sat there completely devoid of any emotion at all." He sniffed again, but he couldn't breathe and shifted to sit up to blow his nose. Tandy handed him a handkerchief and he took it gratefully. He turned to her after he was done, but wasn't sure where to lay. She opened her arms easily, inviting him back to her lap.

"Come back," she said. Another tear rolled down his cheek and he settled back against her belly, holding her tight as his hands wrapped around her waist once again. Her fingers played with strands of his hair, soft and soothing against his scalp.

"The last time, I'm sure you remember the ball before you were sent away. He'd spent the whole day berating me, laughing at me, for thinking there was a future in a marriage I had no part in arranging. I wasn't sure what had brought on his harsh words, but at the time it had been devastating. I thought we had been a perfect match, but was told that you had only been playing the part and many other boys had also enjoyed you. He said it in so many different ways, so many different insults. I told you some of this already, but there was a lot I didn't say. After he insulted you, I gave the King hell like I'd never done before. But he *laughed*. I was angry even before the first sip of wine, though it was never directed at you. After some of the boys in the court were boasting of their prowess and I'd drunk some of that bitter poison, the whole world seemed different," he sighed shakily, no longer crying but his eyes still felt wet and heavy. "It all felt dark and evil, and everyone was set out to hurt me."

"Mariana was also going through the same that day," Tandy asked. He nodded against her, rubbing his cheek on her thigh.

"Much like me, only where I was antagonized and ignored, Mariana was terrorized and hurt," his voice wavered before he fell into another bout of tears, sobbing loudly into Tandy's dress. He couldn't hold them back this time, and could only clutch Tandy desperately. She stroked his hair without a word, offering her comfort in the only way that mattered to him. Just being there was enough. He weeped harder thinking about the way she had been abandoned by him all those years ago.

"I'm sorry, Tandy," he cried. She shushed him, wiping his eyes before running her hands over his back.

"He never raised a hand at me and I never wanted for anything, but he never felt like a father in any sense of the word," he whispered. "I'm not even sure why I'm crying now except that despite all of the hard work I put into the kingdom, it was for naught. He was sabotaging it all along with the incessant parties and Lethe elixirs, and inciting rumors in the Royal court, and I have to inherit a throne undeserving of its kingdom with the neglect it faced at the hands of the previous king, of *me*." The admittance felt like a relief to say out loud, at long last, from *years* of apathy. "Even worse, though, is that I am afraid if I ever am blessed with children, I'll end up the same way and be a father undeserving of the gift I'm given," he wiped away another tear as a sob filled his throat, making him cough as he tried to breathe through his stuffed up nose. Tandy helped him right himself before pulling him into a deep hug. Her knees framed his body, still tucked between her thighs, as she pulled his head to rest against her chest. She leaned her cheek against his head before kissing him where she could reach. Her lips found a tear as it made its escape and he laced a hand through her hair and held tight.

"We've all been treated in ways that children should never have to experience, Davian, but that doesn't mean we are destined to hurt the ones that will grow from my belly. Our children will be like us, from before we were old enough to understand the pain and injustice we experienced, and the difference will be that *we* care. There will never be perfection, but we will do a better job than the ones that raised us because it is a *choice* to be kind and it is a *choice* to show love, and of both we have plenty. Even if we need some help, even if we lose our patience. We will not squander our gifts, should we receive any. And I'm willing to try, despite knowing there will be days I think I'm failing," she kissed his cheek as she nuzzled against him, gripping him tight. He felt her shudder in a breath, almost as though she would cry, too. She only sighed, wiping away the tears on his cheek with her sleeve. "And if we never have any, I'm sure we will be grateful for that, too. Whether we have some, or many, or none, at least we know we will be there together."

"You can't think that it'll be that easy," he said slowly.

"Oh it won't be easy at all, not with the experiences we've had with our parental role models," she said, looking down at him. "You are mourning your childhood, one that none of us truly had. You are facing a lot of firsts, now, and never had the guidance you desperately wanted. Between being a King, a husband, a father, and a son - Davian my love, you were abandoned just as much as I was by the parents that were supposed to love you. I mourn with you, I know how you feel intimately. You are allowed to feel conflicting feelings, and you are allowed to *know* your feelings, too. We are here and we will share the burden of grief together. Tomorrow we will pick up the pieces, but today we will just *feel,*" she said sadly, her thumb tracing his cheek as she cupped it with her hand.

"I am not going to miss him," he told her as her hand cooled his overheated cheek. His lip wavered despite the truth to his words. She only wiped away the rest of his tears and leaned down to kiss his nose.

"I believe you," she said as she slid next to him, cradling his head to lay against her breasts as she played with his hair. He sniffed, fighting back more tears as she comforted him without judgment.

"Thank you," he told her. There wasn't much else he could say, really.

"You don't have to thank me," she tickled his neck, making him huff as he flinched. He wasn't sure how much time passed before he quieted again, but his stomach growled and he realized just how hungry he was.

"I have a tray on the table I brought in when I got here. The tea is likely cold, but it'll be there when you feel up for it," she added. He nodded but tears continued to trail down his cheeks despite the hunger pangs in his belly. He couldn't muster up the strength to stand and find food, and so clutched at Tandy for a few more moments.

"There's a situation with Mariana, but we can eat first before talking about it," Tandy said quietly.

"What happened?" Davian asked.

"Her room was destroyed," Tandy told him.

"Her room was destroyed?" He asked, confused. "What do you mean?"

"Bryson told me to only say that much, he wanted to make sure you were in your right mind to hear it. We can talk more about it when you've had something to eat and are feeling more like yourself," Tandy suggested as she trailed her fingers over his back. "Everyone is okay, though. It was a blessing Mariana was in my room when it happened," she added.

They were quiet in thought for a few minutes as Tandy ran her hands along his body and played with his hair in a comforting way. Truly, he may have fallen asleep for a moment but more memories and thoughts swam to the front of his mind before he pulled himself back to consciousness. He whispered words against Tandy's skin like a prayer, as if she could heal him of his pain.

"Let me bring the food over," she told him finally, moving off the bed. She brought over a plate filled with fruit, pastries, and sandwiches. He gratefully ate a little of everything, finishing the tray with Tandy's help.

"Did Bryson mention anything about the team assigned to the King last night, and why they weren't with him?" Davian asked when his plate was empty.

"He asked the Knights and crossed checked what they said with several other Guards to verify their honesty," Tandy nodded. "The King's Guard were reassigned to the Queen during every ball they have hosted for several years now."

"Who authorized that?" Davian frowned.

"The King," Tandy sighed. "Apparently he reassigned the Guards in order to have sex with his mistresses in private. I'm sure you don't want to hear that though."

"I'm not surprised he has mistresses, but I am disgusted nonetheless. He had them moved from his protection detail in order to fuck?" Davian scowled.

"Essentially, yes. He told the Knights he did not want them to eavesdrop on his secret rendezvous in case it led to scandal with the Queen," Tandy explained. "The Guards were following their orders, and redirected to the Queen as the night progressed and the King left the ballroom."

"That old fool," he sighed, running his hand over his face.

"No one could have foreseen his fate," Tandy said kindly before kissing his cheek.

She cleared his plate as he sat there watching her move around the room elegantly. As she cleaned the crumbs off of the bed, Davian went to the bathroom and cleaned his face. He blew his nose until he could breathe properly again and finally made his way back to his bed. Without his shirt, he sat under the covers Tandy had pulled down and laid against the pillows.

"You can go to your room for some night clothes," he told her softly. He didn't want her to be uncomfortable, of course. She nodded before walking over to the hidden door and disappeared inside for a few minutes.

"Mariana offered her condolences," she told him as she reemerged into the room. He pulled the covers down for her, giving her access to the bed and pulling her into his chest. He kissed her forehead, her cheeks, her chin, her lips. He peppered them over her face softly, gently, nuzzling his nose against her neck just under her ear. She smelled of flowers, a delicate scent, and he kissed further along her neck. His kisses paused over her throat, lingering until a stuttered laugh left Tandy's lips as she fought back a laugh at the sensation. She pulled his chin back up and smiled, giving his lips a gentle peck.

"Go to sleep, you need to rest," she told him. He did need to sleep, but he needed to feel her body underneath him again. He needed to feel her as he filled her, the tight wet heat enveloping his cock as he rolled his hips against hers. She could see his thoughts on his face, and her lips parted as she glanced at his own, licking her lip unconsciously. "It's not a good time, Dav," she tried to tell him. But her voice was already wavering, and he needed her comfort in a way he couldn't explain.

"I need you," he told her, "I need to feel you on my cock again, to *feel* your heart beating," he said before kissing her deeply, his tongue trailing along her lips until she parted them with a gasp. He wasted no time, pulling her dress up and up until he could peel her panties off. He slid them down, not managing to pull them completely off her foot as he pulled himself from his pants. He couldn't wait, he needed her now like he needed to breathe, leaving his pants and shirt on. He didn't want to hurt her, though, and he slid his thumb through the wetness she had, her pussy already dripping for him. She moaned, knees falling to the side to give him complete access.

"Good girl," he told her as he kissed her throat. He twisted his finger until she jolted with a desperate moan, hips seeking the rhythm his hand created. "Ready, or do you need more," he gasped as he kissed her breathlessly, his finger pumping into her with not nearly enough friction. She groaned as she nodded, reaching her hand to his cock and guiding him to her pussy. He gripped tight and pulled her down as he rolled his hips, filling her in the same motion. Tandy's back arched off the bed, hands gripping the sheets as she keened sharply at his intrusion. She opened her eyes and stared at him hungrily as her legs locked around his waist. He filled her desperately, frantically, with every thrust met by her rolling hips. She held him tight, kissing his face and biting the skin on his shoulder as he reached down to grip her ass. He slid his hand behind her lower back, her pert cheek tight in his hand as he tilted her hips upward. The new angle made her drop her head to the mattress, moaning with each drag of his cock along her inner walls. Her fingers twisted in his hair as the other grabbed the pillow behind her, holding onto it as her breathing quickened.

Davian couldn't help but take in how delicious she looked, taking his cock as they were nearly still fully clothed. He leaned down to bite at her breast through the thin nightgown as her pussy squeezed him tighter and tighter. She breathlessly begged him for more, and he nearly came from just the sound of her voice. As she grew closer to orgasm, her breathing accelerated and she tossed her head back and forth through the dizzying pleasure.

"Oh *please*," she begged, looking into his eyes as she moaned. He could tell she was close, she just needed a little bit more. He adjusted his angle a bit more, pounding into the spot that made her see stars only the night before. She wailed before her pussy throbbed around his cock, coming hard around his length.

"Good girl," he told her again as he rolled his hips through her orgasm, milking her for every last ounce of pleasure he could get. He wanted to come, *needed* to come but he had to make sure she was taken care of first. He needed to feel her breathe, feel her body tremble and come undone at his touch. He needed to savor each moment with her because the future was ever changing and everything could be ripped away without warning.

As she trembled under him, he slid his hands under her knees and pulled them up as high as he could, until they were near her shoulders. He pulled out of her almost all the way before slamming back into her, the sound of his cock filling her sending chills through his whole body. *I need her so much*, he thought as his cock ached for release.

"So good," Tandy sobbed under him. He couldn't hold back if he wanted to, and as Tandy scratched at his back and begged him for more, he was helpless to fight the desire. He needed her, he needed to fill her, and with another deep thrust, he lost himself inside of her. Stars came to his eyes as his orgasm hit him suddenly, the pleasure so intense he could only hear a ringing in his ears. He moaned and kissed Tandy, tongue sliding over hers as he rolled his hips gently, chasing the aftershocks as they rolled through him.

"Oh fuck, Dav I'm," Tandy gasped and rotated her hips, meeting his own in a gentle almost non existent motion. He moaned again, realizing that the motion was going to make her come again. He was so overstimulated it was near painful, but the glazed look in her eye as she praised him for how good he made her feel, he pushed through it continued, begging her to climax once again.

"Come for me," he told her, rolling into her again, and again, and again, until she cried out and tensed around his cock. Tears spilled from her eyes as he rocked into her one more time, moaning desperately as a tremor rocked through her body. "Wow," he said as he kissed her, making her laugh breathlessly against his lips.

"Mhm," she agreed with a dazed smile. She panted against his lips as he kissed her again, before rolling away from her. She kissed his cheek before going to the bathroom to clean herself up. When she came back, she brought a cloth for him to wipe himself clean, too, and settled back into the bed once they were wiped up. Davian hugged her to his chest, overcome with emotions he didn't know how to explain. He kissed her softly as she ran her hands through his chest hair,

"I love you," she said softly as he cradled her to his chest. It wasn't a question, more of a sigh as she settled into his arms.

"I love you," he told her, kissing her wherever he could reach as they held eachother. Her physical presence resting against him as her chest rose and fell slowly was comforting. Her heartbeat was gentle under his hand, grounding him in the moment as he took her in. Her blonde hair curled around her face where sweat had beaded on her forehead. He wiped the errant curls from her brow and kissed her cheek, settling further into the bed with a sigh. She laid onto a pillow and cradled her hands under her cheek. They stared into each other's eyes for a moment, just looking at one another before Davian sighed.

"I don't think this will be easily handled," he said. "There is so much that has been going on, and I haven't taken care of any of it."

"You couldn't have known what would happen, it was a shock to us all," Tandy reassured him.

"The way he was found was..." he trailed off, not even sure how to explain it. He shuddered at the memory. Tandy's hand reached out and rested her hand against his. He looked at her again, frowning, as he tried to explain what he saw. "The way he'd been found looked both like an accident, and as a cover up. I don't know what to make of it, in all honesty."

"Maybe it was an accident, but they tried to cover it up out of sheer surprise at the turn of events. Do you want to talk about what you saw, or do you want to leave it be for the moment?" She asked him, no pressure in her voice. He could tell by her look that she meant it, and would be truly unbiased if he confided in her. He sighed again, before nodding slowly. He began to tell her how the Knights had found the king, and what he saw when he was brought to the body. The strange substances on the King, the shade of lipstick, the blanket left over his lap and the expression on his face. He told her everything as she held his hand softly, not saying a word as she took in his words. It didn't take him long to explain, but his mouth felt dry by the time he was finished. As if he'd been talking for hours instead of only minutes. When he finally finished speaking, he trailed off as he watched Tandy processing everything he said. She took a moment before responding, squeezing his hand as she did.

"I think you will need to interview guests in their quarters and have their rooms inspected to find anything that puts them in the throne room with the King. Do you know if maids have been offering laundering services, or cleaning? Or have they only been bringing food to everyone's rooms?" She asked.

"Protocol dictates that should anything befall a Royal, all guests are essentially under house arrest and no one is to leave or enter the rooms aside from the delivery of food items delivered by at least two maids and a Guard to ensure the safety of both guest and staff. Everything should be as it was last night, unless the guests have begun cleaning their own rooms." He said, before Tandy shook her head.

"No one in the Royal Circle would clean their own rooms, so I don't think we'll have much trouble finding the culprit if we begin our investigations now," Tandy said easily. Davian marveled at her analytical mind, much like Bryson. They always held such a wise and steady presence and he couldn't help but be impressed. "Do you feel ready enough to face all of this now, or do you want to go over everything else that has happened?" Davian frowned, looking at Tandy.

"What do you mean?" He asked.

"I mentioned the state of Mariana's room earlier but I'm not sure how much you remember, you were out of it for a while," she said. Davian nodded, remembering then that Tandy and Bryson had mentioned Mariana's room being destroyed. "He ended up telling me what he saw, and made Mariana wait in the room as he showed me so that I could be the one to tell you."

"When did he tell you?" Davian asked.

"Only just now, when I went to get a nightgown. He showed me quickly, and I came right back in here," she explained.

"Let's take a bath while you tell me, so we can get the investigation over with," he sighed as he stretched before making his way to the bathroom. Tandy helped him fill the tub with warm water and added bubbles before she helped him undress. She quickly braided her hair with a ribbon and tied it up and out of the way before dropping her clothes besides Davian's on the floor. Davian was exhausted, and was truly sated, and knew they'd only be bathing together without any lingering touches. But he found himself admiring her lithe form as she elegantly stepped into the warm water and sat across from him. It was nice, sitting with her in the bubbles. She urged him to turn around and began washing his hair before she began to speak.

"Her room was completely torn apart, everything was dumped onto the floor. Dresses, curtains, blankets were shredded and left about the room. There was a red shade of lipstick used to write along the mirrors and walls, Bryson had a hard time reading them. I recognized the lettering though, a very feminine flare despite the obvious intoxication the scribbling implied of the culprit. Most of it made no sense, but one of the scribbles we deciphered was concerning, to say the least. Most of it were just insults, like whore and slut. This one said, 'he had it coming,' and 'it's not over.'" She paused to rinse his hair before making him turn back around to face her.

"It was probably the same lipstick I found on the King," he thought out loud. Tandy nodded before continuing.

"It would also imply, it was added as an afterthought to the king's body and the culprit went after Mariana to make her look guilty. I'm just not understanding why exactly Mariana was targeted, or why the lipstick would write out whore and slut, if the messages were supposed to look as though they were written by Mar," she pursed her lips in thought before a look flashed over her face. "Oh," Tandy said after a minute before looking at Davian.

"What is it?" He urged, leaning forward.

"Mariana has been using my room to sleep in, and has spent the majority of her time with me in my room, one way or another. Martina hasn't been permitted to the room past the Knights in the hallway, *but* her maids haven't been stopped. There was an incident today where one of Martina's personal maids tried to bring me to see you," Tandy told him. "She kept saying you were waiting for me, but Mariana confirmed that it was *not* one of your maids. She recognized her, and so I sent for her family to join us in the palace under you and I as their new masters. I covered their debt to ensure the transition was easy and quiet, and she explained that Martina had been controlling them and all but held them against their will in the Villa," she paused to take a breath.

"However, it seemed as if the maid only came *after* the discovery of Mariana's room had been made. So, I believe this is what happened," Tandy said before Davian nodded for her to finish her thought. "Martina was under the impression that Mariana's room was in between your room and the room on the end. Due to the Knights and guest directory and the first time she had barged into that room, it led her to believe that *my* room was the one on the end. Therefore, the attempt made to destroy the room and paint that room's guest as the culprit of the murder and the cover up, was an attempt at framing *me* for the death of the king. It would also explain why the maid was sent to the correct room today in search of me."

Davian's face paled as his brows rose high on his face. A chill settled over his body despite the warmth of the water and he shook his head, processing everything Tandy said carefully.

"She had wanted to make you lose your place as the crown Princess by making you lose all credibility. She must have hoped to find you in that bedroom to drug you with Lethe, and planned to put the lipstick on you to place you at the scene," Davian considered as he followed Tandy's thought process. It was a lot of *maybe* in that theory, but at the moment it made sense.

"She wanted me to be cast out, the last attempt at getting Mariana to where I am now despite the fact Martina must know now that you are siblings. Which begs the question, what does she have planned for *you* next?" Tandy said slowly. "Because the fact remains, she essentially wants Mariana on the throne. There has to be a man funding the operations that Mariana is going to be promised to, to ensure the throne is secured. It would be quite the bargaining tool, to find someone willing to kill the King and crown Prince for his own chance to be King. Martina must have a partner in this that is funding the plan personally, with Mariana and the crown as their prize." Davian stared at Tandy as he took in her words.

"Honestly, Tandy, if I wasn't absolutely certain that you weren't the mastermind behind this, I would cower in fear before you. You know more than a lot of people would, just by sheer observation and process of elimination. Bryson would have fun training you to be a Knight," he said.

"It's actually easy for me, there's a pattern in everyone's behavior that's not hard to find so long as you recognize them, and hold back your own emotions that they try to turn against you," she said. "There's always a tell, even if you don't know someone well enough to catch it right away. It exposes itself when your cards are played right."

"I just don't understand how they were able to get inside of Mariana's room, with Guards in the hallway," Davian frowned.

"Check the balconies for signs of someone climbing into the room. They likely didn't get in through the hall, or the Guards would have turned them away," Tandy suggested.

They had just finished washing their bodies and dried off before they dressed, when Davian's stomach growled once again. Tandy led him to the table where the tray of breakfast foods and fruits waited for him to eat. Davian was starving and didn't need to be cajoled into taking bites. He ate until he was full while Tandy picked at the strawberries. Finally, they stood and walked into Tandy's room to meet with Mariana. They used the large door so Davian could let the Knights know of his plans of interviewing all guests. One of the Knights sent off to prepare a team to assist him, and they knocked on Tandy's door and waited for their friends to answer.

The door cracked open and revealed Bryson peering through a sliver of the door before he opened it wide enough for them to walk through. They locked the door behind them before Mariana pulled Davian into a hug, tears hot against his collar. He held her tightly and rubbed her back gently, swaying side to side to comfort her. Tandy ran a hand over Mariana's back and they comforted their friend as best they could, though they knew she was in a bad state. She clearly had an idea of what was to come since the maid she had sent to retrieve Tandy had been caught, leaving very little else for them to conclude.

There was only one outcome for this, and if Martina was found to be the one that not only murdered the King in cold blood, but also the one to frame the soon to be crown Princess, she would be tried for treason no matter what. A formal case in which a Royal was harmed rarely even followed their judiciary system as treason had only one sentence: death. Martina would be held to the highest standard of punishment, and despite the obvious harm she had inflicted on Mariana, it was hard for the girl to consider what will no doubt become the future soon enough. After a while, Mariana settled down and they led her to the bed to lay down. They turned the chairs from the table toward the bed to talk to her as she rested, while Bryson called for more tea and made a request for dinner preparations to begin.

"You told him about the maid she sent?" Mariana asked with a stuffy nose, her voice nasally.

"I did," Tandy sighed. Mariana nodded, matching Tandy's sigh. They told her what they'd figured out, what most likely occurred. Mariana's face grew darker and darker until she wore an angry scowl on her lips. She sat up and slammed her hands to the mattress. It did nothing as the mattress was too plush to do any damage but the sentiment was there. Davian understood the frustration, but knew there wasn't much he could say or offer in terms of comfort.

"We're still going to hold a formal investigation, Mar, so you don't need to worry. I don't think it's wise to jump to conclusions and I want to make sure not a stone is left unturned," Davian offered her. She rolled her eyes and let out a sharp laugh devoid of humor.

"We all know it was her, it had to have been," she said. "You should detain her now before she makes a run for it." Tandy looked at Davian with a raised brow, a clear question in her pointed gaze.

"The time will come for when the guilty party is exposed, but for right now I will be continuing along as if I don't have a biased opinion on the situation. It's the best way to make sure we all stay safe," he explained. "We don't want to let anyone know we suspect anything, or they'll try to run." Mariana groaned and flopped back onto the pillow, covering her face under the plush blankets.

"I'm sorry, Tandy" she murmured.

"You have nothing to apologize for," Tandy rested her hand on Mariana's.

"No, I mean to say that I don't want to kick you out but, I'm just *so* tired and I feel like I might also be sick," Mariana's voice wavered as she spoke. "Would it be alright if you go in Davian's room while I try to sleep it off?"

"Of course, Mar. You get some rest," Tandy pressed a kiss to her forehead before standing. Davian offered her one, too, hoping she'd at least feel safer with their presence.

"Whatever happens, we will be okay," he said. "Bryson and I will start planning the interrogations," he told them as he walked to the door, waiting for Bryson to join him. Bryson made his way from the table before looping back to the bed where Mariana lay. He leaned down and brushed his lips to her forehead before following Davian out the door, a heavy clank sounding behind them. He heard Tandy lock the doors behind him and was relieved to at least be able to keep them out of harm's way.

Twenty One

Tandy

When Davian left the room, Tandy locked the doors together, making sure the latch clicked before moving away. She walked over to the bed where Mariana laid curled into a ball, arms tight around her knees. Only her face peered out sadly, staring at Tandy with tear filled eyes, though there was a substantial blush to her cheeks.

"Sleep now," Tandy murmured, tucking the blanket tighter around her shoulders.

"He's going to have her killed," Mariana's voice was thick with emotion, but an anger rested in her brows.

"Most likely that will be her fate," Tandy agreed, wiping Mariana's cheeks gently. Mariana sniffed and sighed, shaking her head.

"I think I am more afraid that she will accuse me of her crimes, and that I too will meet my end," she said finally, squeezing her eyes shut and fighting against the tears threatening to escape. "And yet I am scared for my mother despite everything she has done."

"Let me sit with you for a moment, and then I will let you sleep," Tandy said as she lifted the blanket and slid in next to her. She let Mariana rest her head on her thigh and ran her hands through her long brown hair, playing with the soft strands.

"You and Davian are very alike," Tandy mused. "Your reactions and emotions have always been similar. It's a wonder I didn't notice before," Tandy said. "Your fear is justified, though I would say there's no doubt between Davian and Bryson who the victim and aggressor are in this situation." Tandy paused as she stroked Mariana's hair. "Your sadness is justified, too. She's your mother, but her actions have been anything but motherly." Mariana cried against Tandy's leg and nodded at her words, clutching her waist as she sobbed. She didn't speak for a while, only crying in the comfort of Tandy's arms.

Davian and Mariana's grief were palpable as it radiated off of them in thick waves. Mourning their childhood, their future, and everything they had missed out on. The ones that gave them life continuously disappointing them at every turn. Not only from the lack of love, but the consistent harm they experienced under their parent's words had an undeniable effect on the now grown adults she held in her arms.

She knew she fared no better, but she felt somehow that they'd been dealt a far worse hand than she had despite all that she'd experienced. She was certain Mariana was hurt in more ways than she had been. She had never been physically touched by another in the lessons she suffered through, only ever mortified and ashamed. She couldn't fathom what Mariana had gone through, the physical pain nor the humiliation, and continued to run her fingers through her beautiful hair as she weeped.

"I could have been married by now, with a family," Mariana cried. "No one will want me now! She's only ever used me for whatever plot she concocted, leading me to believe things are changing *every* time. How can I be so stupid?" Her fingers clutched at Tandy's waist, gripping tight to the fabric of her gown.

"You're anything but stupid, Mariana, and you know that," Tandy said as softly as she could as she wiped the hair from Mariana's face. "Your mistreatment and your hope do not make you anything other than *strong*. You've gone through more than any of us, Mar, be kind to yourself." Tandy ran her hand along Mariana's arm while the other continued to play with her hair. They stayed that way until the sun waned in the sky, bathing them in an orange glow. Mariana yawned, making Tandy follow suit as exhaustion filled them.

"M'tired," Mariana said, wiping her face. Tandy sighed as she nodded in agreement.

"Me too," she huffed. Mariana rolled over onto her back and stretched, bones cracking from disuse. She groaned as her body went boneless, running her hands over her face. She looked at Tandy after she sprawled out under the covers.

"Do you want me to let you sleep, now?" Tandy asked.

"Make sure you wake me up when they get back," Mariana nodded as her eyes fluttered closed, heavy with exhaustion. Tandy pulled the blanket higher around Mariana, tucking it back under her as she had done before. She leaned over and kissed her forehead softly, drawing a pleased hum from Mariana. She smiled, eyes still closed.

"Sleep well, Mar," she said as she slid off the bed quietly. She went through the bedroom doors and locked the ante chamber doors. She came back into the bedroom and locked those doors, as well, before finally climbing through the hidden door. By the time she was through to the other side, Mariana was snoring lightly in the bed. Tandy was relieved she was able to find sleep easily, and closed the door behind her.

As Tandy wandered around Davian's room, she wondered for the first time in years where exactly her parents were. Their communications had been minimal to the point that she had come to expect the same level of response from them as she had with Mariana and Davian, and had quickly given up on any more attempts. Her mother only wrote brief correspondence in regards to her betrothal.

It had been a never ending hell in that school but Tandy had been well provided for. Despite the lack of communication, her parents paid for anything that she requested without question. She was able to offer the younger girls, the abandoned girls, the abused girls, just a little bit of help with the funds her parents supplied. It was all she could do at the time, and she still held guilt any time a new student would be brought in, the wails of despair that filled the room as they learned of their fate would never be forgotten for as long as she lived.

As the sunset faded into dusk, and dusk turned into night, Tandy could hardly hold her head up. Exhaustion weighed her down, pulling her to the pillows as the sounds of the night filled the room. She tugged the blankets over her, the smell of Davian surrounding her. For a moment, she was at peace. She breathed deep, falling asleep as she exhaled.

She dreamed as though she were a child again, running through a field of flowers with Mariana and Davian holding onto her fingers. The dream grew dark, a heavy fog filling the field they frolicked in. Suddenly, Mariana was screaming, calling out for Tandy and Davian. Invisible tendrils wrapped around Mariana as she cried out for someone to help her, before a wail left her throat sending chills through Tandy's body.

Tandy jolted awake, hand reaching out for Mariana, as she gasped. As her heart beat loudly in her ears, she finally took in what was going on around her. A crash sounded from outside of the bedroom walls, making her jump.

A woman's voice, a scream, another crash. Tandy tumbled out of the bed as she ran through Davian's doors. Chasing the sound, she bumped her shoulder on the door frame. She made through the antechambers and into the hallway, the sounds of screaming growing louder and louder. Begging, and a man's voice. Tandy's stomach knotted, her steps felt as though she were lost in time. Unable to move faster, the moment dragged on. Tandy urged herself to move and swallowed down the nausea as it bubbled up from her gut.

She ran to Mariana's doorway, chest feeling tight, when she saw the state of both sets of doors as they hung on their hinges. Within the room was chaos.

"You stupid *slut,*" Martina screeched as she raised her hand to hit Mariana as she cried on the floor. Her nose was bleeding and tears stained her cheeks. Her dress was torn, and she desperately covered her hands over her exposed chest as her mother grew closer. A portly man with nice clothing circled behind Martina. Tandy couldn't see his face but knew he leered at Mariana as she trembled on the floor.

"You were supposed to fuck someone else, someone *important! Not* a Knight of all people!" Martina spat, hand still raised.

"I didn't -" Mariana tried to tell her, but Martina's hand came down hard across her daughter's cheek. Tandy snapped back to awareness, time finally resuming around her as her jaw clenched with unbridled rage. She grabbed one of the heavy vases decorating the room and swiftly walked up behind the man kneeling down to grab for Mariana. Tandy raised the porcelain high, and slammed it over the man's head. He hit the ground hard, as Mariana screamed at the sudden noise.

Martina turned to see Tandy standing there, having incapacitated her partner. Tandy wasn't sure who the man was, but didn't care enough to check. It didn't matter either way, it was clear Martina was going to let the man have Mariana however he pleased, broken and bleeding be damned. Tandy felt her body coil with anger, every muscle tightening as she fought the urge to hiss and spit like a feral cat. Martina glared at her, but Tandy felt nothing besides disgust as her face remained neutral and unreadable.

"You whore, you should have rotted in that gods forsaken school," she yelled at Tandy. Tandy curled her lips intentionally to look like a smile. It was hollow, empty of all emotions other than pure rage. Her face looked twisted, she was sure, but she would not allow this creature of a person to harm her friend any longer.

"You can rot in the cold earth once my *husband* is done with you," Tandy forced a laugh. Mariana still sat on the floor, bleeding and confused. Tandy could tell she must have hit her head, she looked more and more dizzy and out of focus as the moments passed. Martina bridled at her words, indignant noises falling from her throat. Tandy laughed harder just to piss her off, though it sounded like a bark with the rage tightening her chest. She wanted Martina to lose herself to anger just from seeing Tandy stand there with a smile.

It worked quickly, of course. Martina was too single minded in her rage to sidestep the confrontation. She raised a hand, intending to hit Tandy. Tandy made sure her smile never fell, and when Martina's hand lowered, Tandy stepped forward into the glowering woman. She grabbed her outstretched arm as it came closer to her simultaneously. The sudden move startled Martina, making her lose her balance. Tandy's foot swung out between Martina's legs and she swept the older woman off balance as her bare foot curled around Martina's ankle. She met the ground heavily, her breath leaving her in a *whoosh*. Tandy wasted no time and descended upon the woman. She grabbed her by the hair and forced her onto her stomach, still holding onto the arm she had used to swing at Tandy, sending screeches from Martina's mouth. She twisted Martina's arm behind her back in order to subdue her comfortably and keep leverage over the woman who weighed more than she did. Tandy twisted Martina's arm harder, pulling it until the shoulder creaked at the angle. Martina screeched in pain, trying to claw Tandy off of her with her other hand. Tandy laughed, a feral glint in her eye.

"I'll break it if you struggle any more," she grinned as Martina stared over her shoulder, glaring at the blonde.

"You worthless wretch," she spat before struggling against Tandy's hold. "You are *weak* and could never hurt me -" Martina's words cut off abruptly as Tandy stepped her full weight onto Martina's arm that was still loose, shifting herself to lean into it.

"I warned you," Tandy said, crushing her foot into the arm she pinned to the floor. She kneeled her other leg into Martina's back before pressing harder against her elbow with the rest of the weight.

"No, stop, you can't -" she screamed again before Tandy looked up at Mariana, sitting there with a dazed expression. Her nose was still bleeding and Tandy could see there were scratches over her shoulders where her dress had been torn off. The poor girl drooped closer to the floor, arms unable to cover her modesty as she tried to keep herself from falling to the ground.

The sensation of ice and a hollow ringing in her ears was suddenly all Tandy was aware of. She didn't know the emotion, or the words to describe it, but she felt completely empty. She felt no remorse, only a sharp sense of duty. Martina's screams filled her ears as she looked at Mariana, now openly weeping.

She pressed harder into Martina's elbow and a sick, pervasive pleasure filled her cold heart as the woman shrieked in pain, the bone snapping with ease despite Tandy's frail frame.

Tandy only heard her heart rushing in her ears, but suddenly was aware of people standing behind her. She turned her head to see who was there and if she needed to defend Mariana from them. A huge swell of relief made her drop to the ground when she saw who had come into the room.

Davian and Bryson, followed by a group of Knights, came into the room. Tandy crawled quickly to Mariana and pulled her to her chest, keeping the men from seeing her bare breasts to preserve her modesty.

"Take them to the dungeon." Davian demanded, the Knights immediately following his instructions. Martina continued to screech as her arm hung limp when they pulled her off the ground, and when they grabbed her by the shoulders to drag her to the cell in the basement of the palace, they ignored her desperate pleas as she begged for them to rest her injured arm.

Tandy held Mariana tightly, afraid she was hurt worse than she could tell. She ran her hand over Mar's scalp to make sure there was no blunt force trauma, and only found a small cut near her hairline. Finally, she felt a bump just on the side of her head that made Mariana flinch when she found it.

"I fell off the bed," Mariana slurred, explaining how her head was hurt.

"Did she make you fall off?" Tandy asked softly, pressing her lips to Mariana's forehead.

"The man did, after I spit at him," she huffed. Bryson crouched low as he approached them after having scanned the room for any-one else.

"Mar, are you okay?" He asked in a wavering voice. His face was pale and his hands shook as he reached out to her cheek. Tandy kept Mariana pressed to her chest to keep her friend's breasts from being exposed, and Bryson could only cup her cheek in their position. He seemed to understand, though, and called out for Davian.

"She needs a blanket, get one from another room. This room needs to be checked thoroughly and I don't want to disrupt any details," he said. Davian glanced fearfully at Tandy as she clutched the brunette, and turned to another Knight to send him for a robe.

"Tired," Mariana murmured as she pressed her cheek against Tandy's chest.

"I know, love, but the doctor has to check on you before we can take a nap," Tandy said. She looked at Bryson who stared at her with fearful eyes.

"Oh, gods, I didn't send for a doctor. Dav," Bryson said quickly.

"I sent for the doctor, don't worry," he assured them. They sighed in relief and kept talking to Mariana to keep her awake. Tandy wasn't sure if it was shock or a concussion that could have caused her current behavior, but assumed it was most likely a little bit of both. She was exhausted, and also had a head injury. She just hoped it wasn't anything serious beyond a bruise and a bit of dizziness.

The Guards came back with a blanket to cover Mariana with, and Tandy gently draped it over her back before helping her lean away, bringing the blanket tight around her chest. Mariana tried to keep her head up but Tandy saw how unsteady she was, just from the simple movement of leaning back. She looked up at Bryson who was biting his lip, wringing his hands with the effort of not reaching out to take Mariana himself. She leaned her lips to Mariana's ear and whispered to her.

"Mariana, do you want to stay with Bryson in his room or with Davian and I?" She asked softly. Mariana hummed, letting out a scoff as she thought about it.

"If I stay with you, will Dav keep it in his pants till I leave?" Her words ran together, but Tandy was relieved to hear the tease. "S'better to stay with Bry," she said with a smile. "He has self control." Tandy looked up to see Bryson nodding, having heard their conversation.

"Let's get you cleaned up in Davian's bath and then I'll escort you to the kindly Knight's bed," Tandy said, making Mariana giggle. Bryson and Davian helped pull the girls to their feet before Bryson picked up Mariana in his arms. He acted as though she weighed nothing, marching her straight to Davian's room. Tandy could tell he wanted to offer to help her wash up but he didn't ask, only looking torn as though he couldn't fathom letting Mariana go, his eyes flicking between the door and the faint woman in his arms.

"I have her with me, you can go conclude your investigation," Tandy assured Bryson. Davian agreed easily, though Tandy could sense a worry in his eyes. Bryson looked out right terrified of leaving without Mariana. "I promise, with the Knights and the healer, we will be alright. We had both just wanted to sleep, that's the only reason we were overtaken," Tandy said. She frowned then, "how did they get through the Knights on patrol?"

"She poisoned them," Davian said with a tight jaw. "It seems that she figured out how to use Lethe as a drug, instead of as only an elixir. She overdosed the King, and the Knights. It was a smaller dose with the Knights, just enough to incapacitate them, but it worked. It can be ingested and inhaled, all she had to do was put it on their face." His eyes looked murderous, and Tandy knew she must have looked the same when she broke Martina's arm. She nodded at him, and they shared a sad look with one another as they knew the palace needed to be swept through again for safety.

"It's okay, Dav, she'll be safe with me, you can go and do what must be done," Tandy told him, glancing at Bryson as the words seemed to pain him physically. He looked helpless, something she never thought to be possible by the tall man. He always had a composure about himself, always level headed and thoughtful. But seeing Mariana injured had shaken him, and Tandy knew their hearts were bound to one another even if they didn't know it yet themselves.

Bryson finally sat Mariana down on the bed and kneeled before her, holding her cheeks in his hands. He gazed up at her with a warmness that made Tandy reach for Davian, holding him tight around the waist as she tucked her cheek to his chest. He held her tight in his arms, kissing her hair as they watched Mariana and Bryson whisper intimately together.

A few moments passed when there was a knock at the door. Despite the fact that it was open, the doctor didn't rush in. Davian called him into the room along with his apprentice, a girl, younger than himself by a few years.

"If you don't mind, Your Highness, my Lord," the doctor said gently. "I'll start checking Lady Mariana as soon as we give her some privacy." Davian and Bryson struggled with stepping away, but acquiesced nonetheless. They kissed Mariana and Tandy's cheeks and left the room quietly.

"My Lady, I will have your friend help you undress so we can see the extent of your injuries," he told Mariana. "I will refrain from touching you as much as possible, but there will be some things I cannot evaluate without putting my hands on you." The doctor and his assistant thoroughly scanned Mariana's frame after Tandy pulled the ripped dress from her body. The poor woman stood there shivering despite the warm summer air, eyes shut as she avoided the doctor's gaze.

Tandy held Mariana's hand throughout the evaluation, dread filling her. The apprentice drew a warm bath in the other room while the doctor looked over each mark left on her body. He asked her when and how the injuries occurred, always keeping her focused on a specific thought.

"I have to make sure you don't have a serious head injury," he explained as he asked seemingly repetitive questions. "Cognitive function would be altered more significantly if you had hit your head any harder."

Tandy bit her cheek at the sight of old and fading bruises on her body, especially the ones that looked suspiciously like hand prints marking over her flesh. Tandy wished she had broken both of that witch's arms. It simply would never be enough for her knowing she walked away with such a simple wound as her daughter sat there in broken pieces.

The girl came back from the bathroom with a warm, wet cloth and began wiping Mariana's bloody nose clean. The blood had spilled down her chest as she'd been unable to stop it from flowing while her mother raised hands at her. Tandy grabbed a cloth too, and cleaned over her chest gently.

"Alright, my Lady," the doctor said as he guided Mariana to the bathroom. "You may take a bath now. I will write down everything I have seen and let His Highness know how you fare."

They helped her step into the tub. It wasn't deep with just enough for the water to reach Mariana's belly button. Tandy found a towel and dipped it into the water before pulling the now warm cloth over Mar's body, hiding her private areas from the world. It wasn't much but Tandy knew that if it had been her, she'd want to be covered. Mariana smiled at her, shivering as the cold air met her skin.

"Thank you, that's warm," she told Tandy.

"Your head injury seems minor," the doctor told Mariana. "Your perception initially was off just slightly but your eyes are clear. There are side effects to look out for in case you do have a concussion, though. A headache is normal with a bump like this but if you start to throw up or your vision changes drastically, you must send for me immediately," he looked at Tandy as he spoke. She nodded, knowing she would be caring for Mar until their boys came back. Tandy thought the doctor and his assistant would leave then, but the old man sighed.

"I'm sorry to ask, my lady, but I must know. Did the man touch you in any way unbecoming of a gentleman? Aside from hitting you," he asked sadly.

"Not today," Mariana answered, looking away with tears in her eyes. Tandy clutched her friend's hand tight, the words like a knife. The doctor nodded as if he had been expecting her answer, before pulling a powder from his bag. He mixed it with a small bit of water and handed it to Mariana.

"Drink this, it'll keep you from catching any illnesses. Those men are pigs and I won't have you getting sick by their repugnant behavior," he told her. She took the glass with an unsteady hand, bringing it to her lips. It wobbled in her grip and Tandy reached out to support her hand as she took a sip. She swallowed it fast and sighed, handing the cup back. Tandy grabbed some of the soap and began washing Mariana's hair, rubbing as gently as she could to avoid the injury hidden under her dark locks. Mariana hummed gratefully, leaning on the side of the tub with her back exposed.

"I've brought medicine for you, you can take it whenever you're ready. There's some that are applied directly to any wound and some that are ingested. I think Duchess Tandanea has it under control," he nodded at Tandy. "If you have Lady Mariana in your watch, I will bid you goodnight now. Call for me if anything changes, though I think she will be fine in a few days. Don't fall asleep for another thirty minutes, just in case anything worsens. I would prefer it if you stayed with someone while you slept," he added. Tandy agreed, and the doctor and his assistant left just as quickly as they arrived. He left a bag on the bed, presumably the medicine for Mariana.

"Let's put some of the medicine on," Tandy murmured. She opened the bag and rifled through until she found a cooling poultice and brought it back to Mariana. She hesitated for a moment, not wanting to distress Mariana but knew she needed the medicine.

"It's okay, Tandy, you can put it on," Mariana said softly as though she could hear Tandy thinking.

"Let's wash you off first, and then apply it," Tandy said.

Tandy continued to wash her friend's hair, rinsing it once she knew there was no trace of any blood lingering behind. She braided it while it was wet to keep it from getting mussed up when she slept then applied the cream over Mariana's scratches and bruises slowly and carefully so as not to hurt Mariana needlessly.

Finally, Mariana was done with the bath and Tandy helped her out. Tandy took a clean robe that was folded on the counter and helped Mariana step into it.

"I'll have to send for gowns to sleep in tonight," Tandy said quietly. There wasn't much to be done when her bedroom and Mar's were both crime scenes. They walked to the table and Tandy helped her sit down. She was wobbly on her feet, but the soak in the bath had brought back a healthy color to her cheeks.

As they sat at the table, Knights led in maids as they carried trays of tea and food. She waited for the maids to leave before Tandy began to serve Mariana a light meal. As she placed a bowl of soup in front of Mariana, could see the bruises on Mariana's face darkening by the minute. Tandy hoped the soup would be easy to eat without any pain. She ate slowly, still clearly uncomfortable.

"I'm sorry, Mariana, I should have stayed in the room with you," Tandy said finally after gripping her own spoon too tight for too long, leaving her fingers numb. Mariana looked at her then, head tilted as she contemplated Tandy's words.

"Tandy, I asked you to give me some time to myself," Mariana sighed. "Besides, it's not your fault my mother did that. This isn't the first time it's happened, it wasn't really much of a surprise for me," Mariana said with an unsteady gaze. Tandy felt ill as she heard Mariana speak so plainly of her abuse.

"Mariana," Tandy murmured. Mar waved her hand and stopped her from speaking.

"Tandanea, you tucked me in and put me to bed. You couldn't have known that this would happen. Davian and Bryson were supposed to be dealing with her. You and I wanted to rest. Martina had other plans that none of us were privy to, though I suppose I should have figured it out first," Mariana continued. "Trust me, Tandy, I learned my lesson after the last time my mother spoke poison to me when we went over the fabric for your wedding. She is cruel, and she is sneaky. We can just be grateful that pig of a man didn't take what he came for," she shivered.

"I'm sorry, Mar," Tandy said softer than before, an apology for something out of anyone's control. She extended her hand to Mariana and the brunette gripped her fingers tight within her own.

"I'm sure Bryson won't look at me the same after knowing that," Mariana whispered. Tandy squeezed her hand tight, gently tugging her arm. Their eyes met as Mariana stared sadly into her friend's eyes.

"Bryson wouldn't care if you had a tail," Tandy said honestly. Her words surprised Mariana, pulling a laugh from her throat. Her cheek was swollen, and her eye crinkled shut tighter on one side, but Tandy could still see her dimples as she laughed.

"Well, I don't believe that even a little bit," Mariana snickered, "but thank you."

"Eat your soup, Mar," Tandy told her.

"What happened when you came into the room?" Mariana asked after a few minutes of quiet. Tandy looked down at her plate, still mostly full as she picked at what she ate.

"I may have lost my sanity for a moment," Tandy said without acknowledging what she did.

"You knocked that disgusting pig out and then *wrestled* Martina into submission," Mariana countered.

"I may have done that," she said, still looking away.

"You *broke* Martina's arm," Mariana insisted.

"I may have done that, as well," Tandy finally met Mariana's eyes.

"So I didn't hallucinate that, it actually happened," Mariana said with a thoughtful look on her face. Tandy felt a wave of anxiety rushing through her at the memory.

"It happened, and I don't quite know *how*," she said. "Well, I do know how. I was very angry, and the thoughts crossed my mind. Only, instead of ignoring my conscience, I acted on it," Tandy admitted. She sighed, certain she sounded like a villain. Mariana surprised her though and let out a sharp bark of laughter.

"I knew you were a volatile minx," Mariana grinned, wiping a tear from her eye. "Tandy with her cold and manipulative wiles, a simmering rage only the lowest kind will ever meet." Tandy only rolled her eyes as Mariana giggled.

As they continued to eat, Tandy noticed a small white envelope on the tray the food was brought into the room on. She pulled the parcel and opened it, reading the note as fast as she could.

To Duchess Tandanea -

The maid you have acquired and the family she is attached to have been called upon. I have sent for them with three Knights minding the carriage and one on horseback. The rider on horseback arrived promptly and delivered the letter I was entrusted with. The girl's family wrote their own letter back in confirmation of the change in master.

The Knight on horseback arrived shortly before seven this evening - the carriage is in transit with all family members and personal belongings accounted for. The girl is in the servant quarters until their reunification. Once they are reunited, the maids will begin their work for you. The girl is currently quite unwell from stress and it is in all parties best interest to leave her to readjust with the other servants as she waits for the rest of her family. For her safety and wellbeing, as instructed, Knights are stationed throughout the servant quarters and there shall be no possible way of interruption or harm in the time being.

Rest assured, the acquisition of the new staff for Duchess Tandanea will be received and trained within the following days. Another message will be sent once they are acquired. Due to the current state of the castle, these new acquisitions will be interviewed in the horse stables and barns so as to keep from adding to the workload of the current staff.

You will be able to call for them when investigations are closed. I will send updates if necessary following the note I send of their acquisition.

Until then,

Madame H. Hollahue - Mistress of Housekeeping

"They already responded?" Mariana asked, wondering how quick of a trip it was to her home. "I guess it isn't that far away," she murmured. Tandy offered her the note to read it for herself. She took it before reading it quickly and placing it back on the table.

"It is a relatively short ride, it doesn't surprise me at all that one of the Knights made it back that quickly. Our ride wasn't that long," Tandy.

"It always feels long to me, I hate that ride. Mother always had them ride faster than what is safe for a carriage, I would nearly fall out each time we were invited to a party in their mad dash to get here," Mariana rolled her eyes. "I think our ride was longer than I'm used to, since we traveled at a proper speed."

"I hope Davian and Bryson come back soon with any word," Tandy said as she leaned back, pushing her bowl away. Mariana nodded in agreement before walking away from the table. Tandy helped Mariana to stand and brought her to the bed. She pulled the covers down and helped Mariana under the covers, much like she had earlier in the day.

"Thank you," Mariana whispered as she laid on the pillows. Tandy tucked the blanket around her and smoothed her hair down.

"I'll be staying awake this time, so you can finally rest like you need to," Tandy told her.

"You don't have to do that," Mariana started to say, but Tandy shushed her gently.

"I know I don't have to, but I'm going to. It has been at least thirty minutes, and your eyes seem to be dilating alright, so it should be okay for you to sleep. I'd feel better, though, if someone watched you tonight. Just in case," Tandy explained. Mariana pouted but nodded in understanding.

"If you insist," she yawned.

"Let's take something for pain relief before you sleep," Tandy said as she tightened the blankets around Mariana's shoulders. Her eyes were already drooping, but she nodded.

Tandy reopened the bag the doctor left for them and pulled out each item. The doctor had labeled them with ribbon and paper tags so sorting through them was quick.

"This is for inflammation, this is for pain," Tandy said under her breath as she sought the best one for Mariana. Tandy took them and poured the proper amount of both into a small cup of tea, so it wasn't bitter and offered it to Mariana. She sipped it slowly and gratefully before tucking herself against Davian's pillow, and promptly fell asleep.

Tandy breathed a sigh of relief that Mariana was safe, snoring peacefully on the bed in the candlelit room. She placed a small swipe of a sweet smelling poultice over the bruises on her cheeks to keep them from swelling any more than they had. She hoped that Mariana would wake up refreshed and not so achy, though she was sure that there'd be at least some discomfort come the morning no matter what they did. Her bruises looked quite harsh on her gentle features, so stark against the gentle curve of her cheeks and the innocence of her brown eyes. Even her lashes were delicate, curled and full, and Tandy couldn't believe that she experienced this level of pain at the hand of her own mother.

Tandy sat at the table going over the medicines when Davian and Bryson came into the room. She had been facing the door to make sure no one came in without them knowing, though it had been unnecessary on their part considering the group of Knights on watch outside of Davian's doorway.

"How is she?" Davian asked as soon as he was in the room. He and Bryson walked straight to the bed on either side and leaned over to see her. Bryson paled at the sight of the bruises, a look of fright over his usually stoic features. He reached a hand out and ran his finger over the bridge of her nose, a whisper of a touch. He sniffed, and Tandy knew he was trying to hold his composure. Tandy turned to sit on the bed along with Davian and Mariana. Bryson looked as though he wanted to slide under the covers and hold Mariana for dear life.

"Why don't you bring her to your room?" Davian suggested. "Or Tandy and I could go in yours." Bryson scoffed, looking at Davian as though he were crude.

"And let you two defile my own bed? I don't think so," he huffed.

"We'll have the maids change the sheets," Dav rolled his eyes. Bryson finally let out a sigh and nodded shallowly.

"I'll bring her to my room, if that's what she would like," he said with a glance to Mariana.

"What happened after you left us?" Tandy asked quietly after a moment of quiet.

"Well, that witch is clearly off her rocker. Hissing like a tomcat all the way down to the dungeons, though the broken arm slowed her down. The man was unconscious for most of the interrogation, and only woke up at the end. I have the Knights working them for more information but there wasn't much else we could do personally. They're locked up, and that's all we can say until morning," Davian told her.

"What happened here, before we found you?" Bryson asked, his eyes bright with the need to put the pieces together. She knew what he saw when they came into the room, but she knew he would want a clearer understanding of the situation. He always had been one to fully invest himself into work, and Tandy knew that this was like another puzzle to solve for him. He thrived on making sense of the pieces that remained, and could only rest once all his questions were answered.

Tandy explained everything that had happened when she found Mariana in the room. She felt a flash of shame as she told them about her part in the madness, of how she knocked the man out and broke Martina's arm. She had cruelty within her, and worse than that, she had no doubt that should another loved one find themselves in danger, she would do the same all over again.

Twenty Two

Davian

Davian stared at Tandy in awe as she explained what happened. When he and Bryson had walked into the room, they knew she must have been the one to incapacitate both the man and the woman as she was the only other person there. Hearing her confirm that she had knocked out a man triple her size and broke the arm of the woman hurting Mariana, all he could do was look at her with admiration.

"We need to put her in training," Bryson said after Tandy explained what she did.

"Without a doubt," Davian agreed. As he looked at Tandy, all he could see were the dark circles lining her eyes and the overall disarray of her dress and hair. She looked exactly as though she had been fighting, still tense from the chaos that had occurred. He walked over to her slowly, reaching his hand to her chin to tilt her face up at him. Her grey blue eyes were dull with exhaustion, but her gaze was still sharp. There was an edge to her lips as though she were waiting to be berated, ready to accept punishment for the acts of aggression she dealt.

"Thank you for protecting my sister," Davian told her.

"I had to," she answered as though it was obvious.

"You are brave, Tandy," he said as he pulled her into a hug, his arms tightening around her. She tensed harder for a moment before melting into his arms, her hands gripping the back of his shirt. He pressed a kiss to her hair as she tucked her head under his chin.

"Do you think Mariana will be okay?" Bryson asked softly, playing with the end of Mariana's braid. He looked lost and unable to express it, torn between duty and love. The struggle was plain on his face as he looked at Mariana lovingly. He had spent so much time running from task to task in order to avoid the call of his heart, but it all had led him back to Mariana in the end.

"She'll be okay, her injuries are superficial and she likely will hardly even scar from the scratches. She needs someone to watch her sleep though, just in case she worsens. I'm certain that won't happen, but I can't sleep after the last time," Tandy explained to them. "I should have been in there with her, it wouldn't have happened if I had stayed."

"Absolutely not, you would *both* have been hurt in ways I *refuse* to think about had you been in the room," Davian said, pulling her tight to his side. "An ambush on a sleeping woman would not have ended well for either of you had you not been able to attack from behind."

"The state the doors were in, Tandy. *Nothing* would have stopped them if you had been attacked, too. It's a miracle you were separated, it spared Mariana another horror," Bryson said through gritted teeth, fighting away the tears.

"Do you want to bring her to your room, Bry?" Davian asked.

"I'm afraid that Mariana would be afraid of me, after what she's experienced," he whispered.

"That isn't true, considering she's trusted you everyday she has known you. If she didn't, tonight wouldn't have been the deciding factor," Tandy offered gently.

"Her *mother* was the one that organized those men to -" Bryson covered his mouth, shaking his head. He wouldn't say it out loud, what happened to Mariana. Davian agreed that it was too horrid to think about, to voice out loud. That she had to physically experience it made him *sick*. Mariana deserved more than she was dealt. Her mother used her as fodder, as bait, to dangle in front of the rich men that lacked any decency and who craved power at any cost.

Mariana stirred as they talked quietly and yawned, stretching her sore muscles. She grumbled before settling against the pillow and looked around the room blearily.

"If you're going to gossip 'bout me, do it quieter," Mariana grumbled.

"We *weren't* -" Bryson and Davian chimed at the same time.

"Do you want some more of the pain relief medicine? I'm sorry we woke you," Tandy said, offering her medicine.

"Hmm, yes, I think so. I'm more sore than I thought I'd be," she stretched again, cracking some of her joints. She turned to Bryson as Tandy filled a small cup of medicine. "Carry me to your room? I don't trust them not to go at it like rabbits while I'm too weak to run away," she pouted. Bryson huffed out a laugh not having expected Mariana's blunt words. He grinned at her before pulling her into his arms easily, and strode to where Tandy held out the small cup.

"Thank you," Mariana told Tandy after she finished the medicine.

"Of course," she replied. "Get some rest, okay?" Tandy squeezed Mariana's hand and kissed her fingers gently. Bryson nodded to them before leaving the room. Davian bid them goodnight before shutting the door and locking it tight behind them.

In a moment of paranoia, he walked over to the door that connected Tandy's room to his own and locked it, too, just in case.

Davian pulled her into another embrace, tucking his nose against her throat as he breathed in her scent. He held her tight, nuzzling into her neck, the smell of her comforting him. He finally let her go and began blowing out the candles around the room. Tandy was in bare feet, and climbed into the bed gratefully as he took his shoes off. It was pitch black, though there was a slight blue hue to the sky outside the window indicating sunrise wouldn't be far off. The Knights would wake them come morning, and he needed to be grateful for the small amount of sleep that he would be able to get.

He climbed in after her, pulling her flush against his chest. She kissed his cheek before rolling over, tucking her hands under her cheek. For a moment, Davian truly only wanted to sleep. But as Tandy's ass pressed against his cock, he found he was desperate for her. His hand splayed out over her belly, and he kissed her neck. His lips trailed up her cheek and he nibbled on her ear lobe. Tandy shivered at his touch, hips squirming against him.

"Just a quick one," she whispered. "I'm exhausted."

"Mmm, so quick," he agreed. "I'm exhausted too, but I need you," he kissed her as she leaned over her shoulder. He pulled her gown up until it rested above her hips and slid her panties down. He pulled her thigh up, and trailed his fingers through her wet heat, drawing a moan from her lips.

"Just give it to me," Tandy huffed as he teased her slit, "too tired to build up to it. I need it *now*," she said before pulling him into another kiss.

"Who am I to deny my Queen?" He teased, pulling his pants down low enough to expose his cock. "Next time, we're taking our time. In the sunlight," he said before lining himself against her pussy. He pulled her ass closer to him, just to the perfect angle, and sank himself deep inside of her.

"*Oh,*" she moaned, pressing against him with each thrust. Her hand curled into his hair, pulling hard enough to hurt. He didn't care, though, and pressed harder into her. Tandy pulled his fingers into her mouth, lathing her tongue around each digit. When she was done, she pulled his hand to her clit.

"Touch me," she demanded as she rolled her hips with a sigh. He ran his slicked fingers over her clit, slowly at first, before speeding up his thrusts along with his fingers. She was so responsive with each touch, he drew out moan after moan as she raised her thigh higher, holding it by her knee as he pounded into her from behind.

"Gods, Tandy," Davian said feverishly, kissing her cheek messily before finding her lips. Their kiss was nothing more than tongue and teeth, sharing air and moans. Tandy's hips jolted with a particular thrust, and Davian continued to find the same angle that made her body tremble with each stroke. Her breath gasped out of her, before her body went taut against him. Davian rubbed her clit harder, keeping his cock deep within her.

"*Oh fuck,*" she cried out as she came, her pussy tightening around his length. He could hardly hold on, and as her body tensed around him through the aftershocks of her orgasm, he came hard. He rolled his hips into her one last time, milking himself inside of her, holding onto the delicious feeling for just a moment longer before he was finally sated.

He slowly pulled out of her and flopped onto his back, sighing contentedly. Tandy gasped next to him, too tired to move. Davian told himself they'd take their time one day. One day, under the light of the sun, he would taste every inch of her body. He would spend an entire afternoon learning each curve in her skin, finding all the places on her that would make her moan. He wanted to see how long she could go before she begged for him to be inside of her. To see just how desperate she could get, before he finally gave her what she wanted. One day, they'd make love.

Tandy sighed and rolled off of the bed, stumbling to the bathroom. He could hear her rustling around for a moment before she came back to the bed. She dropped onto her pillow with a groan, stretching out next to Davian. The sun drew higher still, the sky casting a blue hue over the room. Tandy leaned closer to Davian for a kiss, and he obliged her before pulling her to his chest.

"It'll be a long day," Tandy yawned against his chest.

"I have a terrible feeling," Davian told her honestly. "Martina was crazed when we questioned her, but she was *not* afraid. I think she has something she's hiding close to her sleeve, and I know we won't like it when we figure it out." Tandy hummed thoughtfully, taking his words in before she spoke.

"There will undoubtedly be a very thick web we have to unweave. I think it'll be wise to get as much information out of everyone as possible in the morning. We need to know who works with who, and who's money invests into these plans." Tandy rubbed her hand over Davian's chest, thinking. "It's clear Martina has monetary support from the men she forces onto Mariana, and so we need to assume *any* person with the means to take the throne has ill intentions toward *you*. If they have the desire for power, they'll need to be monitored. Unfortunately, there's no way to know where anyone's alliance lies until we comb through the web. It's unlikely you'll be able to know with certainty, unless there are those that still fear the Crown's power. Our only hope is that the punishment for treason is enough to stir them back to the right path, and either expose those with nefarious goals or intimidate the ones in on the plot that don't have the means to see it through," she concluded.

"I'm glad you came back," Davian murmured against her hair, kissing her forehead. "I'm sorry it took so long."

"I'm not sorry at all, it seems the Royal court has been a terrible nightmare. I'm glad I wasn't here," she grumbled against his chest, startling a laugh from Davian. "I'm not even kidding," she told him.

"I know you're not kidding," he chuckled, "that's why I'm laughing. You have a way with words, and I am nearly always surprised by them."

They fell asleep pressed against each other as the room quickly filled with sunlight.

***

They rested only a few hours before there was an insistent knock on the door, startling them from their very short sleep. Davian jolted upright quickly in surprise, nearly rolling Tandy off the bed. She spluttered under the tangled blankets, much like the morning before, before righting herself and stumbling to the table.

Davian opened the door after nearly losing his footing on a blanket caught on his ankle, revealing the maids with a large breakfast. He heard Bryson in the hallway and supposed the large breakfast was for the lot of them. One of the maids offered them both a large mug of coffee, to which Tandy sighed gratefully.

"Thank you," she yawned before adding cream and sugar. The maids left the room once everything was settled onto the table.

Bryson stepped into their line of view, drawing their attention his way. He helped Mariana to the table, who gratefully walked without much trouble. Her bruises were heavy around her cheeks, but the swelling had gone down from the medicine they had given her the night before. Tandy moved to add more to some tea as they settled into their chairs.

"Let's discuss our next step," Bryson began immediately, wasting no time. How he was functioning, Davian had no idea. Tandy glanced at Dav with a look, both impressed and horrified at his ability to steam through chaos with strategy and patience. Mariana giggled to herself at the look Tandy wore. She handed Mariana the cup of warm tea infused with medicine, and sat back down next to Davian with a yawn.

"Obviously, Martina needs to be tried for her crimes against the throne," Davian began with a sigh. "I just don't want to upset you anymore than necessary, Mariana," he admitted. She waved her hand at him, placing the now empty medicine glass back onto the table.

"Trust me, you don't need to worry. I have no part in her quest for power other than the fact that I was the reward to those in desire of the crown. I know that now, I just wish I had realized it before this happened," she said sadly, "I would have come to you for help had I known the true reason she did what she did." Tandy laid her hand over Mariana's, frowning. Davian knew she was feeling just as guilty as he did, by the way her eyes drew downward.

"It's really the fault of many. That the kingdom was able to be infiltrated in such a slimy way is a crime of its own. I wish I could say we're all guiltless, here, but it's not true," Davian said plainly. "The least of all the guilty parties, though, is you, Mariana. You've been surviving as best you can. It's not your fault she used you for her own gain, Mar. As the Prince, I should have been the one to see this coming, especially since we had been in close proximity for *years*. I let things slip through the cracks, the important things, and the King is dead because of it." Mariana looked at him with a surprised expression, mouth opening in what could only be in his defense. He held his hand up and their mouths closed, waiting for him to continue.

"Trust me, I should have seen this coming. I do *everything* in this palace, I have been the sole ruler for actual years. I'm nowhere near the age at which I'm supposed to hold the title, of course, but it's no excuse. This is costing people their lives, and I have failed not only the King, but the people of the kingdom." He said, his words tapering off as he looked out the window, the lake glistening under the morning sun.

"You're right," Tandy said, looking at him with a stoic expression. He glanced down at her, surprised and yet not surprised at all, though her words made his heart ache. "You are *nowhere* near the age you would have been before taking on the responsibilities of the kingdom. And yet, you have. For easily the last decade, if the last few years before I left were anything to go by," she continued as Mariana nodded slowly behind her. "The fact remains that you were a child when you essentially gained the throne, with no one but the advisors as your support. We know how advisors can be, teetering between masters and finding themselves at the feet of the ones with the money. There is no doubt that you were likely led on by the unspoken coin purse of those hungry for power, much like many others have found themselves embedded in. You are not the first, and may well not be the last, Dav. The only thing we can do is move forward. The past is complete, it cannot be willed into changing simply because we wish it were so, nor can our guilt turn back time. There is nothing to be done, except to see this through. For ourselves, for the kingdom." He was torn at her words, the initial feeling of dread had turned into a surprising warmth filling his belly at her insistent praise. Tandy squeezed his hand and Davian felt a lump form in his throat, and he willed himself not to weep.

"She's right, Your Highness," Bryson agreed solemnly as he held Mariana's hand in his own. "There's not much we can do other than find each strand this web has found us tangled in. The palace needs to be swept through thoroughly, and that is going to be hard in and of itself. But first, you need to decide something."

"What's that?" He asked, swallowing the feeling of tears in his throat.

"What will you do with the Ligotus family and the estate?" He asked, making Mariana turn to him. Her eyes were wide with fear, knowing he could easily have the entire family line wiped out for daring to assault the Royal family.

"Only the guilty parties will be punished, and the estate will fall to the next of kin. Have the entire estate locked down and interrogate everyone. Make sure there is no harm to the home and the people within it, and all guilty parties are brought to the palace, straight to the dungeon. Have that handled, and we will go in with a strong hand today to see the rest of the party guests, now that we have Martina and an accomplice locked down," he said without much thought to it. He had been thinking about it all night, and didn't need another moment to consider anything else, though he still felt heavy from Tandy's praise. He looked at Mariana as her bruises were illuminated in the daylight. Another thought struck him then, suddenly, as he took in his sister's downcast glance.

"Also," he began, making them all look at him, "Mariana will of course be added to the family line. She won't be a Ligotus in name for much longer and will not be questioned outside of what is necessary for the investigation." Stunned faces stared back at him as he spoke, the words heavy as they fell onto the ears of the room's occupants. "That won't leave this room until the rest of the family is questioned, though," he added.

"You don't have to do that," Mariana began, her hand raising toward him.

"I'm going to do it, because it's right and because there is no one who *can* tell me not to. It's my throne, now, and I will claim the family I have left," he told her. Mariana's eyes welled up with tears that she couldn't blink away, leaving tracks lining her cheeks as her lip quivered.

When Tandy pulled herself to Mariana's side, knees on the floor next to her chair, the brunette finally let the tears release. Tandy wrapped her arms around her waist, leaning against her side. Mariana's hands curled around Tandy before she leaned her forehead to the top of her head. The girls shared their breath for a while as Tandy slowly comforted Mariana through the worst of the tears. It was a long time coming, he was sure that this was inevitable. She'd been put through so much that it was a surprise to noone that the idea of her family accepting and loving her, of claiming her as their own, was foreign to Mariana. She clutched Tandy as though her life depended on it, holding her as she grieved the youth that was stolen from her.

"We are going to need to quickly and efficiently go through the guests here, and also consider expediting the wedding. I need to be married before I can officially take the throne, and with the way things are, it must be done as soon as possible," Davian began, running his hand in his hair. "We need to comb through everyone in the palace and in the villa, and find as many leads and connections between Lethe and Martina. It came from somewhere, and we need to find out who," he thought out loud. Bryson nodded along with him before he spoke.

"I'll have the Knights begin to sweep through each room and bring me written information in regards to each guest. I've already swept through most of the Guards, ensuring their allegiance from the moment I arrived. It's in our favor that Martina hurt two of the Knights in her quest to obtain Mariana," he added. "Since that moment, we can rest assured that they will not let anyone get away with anything. Between the King's Guard and the Knights, you have the full support of the Knights in this palace. Majority of the staff have also been consistent with their praise of you. Citing Mrs Hollahue and maids in the kitchen, your policies and treatment of the staff in the castle have been far greater than everything the King and Queen have ever done for them. There are quite the stories within these walls of the things the Royals would do with the lowly servants. Since you've had a hand in the policies and procedures, they have been treated fairly and with respect. It's more than we could have hoped for, knowing they feel this way," Bryson told Davian. He could not quite believe the praise, though. He didn't feel as though he did very much at all, aside from catering to the spread of Lethe through his home. As if Tandy heard his thoughts, she reached a hand out and linked their fingers together.

"You were *born* for this role, Davian, you already know what we need to do. Stop doubting yourself, and be firm with the directions you give," she told him. He sighed, but nodded in agreement. She was right, after all. He had been working towards this his whole life and he would do the best he could with what he was given. He took another deep breath before he spoke.

"We will quickly go through guests, and follow the leads. We will also be planning the wedding for this coming week," he looked at Tandy who only nodded, "and have the coronation as soon as possible after the wedding."

"Can you move the wedding up any sooner than that?" Mariana asked. "I think you should have that sooner than in a week." Tandy looked at her curiously, head tilted in question.

"I know my mother, and I know she has contingency plans for everything. Her webs weave in unimaginable ways and I think until the throne is secured, we are all still in danger. I know she's in the dungeon, and I know the palace is locked down, but there is something inside of my heart telling me this isn't over," she looked up at Tandy tentatively, hands trembling. "I promise I'm not saying this to insinuate you don't have it under control, or that I'm saying this to somehow work with Martina to keep her from being punished, but that's not what I'm doing at all, I just want to be safe, and I -" Tandy reached a hand out for Mariana's and gently placed it in her grip.

"Mar, no one doubts that you have Davian and I in your best interest. I can assure you, there is no one in this room that would believe you have any connections with Martina. If she were let out of the dungeon right now and came to find you, what would you do?" Tandy asked her quietly. Mariana's face went pale and a shiver went through her body as she nervously looked at the door, no doubt looking for her mother to burst through at any moment. Tandy nodded at her reaction, making Davian sigh. He hadn't been worried, but her reaction made it obvious that she was telling the truth. "Your fear is painfully obvious, Mar. I don't think she would be able to use you for anything even if she *did* somehow regain access to you. You've been traumatized enough. Rest assured that we understand, and you are not in danger from us," Tandy said in a near whisper, leaning close to Mariana. With a sniff, Mariana nodded and they all looked to Davian once again.

"Unfortunately, there is a bereavement period for the Royals. The absolute bare minimum for any event, party, or wedding, is at least eight days from the time of death. There's a lot of stories about why exactly eight is the number, but all I know is that there cannot be any ceremonies until that mourning period is over," he explained. "There will also be a *lot* of people who detest this practice. The mourning period can last for months, or even years and there are many advisors that will attempt to delay the wedding. Whether for tradition, or intentional sabotage, it will be hard to tell. Either way, there will be many who are less than pleased about it."

"If they don't even know where the original mourning period length originated, how can they expect you to uphold old traditions?" Tandy asked with a quirk of her brow. He wanted to laugh at her response, but tightened his lips to keep from smiling.

"Tandy, with the hard hitting questions and logical disputes," Bryson laughed from the other side of Mariana. "I think she's right, though, Davian. I'm very well read on the laws and proclamations of the Royal throne since the first King was crowned. I have never seen a document that actually explained what exactly a mourning period consisted of, other than the original statement being that it needs to be at least a week before a celebration is celebrated. Not including the funeral, of course, but nothing explicitly says the appropriate length of time. Of course, traditions look different to many and so there will undoubtedly be pushback," Bryson said, leaning back in his chair.

"There's also the fact that none of those proclamations specifically pertained to the loss of a King," Tandy added. They all looked at her with confused expressions, but she evenly met Davian's eye with a cool expression.

She would certainly make a good Queen, Davian thought, and braced himself for whatever she was about to say.

Twenty Three

Tandy

Tandy kept her gaze locked on Davian, meeting his eyes. She had been explicitly trained in every matter regarding the reign of Davian's bloodline for generations, and knew every law and tradition that had ever been written. It seemed Bryson, despite his knowledge of the kingdom, didn't know of the exact details in regards to the coronation of the next King if the previous one passed away before the coronation. She knew one thing that would supersede the death of a King. The *one* thing that would allow for a wedding to occur before the mourning period was over.

"The Prince and his betrothed may wed irregardless of the mourning period," Mariana said suddenly. Mariana met her eyes, her dimples on display as she completed the thought Tandy had been mulling over.

"If the Prince has a betrothal of longer than eight years, the couple may wed without the mourning period being involved. In fact, we could marry even before a funeral takes place should we wish to. I wouldn't advise that, of course, but as we've been engaged for close to a decade, we can hold a wedding without worrying about traditions or upsetting the advisors. They cannot and will not dispute that once you pull the law from the law books, clearly written by their predecessors with no room for misunderstanding."

"The date you and Tandy were betrothed will be written down somewhere in the records, along with those special circumstances listed. There will be infallible proof you are within your rights to marry tonight, should you wish," Mariana agreed, looking between Davian and Tandy as Bryson stared at her in wonder. Tandy saw her cheeks turn pink as she flushed under Bryson's gaze.

"We'll have to take a walk to the record rooms," Davian conceded. "Bryson, have as many Knights you can spare to put toward the investigation. I want the guest list completed by tonight, it's already been too long to have the guests locked away." Bryson nodded in agreement before Davian continued. "Mariana, are you able to walk and keep up with Bryson or do you wish to stay in this room with Tandy?" Mariana and Tandy shared a look, almost as though they knew what the other was thinking.

"Well, I was thinking," she said, though her shoulders pinched with tension. Tandy reached for her hand again, holding it softly, and nodded in a way she hoped was comforting.

"I was going to suggest that Tandy and I go to the records rooms and find the documents we need while you and Bryson continue with the interrogations," she glanced at Tandy who gave a minute nod in support. Davian narrowed his eyes in thought, a pensive frown on his face as he thought it over.

"I don't feel as though that is a safe choice for you," he admitted regretfully.

"Do you have a superior officer who would be willing to be our guide in addition to the Knights placed in our rooms for protection?" Tandy suggested. "Unfortunately, there isn't enough time in this day to settle the investigation and also the minor facets of wedding planning, and logistics regarding the period of mourning.

We *need* a secondary group working on this today, and I couldn't trust anyone but Mariana and I to know what we are looking for. We are very versed in this, and it must be us that uncover what we need." Bryson's face melted into a gloomy but steadfast expression and looked at them resolutely.

"It can be another Knight that finds it," Davian had started but trailed off. He and Bryson looked at one another and sighed.

"Sir Felton may have arrived by now. The Commander of the King's Guard would be our best option on keeping them safe without worry of corruption. He can be their personal guide if he's back from the training camp. It's a few days' ride, but with notice of the King having been sent post haste he may be here already," Bryson said. "It would be better to have them in the records room if they know the laws better than us. They'll be more efficient in finding what is probably hidden in front of the other advisor's faces. Sir Felton Knighted me, he was friends with my father before he passed. He's a good man and has always been loyal to the throne," Bryson told Davian in a low voice. Davian rubbed his face but nodded.

"We really don't have time to be worrying about that too, so I suppose calling for Sir Felton will be an acceptable option. I'm going to ask that you take at least four Knights with you in addition to him, though, and for the protection of this room I will have additional Knights remain here," Davian said.

"That is very fair," Tandy agreed.

"I'll call for Sir Felton as we begin the formal investigation, I just ask that you do not leave this room until he finds you," Bryson warned.

"We will wait here for Sir Felton," Mariana told him gently, reaching for his hand. Davian swept over to Tandy for a small yet forceful kiss before he headed for the door. Bryson kissed Mariana's hand softly and followed Davian to the door and quietly shut it behind them.

"Do you think Sir Felton is even here or was that their way of keeping us calm?" Mariana muttered as she plopped into a chair at the table once again.

"I imagine we will be waiting for a while," Tandy sighed. "You can nap until they send him to us, Mar. It would be better to rest for your recovery anyway, we should use whatever time we have to help you heal."

"I guess I could nap," Mariana yawned. Tandy helped her into the bed as she groaned from her sore muscles.

"At the reform school after particularly distressing punishments, my whole body would ache despite only being lashed half a dozen times. It was as though every muscle I had would lock in the midst of my panic and fear and the days after would be utter agony trying to recover without so much as a frown," Tandy whispered as she tucked the blankets around Mariana. "We will draw a proper bath for you tonight after we find what we need. It'll help your muscles relax and keep you from feeling so achy in the coming days."

"Thank you, Tandy," Mariana said. "I'm sorry you were sent there." Tandy stroked her cheek, worrying away her frown.

"I'm sorry you were stuck here," Tandy told her. Mariana smiled before yawning. She turned over and pulled the blankets with her and within moments Tandy heard her softly snoring.

Tandy paced by the doors where two Knights stood silently, hardly a sound made from them at all. She nodded to them as she passed by and walked to the windows overlooking the overcast sky. Despite the grey to the clouds, the lake was still quite beautiful as it was framed nicely between Davian's windows and the garden just below.

Tandy turned to the table Davian had set her letters on and took a pen and a piece of paper from his correspondence pile. She began to think of what they needed to provide the advisors with to ensure their wedding was done quickly. They needed a letter stating their original betrothal date occurred more than eight years ago, that she knew was first. They would also need to provide the decree that stated the betrothal of the Royal party existing for longer than eight years meant the wedding could occur even if the Royal family was in bereavement.

She wasn't sure what to expect as far as the record room was concerned, but she knew writing down as much of the laws as she could remember would at least help narrow down where exactly they needed to turn.

She spent about an hour going over everything she could recall before calling for tea and lunch. As she waited for it to be brought to her, she wrote down some more things she wanted to look for. Maids quietly delivered the food and drinks before dispersing with practiced ease, the smell of the fresh bread on the tray made Tandy's mouth water. She skimmed the list she had made as she ate a small portion, still unused to eating her fill.

When there was finally a knock at the door, she stood to receive whoever it may be. Part of her hoped it was Davian and Bryson having finished their investigation despite how unlikely that was. The Knights answered the door for her as she stood to the side.

"Duchess Tandanea," Sir Felton said as he peered through the doorway, a smile lighting up his fair blue eyes. "Forgive me for the delay, it is good to see you again."

"No need for apologies, Sir Felton. Thank you for being our chaperone today," she told him. "It is a pleasure to see you after so long," she smiled at him as he took her hand and dropped a kiss to her fingers.

"I am glad I can be of service," he said. "Now, Sir Bryson did not tell me much of what I was called here for in specifics. But seeing how Lady Mariana is resting, perhaps you can give me the rundown."

"Of course, please have a seat. Lunch was just delivered, would you like some tea while we talk?" Tandy moved to pour the tea into two mugs.

"Thank you, I would appreciate some," he told her with another gentle smile. His eyes looked kind and she remembered his warm presence from when she was a little girl. He was as sweet as he looked, though quite skilled and deadly should the need arise. He trained all of the Knights and also was the one to promote them into Knighthood, a task granted to him after he had served for the King in their youth.

Tandy began to tell him about everything that had happened, sparing no details. She told him most of their theories revolved around one specific person and though she was apprehensive to make assumptions on anyone's character, she was definitely not wrong in her distrust of Lady Ligotus. He nodded and asked questions as she told him everything, and before long he was caught up to all of the drama they had experienced in the last few days.

"I wouldn't want to be wrong in my theories either, Duchess, but it does seem to be quite troublesome in some aspects. I'm sure we are going to find that there are several people like Lady Martina in this situation. A mess like this wouldn't happen if it was solely one investor, the Ligotus family simply doesn't have enough wealth nor reach in the Royal Circle to mastermind this solely through their own finances. She may well be a facilitator, but there must be a larger beast lurking underneath her," he explained.

"I thought the same, but with the other information I am just not sure. You see, with her treatment of her own daughter and her progressively increased agitation while we have been here only a little over a week now, it seems to me she is doing this out of self preservation," Tandy said as she glanced at her notes. "She is getting desperate. There must be something she is doing that is not being recorded to the public, some form of monetary gain. As an ambassador, she should be doing well but her extravagance far exceeds that. Can you recall her acting out in an agitated way before my arrival?"

"She was very handsy and flirted a lot with myself and my Knights, but moved on before long when none of us fell for it," Sir Felton said. "When the Knights were unphased, she moved to the next group. Our salary may have deterred her in the end."

"Her behavior change may be related to Lethe, if she hasn't caused issues before," Tandy thought.

"Well, it *has* been a few years since I was stationed in the castle, Duchess," Felton thoughtfully sipped his tea. "If Lethe made it to the Circle and found the Royal family, I would imagine Lady Ligotus enjoyed it along their side. They were quite the tight knit group for years, before I was moved to the Training Base at least. If her personality is changed, I agree that Lethe would be the most logical cause."

"It is strange to me that after all these years of planning, if we are correct in that she planned to move Mariana into the First Born birthplace, she would risk it all by taking the potion so close to the end. If she managed to find a way to give Davian the elixir whenever she would hand out to others to control them, her reach far surpasses anything I've ever heard of." Tandy said as she skimmed along the rest of her notes. "We are missing something, clearly, which is why we need to go to the record room to clear it up."

"We can let her rest a bit longer and wake her for lunch before we head down there," Sir Felton offered. Tandy nodded, agreeing with that plan. She made herself eat some fruit and a small finger sandwich before she went to wake Mariana.

"It's time to go, Mar," Tandy said softly as she ran her hand through her hair. Mariana woke slowly with a stretch and sat up, groaning as she cracked her stiff joints.

"I don't know if I *can*," Mariana grumbled as she eased her feet over the side of the bed. Sir Felton stood toward the door with politely averted eyes as he waited for them.

"We'll take our time walking and then you may sit in the records room," Tandy offered. "I can't go without you."

"You'll be fine without me, you know what to look for," Mariana said as she continued to stretch her shoulders and legs.

"I'm not worried about myself, Mar," Tandy admitted. She would not be able to focus even with her training if she left Mariana alone in her room again. She wasn't sure she'd ever really be able to leave her behind again, with all that had happened before. Mariana frowned but said nothing so Tandy readied another dose of the medicine to help with her pain. She offered it to her and Mar took it gratefully, though still made no effort to put her feet on the ground.

Tandy waited patiently for Mariana to make the decision to come with her, though she knew full well she would not be leaving without her no matter how long it took. Still, silence generally brought with it a reward. If she waited long enough quietly enough, Mariana would come around eventually. It took a few minutes more before finally Mariana stretched again with a loud yawn and placed her feet firmly on the floor.

"Do I have to change?" She asked.

"There will be no one but us, the maids, and the Knights. Every guest is in lock down until Prince Davian gives the go ahead on releasing everyone," Sir Felton told them.

"Plus everything we owned was destroyed in both of our rooms already this week, I'm afraid there's not much to change into even if we could," Tandy added. Mariana groaned but nodded.

"This will be the most unkempt I've ever looked in public," she laughed. Mariana put on soft silk slippers as they neared the door. "And my slippers are soft on my sore feet," she sighed. "I don't know the last time I dressed comfortably."

"Are you ready to go?" Sir Felton asked them with a glance to the Knights. They parted wordlessly and opened the door, letting them through. Tandy laced her arm through Mariana's and used her height to her advantage. Mariana was a bit shorter than her which helped Tandy hold her friend's arm as they walked down the long corridors and down the steps. Mariana grunted with each step down the stairs before she asked for them to pause.

"My legs hurt so much, I just need a moment," she panted.

"Would it be okay if I held your other arm to guide you down? If we both help you on the stairs it would alleviate your pain," Sir Felton offered. She knew he hadn't wanted to approach her without Mariana's permission first due to all of the poor girl's experiences with men but her distress made it hard to wait for Mar's choice to arise from her first.

"Yes, thank you," Mariana said gratefully. Sir Felton smiled and easily held Marianas other arm and they began descending the stairs again. With the two of them supporting under her arms, Mariana hardly had to lift a finger before they made it to the bottom of the stairs. They kept their grip on her as they neared the records room near the offices and meeting rooms. It was quiet in the belly of the castle with a heavy weight to every piece of furniture and decorative piece adorning its walls.

Finally they reached the records room, pushing through the dusty doors. Only the light from the halls filled the rooms leaving everything dim and dreary. Tandy looked around the small portion of the room that was bathed in light and noticed lanterns and candles placed on top of the table facing the doorway. She let go of Mariana with a nod to Sir Felton and grabbed the lantern. With a twist to the dial, a flame burst to life and illuminated the dark room. Several other lanterns lined the shelves and the table that laid from the doors to the furthest shelf. Chairs and pens littered the space, clearly once very used but neglected in the years before they came here.

After lighting the lanterns, Sir Felton and Tandy led Mariana to the table as the Knights stationed with them remained at the doors. One followed them dutifully while the others kept watch in the hallway. Once Mariana was settled, Tandy moved to the other side of the room to begin her search.

"I'll bring you anything I find, you don't have to move. Rest your legs," Tandy told her. Mariana nodded and laid her head on her hands with a sigh.

Tandy took a lantern with her as she headed to the back of the room. She wasn't sure how the shelves were organized so aimed to look around first before settling into a spot to begin reading through the records. She walked past the shelves in the middle and through to the entry doors, crossing Mariana again before heading down the other side of the room. She looked through everything lining the shelves, at the names of the books and kept moving. Just as she was about to cross over to the shelf she had started at, her eyes were drawn to the very end of the aisle.

Almost flush to the shelf and the wall sat a chair. She could only see a portion of the leg and the armrest from where she stood, but it seemed oddly out of place. She walked towards the chair and noted it was nearly untouched by dust, only a very fair layer sat on the chair as if it had been used recently, or at least recently considering it was still covered in dust. The rest of the room had a denser layer of it, though, which stood out to her as she looked at this strangely placed seat.

She pulled the lantern closer to it and noticed a small broach pinned the inner cushion, almost under the armrest. She leaned in until she could make out what was on the broach. A small filigree read the initials LT with a large Q in the center. Tandy frowned as she looked at it, a beautiful trinket with colors matching the insignia of the Royal family.

The blood drained from Tandy's face as she realized who this broach belonged to. She immediately began picking at the chair for anything else that may be hidden, prodding gently. She nearly moved to the shelf to begin her search when she nudged the chair slightly. It was heavier than the one they had moved for Mariana but it was certainly the same chair, there was no reason for it to be heavier. She hit the ground and looked underneath the cushion.

Under the chair carefully wrapped was a parcel. It was tucked into the chair in what looked to be a small embroidered piece of fabric sewn with small button knots to hold in under the chair within the frame of the cushion. Tandy put the lantern on the book shelf and bent to the chair, turning it onto its back. She exposed the belly of the seat and brought the lantern back down with her. The fabric holding the parcel tight to the chair was needled with the same initials over and over again. With shaky hands, Tandy grasped the parcel and pulled it from its hiding place. She held it to her face, but it was in a sealed bag. She held it to her chest to scan the pocket for anything more and found a small envelope. She opened that first, reading the careful script scrawled on the parchment.

If you are reading this, you will be looking for a specific decree and details on a betrothal. You will not find it in the shelves, I have saved it from the fireplace that would have been its fate years ago. It was kept in the office of the Royal King until I was able to find it and protect it.

Everything I have done, I have done with solely my son at the forefront of my heart. Though my mind may not remember for much longer, there will be nothing that stops me from ensuring the safety and wellbeing of my son, the crowned Prince.

You are my heart, my love.

LMT - Lorraine Eugenia Tolzari, Queen of Kronevalta

Tandy gasped as her theory of the origin of the broach was confirmed. Her hands trembled as she clutched the letter in her hands. Footsteps approached her as she shook on the floor in shock and fear as she read what was probably the last coherent thought the Queen ever had.

"What happened?" Sir Felton asked with a Knight close behind. She wordlessly offered him the letter and began opening the small parcel.

"We need Davian and Sir Bryson immediately, Sir Felton. I'm afraid this cannot wait, irregardless of guests and interrogations," she said as she pulled a very heavy and dense book from the burlap parcel it was contained in. Sir Felton told the Knights to send for the Prince and his night and for additional men to be gathered to ensure their safety as well.

As she opened the book to the first page, she realized quickly that this book was a journal of the Queen's and likely had the answers they were looking for for everything. She turned the pages, skimming briefly until a rolled up and tiny parchment slid from the binding of the book. Tandy tentatively but resolutely pulled it from where it hid and placed the book on her lap. She held the small piece of paper and unrolled it slowly so as not to damage it.

Betrothal Agreement of Duchess Tandanea Isodora Leighton and Prince Davian Elroy Tolzari

Tandy's eyes blurred as she read the document. She felt dizzy as she took in the dates agreed upon between her mother and father, and the King and Queen. Their signatures lined the bottom of the document, perfect filigree with each stroke. She took a deep breath to settle her nerves and continued to read, counting backwards of the years and months that led to their original date of betrothal versus the year her and Davian were even made aware of it.

She nearly dropped the book altogether when she realized just when she had been betrothed to Davian.

"I was nought but six months old when I was promised to him," she said in a whisper.

Twenty Four

Davian

"Should we see to your mother first?" Bryson asked as they began the trek down the hallways to begin their formal interrogation of the guests.

"I don't think I'm ready to face her just yet," Davian said quietly. "I suppose that makes me a coward, though."

"Not at all, you're grieving and we don't know what hand she had in this yet either. We can wait for her," Bryon said. "I'll call on the Knights to ensure her safety until then and have maids wait on her, as well." Davian nodded, grateful for the thoughtful suggestion though he couldn't find the strength to visit her first. The guilt of wondering if she was afraid or lonely was too much to handle, though, so he immersed himself in questioning the guests with as much intensity as he could.

By the time they made it to the fourth room for interrogations, it was obvious they'd be done by lunchtime with all the evidence they needed in order to try Martina for her crimes against the crown. Bryson and Davian painstakingly asked question after question, the same ones over and over, and the majority of the guests all generally had the same response.

"I saw them leaving together, but I felt as though my body were suspended in a strange state," one woman said.

"I wanted to follow my friends and business partners along, but my feet melted to the floor. I couldn't move, I could hardly even think," a man told them.

Everyone agreed they could not explain the strange sensations that befell them during the ball. Most felt sick as they had woken up and wrote it off on the wine and mead that was served. They left each room with solid evidence and witnesses that the King left with Martina the night of the ball and hadn't been seen again.

There were a select few of the guest list that hadn't mentioned feeling strange, even with gentle questioning to lead them towards an explanation on the behavior of everyone at the ball. For the ones that acted as though nothing was wrong, Bryson and Davian agreed that they would revisit them with a secondary interrogation, but they would send home the guests that were not perceived as a threat.

By noon, they'd made it through more than half of the guest list. The Housekeeper followed behind them diligently as guests were allowed to slowly make their way from the castle with stable hands guiding carriages to the front entrance. It was good that most of them had needed a day to sleep off the adverse effects of the Lethe, though most hadn't known what had happened or what they were even exposed to.

"We'll have to send for them to come back soon to make sure no one suffers ill effects, but I don't think telling them about the elixir would be helpful. It may cause them to seek it out once they know of its name," Davian had murmured to Bryson before leading them into another room.

"It would be risky to expose them and then also give them the name and location of the elixirs," Bryson agreed.

Another hour passed when a group of Knights approached them after they left one of the last rooms they needed to question.

"You're needed in the records room," the Knight in front told them quietly. Bryson and Davian shared a look before following the Knights with trepidation. The walk was agonizing but Davian knew it was a short distance from the guest wing despite the feeling that he was walking in slow motion.

As they made it to the doors, the Knights wordlessly stepped out of the way and allowed them in. They were cast into a dark room but followed the candlelight illuminating from behind a shelf towards the back. They stepped into the narrow aisle that held books and records and found Tandy sitting on the floor next to an overturned chair.

Tandy was holding a leatherbound book thick with pages that were heavy with text scrawled across the pages in neat and tidy lines. She turned a page before they all looked up to see Davian and Bryson standing there.

"You'll never believe what we found, Davian," Mariana whispered as she delicately held a parchment in her hands. Tandy said nothing, only continued to read the book in her hands with her feet tucked underneath her. Davian stepped closer to Tandy, nodding at Sir Felton as he stood in the space between the shelf and the wall of the next aisle.

"What happened?" Davian couldn't help but ask.

"We have the answers we need, Davian," Mariana told him.

"Duchess Tandanea made quite the discovery, Your Highness," Sir Felton added. Mariana handed him the piece of paper she held in her hands. He held it to his face and squinted in the dark before he turned toward a lantern to better see what was on it.

He recognized the script immediately and his heart dropped.

"My mother," he said. Bryson pushed closer to him to read over his shoulder.

"You've been betrothed Tandy's *whole* life," Bryson said in shock.

"Not only that, but the Queen foresaw everything happening now, and made an effort to hide the documents we needed most," Mariana explained. "We have the decrees and laws we need in this book and the hard copies of them, too. Your mother folded them up and hid them for your safety, Davian." Mariana handed Bryson the rest of the papers she had held on her lap and he looked over them. He read the decree out loud for them to hear.

"*I, King Jerem Borix Tolzari, decree that a betrothal existing for longer than eight years shall be exempt from any period of mourning as it has been upheld by both parties in its purity. The mourning period does not supercede the longevity of the betrothal in this instance and only in this instance, no matter the loss. The enduring betrothal will be the only exception to the mourning period as it demonstrates not only an exceeding loyalty to the promised, but also to the throne, to the Royal bloodline, to the kingdom.*" Bryson finished.

Davian was at a loss for words as he held a letter written by his mother when he was very small that supplied them with everything they needed in order to get married without waiting for the mourning period to complete. Though they had Martina locked down, the risk to them and the throne was still a concern as they did not know how far the tendrils of deceit went.

"Your *whole* life," he murmured in dismay, shaking his head.

"What does the book tell us, Tandy?" Bryson asked.

"So far it is an incredibly detailed documentation of *everything* that occurred in the Royal Circle when we were just babies," Tandy said softly, still skimming the pages. "The Queen was unseen in a lot of what occurred and generally moved in the shadows in order to save this for you, but she knew she would be overtaken by the Lethe at some point because of the King and Martina's imbibing of it. It's been around for a *long* time, Davian. Long before it was even in the poor districts, it was here." She looked up at him as she held tightly to the book as though she were tethered to the ground and only those pages could keep her from floating away. She looked small, but she was breathtaking in the candle glow. He reached his hand down to her to pull her to her feet.

"Bryson, you're Knighted, correct?" Davian asked, making them all frown in confusion.

"Yes, Dav. You were there at the induction, if you recall," Bryson rolled his eyes with a chuckle.

"You have the ability to stand in as an officiant as well, yes?" Davian continued as he held Tandy's hand in his own. Mariana gasped from where she was perched on the overturned chair, jumping to her feet and jumped in excitement.

"I am able to stand as an officiant, yes," Bryson said with a smile.

"Well, I can't imagine a better place to wed my bride," Davian told them. Mariana was nearly breathless as she danced with joy. "I don't want anything fancy, I don't need anything extra. The most basic of vows will be perfect," he added.

"Oh, Davian, always the romantic," Tandy said flatly as Mariana groaned at his words. "The accumulation of my lifelong engagement, to marry in a dark and dusty library," she rolled her eyes. In the dark it had always been easier for her to share her emotions with Davian. To see her small smirk quirk up at the corner of her mouth was all he needed to see to know that this was the right choice.

"If you must marry in the dark like forbidden lovers we need just a *little* romance, Davian. I could hardly bear it otherwise," Mariana protested though she still couldn't stifle the giddiness emanating from her body.

"Keep it short and simple, please. Mariana and Sir Felton, will you act as our witnesses?" He asked, pulling Tandy to the center of the room so they weren't quite so cramped.

"Of course, Your Highness. I can even complete the documents you need in order for it to be recognized by the kingdom, without bringing it to the attention of those within the kingdom. We can, on paper, have it completed before the wedding ceremony itself," Sir Felton offered.

"Thank you," Tandy told him without taking her eyes off Davian. She hardly looked nervous and even though Davian had made the suggestion himself, he felt like he was shaking in his boots.

Bryson stood in front of them, taking his place as officiant. Mariana and Sir Felton stood off to each side, her with Tandy and him with Davian as witnesses. Bryson bowed his head for a moment, hands crossed as if in prayer as he gathered his thoughts for the vows. They patiently waited for him another minute before he straightened. With a nod, the Knights in front of the doors backed up a few more steps until they were nearly in line with the Knights outside of the door. They formed a sturdy wall between the goings on of the records room and the empty hallway outside of it.

"Ready?" Bryson asked with a gentle smile as he glanced between Davian and Tandy.

"Yes," they said together as Mariana squirmed excitedly behind them.

"Prince Davian Elroy Tolzari," Bryson began. "Do you accept the bride offering her hand?" Davian held Tandy's hands tight in his own.

"I do," he told Tandy.

"Duchess Tandanea Isodora Leighton, do you accept the groom offering his hand to you?" Bryson asked her.

"I do," Tandy told Davian. Davian could hardly look away from her eyes as they were illuminated by the lanterns around them.

"Please recite your oath, Prince Davian," Bryson directed him.

"I offer you my hand and a throne by my side,
the kingdom together we shall abide.
I bind thee to me and our lives shall entwine,
My duty to you and my crown for all time.
With you in my heart and my crown up above
We will share our burdens, honor, and our love.
You will produce from your body heirs I bestow,
As many children the gods deem for you to grow.
I entrust you to bring forth my offspring,
To ensure the growth of my seed as your King.
Henceforth shall be your duty and charge as my bride
Bear the fruit of my loins from your womb to earthside.
You will regard me with reverence and ardour,
As I promise my life and devotion forever more." Davian finished his oath, hardly containing his nerves. The entirety of the promise sounded vulgar and inhumane but it was required for the eldest son to recite that specific variation of vows in order to inherit the throne. For each subsequent heir born to the king, there would have been a different vow for each to be recited to be considered a legitimate marriage. Though the wedding ended up being extremely small and anything but lavish, on paper Davian would ensure it was honored and nothing could be said about it being illegitimate later on. Tandy's lips curved up once again as Davian finished speaking, as if she could see the sweat beading on his brow. He savored the small smile and thanked the candlelight for mak-

ing her feel safe enough to emote, even if it was only a tiny quirk to the corner of her lip.

"Please recite your oath, Duchess Tandanea," Bryson told her. She raised her head higher and began to speak, voice strong and unwavering.

"I ask for your hand and to stay by your side,
Your kingdom together we shall abide.
You bind to me and our lives shall entwine,
my duty to only you for all time.
With you in my heart and your crown up above,
We will share our burdens, honor, and our love.
I will produce from my body heirs you bestow,
As many children the gods deem for me to grow.
You entrust me to bring forth your offspring,
To ensure the growth of your seed as my King.
Henceforth shall be my duty and charge as your bride
To bear the fruit of your loins from my womb to earthside.
I will regard you with reverence and ardour,
As I promise my life and devotion forever more." Tandy completed the oath in a level but quiet voice. Davian felt as though he had stumbled through the words himself despite the lessons he learned to memorize them from an early age, yet Tandy held onto her composure and pride with each verse she recited. She made it look easy and he couldn't help but smile and squeeze her fingers as they held hands.

"It is my honor to recognize you as husband and wife as you have completed your sacred oath to one another. Your Highness, you may claim your bride with a kiss," Bryson smiled and raised his brow. Mariana squealed behind them as Davian took Tandy's face in his hands and pulled her into a chaste kiss.

"We're married," he grinned at her as he pulled away.

"I waited my whole life for this," Tandy said, making Davian and Bryson chuckle. Mariana leapt at them and pulled them into a tight hug.

"Congratulations," she cheered.

"Thank you," Davian told her. "And thank you Bryson and Sir Felton," he added, grateful for their help.

"I think it would be wise to continue where we left off before your wedding, though, Dav," Bryson told him hesitantly. He understood and nodded, they had to complete the investigation as quickly as possible.

"Sorry Tandy, I'll be back by dinner I hope," he told her with another kiss.

"Don't worry, we'll be fine," she said. "Do what must be done."

"I'll have the documents signed and notarized as soon as I've escorted the ladies to your chambers, Your Highness," Sir Felton told him. "After your signatures are acquired I will have them officially processed right away and with most of the advisors currently being held in their rooms, it would be easy for this to be overlooked. It likely will be forgotten until you decide to throw a public wedding or reveal it to your advisors later on."

"I appreciate that, Sir Felton," Davian said in a serious voice. "Make sure the ladies make it to my room safely."

"Of course, Your Highness," Sir Felton bowed and headed to the door, offering his arms to Mariana and Tandy. Before Tandy took his arm, she grabbed all of the papers and his mother's journal. They left with a group of Knights and Davian and Bryson were left in the dark room.

"I suppose I should see my mother, now," Davian sighed.

"It won't be an easy task, but we will have to try to gather information from her," Bryson agreed as they walked into the hallway. The Knights remaining in the hall fell into step behind them. Only their footsteps echoed through the barren halls and Davian could hardly swallow the lump forming in his throat.

He owed it to his mother to stand strong, though, especially considering the information that Tandy had uncovered. Though their wedding was an unexpected turn of events, he was relieved it was over. Once Sir Felton helped them with the paperwork, they could finally breathe without a concern for the safety of the crown. A proper ceremony would be a worry for another time, a time when they could trust that Lethe wouldn't be distributed amongst the guests.

"Do you know where they're keeping her?" Davian asked quietly as he realized Bryson had been leading him through the castle on a route he couldn't make sense of.

"She's in the infirmary," Bryson told him. He recognized it the further they walked into the medical suites as the white and sterile walls greeted them. It felt like he was in another time, another place. It was half underground so as to keep the medicinal stores safe from harm, but windows still lined the adorning walls in the patient rooms from ceiling to midway from the ground. The view looked out into the gardens though the vines had begun to creep along the window frames. It was a soothing sight to see during recovery of illness or injury, he could remember the times he had spent there.

Davian saw his mother just as Bryson did. She laid on a cot with a white blanket tucked under her chin, her hands folded under the cheek she had resting against the pillow. She looked young with her hair laid out in loose waves. She hardly had any grey hair and it was easy for Davian to see her as the little girl she had been when she was engaged to his father.

"She deserved better," Davian muttered as he kneeled next to the bed, reaching his hand out to touch his mother's.

"She was very brave," Bryson said stoically.

"Your Highness," an older man approached them. "I didn't hear you come in, forgive me." Davian recognized him as the doctor that had helped Mariana just the other night.

"No forgiveness needed, Doctor. How does my mother fare?" Davian asked.

"She has been sleeping for a while, but I'm suspecting that that is normal for her condition," he began. "Unfortunately, she is very weak and I don't suppose she will be of much help to your investigation. The only thing she would say was something along the lines of, she is the key and the answer lies within her heart."

"I wonder what that could mean," Bryson said as he began pacing, deep in thought.

"She did not say much else, always in a frantic state of distress. I thought it would be best to offer her a sleep potion that works temporarily so as to give her a semblance of rest for a short while," the doctor continued to explain. While he spoke, Davian's mother's eyes opened. She reached for him, a strange look of concentration on her face that he couldn't remember seeing before.

"Is it done?" Lorraine asked as she laid the palm of her hand on Davian's cheek.

"She will be punished, Mother. We know what happened," he told her weakly, surprised by the lucidity in her gaze.

"Is *it* done?" She asked again, urgent this time.

"It is done, Your Majesty," Bryson told her as he stepped closer behind Davian to see her better. She looked relieved and squeezed Davian's cheek before resting back against her pillow and falling back to sleep. They all paused for a minute before Bryson began to urge him away from his mother. When they were out of earshot of the medical wing, Bryson turned to Davian.

"She was asking about your marriage. She wanted to know if you had done it yet," Bryson explained in nothing more than a whisper.

"How do you know?" Davian asked.

"She said the answer lies within her heart," Bryon said simply. "She said it another time, too, just recently."

"When?" Davian felt annoyed that he wasn't comprehending what Bryson meant.

"In the letter Tandy found, she called *you* her heart. She alluded to it again with the doctor, too. We have to check your room for the other copies of documents, or if she hid something else important within your rooms. With that clue alone I would say Lorraine has more memory left than we thought, not to mention the way she had grabbed you with such intent." Bryson hurried his feet and Davian followed to catch up to him, still taking in everything they had learned in such a short time.

"We will finish the final few interviews and have Sir Felton with a team of Knights do the second rounds of the guests we found suspicious," Davian murmured as he matched Bryson's hurried pace.

"Let's call for the maids to clean Tandy and Mariana's room now that we're certain of the crimes that were committed," Bryson suggested. "There is certainly no more need to study the crime scene when it is completely verified *with* witnesses that Martina was masterminding an elaborate coup attempt along with illegally distributing Lethe. We have enough evidence that she can be sentenced to death without a formal hearing."

"Let's send for the maids to bring dinner to our rooms, as well. I anticipate completing the interviews by then," Davian continued. "We should also inform Sir Felton of the next steps."

Davian and Bryson found a group of Knights and had them split up to send for dinner and for Sir Felton to prepare for the upcoming following interviews. Davian was certain the man could decipher the guests' body language well enough to exonerate them, or if they too should be tried with Martina. He braced himself to spend the next hours asking question after question again.

***

The interviews were finally completed well after dinner time. Bryson and Davian suggested having the meal delayed so as to ensure it was kept warm and trekked on through the rooms of the last handful of guests. The guests that would require an additional screening totaled two women and six men. They seemed to have knowledge of the goingson of Martina but withheld quite a bit of details as well as fabricated information that was contradictory. Their deceit had been poorly constructed and easy to see through but he would have Sir Felton and his selected Knightsmen to check for anything he could have missed.

Davian was confident that should the public ask him why he had a Lady sentenced to death, his subjects would readily agree with his ruling. He had been a lenient but firm ruler so far in his life, even without being crowned just yet. He just wished he had noticed a long time ago so as to save his family and kingdom from any harm they faced in the last few years.

"I'm starving," Bryson muttered as they walked back to Davian's room long after the sun went down.

"Dinner better be hot and waiting for us," Davian agreed as his stomach grumbled pitifully.

"I'm sure your wife saw to that," Bryson said with a quirked brow. Davian stumbled as he remembered what they had done today.

"Oh gods, I forgot," he said in a near whisper. Bryson only laughed in response.

As they made it to the door, Davian greeted the Knights and sent two of them to Tandy's room to stand watch on the halls. They opened the doors and instructed the Knights still inside to return to their post in the hall with the others, and to await their shift change as per the Commander's orders. Bryson and Davian closed the doors behind them and locked it, sighing heavily as they finally turned to the girls.

"We waited *ages* for you to finally eat dinner," Mariana said, exasperated. "Sit down before I starve to *death*," she added with a groan. Tandy said nothing but raised her brows as if she was in agreement.

"Forgive us, my Lady, your Grace. We had a troubling afternoon as it were, and I would love to join you for dinner," Bryson said as he sat heavily in his chair. The plates were sitting on the table with serving lids atop them, keeping in the heat. Davian barely made it to the table before his stomach growled again painfully. Mariana snickered but said nothing, but as soon as Davian touched the lid on his placemat, the rest of them followed.

"Oh thank the gods," Bryson said as they all stared at a plate full of steak, summer vegetables with potatoes and bread. Davian immediately dug into his meal, scarfing it down quickly. While he ate, he glanced at Tandy to make sure she ate something as well. He was pleasantly surprised to see her eat nearly half of her plate by the time Davian was finished his own.

"How were the rest of the guests?" Tandy asked as she placed her fork down.

"We're having Sir Felton field through the ones we deemed most suspicious, but we were able to send the majority of the guests home," Bryson told them. Mariana looked at Davian as she pushed food around her plate with her fork. He met her gaze but could not lie to her.

"It is apparent that Lady Ligotus was distributing Lethe throughout the Royal Circle and the inner cities. It is also apparent that many of the guests placed Lady Ligotus as the last person seen with the King," he said. There wasn't much else he could say about it but Mariana only nodded.

"I am not surprised," Mariana said slowly with a frown. "She's brazen, though I must admit I didn't think she would be smart enough to mastermind anything like this."

"It is also certain she will face her crimes with her life," Bryson added, though his voice carried low across the table. Tandy only blinked as she glanced to Mariana as they waited her response.

"Am I going to be questioned for having been associated with her?" She asked, not reacting to Bryson's statement.

"Have you withheld evidence from the investigation, or gained anything from Martina's pursuits?" Davian asked.

"I have never received anything but punishment, and if I helped her it was not of my own free will. It is obvious what she had me do, offering me to men decades my senior. I don't know what she gained from it nor if the *suitors* were pleased with me. Though it didn't matter, they took even what I didn't offer," she shook her head. "But if I were involved, it was done kicking and screaming and not of my own accordance," Mariana crossed her arms, her words cold as they gaped at her. Davian had known from what she had mentioned before, of course, but she hadn't gone into much detail.

"We had a lot of time to talk it over today while you were investigating," Tandy said in a gentle voice while Mariana sighed again, drooping her shoulders as she placed her hands on her lap.

"A very lot of time," Mariana agreed. "Enough time to rationalize the abuse and finally put a name to it. She is a despicable woman, she deserves what consequences she made for herself." Mariana rubbed her eyes before putting her hands back onto her lap and turned to Bryson. "I know I've brought up wicked and dirty pieces of my past, but I am afraid to go to bed alone. Would you stay with me?" Bryson blinked at the request, looking surprised.

"Of course, Mariana. You will be safe with me," he smiled.

"I know," she laughed. "I am very tired and would like to go to bed, now. Shall we leave the newlyweds to it?" Bryson chuckled and agreed, standing. He offered his hand to Mariana and she took it.

"Goodnight, then," Bryson said as they opened the door. Tandy nodded to them and they left hand in hand.

"Let's get ready for bed," Tandy told Davian. She stood and reached her hand out and he took it into his own.

She led him towards the bed and Davian's brows raised with curiosity. She continued to lead him past the bed and into the bathroom where she began to fill up the tub. Once the drain was in, Tandy turned around to face Davian, dropping his hand from her grip. She placed her hands on his chest and pushed him back a few steps.

"What -" he asked, but she stepped back from him. His jaw dropped as she pulled the sleeves off her gown and let it slide down her legs and to the floor. She raised her brows at him as she stood in only her panties, but he could only look at her. She ran her fingers along the waist of her panties before she pulled them down and kicked them off. She looked up at him with a mischievous glint in her eye before she leaned over to touch the water. He couldn't hold back as she held her ass in the air, a perfect height for him to grab.

"Gods, Tandy," he said as he gripped her hip in one hand and slapped her ass with the other. She gasped, gripping the side of the bathtub.

"You must really like baths," Tandy said, making Davian laugh.

"I might just like you in the bath," he told her as he let go of her. "Go ahead and show me how you look nice and wet for me." Tandy peered at him over her shoulder with her lips drawn in a line, almost as if she fought back a smile. She obliged him, though, and sank into the warm water before running her hands along her body and through her hair.

"Are you going to join me?" She asked, her hands trailing over her belly. He nodded as he enjoyed the view of her soaking in the tub before he slowly began to strip himself down. When he was bare before her he stepped closer to the tub but was surprised by Tandy as she raised herself up to the edge and leaned into him, pulling his waist towards her. As she kneeled in the tub, she was a perfect height to reach his cock and she certainly seemed to want to take advantage of it. Tandy opened her mouth and swallowed his cock, resting her lips against his dark curls.

"Oh my *fuck*," Davian gasped. She swallowed around him, the pressure pulling a moan from his lips. He ran his fingers through her hair and tightened his grip, pulling her off of his cock. "You feel so good, baby, but I want to be inside your pussy," he told her, running his thumb along her cheek.

"But you taste so good," she told him, licking her lips. His knees felt weak as she looked up at him, her hand tightening around his cock. He stroked his hand along her jaw before he wrapped his hands through her hair. He ran his other hand over her lips and slid his thumb into her mouth. She opened for him easily, her tongue rolling over his finger. He pulled his hand away for her mouth and tightened his grip on her hair before pulling her back onto his cock roughly. She gagged at the sudden motion but kept her eyes locked onto him, not pulling away. His other hand found her hair and he pulled her from his cock before plunging back down her throat. She moaned around him, eyes rolling as she let Davian guide her mouth over his cock.

"Fuck, baby, you're so good for me," he groaned, the view alone enough to make him want to come. "You like getting your face fucked?"

"Mmm," she moaned as her lips wrapped wide around the base of his dick.

"I'd like to come from this," he told her, "but not tonight. I want to come in your perfect little pussy tonight." She moaned again, the vibrations spreading to his cock. He clenched his jaw with restraint to keep from rutting his hips into her face again. He pulled her hair to lean her off of his dick and leaned her back into the tub. He stepped in after her and sat in the warm water, stretching his legs out in front of him. He pulled Tandy over his lap, sliding her ass until she was pressed flush against him. He held her with her back to his belly and placed his hands under her knees to lift her legs. He placed her feet on the rim of the tub leaving her pussy on display under the water for him to play with.

"Don't move your legs unless I give you permission," he told her evenly, making her shiver. He placed his hand around her throat and pulled her back until her head rested on his shoulder, tucked into his neck. Her tits rose and fell from the water with each breath she took and his cock throbbed with want as it pressed against her slit. Tandy's hips undulated as she sought the friction she knew was nearby, but Davian knew he needed to catch her up to him before he fucked her, or he'd finish first.

Tandy whined as he held her still in the water that way, one hand on her throat while her legs were spread wide. He trailed a single finger down her face, her cheek, her chin, all the way down to her neck. He circled her nipples until they hardened and massaged each breast with a full grip. She panted and wrapped her hand around his that lay on her throat, adding pressure to his grip. Her other hand reached behind her to find a handful of his hair.

He continued trailing his fingers slowly down her body, down her ribs and down her belly until he came to her thighs. Her legs began to tremble and shake with restraint from holding them up. He paused his ministrations to take her ankles and tuck them off the side of the tub, now letting gravity hold her legs open for him. It immediately made her roll her hips at the sudden change as his cock nestled itself against her pussy with the shift in position.

"Please, Dav," she told him, voice rough as he held her throat in his hand still. He loosened his hand slightly so she would moan louder for him as he finally trailed his fingers to her clit. She cried out as he roughly rubbed at the sensitive area, knowing it would overstimulate her and make her desperate. With her legs hung over the sides, she could hardly move as he did what he wanted to her, and he couldn't help but feel a thrill over the control she allowed him.

He slowed his movement until she began to roll her hips in time with his fingers. He ran his hand through her lips, feeling every inch of her. Despite the water in the tub, he could still feel how wet she was for him, how slick she was with need. He kept playing with her pussy, never in the place she wanted it most. He brought moan after ragged moan out of her before he slid his fingers further, prodding the entrance of her ass. She jolted in surprise, but moaned hard at the sensation.

"Gods, Dav, please give it to me," she said as he pressed his little finger against her hole until he broke through. Though it was only his smallest finger, she writhed on his lap as if he'd filled her with his cock.

"We can play more with this another day, when I'm more prepared," he promised her. "This will be good for now." She nodded against him, pleas bleeding into moans. He curled his finger as best he could with the angle they had, trying to find the angle that would find the walls of her pussy and massage the nerves there that always brought her to orgasm. He wondered if she would come like that, if she *could* come like that, but as she pleaded his name he knew she definitely could, just not tonight. Tonight he needed her, to fill her completely. He pulled his finger out of her and ran his other fingers along her pussy before sliding his middle and pointer finger inside of her.

He curled his fingers immediately and held onto her as hard as he could without hurting her as her back arched and hips rutted without her control. She was lost in the sensations with nothing but moans and gasps leaving her mouth. He pressed his fingers into her as deep as he could and curled them before shaking his hand repeatedly against her and inside her, nearly vibrating with motion. He didn't pump his fingers, just kept the frequent shake of his hand as her cries grew louder and louder.

Just as she was about to come on his hand, he pulled out of her. She cried with near anguish at the loss of the orgasm but he lifted her waist and guided his cock to her pussy.

"Oh yes, oh *yes*," she begged, reaching her hand down to help guide him into her. Her whole body trembled, legs still dangling from the tub.

Finally, his cock filled her pussy. Tandy moaned, squeezing Davian's hand around her throat tighter than before. Her voice sounded rough in his tight grip, but he didn't pull away from where she pressed his hand. She could still breathe, it was only her voice that seemed to be affected. He used his free hand to feel the space where their bodies joined. He felt her pussy spread around him, he felt his cock where it met her skin. He leaned over her shoulder to take a look at how perfectly they fit together.

"Oh my gods, Dav," she told him, the angle deepening as he leaned forward. He couldn't take it any longer and let go of her throat, using both hands to lift her hips onto his cock. He pulled her down hard, sliding his hands to grip the underside of her thighs. She held onto him with her hands around the back of his head and neck, leaning to kiss him roughly, barely meeting his lips with more than teeth and tongue. He bit her back as he circled her around his hips.

Tandy suddenly pulled her legs back into the tub before leaning over the edge. She looked over her shoulder and wiggled her hips, and Davian wasted no time in sliding back into her pussy. He placed his legs between hers, spreading her open so he could look at her ass as he fucked her. With the better view, he spread her cheeks before circling his thumb over her hole, this time a bigger finger. Tandy moaned and pressed back into him, matching his thrusts and squirming for whatever else he would give her. He leaned forward and spit on her ass and spread it around with his thumb as he pressed into her. He spit again and entered her ass with his finger, curling it under he could feel the slide of his cock under his finger. Tandy's hand gripped the edge of the bath desperately before she screamed.

"I'm going to come, Dav, *please*," she begged him. He fastened his pace and spit more onto his thumb where it met her ass and began to shake it like he had to her pussy only moments before. Tandy could only moan, but Dav wanted her to come harder than she had before and reached his other hand around to stroke her pussy. The angle was off, so he lifted her leg from the water and placed it on the rim again before dipping his hand under her raised thigh to rub her clit.

"Come for me, Tandy," he told her as he leaned down to kiss her desperate lips, his body filling every part of her. She went silent for a moment before her body tightened and nearly snapped under the pressure of her orgasm. She screamed, writhing against his hands and his cock still buried inside of her. She cried out again as another wave of pleasure rolled through her. He pumped his fingers and cock into her again and again, following the ebb of her orgasm until she panted beneath him.

"Now it's your turn," she said, pressing her ass against his cock and rolling her hips. She bucked against him repeatedly, he hardly had to move to fill her pussy. She ground against him and finally he reached down, draping himself over her to grab her breasts. He kissed her with tongue and teeth as he fucked into her with no regard to the water splashing onto the floor.

His thrusts grew erratic and he gripped her tits hard, pumping into her twice more before he orgasmed and filled her with his come. His vision went white as the pleasure continued to roll through his body. He rutted his hips into her until he was sated though he made no move to pull out of her, the heat of her core too perfect that he couldn't stop just yet. He gasped into her neck, rolling his hips one last time before he reluctantly leaned back into the water with a sigh. He pulled her back and draped her over his lap, tucking her under his neck once again but with gentleness this time.

"Wow," was all he could think to say. He missed her *so* much.

Twenty Five

Tandy

"Wow," Davian breathed against her cheek. Tandy could hardly disagree, her body felt warm and tingly as he held her in the water. From his lap she could see over the walls of the tub and noticed all of the water pooling on the tiles. A small huff of a laugh bubbled from her throat, surprising Tandy. She simply felt too relaxed to be able to lock in the giddiness that filled her after what she and Davian had done, though she was sure she'd sober herself soon enough.

They soaked in the tub for a few minutes longer until the water was nearly cool before they stepped out and dried off. Tandy dried her hair with a towel as they sat on Davian's bed, talking over the day they had.

"It wasn't quite the wedding promised, but it *was* intimate," Davian told her. She rolled her eyes playfully before sliding under the covers next to him.

"It was a good wedding," Tandy said. "Preferable to the ordeal a classic Royal wedding would have been, if I'm being honest."

"I thought so, too," he said, running his finger along her nose. "We should get some sleep now. It will be a long day tomorrow. I have a feeling it will be a rough one, too," he admitted.

"I feel the same way, it doesn't feel as if we are near the end of this," Tandy agreed. She had been thinking about it all day, really. Something didn't bode well for them. She wasn't sure if it was just paranoia, but she couldn't help but think there would be another death amongst the Royals soon enough, though she hoped she was being pessimistic. She knew she couldn't tell Davian that, though. He would worry even more than she could if it came down to her and Mariana's safety.

"It is strange, though," Davian said quietly after a long moment. "I didn't find Lord Ligotus to be of much use, if any, to the investigation. He seemed just as unwell as my mother had the last few years."

"It would make sense she would make him a docile pawn. She couldn't have allowed for her husband to take notice of what she was putting Mariana through and risk upsetting her plan," Tandy said. "She would have most likely been married by now if Martina hadn't drugged everyone in her life," she mused sadly.

"I'm sure wedding bells will be in her future," Davian told her with a kiss to her cheek. "Let's go to sleep and try to be well rested for the morning and whatever comes with it."

"Goodnight," Tandy yawned, tucking into her pillow. Davian kissed her hard on her lips, pulling her into his arms.

"I love you, my wife," he told her through his kisses.

"I love you, my husband," she smiled, kissing him back. She fell asleep facing him, hands under her cheeks.

***

Tandy blinked her eyes open in the dark room. She wasn't sure what had woken her, but she knew it was something in the room.

She rolled onto her back, eyes still scanning the room as she tried to make out what was beyond the shadows when she realized what had woken her. She turned to Davian as he lay sprawled on the bed, blankets kicked off of him. He breathed deeply, still asleep, but he had pulled the covers from Tandy's body and she was chilly in the cool night air. She went to pull the sheets back over herself and Davian when she noticed something *else* in the darkened room. She nearly licked her lips as she saw Davian's cock standing proud beneath his bedclothes. She kneeled and crawled over him as he slept soundly and slipped her panties from beneath her nightgown. She wasn't sure if Davian would wake up right away and wondered how far she could go before he realized he wasn't quite dreaming.

She gently pulled his waistband over his cock eliciting a sigh from him as he shifted beneath her hands. She gently draped her leg over his lap and settled against him, pressing her ass against his length. She wanted him inside her, but wouldn't be so brazen unless he was awake and willing, though she had to admit the temptation was strong.

"Tandy," Davian whispered, still asleep, though his hands found her thighs. She rolled her hips as she leaned down for a kiss and ran her tongue along his lips. He gasped gently into her mouth before his hands were in her hair, pulling her closer as he kissed her back fervently.

"I want you," she told him.

"Next time, I'd like to wake up with my cock in your pussy," he told her before he slotted his cock at her entrance. She shifted to accept him inside her, pressing down until her ass rested against his hips. He rolled his hips into her and she and met his thrust eagerly, eyes rolling in pleasure as he found the perfect angle to reach the nerves deep inside of her that curled her toes.

"As you wish, my King," she moaned as he gripped her ass with his hands, pulling her roughly down onto his cock with each thrust.

"I'm going to take my time with you tonight," he told her as he sat up, ceasing the roll of his hips as he kissed her gently. His tongue met her lips softly until he filled her mouth, drawing a soft moan from her. He slid his hands down her back and spread her knees further to the side to fill his cock deeper into her pussy. He didn't move beyond that, and Tandy couldn't help but pant with need at the agonizing feeling of being filled without relief. She felt like she could orgasm from just sitting on his cock and grew desperate, panting hard before pulling him into kiss after kiss.

He let her take control of his mouth as he gripped one hand in her hair at the base of her neck and the other against her lower back. She moaned as he tightened his hands and the slightest change in the depth of his cock sent sparks of light through her vision. Just as Tandy was about to go mad with need, Davian leaned onto his knees and laid her slowly back onto the bed keeping her spread open on his cock. She liked the feel of his weight on her, pinned beneath him as she kissed him deeper than she ever had before. The flush of helplessness under his frame made her belly flip and roll and she tightened her knees around his waist in response.

Davian pulled away from her lips and looked at her in the moonlight. He raised a brow before taking her wrists into his hand and pulled them above her head. He pinned them there, hard enough for Tandy's wrists to strain. She moaned pitifully as she tried to wriggle her hips for friction, desperate to feel his cock pounding into her once again. He pressed her wrists harder and placed his hand under her ass, lifting her to his hips. She moaned again, back arched near painfully.

"You like getting held down, you little slut," he told her with a sweet voice. She couldn't help but nod, he was right and they both knew it.

"Yes," she said, still squirming.

"You like to be helpless," he said, almost a question. "You like how I'm holding you here and you can't be free unless I wish for it." She nodded her head again, harder, the desperation near painful as she felt his cock twitch inside her pussy at her admission.

"I want you to move, Dav," she said as she gasped.

"You want me to move my hips like this?" He said with one deep thrust, sending his cock hard into her pussy. She thought she saw stars as she wailed at the pleasure that filled her.

"Oh *please*, I need you so badly," she begged.

"I don't think you sound desperate enough," he teased as he slid his cock out of her. She protested, but he only tightened his grip on her wrists. "I'm going to leave your hands here, baby. If you move them I'll smack your ass." She shivered with anticipation, hoping he'd give her what he wanted before she passed away from need.

"Yes, Your Majesty," she told him as her voice trembled. He let go of her hands and she gripped the footboard in her hands, trying to keep them from grabbing his hair. He slid down her waist before he kissed his way to her clit and sucked it into his mouth. She cried out as her feet slid along the blankets for support. He gripped her legs and draped them over his shoulders, pulling her closer to his mouth. He ran his tongue from her clit and down her lips until he reached her pussy. He widened his tongue and licked into her, filling her as deep as he could. Tandy screamed as an orgasm teased her, just out of reach, as he changed his tongue's motions continuously until she could hardly think straight. Her hands found his hair as she neared her climax, when suddenly Davian pulled away.

He flipped her onto her belly so suddenly, she hardly knew what happened. When his hand struck her ass, she realized she had disobeyed him by moving her hands from the bedframe to his hair. He smacked her ass harder, again and again, and though it stung she only begged him for more. She lost count of how many blows she took, but with each one Davian would massage her sore flesh before smacking it again. She felt delirious with desire as her ass burned from his hand. He slowed his hand before landing one last blow to her sore cheeks and raised her onto her knees. He pressed in between her shoulder blades so her ass was raised in the air. She wasn't sure what he was going to do, but she vowed she would be a good girl for him this time.

She felt his breath on her ass before she felt his tongue tracing her pussy. He plunged back into her pussy urgently, sending her keening as her ass remained in the air. He pressed into her to keep her from sliding back down and she couldn't understand how *good* he could make her feel.

"I need more," she begged him. "Please let me come."

"Not yet," he said against her slit and smacked her ass without warning. A roll of pleasure filled her at the feeling of his tongue inside her as he smacked her at the same time. She wasn't sure what could be wrong with her, but it was undeniable that his hands abusing her skin were delicious and addictive. He tasted her for another agonizing moment, bringing her close to the edge only to back off to bring her down. She wasn't sure how much longer she could survive his torment and could only beg and plead for him to have mercy on her. Davian drew away from where she lay and ran a gentle hand over the globe of her ass still on display.

"What a lovely bride," he told her. "For our honeymoon, I should like to see my handprint on your ass in the daylight." Tandy moaned at the thought of his mark on her skin, something she could carry with her for a while even after they had left their bed. Davian laughed at her reaction and continued to slide his hand along her body. He turned her onto her back slowly and soothed her trembling. She hadn't realized she was shaking until he held her hands and thighs in comfort. He kissed along her belly before resting his weight above her once again and drew her lips to his. He overwhelmed her mouth with licks and bites and she could only accept what he offered. Her limbs felt distant to her and she wasn't sure if she could move even if she tried. Davian spread her thighs apart with his knees and ran his thumb over her pussy, before he rested his cock at her entrance once again.

"You're dripping for me," he said. "So good for me."

"Just for you," she told him, aching painfully as the head of his cock sat at the entrance of her pussy. "Please," she begged as she tried to roll her hips. He slowly slid inside of her, pressing his whole body along her own. Tandy's mind nearly went blank with lust, unable to make any more requests with her voice. She felt primal, instinctual. All she wanted was for Davian to stay inside of her, to fill her until she couldn't bear it any longer.

"You feel so good," he whispered as he peppered kisses along her cheek, trailing them into her neck until he traded his lips for teeth. He bit her softly just under her jaw, nipping at her skin. Tandy couldn't tell if she was making individual moans or one elongated moan, all she knew was that Davian would ruin her if he kept this up.

"*Oh,*" she cried at his words, scratching her hands along his back.

"I wanted to take my time with you," he told her through his lips as they traveled their way across her skin with love bites planted at random, savoring her. "We're always so rushed, even when we first made love. Remember that night, Tandy?" He shifted his hips with a sigh, bringing a deep moan from Tandy.

"I remember," she gasped, holding onto his waist with her knees.

"I had not taken my time with you, but the look on your face when my cock filled you," he paused to kiss her hard. His tongue filled her mouth with his tongue in the same motions as his cock as it ground into her. Tandy cried out, pulling his hair and tightened her grip on his waist with her knees. "You came *so* hard for me that night, and so quick too. I have craved you ever since."

"Please, Dav," she begged him, tears brimming in her eyes. She couldn't handle it, she needed him to fuck her and put her out of her misery. He was *so* good, filled her so perfectly she felt she would burst.

"You begged me just like that our first time," he grinned down at her. He wiped her eyes as they flooded with tears but he kept his hips locked against hers. "Was it your first orgasm, too?"

"Yes," she panted. He looked down at her with his brows raised. He pulled his cock out and slammed back into her and she screamed, the pleasure too much for her body to ignore. She orgasmed hard around his cock as tears fell from her eyes at the suddenness of the sensations. She clawed at Davian's back but he made no moves to fuck her through her orgasm and only observed her falling apart as he held her still.

"What a good girl," he plunged his tongue into her mouth roughly, pulling another moan from her lips. As Tandy's body recovered, she found she felt nearly the same level of need as before. "I quite like having you spread like this," he told her as he leaned up slightly and pressed her knees into the mattress. He slid her knees up higher, tucking them near her upper arms, leaving her toes midair. He took her hands and wrapped them around the underside of her knees.

"You will hold your legs just like this," he told her.

"Yes," she told him before she let out a wail. Davian kneeled and brought her ass slightly higher and fucked into her pussy with one thrust. The snap of his hips sent stars to Tandy's eyes, she could only grip her thighs in desperation. Through her moans she begged him to fill her. He snapped his hips again, bringing tears once more from Tandy. She was so overstimulated, her pussy was begging her for relief. She could only gasp and cry out as he paused his hips once again. She looked up at him as she lay there, taking in the sight of his body where it met hers. She moaned again before reaching down to feel where they joined, running her fingers along Davian's cock. He quickly pinned her hand back to her thigh before pumping his hips into her several times in succession. She threw her head back with a gasp, but he stopped his dick from penetrating far enough to reach the spot inside of her that could bring her to orgasm. She groaned in frustration, nearly losing her sanity as he rolled his cock *so close* to where she needed it most.

"Davian, *please,* I can't take it," she begged him, wrecked sobs spilling from her throat.

"You'll take what I give you," he told her, not the least bit phased by how crazy he made her feel. He pulled nearly completely out of her before rutting right back in. She couldn't stop the moans from leaving her throat, it was impossible.

Davian suddenly moved and pulled her to the side of the bed where he stepped onto the floor. He lifted her and the sheet from the bed, inadvertently pulling himself from inside her and carried her to the window. The moon shined brightly as he carried her there and opened the door leading to the balcony.

"In the moonlight," Davian said before kissing her. He carried her to the far corner of the balcony where a trellis covered in vines and flowers grew. She saw a partition there, blending in with the trellis and the wall. Behind the partition was a lounging bed, protected by an awning. Davian placed Tandy on the bed with the sheet from the bedroom and tucked the awning back against the wall, illuminating the dark corner with the moonlight. Tandy kicked the blankets to the corners before Davian crawled up the bed, sliding himself between her thighs once more.

He was stunning under the light of the moon, quite nearly god-like in his image. Tandy could only run her hands over his cheeks and into his hair. He kissed her softly before he grew passionate. Tandy reached down for his cock and stroked it before bringing her hips lower down the bed. She pressed his cock against her entrance and rolled her hips, enticing him inside. Davian moaned through his kiss as he met her hips halfway, filling her to the hilt. Tandy moaned as she looked over his shoulder at the sky, bright with stars. Davian drew her gaze to his eyes and slowly began to roll his hips into hers. He kept a slow and even pace, the pleasure curling Tandy's toes as she moaned each time his cock filled her. He kissed her lips, her cheeks, her breasts. She kissed his jaw, his neck, his chest.

"I love you," Davian told her.

"I love you too," she told him. Tandy used her feet for leverage and managed to push Davian onto his knees. She rose with him, straddling his lap. She pressed harder against his chest until he fell back and she was left on top. She couldn't take it anymore, she needed him to fuck her. She slammed her hips down and sent his cock deep inside of her pussy. "*Yes,*" she cried. "*Just like this,*" she panted as she pounded his dick into her.

"Fuck, Tandy, let me make love to you," Davian gasped as he held her hips tight with his hands. She nearly screamed in frustration, but Davian ignored her and sat up, draping his legs over the side of the bed. He kept her on his lap with his cock still deep inside of her.

"I need you," she begged him. "*Please.*" He kissed her hard before he pulled her hips up and back down. Tandy gasped at the sensation and immediately met his pace as she used her knees on the side of Dav's hips. They looked into each other's eyes as they increased their pace, each of them never wavering in their movements though Tandy's legs were certainly getting tired. The feel of his cock in this position sent sparks of pleasure through every inch of her body.

"Do I make you feel good?" She asked him as her orgasm approached deliciously slowly.

"Feel so good riding me," he told her as he grabbed her ass with both hands. She held his hair tight and licked and nipped at his lips. She filled his mouth with her tongue, tasting each of his moans as they fell from his lips. She felt a warmth spread all throughout her body and knew she would come soon. Davian must have felt the shift in her motions and greedily followed the rhythm her hips took as he used her hips to fill her pussy on his cock. She pulled his hair and arched her neck as the feeling spread further, threatening to break her in half.

Stars exploded from behind Tandy's eyes as her orgasm overtook her. It was slow to build, but the fire it ignited made her scream with no regards to who could hear it. She rolled her hips onto his cock, following the waves of pleasure that rippled through her. His cock was still hard inside of her and it brought another wave of bliss. She trembled on his cock but Davian continued to pump her hips onto him, allowing for no recovery. She was nothing more than a wanton slut as she begged him for even more than he'd already given.

"Come for me," she begged him as he quickened his pace to reach his own orgasm.

"Yes," he said, biting her lip as he rutted against her. He moved her to lay back down, never moving from inside of her. He raised her knees so they draped over his shoulders and Tandy could only take it, the depth of his cock sending her to the stars themselves. She arched her back and gasped as another orgasm threatened to sweep through her. She licked her fingers and reached down to rub her clit, still begging Davian to come for her. As Davian saw what she did with her fingers, he moaned. His hips sputtered as he trembled but Tandy only continued to moan.

"Oh *fuck*," Tandy exclaimed as her body tightened around Davian's cock. Like a bolt of lightning, the orgasm hit her. Davian's hips thrusted deep, once then twice more, before he came inside of her.

"*Yes,*" Davian moaned into Tandy's ear as waves of pleasure rolled through him. Tandy pulled him into a feverish kiss as he ground his hips into her. He pumped his cock into her one last time before collapsing on the bed next to her, finally sated. They laid under the moon curled around one another and gazed at the stars.

"Wherever did this even come from?" Tandy asked finally. Davian laughed, pulling her tighter to his chest where she laid.

"One day I wished to be under the stars and thought, this would be better with a bed," he explained. "I had a mattress brought in that was suitable for the elements and with partitions and the trellis with vines to help cover the area even more, I had an outdoor bedroom. It's been a long time since it's been used, though."

"It's lovely out here, I forgot how warm it could be," she told him.

"Let's go to bed, Tandy. Tomorrow will no doubt be tedious," Davian said with a yawn.

"You may have to carry me, my love. I am quite sore," she admitted as she mirrored his yawn. He obliged, pulling her with him before bringing her back to his bedroom. He rolled the other sheets over her body before closing his balcony door and tucked himself into bed next to her. They gave each other a good night kiss and fell asleep quickly, completely exhausted.

***

Dawn brought with it a team of Knightsmen sent by Sir Felton to retrieve Davian for the final rounds of interviews. They also brought their wedding certificate and had Tandy and Davian sign their names, still blinking with exhaustion as they wrote. Tandy yawned as she stood in her robe as Davian dressed. She wished to go back to sleep but didn't want to waste the day considering Mariana's mother would shortly be on trial, *if* she was tried at all.

"Will the trial begin after the interviews?" She asked him with another yawn.

"If they go as I expect them to, there will be no need for a trial. The evidence as it is is extremely damning," Davian said. "She's essentially undoubtedly guilty from several different crimes, most of which call for execution. Even if I wished to be lenient, she is not only guilty of mass distribution of an illicit drug and plotting against the crown, but drugging the Royal family *and* of murdering the King. Of course I suspect many more civil suits as well from other members of the Royal Circle as she essentially stole their fortunes through deceit and drugs, as well."

Tandy ran her hand along the journal the Queen had left for them to find as he spoke. She knew this book would be its own great source of evidence as well, but she was afraid to offer it to Davian in case it was mishandled. The Queen's whole soul went into ensuring its safety as it had been her only way of keeping Davian safe.

"I read some more of it after our wedding, but I felt as though you should read it first," Tandy explained when Davian noticed what she was looking at. She had desperately wanted to read it with Mariana when they were locked in the room all day but she could not fight the feeling that it hadn't been written for her eyes, but for Davian's.

"You can read it for me today," Davian told her as he stepped close to her, kissing her temple.

"I do not wish to overstep your mother if she wrote it for you," Tandy said quietly. Davian shook his head and pulled her into a hug.

"Don't think of it that way," he told her gently. "I don't think I'll be able to give it the attention it needs, if I'm being honest. The mere idea of it being the only part of my mother left... I do not think I can handle that currently. Perhaps after the trial, if my mother begins to show more improvement. But right now I cannot, and need your help." Tandy hugged him back tightly as he spoke.

"Of course," she said. There was nothing more to say about it. He kissed her gratefully one last time before he opened the door and joined the Guardsmen. "Be safe," she called after him as Bryson joined them in the hall.

"You too, my love," he smiled before they disappeared down the hall. The Knights that were left stayed outside Bryson's door and Tandy's. She was grateful there were so many, though she knew there wasn't much of a chance they were in any danger at all.

"Call for a full breakfast, sir. With coffee and tea," she asked a Knight. He nodded and walked down the hall to find a maid to send in her order. "Thank you," she told him before closing the door.

Mariana arrived just as the breakfast was laid on the table. Tandy had begun reading the journal while she waited for them and placed it to the side. They sat quietly together while the maids filled their coffee mugs and readied their plates. For the first time in a long time, Tandy felt like she was starving. She couldn't eat in front of the maids and waited as patiently as she could before they left the room finally.

"Davian let you read that, then?" Mariana asked through a yawn as she reached for her coffee.

"He said he couldn't yet but did want me to read it through," she agreed as she brought the mug to her lips.

"I don't blame him, that book is like holding the last twenty years worth of his mother," Mariana said. Tandy agreed, taking bites of the fruit and pastries. She tried the bacon and sausage as well and was surprised to find them palatable, she wasn't sure the last time she was able to eat so much meat without feeling ill.

"Tandy, are you already pregnant?" Mariana asked her with her brows raised.

"*Excuse* me?" Tandy said after she swallowed a mouthful of food. "It has hardly been long enough for an heir to have taken to my womb," she sputtered on the food as it scratched its way down. "I eat one normal breakfast and I'm suddenly a broodmare." Mariana laughed as she bit into a danish, sending crumbs from her lips.

"Oh, Tandy, it is so easy to rile you. But you will tell me if you *do* take?" Mariana asked through giggles.

"No," Tandy said as she pretended to frown, only making Mariana laugh harder.

"Careful Tandy," Mariana grinned. "If you're too much of a bitch, you may just end up with a litter of pups in there instead." Tandy shook her head as Mariana laughed, struggling to hold her composure.

"You're quite unwell," Tandy said, though the laugh that echoed through her words took most of the heat from her tone away. They continued to eat in silence for a while before Tandy spoke again.

"I wonder if they'll let us go to the garden today. I don't think I can stay in this room one more day," she said.

"I suppose we could ask the Knights," Mar said with a shrug. "It may be a bad idea though." Tandy knew she was right but stood from the table and went to the door anyway. She pulled it open to ask the Knights to accompany them to the garden. She didn't expect much but they told her they would send word to ask Davian for permission and would let her know soon. She went back inside and they sat together to read more of the journal before finally there was a knock at the door.

"I'll get it," Mariana offered with a sigh. They braced themselves for bad news but were pleasantly surprised when the Knights agreed to escort them to the gardens.

"His Highness has nearly completed the final investigation and will join you in the gardens for a late lunch," they explained.

The girls dressed with the maids' help before the Knights brought them to the garden. Tandy made sure to bring the journal with them so that she could look it through while they waited for Bryson and Davian. She wasn't sure what she would find, but she knew the Queen deserved to have her story told.

The sky was grey and the wind picked up as they stepped outside, but Tandy didn't mind. She had always loved the Royal gardens and was grateful to be there once again after so many years away.

"Thank the gods," Mariana said as she breathed in the fresh air deeply. They headed to the gazebo and sat in the lounge chairs, sighing contentedly. Three Knights took their places around the perimeter of the gazebo while another Knight stood by the stairs leading into the rear of the castle. The wind blew around them, sending petals and scents through the air. The only sounds Tandy could hear were of the leaves and the birds.

Tandy opened the journal and leaned back to read it while Mariana sat beside her in the large chair. She read over Tandy's shoulder, cheek resting against Tandy's sleeve. As they read, Tandy noticed a strange entry in the journal that left her unsettled.

I feel as though I am a stranger to myself. Though I certainly limit my interactions with the Ligotus potion, it seems to somehow hold me in its grip. It also seems to be that Lady Ligotus has noticed my apprehension, though I had thought my secret to be well hidden.

I can not know if it is my mind playing tricks on me, or if I may still trust myself. It seems as though she is slippery like a serpent and nothing can keep her contained. A locked door cannot hold her. On several occasions she has made her way into a room protected by key. She is somehow able to find her way despite all reasons otherwise, namely the rooms that had only one key made that were in my possession. There would be no way to enter a room under lock and key in this way, not without the key I hold on my person at all times. Is my son safe in his own suite if locks are now meaningless?

The locks I recover are misshapen and damaged, and perhaps it is nothing more than a pick lock with little experience, or perhaps it is poor craftsmanship. That is not what I believe, though. It may be the potion taking its hold on me that I am thinking of such ludicrous plots, but it is as if her breath is the very poison in her body, her blood a potion in which she can dissolve even the most complex of locks.

It is hard to trust myself when I feel so out of control, but there is something not quite right with Ligotus' ability to find her way through anything. For her to appear in those rooms I attempted to hide myself away in, to hide my child, my secrets. It is most disturbing, especially as she is very tactile in her movements and could pose a risk to anyone she touches if my paranoia is correct. I fear she is becoming the very potion that which threatens the life of my son, my heart. Each time she lays her hand on my arm I can't help but feel as though she burns me.

I fear I may be going mad already.

"Do you smell that?" Mariana said, suddenly sniffing the air. "It smells like..." Her voice trailed off as she kept taking sniffs of the air. Tandy followed her, noticing a rather sweet scent on the breeze. She couldn't smell it consistently, but with each thick gust of wind the scent grew clearer. Her stomach rolled as she thought over the passage in the journal, of what it could mean if Martina truly was Lethe come to life. If her hands and her touch, her very breath, were strong enough to erode the metals of door locks as the Queen believed, what could stop her from finding her way from the dungeons?

"Is it the flowers?" Tandy asked, unsure. She had a bad feeling that something was headed their way. Mariana's eyes widened suddenly before she stood up, glancing frantically from each side of the gazebo. Tandy also stood and looked around, trying to glimpse the area but could only see petals and hear the wind.

"Tandy," Mariana said in a fearful voice. "Something is wrong."

"It'll be okay, Mar. Davian will be here soon," she said in a comforting voice though she knew something was indeed very wrong. The scent grew stronger and Tandy felt her stomach dip again. She scanned the garden but saw nothing.

Suddenly, a heavy *clunk* sounded behind the gazebo. Tandy and Mariana watched in horror as one, two, three, of the Knights collapsed to the ground. One after another. The Knight by the stairs noticed and ran toward them, but he fainted just as he neared the grass surrounding the gazebo. The scent grew stronger and stronger until Mariana and Tandy covered their mouths and coughed, hardly able to breathe through the thick plume.

"Oh, Mariana my darling," a shrill voice cried out until the woman attached to the sound stepped into the gazebo. "I will make sure you end up on the throne, my dear, never fear," Martina told the girls. "With that slut out of the way," she glared at Tandy, "you will make an amazing Queen."

Tandy and Mariana stepped back but they swayed on their feet. Tandy didn't know what was in the air but she *knew* it was Martina's fault. She felt dizzy and sick, but she still tried to step between Mariana and Martina who's arm hung wrapped in cloth,

"Oh, no, no, no, that simply won't work for me," she nodded behind Tandy. A big man stepped over the edge of the gazebo and grabbed her, covering her face with a rag soaked in a thick and heavy sweet scent. "You will not be marrying the Prince, my daughter will. It will be the *only* way this works. I will see to it," she assured them. "When that wretch gives birth, I will give it to you to raise as yours and the Prince's. The boy will be infertile, what with the Lethe he's been fed all these years. The only way to ensure the lineage. You will take the whore's child and act as its mother. The Prince is daft enough he will not notice, Mariana, no matter who the child's father may be."

Tandy's vision spotted around her but she scratched and kicked at the man holding her. Mariana tried to hit him but he held her with his other arm and slammed her against the wooden post. Martina stepped closer and laid a rag over Mariana's face roughly with her uninjured hand. The girls fought to pull the cloth away from their faces for as long as they could, before Tandy could not feel her limbs any longer. She could hardly see as Mariana's body drooped lower next to her own, both of them unable to struggle against the hold of the drugged cloth. Tandy felt as though she were falling slowly as her eyes could no longer see the bright colors of flowers that had surrounded her. Everything was muffled around her as though she were underwater. The wind stopped, the birds no longer sang.

Tandy was swallowed up by darkness as she cried out for Davian, though no words left her lips.

Twenty Six

Davian

Davian and Bryson walked to the throne room where Sir Felton instructed them to hold the final interviews. As they walked, the Housekeeper intercepted them.

"Your Highness, I have the list of staff you requested," she told Davian, out of breath. "I hoped to find you before you began your interviews, in case any of the names were relevant."

"Thank you, Mrs Hollahue," Davian exclaimed, taking the notebook she presented him.

"This will be extremely helpful, Mrs Hollahue," Bryson said, taking the book from Davian to look over the pages.

"I will continue on my way, then, Your Highness. Please call for me for anything else you may need," she said emphatically before turning around and walking away.

"Thank you," Davian called after her, more grateful than he could begin to explain.

"I'll look through this when Sir Felton begins the questioning. Perhaps we will be able to narrow it down as we go through it," Bryson said as they continued to the throne room.

"Good morning, Your Highness," Sir Felton said as they entered the sun filled room. "Are you ready to begin?"

"No," Davian said honestly. "The only way I'll be able to stay in this room is if the chair my father died on is destroyed. I am not sure I'll be able to bear to be here otherwise," Davian told Bryson and Sir Felton. He wasn't exaggerating. There would be no way he could handle it without being ill and fleeing the room. Even as they had stood there for only seconds, Davian could feel his heart beating rapidly in his chest as sweat beaded on his brow.

"Of course, Your Highness," Sir Felton agreed. "That is a reasonable request and I should have considered that prior to calling you here." The Knights and maids emptied the room of anything even remotely related to the King. As they waited, Sir Felton shared his plan for the day.

"The King's Guard will lead the interviewees into the room where I will direct the questioning. Davian will sit on his throne and oversee it. The goal is to intimidate them and ensure they reveal the half truths they concealed just the other day. We'll make sure none of the guests are able to converse with each other, which is easy considering they have been detained since the ball. The Knights assigned to their rooms will make sure they are led to the Throne Room directly," Sir Felton explained. "I will ask the questions, you will look brooding and disdainful. Share looks with one another as though you're uncovering the truths to their lies and we will be through this quickly. It is inevitable they will face a trial as the evidence supports their involvement in conspiracy. However, it is not obvious the depth their deceit goes which is what we will be ascertaining today."

"A good plan," Bryson nodded before offering Sir Felton the notebook Mrs Hollahue gave them. "Glance through this in case any names can be narrowed down for this investigation." Sir Felton took the book from his hands and looked through it, skimming over all of the names on the list.

"None of the names match those we are currently interviewing. They could perhaps be servants of these families, though, we will have to look into them further," Sir Felton said with a frown.

"That's okay, I'm sure there is a connection somewhere," Davian said, shrugging despite his disappointment at Felton's words.

"I will take notes in case not all is what it seems," Bryson offered.

"Thank you," Davian said. "How long do you suppose this will take?" Davian couldn't help but ask as the sun beamed through the skylight.

"As long as it takes," Sir Felton smiled charmingly. "Lead the first one in," he told the Knight's Guard.

A Knight led a middle aged woman into the room. She wore a garish dress decades out of style, but her eyes were wide as she took in Davian on the throne as he glared down at everyone below him. If Felton wanted him to look the part of angry Prince, he would surely give it to them. It was an easy task.

Felton's questioning was piercing and direct, and Davian hardly knew where he would lead or how much time between each question. The woman could only weep under such pointed ire, but Felton had no mercy. Davian was impressed, if he was being honest.

"What were you offered by the Ligotus family to assist with the distribution of the Elixir of Oblivion?" Sir Felton asked.

"I - we did not - there was nothing going on," the Lady answered.

"The funds you received were added to your treasury. You will provide me with the details on this transaction," he told her. "You are being remanded until a formal trial takes place. I have all of the evidence I need. Right now, I want your compliance. Every other guest has already completed their interviews and now only you remain. I know everything and you will comply." Sir Felton told the woman coolly. She immediately broke down in tears and nodded. Davian knew she was the first one they had drawn for a formal interview, but the Lady did not and would hopefully reveal the truth quicker upon believing Felton's lie.

"Lady Ligotus needed the support of my family as we have a long standing relationship with the inner cities in the southern and eastern regions due to our familial line. She wanted access to some of our rental properties. She didn't say why but I originally assumed for Lady Mariana's betrothal, though that never occurred," she explained as thick tears fell from her eyes. "I was told that I needed to be a friend and provide these without a question."

"You aided in the murder of your King because you were trying to be a good friend, is that what you are saying?" Sir Felton asked after a lengthy pause. The woman's eyes widened and she stammered frantically trying to explain herself.

"I did not mean it that way," she said through tears.

"I think it is high time you explained the full truth, Lady Penser," Felton said.

"Lady Ligotus introduced us all to a strange new wine that everyone loved. She said it was made from her own personal gardens, and it became very difficult to say no to her. In fact, if I ever uttered the word, I would be overcome with a despair and rage so great I was afraid for my own life. She had us take part in most of her dinner parties, until it came to the point where many of my friends became desperate for it. It thrilled her to see them act this way, I am sure she assumed all of us felt the same about it. Once that happened, she began demanding items from us," she explained as she looked up to Davian with pleading eyes. "Funds, estates, horses and carriages for distribution. We were promised some of the profit and that our donations would be returned at a certain point. It was never returned, only offered the potion to appease us. We are *broke,* my Lord. She has taken more than we even have, and has been doing it for years. My family is doing well by my husband's hands so we do not suffer unduly with the financial loss, however most of my inheritance is gone. I do not know how she was able to access it and transfer those funds. She stole the lot."

"Are these actions recorded in the treasury or within the Penser documents on the estate?" Felton asked.

"Both, my Lord. I was instructed to destroy correspondence between Lady Ligotus and myself, however I was unable to do that. I saved the documents under lock and key along with the formal bookkeeping and the informal bookkeeping. If Lady Ligotus saw the real information on the Royal charter and treasury forms she would *not* have taken it well. I felt the need to ensure the truth was easily made out in the future. Unfortunately I had hoped the King would be wise to it sooner rather than later but he never realized. The only true concern we had was the fact that Lady Ligotus was strong enough to break through locks, something witnessed when we had dinner parties and things didn't go according to plan."

"Elaborate," Felton demanded.

"She seemed to be able to break a lock in her hands. Perhaps she used firing jelly from a pistol, but her strength and vitriol were unmatched the day we saw her do this,"

"Can you name the others involved?" Felton asked.

"Will my family be spared from the investigation?" Lady Penser asked.

"As of right now, it is unlikely you and your family will be spared from the investigation. However, if what you say is true, the trial will not affect you in a negative way. You will still be considered an accessory to the crimes the Ligotus family committed, however if it was due to extortion or your health and safety were put into jeopardy by the accused, you will be protected," Felton told her. "There would need to be quantifiable and definitive proof of your involvement being exclusively that of a victim."

"I have proof," Lady Penser said, wiping her eyes. "I kept our true records safely hidden. I had to change my security measures when Lady Ligotus entered the locked door of my husband's office, but gratefully she never caught wind of my secrets." Davian frowned at her words. He wasn't sure what she could mean, that Martina would be able to break through the locks that way. It unsettled him greatly, though, and he shifted in his seat before glancing at Bryson. He wore a similar expression on his face, brows raised.

Sir Felton dismissed the woman with the promise to send Knightsmen to her home to collect the documents that would prove her involvement only occurred because of Martina's manipulations. He also told her a few of the Knights would stay for the duration of the investigation in order to protect her family. She smiled gratefully before curtsying and turned to leave in arm with a Knight.

"Thank you, I should like to be able to live in peace again," she said as she looked back toward Davian on the throne. "I will assist however I can, please forgive me for attempting to hide my involvement originally. It has been incredibly hard to live this way," she told him before they swept through the doors and she was gone.

The rest of the interviews went about the same, though the majority of them were in fact dependent on Lethe. It was easy to see how Martina was able to collect a small group of assistants and assure they complied with her demands, the addiction was how she controlled them. The poor souls were suffering now that they had been without the potion for a few days, though their eyes seemed clearer than the day before.

There was a lot they still didn't understand, though, but not because of the interviews. The collective group did not have specific answers to the most important questions, namely how Martina was able to manipulate so many in the kingdom and the Royal Circle without the King's Guard catching on years ago. There was no answer for how long she had been doing this, or who she had brewing the elixir. They didn't know where her ties ended, or how she was able to do this while also imbibing the potion that took many a good soul away from their true character.

As they were discussing details on the funds the Ligotus family stole from the Leions' family, a Knightsman abruptly entered the throne room. He was out of breath with sweat on his brow, struggling to reach the throne. Sir Felton noticed and immediately dismissed Lord Leions and a Knight escorted him back to his room. In the time it took for the Knightsman to reach the stairs leading to the throne, the Lord was already through the doorway.

Davian felt queasy and stood to meet the Knight at the stairs. Bryson met him first and reached his hand out to steady the man. He was nearly white with a sheen coat of sweat on his brow and he stumbled despite only just standing there. The Knight's knees went weak and Sir Felton caught him. They helped the man sit on the stairs before Felton pulled the frantic words from the Knight's throat.

"What happened?" Felton demanded.

"The Gardens," he gasped. Davian's blood ran cold though he wasn't sure what had happened. Briefly, the words of Lady Penser ran through his head. *She can break through locks.* He took off running toward the Royal Gardens where he knew Mariana and Tandy had been waiting for them for lunch. They would have been there within the next half of an hour to eat in the fresh air, so close from now.

Bryson and the Knight's Guard followed behind him, though he was faster. He cursed the size of the castle for a moment as he ran through corridor after corridor before he finally made it to one of the side doors, bursting through it. He ran past the vines and the tulips, he passed the arches of wisteria, through the rose bushes.

"Tandy!" He called out, searching for her blonde hair. "Mariana!"

He didn't see anyone, but Bryson joined him as they yelled their names as loud as they could. Davian wanted to cry, he couldn't process what was happening. He needed to find Tandy and have lunch with her, she would *be* in the gardens like she was supposed to be. Bryson called out their names once again as Davian could only gasp from running so fast.

"Tandy!" Davian yelled out again despite the wheezing of his chest. A pit of dread filled his stomach, a quiet burning rage simmering beneath it.

A small hand curled on the ground as a woman's body lay on the floor of the gazebo. He couldn't tell who's fingers they were but Davian and Bryson sprinted the last few feet desperate to know. He would *kill* whoever harmed his wife and sister, he swore. With his *bare* hands.

"Mariana," Bryson yelled as he dropped to his knees on the ground next to her. He pressed a shaky hand to her throat, checking her pulse. "She's alive," he breathed. He held her in his arms and tried to bring her back to consciousness. Davian continued calling for Tandy frantically, his vision swimming as his heart raced.

"Mar, wake up," he told her. "We have to find Tandy." Mariana was silent in his arms and said nothing. Bryson stood with her in his arms as she remained unresponsive. She only breathed slowly and deeply as though she were sleeping. As Davian walked around the gazebo, he saw another Knight on the ground in much the same way Mariana fared.

"Tandy!" He called out again as the Knights following after them along with Felton began shouting orders. "What the fuck is going on?"

"Don't touch anything around the area," Felton announced loudly to everyone around the gazebo.

Bryson directed a Knight to check over Mariana for signs of a struggle and laid her on the nearby bench. After assessing that she wasn't injured, he pulled a small aid kit from his pocket and removed smelling salts.

"I am going to rouse her, my Lord," he told Bryson. Though Davian continued to call out Tandy's name desperately, he listened to Bryson and the Knights and waited with his heart racing for Mariana to wake up and tell them what happened. He walked towards them, though his limbs ached to run after Tandy, wherever she was. His fists clenched and unclenched as he fought back the urge to hit anything in his reach. The Knight ran the salts under Mariana's nose causing her to gasp awake, startling Davian and Bryson.

"Tandy!" Mariana cried out before leaping to her feet. Davian caught her as she swayed where she stood. "Where is Tandy?" Mariana asked desperately, looking around the garden. "Oh, gods, *no*," she wailed. Bryson placed his hand on her shoulder.

"What happened?" He asked.

"Martina and a man were here, we have to follow them," she yelled trying to push her way between Bryson and Davian. "I knew it wasn't a good idea to go outside. She insisted on being in the fresh air. Why did I let her go outside?" Mariana cried. "Please let me go find her," she begged them. Davian was not far off from his own reactions matching hers. He was going to lose the battle of remaining calm as he trembled with rage.

"She is not in the gardens, Mar," Bryson told her with a shaky voice. Davian felt unsteady on his feet and swallowed hard at Bryson's words. Anger pooled in his gut and he tried to remain in control. *Tandy could do it,* he told himself desperately.

"She can't have taken Tandy," Mariana said with tears running down her face.

"What happened, Mariana? How long ago did this happen?" Davian pleaded, holding her arms tightly. He couldn't let go, though he absently thought he might hurt her if he didn't stop squeezing. She looked into his eyes and gripped his shoulders just as tightly, saying nothing about his hands leaving marks on her skin.

"What time is it now?" She asked with a trembling voice. "We had only just come outside when Martina appeared. It hadn't been but ten minutes since we sat down *maybe*. It felt like we had sat down a mere moment before," she told them as she clung to Davian.

"Fuck," Davian said, squeezing his eyes shut. "You were escorted outside early, just after breakfast," he told her. Tears spilled from her eyes as though she knew what he would say. Davian's vision blurred and he vaguely realized he was crying, too. He hoped that the tears would dissipate his hysteria, though he was certain he would land his fist on the next disturbance he met. He couldn't *breathe.* He loosened his hold on Mariana's arms as best he could and tried to stay level headed.

"It's well past two in the afternoon," Bryson finished. She tightened her fingers into Davian's arms desperately. "What happened?"

"She came out from behind the gazebo with a man. They used something on a handkerchief to incapacitate us. It was sweet smelling, a scent I've smelled on her countless times. I could feel it in the air moments before she appeared," she shuddered.

"Send as many Knights that we can spare in pursuit of Tandanea, follow *every lead!*" Davian shouted at the Knights around him. "Why the fuck did this happen? Where *were* you?" He shouted at the Knights. "How was the Queen not protected in her own home?"

"The Guards assigned to the Queen and Mariana were within their assigned posts. All of the Knights that were within the view of the gardens were incapacitated due to whatever potions she had used against them," Sir Felton explained as he crossed the garden to Davian. He let go of Mariana as he listened to his words. Mariana continued to cling to him, weeping against his chest as her fingers curled around his lapel.

"Because of their arrangement and close proximity, they all unfortunately fell victim to the potion. With each assigned Knight unconscious upon first contact, no one was able to send an alarm until the Knight closest to the rear stairwell was roused," Sir Felton continued. "We have underestimated what we were up against, Your Highness, and we will do everything it takes to remedy that."

"How are you going to do that?" He asked, voice hitching as he felt his throat tightening, his breath harder and harder to find.

"Horses have been sent after for any leads, Your Highness," the nearest Knight said. "We already have men looking at every part of the trails leading out of the grounds. We also sent them in between any known path that may be taken. Sir Felton also sent the King's Guard to survey the gardens to find any footsteps or clues that may help point us in the right direction." Davian wanted to feel grateful for their words, but he only felt desperate and angry.

"What we know currently is that the Duchess is missing. There was a man with Lady Ligotus approaching the gazebo before they lost consciousness. We did recover a small piece of fabric that tore on the wood of the gazebo," Sir Felton said before turning to Mariana. "Will you explain your recount of the events?" He asked her.

"She was behind us in the garden. The scent was in the air, it's what I noticed first. The Guards collapsed before she made it to us," Mariana said, brows tight as she remembered. Bryson pinched the bridge of his nose, frustrated.

"What else did she say?" Davian asked, fury growing.

"She said she would take Tandy away until she gave birth," she paused before she frowned, eyes cast to the side as she remembered what happened.

"What the fuck would she say *that* for?" Davian growled.

"I don't know, but the wording is strange," Bryson commented. "What else did she say?"

"She said that Davian is infertile because of Lethe and that she would have me pretend that Tandy's baby is *mine* and you'll raise it as your heir none the wiser. She would have me be Queen by marrying you, it seemed." Mariana wiped her tears before reaching for Bryson's hand. He pulled her close and ran his hands on her back soothingly.

"Is she planning on *making* Tandy pregnant?" Davian said in a low voice, though a small part of his mind prickled at the mention of him being unable to have children. While upsetting, it was not nearly as upsetting as the idea of Tandy being forced into bearing children as a broodmare and the trauma that was to come with that.

"I think what we can be grateful for right now is that Martina plans on holding Tandy until she becomes useful again, which gives us a few days to find her at the very least," Bryson said as he paced around the gazebo. Davian glared at him but he raised a finger, gesturing for him to wait. "Do not mistake my words for callousness,

Davian. If Ligotus has an ulterior plan that involves Tandy being and *staying* alive, that is good news. Bruised or broken, she will be alive and home soon enough." Bryson turned to Mariana. "Can you tell us anything else?"

"It happened so fast," Mariana admitted as she sat on the bench. "Tandy was grabbed first and then the man grabbed me. He put the cloth over Tandy's face, and my mother put it on mine. The man was big, he used one hand to hold Tandy and the cloth and I tried to attack him to get her away. He tossed me against the side of the gazebo as if I weighed nothing. After the cloth was on my face it felt as though I was falling, but I could do nothing to stop it."

As Mariana explained the man's size and strength, Davian felt sick. He would castrate that man if he dared to even *think* about touching Tandy. He prayed to every god he knew that Tandy would be safe from harm, that she would return to him just as she had been taken. Not a hair out of place.

"Did you recognize the man?" Bryson asked. "Had your mother introduced you to him before?"

"She may have introduced us a good while back," Mariana thought. "There had been no untoward meetings like she usually orchestrated. He looked different though, so I don't know for sure if it's the same man or a relative." Davian's heart was beating hard in his chest with each passing moment, he wasn't sure what he could do to stay sane and rational for another minute.

"What is the man's name?" Davian asked as he clenched his fists so tight his knuckles turned white.

"He was introduced as Lord Vildegard," Mariana told them.

"Send Knights to the Vildgard estate immediately," Davian told Felton.

"Of course, Your Highness. I will have the rest of the gardens looked through and follow up with the others for any leads on where Duchess Tandanea may have been taken," he told them. "We will interview the stable hands and anyone else who may have seen a horse or carriage leave the grounds."

"We will find her," Bryson told Davian and Mariana.

Sir Felton bowed before dividing the Knights into groups to send to the desired areas. Five Knights were left with Davian and led him back to his rooms, though he found he could hardly stand the thought of going anywhere near his bed without Tandy in it with him.

"I shouldn't have let you go to the garden," he muttered as they walked slowly along the corridor.

"If she had enough of whatever drug strong enough to put both Tandy and I to sleep along with the gang of Knights you sent with us, I have a feeling she would have been able to get into the bedroom we stayed in just as easily," Mariana sniffed, wiping her eyes. "Even with a broken arm she holds no regard for humanity or pain."

"She would have done it either way," Bryson agreed.

"I didn't have to make it easy for her, though, did I?" Davian shouted, furious with himself. "I thought they would be safe with Martina behind bars and yet it *still* wasn't enough. I'm unfit to rule if I can jeopardize my own wife that way." He walked faster, breaking away from them.

"Wait, Dav," Mariana said as she grabbed his hand.

"I think Tandy is as good as dead and I hand delivered her to it," Davian spat. He tried to pull away from Mariana's grip but she held tight.

"You know that is *not* true, do not say such a thing," Mariana snapped at him. He said nothing, feeling the loss of his wife by his side as rage simmered inside of him.

The Knights followed them into Davian's room, closing the door behind them. Two of the Knights remained at the door and the others went to the balcony and the doorway there. Davian sat heavily in the chair he pushed near the painting, running his hands through his hair. He didn't want to think about anything anymore, he just wanted Tandy to come back to him. Mariana sat at the table across from Davian as he huffed.

"Tandy will be the only one of us that would get out of this unscathed. Martina is the one who will need to be rescued from her," Mariana said. "She broke her arm within seconds of disarming her, knocked her straight to the ground with a smile on her face." Bryson's brows rose, impressed at Mariana's words but Davian just slouched further into the chair feeling as though his limbs were made of lead and his head was stuck within a glass bowl. He wanted to break something, he wanted to scream and blame *anyone* else for this. He couldn't process the conflicting emotions he was feeling. He huffed again and swiped his hand over the table, sending the stationary and decor to the floor with a loud *crash*.

"Feel better, now?" Bryson said as he brought his chair closer to him. Davian felt him move, saw him sit down. He just couldn't react, his vision narrowing around him as his heart raced with dread that Tandy was gone forever. He groaned, clenching his hands before running them through his hair.

"Davian," Bryson said again. He looked up and met Bryson's eyes. "Tandy has the survival skills she needs in order to make it through *one* day. It will be one single day, I will make sure of it. As soon as you are calmed down, as soon as we hear back from Sir Felton where horse tracks have been made, we *will* be riding after her. There will be no way to stop us, Tandy *will* be found."

"Martina has a lot at stake right now, her plan may evolve within the next few hours as she weighs the pros and cons of keeping her as a hostage for money, or for what she had said in the gazebo earlier," Mariana said. This stirred Davian and he leaned his elbows onto his knees and dropped his head into his hands.

"If we don't find her soon enough, will she have someone impregnate her until she can harvest the child?" Davian said through clenched teeth, hardly managing to swallow down a gag.

"That won't happen," Bryson and Mariana said simultaneously.

"I'll kill that woman myself," he said through his teeth. "With my bare fucking hands."

"That's the energy we need right now," Bryson told him. "We will give you that opportunity. Now, let's get changed and be prepared to ride after Tandy." With a gentle nudge, Davian stood and Bryson led him to his dresser and wardrobe next to the bathroom.

"Do you need a maid to help or can you find riding clothes?" He asked gently. Davian only waved him away.

"Don't leave him unsupervised," Bryson told the Knights. "Have a Knight and a maid assist Lady Mariana in finding suitable clothes for a horseback ride. Do *not* put her in a dress. I want to see riding pants and boots and a shirt with full coverage. We have no idea what we'll encounter today and I don't want skirts being the reason we are ill prepared."

It didn't take long, though Davian wasn't quite sure he could tell how time passed when he felt this way. Sluggish despite the racing of his heart, tired despite the anxiety in his veins, sad despite the rage boiling through his veins. He felt like he'd drank an entire pot of coffee, jittery and flustered. He stood there dressed in his riding clothes and struggled putting his boots on. He knew he could call for a maid, but he didn't want to waste time. He took a deep breath and focused on lacing his boots until finally he was ready and headed to the hall.

"Let's go," Bryson said as he stood there in an outfit similar to his own, with Mariana at his side. Her pink blouse and beige pants looked brand new, and just slightly too loose around the collar. He wondered if she had borrowed it from someone else's closet or if it was something she had never worn before.

"Is there news?" Davian asked as they headed to the stables.

"Not yet, but I assure you, there will be news once we are saddled and ready," Bryson told him. "We do not want to rush and miss anything. If you feel tired or hungry, make sure to say something. This will be a long night," he told them.

"It's still only early afternoon," Mariana said, though her voice wavered as though she doubted herself.

"In an event like this, the hours will pass both quickly and slowly. It's past three in the afternoon now, the sun will be lowering soon enough and lanterns will be our only option unless we choose to camp somewhere," Bryson explained patiently. "I've arranged for Knights to follow after us with a carriage containing food and medical supplies just in case."

Three stable hands brought each of them a horse already saddled and ready to go. The horses were friendly and sniffed at them looking for any treats they had hidden away. Mariana giggled as the mare she was given nuzzled her neck. No matter where she turned, the horse followed. Her high bun gave the horse plenty of room to sniff and prod at Mar until she finally hugged her face and rested a cheek against the mare. She sighed, smile dropping as she leaned against the large creature and caught Bryson and Davian's gaze.

"Are we riding now, or waiting?" She asked.

"Now," Davian and Bryson said together. Bryson easily climbed into the saddle of his brown gelding, his personal stead. Davian's mare was large with black and grey coloring and had been his friend since she was born a few years prior. She was mild tempered and had been easy to train, always obedient and docile.

"Sweet girl," he said as he climbed into her saddle, stroking her mane.

"Ready," Mariana said as she settled into her dappled mare's saddle as well.

The stable hands led them to the gates and opened them. With a brief thank you, Bryson brought his horse to a trot and guided them to the gazebo. They scanned the area, looking for anything they missed while on foot. The Knights that shadowed them stayed close, with some on horseback and some on the ground.

"Better view this time," Bryson said as he looked over the area where a piece of fabric was found on the wood, still flowing in the breeze. "Mar, did the fabric match what Tandy wore?" Mariana squinted and looked at it.

"Maybe, it's hard to tell. We all have lace in our gowns and that only looks like a piece of lace. It could be any of ours."

"We should call for the hounds," Davian said. Bryson nodded and whistled for one of the Knights that waited behind them.

"Are the hounds still on the grounds?" Davian asked him.

"I will have someone call for them, the groundskeeper will have them in the kennel if they are still here. They are taken to training every so often throughout the year and may not be back yet," the Knight said. He quickly rode off and left the other Knights behind with them.

"You should be prepared that the dogs will not be of any help," Bryson warned him. He nodded, remembering how they had acted last time.

"They could not find their way out of the corn maze," Davian said. "They instead followed the trail of sweet treats left behind by children. They're not much more than spoiled pets of the groundskeeper, but I would exhaust *every* option we have."

Bryson was about to speak when Mariana gestured behind them. A Knight galloped towards them on his horse and they rode to meet him halfway. Davian waited with bated breath, praying to every god he could that Tandy would be found safely. He felt sick with worry, even more angry as each moment passed. He desperately needed the Knights to find her location so that he could rest easy again and punish those that wished her harm.

"Your Highness," the Knight said. "We have a lead. Horse tracks are headed off the property, not following a trail but heading toward the western lakes."

They all looked at one another and nodded, realizing that Martina was headed toward the lakeside villa, not far off from her estate. The Vildegard estate was in the north, and not near a lake.

"Let's go," Davian said, bringing his mare to a trot. "Bring the Knights around with the carriage and as many men we can safely spare, I want the grounds protected!" He called behind him. Mariana and Bryson flanked him, following his stride.

"Let's get Tandy," Davian said as he brought his horse to a full gallop, praying all the while.

Twenty Seven

Tandy

Tandy had undergone extensive training at the reform school, significantly more than she had told Davian. Not only were there lessons in which she was inflicted with pain or humiliation, but also survival training. She had been ingrained with techniques and strategies that ensured she could withstand anything, whether she was ransomed or assaulted. As soon as the handkerchief covered her nose and filled her body with a numb and tingling feeling, she knew what she needed to do. Though her body felt detached from her, she focused her thoughts together and waited for her body to regain control once again.

***

Tandy woke slowly, feeling dizzy as she regained consciousness. She was painfully sore and blinked her eyes open to look over herself. Bruises covered her arms and she was sure her legs too, though she couldn't see under her skirts. She was going to make Martina wish she hadn't kidnapped her. Her anger made her feel cold yet overheated at the same time.

She looked around the room as her vision spun, taking in as much as she could as quickly as she could. Her arms were tied behind her as she sat on a chair in a dark room. It was a storage room in a barn or a shed of some kind, damp and dilapidated. There was dirt on the floor, some tools and boxes in the corner. She was alone and could hear nothing but nature beyond the cracks in the walls. She pulled against the binds on her hands as she took in the items in the room, planning her escape.

Martina would have had to take her to the Ligotus lake house, as it was the furthest estate Martina had access to without needing a host and closest for same day travel that had enough space to hide Tandy's presence. With Martina's plans changed last minute, Tandy was sure that she would not have had another location prepared so soon. The lakehouse was the only place she could be. She listened to the sound of wildlife and the lake's waves against the shore as the frogs croaked in the night.

As Tandy continued to pull on the binds, she squirmed in her chair as she felt her bladder twinge. It had been hours since she had last relieved herself and she desperately needed a toilet. She bristled at the thought of stewing in her own bodily fluids, but feared she would be unable to do anything about it if that time came. She emotionally prepared for the humiliation of wetting herself and pulled harder against her wrists.

The rope that was used felt scratchy and scraped at her skin with each tug. She ignored it and pulled harder until it creaked under the strain and snapped, freeing her from the chair. She stood on tired and shaky legs and froze as the wood beneath her creaked under her weight. She couldn't ignore her bladder for a moment longer, though, and took step after step until she was at the door frame. She peered beyond it, searching for a face or a voice, but found nothing but darkness. She ran to the grass and gratefully dropped down and lifted her dress to go to the bathroom. She tangled in her undergarments but managed to keep her clothes dry, thanking the gods for sparing her the embarrassment.

"Where is that open legged slut, Damassius?" Martina called out from the distance. Tandy froze, steps away from the door to the shed. She wasn't scared, she only felt a calm sense of fury. Martina's voice was slurred but far away, but Tandy couldn't make out from where it was.

"She's in the tool house, Mistress," a male voice called out with a heavy accent. A city boy, she was sure.

Tandy had made up her mind on how to handle this situation long before she stepped out of the chair. She had weighed her options, narrowing them down to either running away or playing docile and feeble. She could return to the shed and feign sleep, slide her hands back into the twine that bound her. The other option would be to run clear across the field and hope to find a tree with enough coverage to hide her. Tandy knew Martina wanted to see Tandy humbled, to watch her crack and crumble under the strain of fear and desperation. She would play Martina's game and set a trap for her.

Before she made her way back to the chair, she looked around for anything that could be a weapon. She saw a broom stick that was missing its broom and quickly picked it up, delicately stepping on the floor to avoid the creaking. She turned around once more and her eyes caught on to an item that was out of place in the mess of the dilapidated shed. The cloth that was used to drug her lay on an empty carton by her chair, likely tossed there after they had tied her in. She took the items and sat back in the chair, tucking the cloth under her ass close enough to her hands in case she needed it. She placed the broom stick next to her skirts, sliding it flush against the chair legs. She fluffed her skirts until they covered everything completely and sighed, waiting for the footsteps just outside to barge into the room. Tandy drooped her head until it lolled onto her shoulder and closed her eyes. Her hands had slid back into the twine that was used to bind her originally.

"She's still fucking sleeping," Martina hissed as they flew into the doorway, wood creaking under the strain of their footsteps. Tandy didn't move even as the footsteps drew closer and closer. Though they neared where she sat pressed to the wall, they made no notice of the wooden rod she had pressed under her skirts.

Suddenly a hand struck Tandy across the cheek with a harsh *crack*. Tandy remained still, but chose to blink her eyes slowly open and blinked at Martina.

"You will wake, now," Martina hissed at her. Though the man behind her carried a lantern, it was still dark in the small shed. Tandy only stared at her with a blank expression, giving her nothing despite the stinging of her cheek.

"You ruined *everything*," Martina continued, hands waving about. She stomped around the wooden floor though it protested heavily under her feet. "It was going according to *plan* until you arrived and ruined it all."

"You killing the King was not of my doing," Tandy said with a calculated smile.

"That old fool only had to claim Mariana as his own but -" her words cut off as she realized what Tandy said. Her eyes were crazed in the dim light, though Tandy hardly felt intimidated by the madwoman. "You shut your mouth or I'll let him have his turn with you right now," she said. Tandy only blinked, unphased by the threat.

"I wonder how badly your plan must have failed to sentence your daughter to marry her own brother." Tandy said pleasantly, ignoring her threat.

"Shut the fuck *up*," Martina spat.

"I imagine that when the King didn't claim your daughter, you lost the coveted eldest child's birthright to the throne. You had planned for Martina to be the Crown Princess, and take the throne as Queen," Tandy continued. Martina glanced around, the whites of her eyes exposed and bright under the lamp.

"Stop speaking," Martina said through clenched teeth.

"You lost the wallet that was funding such an ambitious endeavor when your attempt at changing the birth order failed. You failed to gain the King's favor of Mariana, you failed to gain the King's favor of *you* and now you have nothing to show for it," Tandy said with a brutal smile. Martina rose to the bait and raised her hand to slap Tandy across the face again. Tandy let it land and laughed once it did, jarring Martina and the man that stood behind her. They gaped at her, shocked and unsure of what to make of her.

"You had decades to solve this problem, Martina, and you failed spectacularly. What will become of you when the Prince realizes what has happened?" Tandy asked.

"He will not know anything I do not wish for him to," she stammered, pacing the floor.

"Oh, so you killed Mariana, then? So she will not be able to speak of the kidnapping?" Tandy said, glancing between the two of them. "As I can recall quite clearly what transpired this morning. They are most likely already on their way."

"They won't know where we even *are*, bitch. You talk in circles to unsettle me and it won't work. I have *won*," Martina crowed as she leaned close to Tandy's face.

"I'm sure they quite recall the Ligotus Lakehouse, my Lady," Tandy deadpanned. Martina's face fell and she stepped back from her, continuing her path along the creaking floors.

"This isn't how it is supposed to go, this is all *wrong!* You broke my fucking arm before we could complete the plan!" She screamed. "You were to fuck the man I brought to that room, the Prince was to see you and break the betrothal on infidelity charges, and Mariana was to marry the Prince! Mariana shouldn't have been there, it should have been *you!*"

"You poisoned my husband and took away our chance of bearing children," Tandy said in an icy tone.

"No one could have predicted the loss of fertility," She said, kicking an empty bucket across the room. "That's why we planned on *you,*" she pointed at Tandy, "being the broodmare for the Prince and Mariana. Bear the children, supply them to the crown. Make some use out of you, a worthless slut," Martina's voice grew louder and louder with each word.

"If the King had claimed his own child as he was *supposed* to, Mariana would have been on the throne without any use for you or Davian. I would have allowed you to keep the betrothal as it was of no use to me so long as the eldest Royal child was in their rightful place," she spat.

"Your plan was haphazard at best, Martina. You think too highly of yourself, and wouldn't be in this mess if you had actually known what you were doing," Tandy said. Martina bristled and shook her head, but Tandy continued. "Only one of us is a whore, and it isn't me. You'd have known who fathered your only child if you had spent *five* minutes with her as a mother. Your ego is your downfall, Martina, and here we are in a broken down building with nothing but the rodents for company and *still* you think the King won't flay you alive personally when he catches you."

Martina screamed at her and once again slapped her across the face. Tandy laughed to instigate Martina, stalling for as long as she could before Martina grew bored. Though her cheek burned and her body ached, she couldn't risk Martina knowing she was only being held by her own free will.

"Is it time for my contribution, yet?" The man asked, impatient with Martina's delay. Martina rolled her eyes but nodded to the man.

"Oh yes, do be quick about it. There's plenty of places to tie her that will suit your needs," she said, standing there as though she was prepared to watch him assault Tandy.

"Well, then, I can't do it if you're watching, my Lady," the man said as he crossed his arms. "And I expect the money when I'm done with her," he added. Martina huffed but headed to the door with a sharp nod, stopping to look at Tandy. Tandy met her gaze with a cold and unblinking stare.

"You'll be rewarded for bearing a Prince, dear. Don't try to make this difficult, your Queen requires your service as a loyal subject," she said in a sickeningly sweet voice. Tandy fell into the training she was used to, numbing herself of all feelings as Martina stepped into the darkness. As she left Tandy and the man alone in the shed, she swallowed any sense of fear and hardened her gaze, bringing all of her rage to the forefront of her mind.

The man approached her as he unbuckled his belt. She needed him to get closer in order to use the rag with Lethe on it, the scent still softly permeating the room. When he was close enough, she would strike.

He reached over Tandy's chair for her wrists, but Tandy slipped from the binds quickly with the rag. The man fumbled behind her, reaching for where he thought his wrists were. She brought her arm around the back of his neck, and at the same time, pressed the rag to his nose and mouth as hard as she could. With his body off balance as his arms were stretched over the back of the chair, he fell to his knees, weighing heavily against her where she sat. His hands flailed behind her as he grabbed at her hair, but Tandy held tight to him despite the struggle.

After a minute, an hour, she wasn't sure how long, the man finally succumbed to the potion. She held it to his face for an extra moment to ensure he was completely unconscious and let him slowly roll to the floor. She quickly tiptoed to the lantern they had brought in and made a desperate search for stronger rope but only found twine.

Tandy rolled the man onto his stomach and tied the twine in a tight knot around his wrists. She pulled the thread around once more where the strands met in the middle, knotting it tight between his wrists. He would be unable to pull his hands free with the tension of the twine as tight as they were. To make sure he didn't escape, she tied his wrists to the hole in the floorboards. She left the rag under the man's face, hoping that the scent of the Lethe would remain strong right under his nose. Her eyes flicked to the belt he had been removing from his waistband, and she reached for it. She would use it as a restraint on Martina when the time came, wrapping it around her own waist to hold it.

Tandy grabbed the lantern and the wooden rod and headed to the doorway, pocketing the remainder of the twine. She wasn't sure what awaited her out there, but it didn't matter. She would kill Martina if need be, something she wouldn't feel guilty over. Sweat dripped down her nose, itching her skin. She paused a moment to listen for any sign that someone was nearby, but heard only the crickets and frogs. She wiped her face on her gown, drying the moisture and braced herself for what was next.

She lowered the flame in the lantern before stepping into the grass. With her first step, she lowered herself to a crouch. Her dress made it hard, but she ignored it and shuffled next to the side of the shed as best she could in an attempt to conceal herself. Her lantern was no more than the glow of an ember, and she hoped it appeared to be a firefly from a distance should Martina be watching. She listened for the sounds of footsteps or noises, but only heard the sounds of nature and hoped for the best.

As she neared the last corner of the shed, she realized the lake house was just beyond the hill. The shed seemed out of place, broken down as it was. As she walked, she neared the garden patio and noticed nearly every plant was overgrown or wilted. Though the lantern only brought with it a small beam of light, she was able to see each flower pot and garden bed as she walked by. It was as though the garden had been left to fend for itself.

Finally, Tandy neared the back entrance to the lake house. Much like the garden, the door frame was in shambles. Pieces of wood and brick laid on the ground, scattered as though kicked around over the years. She peered around the area, looking for a way inside that wouldn't alert anyone of her presence. As she crept along the side of the walls to find another way in, she heard Martina's voice.

"I'm nearly out of ingredients to make another batch," she whined. Tandy couldn't see her yet, but followed where the sound was coming from. She came across another broken doorway that was nothing more than a pair of hinges and splinters. She crouched lower, placing the lantern quietly on the ground and looked carefully beyond the entrance. Her brows raised in surprise as she saw what Martina was doing.

"When Mariana gets her crown, I'll enlist the servants to do this for me," she said, stirring a large vat of a purple liquid. It smelled sweet where she stood, the chill breeze bringing the scent of Lethe with it. Martina stopped stirring to reach into her pocket and pulled out a bottle of another ingredient, though Tandy was unsure what it could be.

"When the servants are done mixing the ingredients, I'll simply add in my addition and *profit*," she poured the black ashy soot into her hand still wrapped in a sling. She leaned down and kissed it, breathing it in deeply as she pulled away. As her lips touched the mysterious powder, it started to let off an ominous glow in her hand. She dumped it into the vat and mixed it quickly, agitating the liquid until it was glowing with whatever the ingredient had been.

"Just a bit of ash from the bones of a sorceress shall do," she laughed over the vat as she stirred with her one good arm. "The King never suspected me of Dark Magic, though that Queen certainly tried to gain his attention. She was not strong enough against me, of course," she giggled to herself as she leaned over the pot of the incandescent substance. "Truly, what an idiot for him to have been unable to see where I spread Lethe around so bountifully. The Queen was really all I had to hide from, and in the end she was of no more threat to me than that of dirt on my shoe."

Tandy couldn't believe that Martina had not only been the one *making* the elixir herself, but also *distributing* it, as well. The fact that Martina was using Dark Magic to create this elixir was not what Tandy expected to hear, but it made sense on how the elixir was being spread through the Realm in such an insidious way throughout the years. With a Magic ingredient, the Realm was helpless against the elixir. She wondered if there was a possibility of a Magic potion that could cure the effects of the elixir, since it was clearly not an apothecary that had created the potion in the first place.

She didn't know much of the realm of Magic or witches, least of all sorceresses, but knew Martina had to have done something horrible to obtain those ingredients. She doubted that Martina had the true gifts of a sorceress, though, because if she did, there would have been so much more she was capable of to obtain the power she craved. All she could do was make a potion that allowed her to slowly overtake people, and that was over a decade in the making.

Martina continued to speak to herself into the pot, never once changing the speed of her hand. Tandy wasn't sure she was even speaking to herself or if she was having extremely vivid hallucinations. She looked up from where she stirred and nodded or frowned and spoke at random. Tandy almost believed there was someone else in the room that she couldn't see from her position, but she knew that couldn't be. Their voice would travel just as Martina's through the cracks in the foundation, windows, and empty door frame.

"No, I *told* you it would work. They'll be none the wiser when I deliver a baby to Mariana," she said. "How was I supposed to know it would make it impossible to conceive?" She rolled her eyes and stirred the pot with a frown. "If that stupid fool had just taken her as his own daughter like he was supposed to, we wouldn't be in this mess!" She groaned loudly, rolling her eyes. "Well it is unreasonable to have known she was the King's daughter until recently - *stop* saying I was impatient!" Tandy raised her brow and continued to listen to her ramblings.

"This should have been resolved years ago, truly. The throne would have been mine and - *no* that is not true. The girl was an unruly and misbehaved child. There is no way to have known she was the King's, she had to take my *face!*" Martina dropped the spoon and pointed at herself. Mariana had been nearly identical to Martina, something that caused quite the resentment in her. "I paid as much attention to her as I deemed her worthy, it is not *my* fault she bore only my resemblance. Of her smile? How would I have seen *that?*"

Despite the lack of parenting Tandy had had, her mother hadn't been entirely cold to her when she was a child. She had at least provided affection and laughter when she could, though sparse as it was as she grew. Tandy couldn't remember how Martina acted with Mariana, but she did recall the nannies and maids at the girl's side through most of their play dates. The cold sense of wrath filled her veins once again as Martina spoke so callously of her treatment of Mariana.

Martina straightened suddenly, spinning around to knock over the assortment of items on the broken counter. She screeched as everything crashed to the ground. Tandy tensed as she sat in a deep squat, ready to move when the time came. Martina picked up the bag of ashes and walked to the broken door before dipping her finger in it. She poked the door knob and it fell open, allowing her space to pass. With that trick, Tandy supposed she knew why and how she was able to escape from the dungeon and how other doors posed no risk to her as she had read in the Queen's journal.

The curve of the wall gave Tandy protection from her eyes as Martina headed through the garden to the shed. Tandy nodded to herself and stood, still holding the rod and lantern. She walked into the remains of what must have been the lounge and sat the lantern on the counter.

She quickly searched the room for something more powerful than a large stick but only found debris and dust. She wandered further into the chateau, relying on memory of the layout to find her way through as the sky lightened near dawn through the broken walls. She hoped Lord Ligotus had left behind a pistol or a sword, but she did not seem to be lucky enough in those regards and headed back to the room with the Lethe. The smell was overwhelmingly sweet, like honey had been left in the sun with wine and fruit.

A scream fell through the air. Martina must have found her lackey in the shed and would be back in only moments, so Tandy needed to be ready. She looked at each entry point to the lounge and saw only one door leading deeper into the home. She ducked behind the wall and waited for Martina to enter. She held the wooden rod in her hands, ready to swing it at Martina and end this for good.

She waited for a few moments until she heard footsteps approaching quickly. She braced herself with her wooden rod and held it where she thought Martina's face would be. Feet echoed through the broken mess beyond the room full of Lethe, growing closer and closer. Finally, Tandy heard Martina's voice gasping through the open doorway, pushing through the debris until she was right next to the doorway where Tandy waited for her.

As Martina crossed the threshold, gasping and muttering incoherently, Tandy swung the rod. She made full contact with Martina's head as she ran past, dropping her hard to the floor with a heavy thud. Sprawled out like a marionette without its strings, Tandy swung the rod onto her again to make sure she was completely unconscious.

She followed Martina to the ground where she had landed on her side and immediately pulled the belt from her waist and rolled Martina onto it. As she looked at Martina's arm that was wrapped in a sling, she paused. A moment of empathy plagued her as she wondered if moving her already broken elbow was humane, but the thought passed quickly as she remembered what she had done to Mariana and what she had planned to do to Tandy, as well. She looped it over her arms and buckled her to the last prong that she could go, pulling the sling out of the way. Martina's broken arm cracked and moved in disturbing ways as Tandy tightened her into the restraints, but with each *crack,* Tandy found her lips curling in a gruesome parody of a smile.

With her arms tucked behind her and the belt tight around her elbows and ribcage, she would be unable to use her hands effectively without dropping her own weight to the floor. Tandy used the last of the twine to tie Martina's wrists together much like she had to the man, and looped it around to her knees. Martina would be unable to do anything but kneel when she awoke, Tandy made sure of it.

"It better hurt," she said as she scanned over the restraints one final time, satisfied with how it looked and felt.

Tandy remembered the ash the woman had tucked into her gown and rifled around her dress to find it. It was right underneath her breast in a small pocket, loosely closed as it rested there. Tandy placed it between her breasts, tucking it as far as her bodice would allow. If Martina was able to open doors with it, it was clearly powerful and Tandy needed it far from Martina's hands.

Martina groaned on the floor, squirming by Tandy's feet. Tandy kicked her shoulder, sending her onto her back. She grabbed Martina's foot and dragged her further into the room with Lethe, pulling her out of the doorway and into the light. She propped her against the wall and waited for her to wake up. She moaned pitifully as she slumped over herself, but it only made Tandy feel a perverse sense of pride. She wanted the woman to be aching as she laid there in a tight restraint that Tandy herself had put her into.

Martina let out another pained groan before she tilted her head up, still slumped. She tried to right herself but struggled with her arms tight to her sides, whimpering as her elbow was twisted. Like a bug stuck on its back, Tandy let her squirm. Finally, Martina sat herself upright and looked around the room. Her eyes landed on Tandy and she screamed, shoulders flinching with pain.

"You fucking *bitch*," she snarled, trying to stand. As she changed positions, her arm pulled against the ties and she screamed, stuck where she was. She couldn't move, making Tandy laugh sharply. She knew it would infuriate Martina, and Tandy was rewarded with her indignant screech.

"Oh, shut the fuck up, Martina. It's just you and me," Tandy laughed. She trotted over to Martina and stood there, golden curls highlighted by the sunrise behind them.

"My *arm*," she cried, shaking her head and trembling with the strain of the belt and twine pulling hard at her broken bone.

"My *virginity*," Tandy mocked. "Let's not act like you didn't just murder the leader of our country and attempt to use me as a human broodmare and steal my innocence, Martina. Tit for tat, if you will," Tandy said leisurely. Martina looked at her with narrowed eyes before she scrambled around, looking down at her chest and straining to pull her hands from the restraints without damaging the broken elbow. Her knees squirmed with effort, trying to gain traction to straighten but were held tight around the ankles to her wrists, locking her in the feeble position. Tandy watched as Martina shrieked in agony, attempting to reach into the pocket she had held the ashes in.

"Where - I *need* -" she grunted as she huffed, turning red from exertion.

"Awe, Martina. How pathetic you are," Tandy said, her grin taking a dark edge. "I hope your arm hurts right now," she said, stepping closer but far enough away to avoid her if she chose to use her weight against Tandy. She pulled the bag of ashes from her breast and held it in front of Martina. She gasped, eyes wide as she realized what Tandy had.

"Looking for this?" Tandy laughed, dangling the small coin purse filled with the ashes. Martina sat there for a fraction of a second before she shrieked, kicking her feet on the ground as she let out a full blown tantrum. As Tandy held the bag in her hand, some of the ash spilled onto her palm. She grew impatient with Martina's grating voice and pocketed the bag back into her breast. She leaned down, kneeling before Martina and grabbed her by the hair. With the hand still dirty from the ash, she slapped Martina as hard as she could. Her hand burned where she met Martina's skin and for a moment, the woman was stunned.

Tandy's hand burned harder as the seconds passed and Martina's screams turned to wails of pain. She rubbed her cheek against her shoulder, a sooty smoke billowing from her flesh. Tandy stood and backed away from Martina, looking at her hand as she watched it blister where the ash had touched it. Though it hurt, the pain was dull on Tandy's mind. She was too far gone with apathy that she could hardly register what the strange powder had done to her. She looked up to watch as Martina writhed in pain as her cheek charred in front of her. Tandy waited until Martina quieted, weeping as she leaned against the wall in defeat.

"You could have done much with the Magic you found in those ports you frequented. You chose to dishonor the crown and destroy a long lived family for your own endeavors," Tandy said.

"Mariana will marry the Prince and become the Queen, you have already lost," Martina scowled. Tandy laughed, shaking her head.

"I am and always will be the promised Princess, Martina," Tandy snickered.

"Mariana *will* be your Queen, you slut," Martina seethed. "You better beg me for forgiveness before it is too late."

"Oh, but you are missing something quite important, my Lady," Tandy said in a mocking conspiratorial tone. Martina narrowed her eyes, tears dripping over her burned cheek. "I *am* the

Crown Princess. I was married to the Prince the night before you brought me here, Martina. I have *won,*" Tandy's smile bordered on feral as she stared unwaveringly at Martina.

"You are *lying,*" she hissed, adjusting where she sat.

"I am not," Tandy bared her teeth, dropping the smile she had been faking and allowed her true facial expressions to rise to the surface. "I *am* your Queen, Lady Ligotus. You kidnapped the Crown Prince's wife. Death will soon find you, though I cannot say if I will show you the way to the next life or if my dear husband will. You can trust that it will not be quick, though, and I do find I enjoyed how that strange powder felt as it ruined your beauty. I wonder what else it can do," she told Martina as she walked toward her. Martina could do nothing but lean away from Tandy's hands, powerless as she sat there broken.

"Please," Martina whimpered. "Forgive me," she cried out as Tandy pulled her up by her hair. Tandy pulled her through the broken doorway she had come in from. In the sunlight, Martina's cheek steamed where the ash still sat in her skin, melting deeper into her. Tandy pushed her to the ground, not caring how she landed. She turned back into the house and placed her foot on the edge of the large vat of Lethe, kicking it over. It spilled all the way down the hall through the doorway they were in, filling the air with that sweet scent once more as it cast the whole of the halls with a pink glow.

"No! It must stay within the cauldron or it will not *work,*" Martina screamed out, struggling from where she lay sprawled out on her belly.

"Good," Tandy said as she watched the color slowly draining from the Lethe. She pulled the powder from her chest and placed it into her palm, the weight settling gently into her grip. "Now we can discuss your past," Tandy said, sitting on the ledge that jutted from the window. "And your future," she added, ashes spread over the blisters on her finger tips.

Twenty Eight

Davian

"For fuck's sake," Davian said as he waited for the carriage to catch up to where he sat on his horse. "How many holes will that fucking thing find?" He gritted his teeth, looking ahead as he listened to the men struggle to pull the wheels from the mud.

"It's too dark, Davian," Bryson told him calmly beside him. "Let them set up camp."

"I'm not staying here, Bry. I'm going to get Tandy," he said, urging his horse forward.

"Tell them to set up camp, Dav. The horses will break their legs on these old roads, and then we won't be able to get to Tandy for even longer," Mariana agreed gently.

"You can stay, but I'm going," Davian growled, trying to lead his horse away from them. They blocked his path, though, and prevented him from moving forward. He yelled, covering his face with his hands in frustration.

"It's time to rest, Davian," Mariana continued, pulling his reins and leading him back to the carriage. Bryson trotted ahead, telling the Knights to set up a simple camp.

"Your Highness," Sir Felton said as he neared. He jumped out of the saddle angrily, desperate to keep going even though it was too dark. "We've gone further than we could have hoped in such a short time," Sir Felton told him in a soft voice. "I know it is certainly not what we want, but your wife will be able to survive for a few hours more, I am sure of it."

"She could already be dead," he huffed, dropping onto a fallen log.

"She has more fight in her than that, Davian," Bryson rolled his eyes. "Give her some credit, she's survived the Fine Etiquette and Reform School." Some of the Knights gasped as they heard. Sir Felton's brow raised as one of the Knights brought a flame to life.

"Is that where she has been, Your Highness?" Sir Felton asked.

"It is," Davian said, guilt lacing his tone.

"I am certain she will not need assistance when we arrive, then," Sir Felton said with a gruff chuckle. "Surely it will have been handled by the time *we* arrive."

"What would you wager?" Bryson said, nudging Davian's shoulder.

"I'll give you a silver if the Duchess fucks up that Ligotus bitch," a Knight called from beside the carriage, unrolling blankets.

"I'll give you a gold if she kills her," Mariana said, bringing a titter of laughter through the group. "If she can break an arm, who knows what else she is capable of," she added, causing the Knights to look at Davian with impressed expressions.

"Don't bet on your Queen's life," Davian snapped, but paused as he thought of Tandy's actions and words over the last few days. How she protected Mariana and was able to break her arm and incapacitate a man in a matter of minutes. "She's at the very least making Martina wish she was dead," he said finally. She would be fine, he knew. There was no alternative to this incident. There was only one way this ended, and that was with Martina dead and Tandy by his side on the throne.

The Knights quietly brought everything around the campfire. They had a small meal and laid in their sleeping packs and waited for the sun to rise, though Davian was sure he wouldn't be able to sleep at all.

"We will take sleeping shifts and rotate through men, Your Highness," Sir Felton told him quietly as Mariana settled into her blanket. "I will be sure to wake you just as the skies are about to lighten."

"Thank you," he said. He laid in the sleeping roll and stared up at the stars as the flames warmed him.

Davian tried to sleep but couldn't settle his thoughts, no matter how hard he tried. Though he was able to doze lightly, he remained conscious and aware of his surroundings. He listened to the Knights as they whispered amongst themselves as they traded sleep shifts. Davian's joints ached as he forced himself to rest, praying for his exhaustion to be healed. He just wanted to find Tandy.

He wondered what he would find when they arrived, if Mariana could have predicted the outcome. With how Tandy was able to fall into apathy to assure her own self preservation, and that she was able to defend herself and Mariana with brute force, it was evident that Tandy would be recovered with minimal risk of injury. He just wasn't sure what her mental state would be after this, or what was inflicted to her while she was unconscious.

Mercifully, the sky lightened to a dark blue and the birds in the trees began to chirp. Davian sat up and stretched, quickly pulling himself out of the blankets. He looked around and saw that a few of the Knights were putting away the equipment that wasn't in use anymore. He walked to his horse with the hope that the sun would be high enough by the time he reached her and he'd be able to leave immediately.

Though it was still dark, he gently ran his hand over her nose. She leaned into his touch, sniffing his pockets for any treats he may have hidden. He climbed into her saddle after unhitching her, and headed to the edge of their camp. He waited until the sky was a deep blue, and looked back to see if anyone else was awake yet. Felton nodded to him from afar, and approached him with a small bag.

"Take this," he said, offering it to Davian. He took it and saw two small breakfasts and looked up at Felton. "For the Duchess," he explained. He offered Davian's horse an apple, patting her on her neck.

"I'm getting my wife," Davian told Sir Felton, though he suspected he already knew what Davian's intentions were.

"We will meet you there," he said simply, stepping back, making room for Davian to leave.

Davian wasted no time and led his horse onward. He moved slowly while the path was still darkened by the lack of sun, but quickened his pace as the morning light rose over the horizon. The sky turned from indigo to gold slowly, and then all at once the world was lit once again and he brought his horse to a gallop. It was a long ride, but he made good time after leaving the caravan behind.

He rode for well over an hour, alternating between a trot and a gallop to let his horse catch her breath. He didn't want to push her too hard in case he found Tandy in a poorly state when he found her, but managed to reach the lake house just as his steed grew weary. He felt both relieved and anxious as the large building fell into view, but slowed down and jumped to the ground. He led the horse to the hitching post on the pathway, taking in the sight of the decrepit estate.

"What the fuck happened?" He asked himself as he looked around the nearly rotted roof accented by fractured windows and walls. He approached the front door but it was too broken to move from where it was, and followed the weed covered path to the back of the house. As he rounded the corner, he heard screaming. His stomach dropped at the sound and immediately started running towards it.

Another shriek split the air as he ran through the gardens. The patio that led into the home from the garden was on display, yet severely damaged by time and weather. Nothing looked the same, but he nearly collapsed when he saw Tandy standing there. She had dried blood dripping from her nose and lips, but she was standing as though nothing was wrong. Her expression was terrifying, all teeth and no empathy showed on her face. He approached slowly so as not to startle her, but finally understood what the screaming had been coming from.

"Please stop! *Please,* I beg for mercy!" Martina wailed from where she lay sprawled out on the stone. Her arms were bound and her face was severely burned, but Tandy hardly moved at her plea. Davian stepped closer, but she didn't acknowledge his presence and he wasn't sure if she could even see him at all.

"Did your baby girl beg for mercy when you fed her to the wolves?" Tandy asked, voice steeled with fury. Davian could only gape at her, so much like Tandy yet someone new all the same stood before him.

"I only did what was best for her," Martina continued to beg.

"You prostituted your daughter so you could be connected to the Royal family," Tandy said, dipping her hand into a small coin purse. She pulled out a shimmering ashy substance that Davian didn't recognize but Martina surely did. She wailed and tried to kick her feet at Tandy, trying to get away but unable to with her bound and broken arm.

"You poisoned my husband and sent me to prison. You used your daughter as bait. You entrapped people, you destroyed livelihoods, you *killed the King*," Tandy seethed, holding the powdered hand out higher and higher as she rose to strike Martina. Davian did nothing, allowing her to act out her own justice as he watched and waited.

"No, please," Martina sobbed, rolling over to protect her face despite the pain of the broken arm bringing a wail from her throat.

"Is that what your little girl begged you and those men?" Tandy asked, reaching her clean hand down to tangle in Martina's hair. She pulled her head back brutally and raised the ash covered hand. She slapped her across the face, sending blood onto the stones. No sound came from Martina right away but she wailed after the pain registered to her. Davian could smell burning but didn't know how until Martina rolled over and exposed the blistered and bubbling skin on her face where Tandy had struck her, a perfect hand print on each side. Davian gasped as he took in her broken skin and finally rushed towards Tandy, arms reaching for hers to inspect what the powder had done to her hand as Martina writhed in pain on the ground.

"What is this?" He asked frantically, grabbing Tandy as she pushed away from him. He held tight to her wrist and pulled it to him, inspecting the ashy hand. "You are burned," he said with a pained voice, looking into her eyes. She didn't look at him, avoiding his gaze as he checked the rest of the marks on her. He could tell she was lost in the adrenaline of the situation, falling back into her dissociative ways that she had been trained to do under high duress. She likely couldn't feel the pain yet, but would realize soon enough. He hoped she'd remain this way until after the carriage with medical supplies arrived.

Martina continued to scream as Tandy stared at her coldly, though Davian could tell the facade she had built for herself was close to crumbling. She had been in survival mode for hours, starving and exhausted, and reality would hit her soon.

"Let's go," he told Tandy as gently as he could before he turned around and addressed Martina. She groaned on the ground as Davian glared down at her. He hoped she was in pain, it was the very least she could do after everything.

"Stand up, Ligotus," Davian snapped. Wordlessly, Tandy pulled away from him and pulled on Martina's arms until she kneeled. With her hands, she snapped the twine that held her legs bound to her wrists. Martina looked up at him with tears in her eyes, though he couldn't see guilt anywhere on her face. He didn't help her to stand and waited for her to struggle to her feet, pulling Tandy back into his arms as they waited. Finally she shakily stood up.

"To the front," Davian commanded with a nod in the direction he wanted her to go. They walked around the house slowly, only the sound of Martina's whimpers and cries filling the air. Davian led them toward his horse who grazed by the hitching post, unperturbed by the noise.

"Kneel," Davian told Martina, pointing to the front entrance of the lakehouse. She continued to whine but complied and sat on her knees in the grass.

Davian knew that Tandy would most likely not eat until she felt safe. She had been shut down emotionally for who knew how long and had amplified it by taking her rage out on Martina. Though it was self defense in Davian's eyes, he knew Tandy would find her behavior hard to wrap her mind around. Instead of offering her food, he offered her a sip of his water pouch. She only took a small sip but he was grateful for it all the same.

"Good girl," he told her, kissing her forehead and pulling her into a tight hug. He kept his eyes on Martina the whole time he breathed in Tandy's scent. "They'll be here soon with supplies for your injuries. I only have rudimentary supplies in the saddle bags. I will hold you until you are ready to talk, or eat," he murmured into her hair. He reached for the one small blanket he had packed and laid it on the ground next to the hitch. He brought the small first aid kit and the breakfasts Felton had given him and pulled Tandy to sit with him.

He cleaned her hand thoroughly where the ash had stuck to it until it was cleared of the material. The pink and oozing blisters looked frightening, but not as bad as he had originally thought. He wiped on a salve and wrapped her hand in a strip of linen, sealing it with a kiss.

"Where is the bag, Tandy?" He asked her gently but firmly. She had tucked it back into her gown, but pulled it from her breast. She handed it to Davian without protest, face still empty of emotion. He was glad she had given it to him so easily, relieved that there hadn't been any after effects from using it. Though he wasn't sure what exactly it was, he knew that if Tandy had found it she had most likely taken it from Martina and used it against her.

Davian placed the powder into his saddle bags and sat down beside Tandy. She was rigid where she sat, tight and bound with anxiety though he could still see no emotion in her. He knew it would come, and waited by her side for the rest of the Knights, for Bryson and Mariana, to finally arrive.

They sat and stared at Martina under the warmth of the sun silently. After an hour, Davian could hear the sound of horses in the distance as they approached. Relieved, Davian stood up and reached his hand out for Tandy. She stood with his help, and they turned to the approaching caravan. Three horses raced toward them ahead of the Knights and the carriage. Bryson leapt off his gelding first and ran toward them, quickly followed by Mariana and Felton.

"You found her!" Mariana cried out, reaching for Tandy. Davian let her close but made sure to watch Tandy's reaction in case she responded with the same violence she used on Martina, though unlikely. She was still locked in a survival mindset and he wanted to ensure everyone's comfort and safety.

"You found *her*, too," Bryson nodded toward Martina as she still kneeled in the grass. "I'll handle that with Felton. Just bring the girls to the carriage and set home," Bryson told him softly. Davian nodded to him as Felton approached, ready to go home.

"Mariana, did she ever give you comfort or medical care after selling you to those men?" Davian asked with an edge to his voice. She hesitated for a minute as she held Tandy but shook her head.

"No, I healed on my own with the occasional maid to help me," she admitted.

"Even for serious injuries?" He asked.

"Even when it was serious and I begged for mercy," she told him.

"Ligotus is to get no compassion from any of the Knights or healers. She has made her choices, and they will be reciprocated," Davian spat, glaring at the woman as she pleaded in the distance.

"Of course, Your Highness," Bryson agreed.

Davian led Tandy to the approaching carriage with Mariana's help. She began to tremble on weak legs as they walked and Davian feared they wouldn't make it before she began to express the emotions she had bottled up over the last twenty four hours. He scooped her up and ran to the Knights as they opened the carriage doors, Mariana tight on his heels.

"We stay here until Duchess Tandanea has calmed down. Then I will return to deal with this," he told the Knights as they entered the coach. They nodded and closed the door behind them.

They sat Tandy down in the center of the bench as Mariana and Davian sat across from her. Davian quickly kneeled before her as her trembling grew stronger, holding his hands at her waist in comfort.

"Do you want to talk about it, or would you just like me to hold you for a while?" He asked her, not expecting an answer.

"I," Tandy croaked, squeezing her eyes shut. "I have to say it," she whispered as her teeth chattered with adrenaline as it fled her system.

"You can wait to talk," he offered, surprised she had managed to say that through the trembling in her lips. Her pained look made him want to protect her for longer.

"I will say it," she breathed through her mouth, finally looking down at him. "It will be harder to speak of it if I wait until the adrenaline is gone," she said as her eyes filled with tears.

"I woke up in a shed where she hit me and offered me to a man that would bear the Royal children," she said, stuttering through her words. Davian bristled at the thought she had been touched by another man and swore he would kill him himself. Tandy placed her hand on Davian's cheek, running her thumb over the crease of his furrowed brow.

"He was handled easily, currently still tied up in the shed I woke up in. He did not harm me," she told him. "The training I underwent was more thorough than I let on," she hesitated. "It involved a lot of survival scenarios such as this." Mariana kneeled down next to Davian and squeezed her arm, tears filling her eyes. Tandy's eyes dripped with tears as they fell continuously down her cheeks.

"I found Martina with illegal substances from the outer cities, where Magic and such are accessible near the Ports and Trading Posts. She admitted things, some of which we already knew," she continued, her voice steadily growing more and more distressed.

"Is she a sorceress?" Davian asked, concerned with Tandy's admission.

"No, surely not," Tandy spat. "But she had the ashes of a sorceress," she said, looking down at her burned hand.

"Is that what that was?" Davian asked.

"That's disgusting," Mariana shuddered.

"She was easy to subdue, and I went easy on her. She should have suffered more," Tandy said through gritted teeth. She shivered again, eyes squeezed shut. Davian could only sit beside her and pull her into a tight hug. He hoped his hands could offer the comfort she needed, though he was sure it wouldn't be enough.

"I'm so sorry I lost you," he told her, nose pressed into her hair. Mariana sat beside them, running her hands over Tandy's bruised legs gently.

"It was no one's fault," Tandy said, voice heavy with tears. "And more importantly, I was able to reveal her plan, or lack thereof," she told him. "The original plan was to have Mariana marry into the throne, which is why our betrothal was targeted. When she realized Mariana's paternity, she was heavy handed in her method of controlling him and he overdosed on Lethe before he could claim Mariana as his eldest. She used people through bribery or blackmail, and the ashes as a means of breaking through opposition, literally. She distributed it herself, made it herself. Such an easy arrest to make, she revealed what we did not know."

"Your safety is more important to me than anything else in this Realm," Davian rasped, hardly managing to get the words past the lump in his throat.

"The kingdom is more important, Davian," she scolded him through tears. He couldn't help the desperate laugh as it bubbled from his throat, relief and terror fighting for release in his body. She was so stubborn, even after being kidnapped and rescuing herself. He squeezed her tighter, holding her as hard as he could. She gripped his hair in one hand and Mariana's hand in the other, just as desperate for connection and reassurance as they were.

"I'm so sorry, Tandy," Mariana wept, cheek pressed to Davian's shoulder.

"You were a victim of Martina long before I was, Mar," she said softly. Her tears fell heavier than before as she clung to them. She sniffed, pressing her cheek against Davian's chest. Sobs fell from her throat unfettered, and Davian knew she had held onto her emotions for as long as she could before giving in to them finally.

Like a storm, he had known it was coming and could only brace himself while it lasted. He held her tight as she wailed and cried and screamed, nothing but gentle hums and reassurances falling from his lips. Despite her anguish, her rage and despair, he held her through it. Mariana cried with her, knowing her fear even clearer than Davian wanted to know. After a while, she quieted. She had spent all of her energy surviving, and fell asleep against Davian's chest. Mariana moved to the other bench and sat down, giving Davian room to lay Tandy down. He sat next to Mariana and sighed, rubbing his face as he braced himself for what was next.

"What will you do?" Mariana asked.

"A gentleman doesn't harm a woman," he said sagely. "But fuck if I don't want to kill her with my bare hands."

"Give her no mercy," Mariana told him, turning to him with fire in her eyes.

"She will be punished," he agreed. "I'm sending you home, make sure she knows I am right behind you," he told her as he reached for the door. He gave her one last smile before stepping back onto the ground, sending the carriage home. Davian walked towards Martina as she still sat on the ground.

"The man's in the shed," he told Bryson who nodded and sent a few men to detain him.

"What are you thinking?" Bryson asked him as they waited. Martina looked up at them from where she sat with a steady glare. Davian told Bryson everything that Tandy had told him within Martina's earshot. Her eyes widened as he murmured but he ignored her until he was done speaking to his friend, and then finally glanced at her with disdain.

"We need to get a full list of victims out of this bitch, by any means necessary," he met her gaze evenly.

"You won't get shit out of me," she spat on the ground by their feet, though her wide eyes said otherwise.

"How sweet," Davian said, stepping forward. "She still thinks she has a say in this," he pulled the ashes from his pocket. She flinched when she saw it, but kept her glare pointed at him.

"You will give me what I want, *and* I will punish you. You will not be able to barter your secrets for your safety. I will harm you just as much, if not more, than you have harmed those around you. For harming my *wife*, the *Queen*," he growled, "you will face my full wrath."

Martina stared at him, silent and fearful. He smiled as the man that intended to rape Tandy was brought into view and glanced at Bryson.

"I'll have everything set up," Bryson told him.

"We'll need someone to take down the names and damages that Lady Ligotus is guilty of," Davian said.

"I won't tell you *anything*," Martina spat. Davian turned to her and grabbed her by the arm Tandy had broken. She screamed but he pulled her to her feet, not caring for her comfort in the slightest.

"You'll tell me everything," he yelled into her face. "Every person you so much as said hello to in the last twenty years. I want names from every theft, every bribe, every human being you bartered for your own pleasure," he continued. "I want to know *everything* Mariana experienced at your hand, by sending her into the beds of men unfitting for the horse shit on the bottom of my boot."

Behind him, Knights guided by Bryson brought chairs and a small table. They were dirty and weathered, likely from within the once beautiful chateau. As they approached, Bryson handed Davian a notebook and pen to take notes. Another Knight sat down with a large stationary set and readied his pen. Davian dropped Martina's arm, sending her tumbling to the floor. She sobbed in pain, but he did not care. Any empathy he had was with Tandy and Mariana, and they were miles away.

"We're waiting, Martina. Who, when and where are these ashes from? When did your plan to destroy a long standing family begin? What families did you destroy? What are the names of the men that you bartered your own daughter with?" Davian fired off question after question, hardly stopping for a breath. When she made no move to respond, he held the small bag in his hand and opened it slowly.

"I wonder if this will hurt me just as much as it hurt you," Davian asked. "Well, it hadn't hurt Tandanea at all. It must not be that bad," he shrugged as he dipped his hand into it. Martina visibly flinched, and Davian waited for her to speak.

"Gods *damn it,*" she whined.

"When did it start, Ligotus? When did your treachery begin?" He asked again, rubbing the ash between his fingers. He raised his hand as though he would strike her and held the pose, though he had no intention of doing so. He wouldn't have his reputation marred by this woman.

"The moment I knew I was pregnant," she hissed. Davian shook his head in distaste, lowering his hand.

"Have her walk behind the horses the whole way home," he said. "I don't care if your feet are bloody from the trek or if you're dragged behind."

"You have quite the long list to bring us through, Ligotus. It would be in your best interest to share who was affected by your plans," Bryson said as he nodded to Felton and the scribe.

"I won't say anything more," she said. "I don't think the Prince is man enough to make me talk," she spat as Davian stood there. He raised his hand quickly and pressed it hard to her throat. She tried to gasp but couldn't as he squeezed the breath from her.

"There is very little I am unwilling to do to you," he said in an eerily calm voice. "In fact, there is *nothing* I would stop my Knights from inflicting upon you, either. Martina Ligotus, you are purely at my mercy now," he squeezed tighter and watched as her legs flailed pathetically. His hand started to burn from the ash and he dropped her to the ground.

"You will speak of all the crimes you have committed, you will expose every secret and every name of anyone you have slighted in any capacity. This is your final warning," he told her. He turned to Bryson and the other Knights before he spoke again. "I would prefer to do this while we are on the way home. Can you scribe on the back of a horse?" The Knights nodded, cleaning up the items they had just laid out. Davian didn't feel bad for making them change positions, he only wanted to be home and away from the barren lake house.

"You will tell us everything," Davian looked down at Martina as she still coughed in the dirt, catching her breath. "You will not rest until it is done." She glowered up at him but said nothing, but he knew she would submit as her legs grew weary and she was threatened to be dragged behind as they waited for her answers.

"Is there anything else you need from this place?" He asked Felton and Bryson.

"I think we have everything we need from this location. All the clues have been documented and now we simply only need the confession, though at this point it is hardly necessary for arrest and conviction," Felton told him.

"I do think we will be able to unravel the web she wove all these years, and the threat of the Crown against any titled families in the Royal Circle would be wise to admit their compliance or their unwilling manipulations in order to remain titled," Bryson said. He nodded, accepting their words as they made their way to the horses.

Davian climbed into the saddle of his ever patient horse after untying her from the post and headed toward the main road. Bryson followed closely behind while Sir Felton stayed back.

"We will be right behind you, Your Highness," Felton called after him as they began tying a rope around Martina's waist. The man lay unconscious and a few of the Knights had to lift him into an empty saddle on a horse with no rider. They began to walk the long trek home, and despite the desire for Davian to rush ahead and meet up with the carriage, he found he was unable to do so. He couldn't leave the vile woman behind in case she managed to escape his grasp once again.

He would have her executed the moment she completed her confession, and vowed to ensure she left *nothing* out during the hours-long walk they had ahead of them. His body was tired, but he could only feel bloodlust at the thought of finally ending the curse Martina had left on his family. It would finally be the end of her reign in the shadows.

***

By midday, Martina's body sagged with exhaustion. Her feet were red with blood as blisters filled her shoes. The scribe had managed to get down several names and accomplices from Martina as she continued talking the whole way. It was evident she liked to be at their beck and call, despite her predicament, and made each answer difficult to extract as she spoke in circles. When that happened, Davian brought the group to a faster pace, leaving Martina gasping for breath as she caught up.

The heat wore on her, though, and he could see the exhaustion on her body as they neared the castle. Any moment now, she would beg for rest and sustenance and would only receive them when she revealed her final crimes.

"Water," she begged, coughing and stumbling behind the horse she was tied to.

"Answers," he replied coolly. Another hour passed that way before she wept, finally giving them the truths they needed.

She revealed the families she had affected, the ones she stole from or bargained with. She exposed the names of those she drugged or had offered Mariana to in exchange for monetary support or affluence. She revealed the families she forced into servitude, the other girls she had facilitated marriages to in exchange for money or Lethe. Many of the men had told her of the girls they wished to acquire, and she would take their money and manipulate the girl's parents until a betrothal or forced wedding occurred. He would make sure that the men working with Martina to arrange marriages against the daughters of noblemen were arrested. He planned on absolving the marriages made with coercion after full interviews were made with the girls.

"Find the men that stole their brides, and bring their families here. We need to fix this before it goes any further, and I will not have honorable bloodlines destroyed over this," he told Byrson as they walked home. "We need the cities ransacked for any trace of Lethe left behind and if *anyone* is in possession of it or found to be brewing it, they will be jailed." Bryson sent two of the Knights ahead to gather documents for the dozens of arrests they would be making to have it ready for them by the time they arrived to the castle, along with new orders for the soldiers in the far reaches of the Realm.

With each passing admission of guilt, Martina's list of crimes continued to grow until finally, she revealed her hand in Tandy's exile.

"I had a servant I paid to alert me when letters from the north were delivered. She hid them for me until I arrived with Lethe and dosed Mariana and you with them in a brew that intensified negative emotions. You would never have been able to read what that girl sent, I made sure of it all in order for Mariana to be your chosen one," she had rambled. "It was a blessed day when I realized where they had sent her, so far away from you."

Martina was without any empathy for any of the crimes she revealed, and the tears dried on the burnt flesh of her face were only shed for herself. It made Davian sick that someone such as this had been haunting the halls of his home. So many people were affected but none were able to stop her as the Lethe and ash had been too powerful to stop. The only thing the families could do was do as she told them to, to save themselves from additional hardships she inflicted upon them. The more she told them of her history, the more they collectively felt despair, and then rage. As she admitted to drugging both Martina and Davian in small doses to ensure they never looked for Tandy when their curiosities for the girl rose, all Davian felt was a cool wash of anger.

"How did this go undiscovered for so long?" Davian shouted at Sir Felton multiple times throughout the day as more truths were revealed. Martina's answer filled him with even more rage than before, and he couldn't wait to have her sentenced to death because of it.

"Anyone that attempted to reveal my plans was dealt with," she had said after his final outburst. The truth was that she would dose them with enough Lethe at the slightest hint of betrayal, enough that would render them mad with the elixir. It would eliminate their ability to communicate effectively with anyone, let alone reveal those truths to the King's Guard and the King himself.

By the time Davian walked through the doors of his castle, he had heard enough from Martina to issue his sentence. There was nothing more to be done until the public was called to the hearing and the additional arrests were made. Until everyone connected to Martina's crimes had shared their testimonies, she would remain alive. He would *not* let her be in peace in the meantime, though. He stormed down the hallways and escorted the Knights along with Martina to the dungeon. He gathered the keys perched on the arch of the entrance and led them to the smallest, dankest cell there was.

"Untie her arms and strip her down. She is to wear the prisoner's garbs," he said. The Knights complied immediately despite her protests. "Two Knights at the cell doors at all times, and two at the exits," he ordered as he locked the cell as Martina shivered with her bruised arm and bloodied feet. He looked down at her and shook his head.

"What is most unfortunate, Lady Ligotus, is that had you come to *me* with the accusation that Mariana was my sister and of my father's blood, I would have granted her place in the family line. It would have fallen to both my and Mariana's discretion when it came to the throne, but I would have assured your place in the Royal Circle and the Royal Quarters no matter the outcome, as well. Now, your daughter still has a place here but unfortunately for you, you do *not*." He turned away, intending to leave when Mariana called out to him.

"There's a cure!" She cried, reaching through the bars. He was unmoved by her plea, though, and did not believe her. "It needs magic to be made, but a cure *exists*," she insisted. "Please, I can acquire the cure and bring it back if you grant me mercy!"

He ignored her and made his way through the dungeon and headed to his rooms where he hoped to find Tandy and Mariana. As they walked, the Knights told Bryson they had all of the documents ready for the arrests, and planned on sending for the men and families for the trial.

"When you return, the trial and sentencing will begin. Make haste, I do not want to risk the prisoner falling ill in the dungeon before the trial," Davian warned. "I want the inner cities raided for any more illegal substances, and any apothecaries with unapproved ingredients looked into." With a nod, Bryson looked over the paperwork before nodding to them. "We need to find out if a cure is a possibility," he added. "Though I don't believe her, I do need to figure out if it's possible to cure those affected by her treason."

"On it," Bryson agreed. "Everything looks to be in order in these documents, send men to each estate. Make sure they believe leniency will be granted for those loyal to the crown and those with additional charges to be made against the Ligotus family," Bryson told them. "And what of Lord Ligotus?"

"Lord Ligotus cannot be retained as a witness as the Lethe seems to have done him worse than the Queen," a Knight told them as they neared Davian's doors. "He's still in what can only be described as a coma, speaking nonsense. At best, we can use him as the evidence of what Lethe is capable of, but nothing more."

"That's unfortunate, but truly will not affect the case we have against Martina," Bryson told them before dismissing them to their next task. Davian wasted no time pushing through his bedroom doors and found both Mariana and Tandy resting peacefully in his bed. He sighed, relieved to see them, and told Bryson to take his woman and leave.

"She is not my woman unless she declares it, but I shall take her to another room anyway, Your Highness," he chuckled as they neared the bed. "Mariana, I am here to relieve you of protective duties," he said softly, running his hand over her arm. She sat up quickly, looking around the room in surprise, but calmed when she realized who had woken her. With Bryson's help, she climbed from the bed and left Tandy rubbing her eyes as they left the room. When they were gone and the Guards updated on their assigned positions, Davian pulled Tandy to her feet and wrapped his arms tightly around her. She squeezed him back, breathing into his neck. He felt her heartbeat, the breath she breathed.

"We must scrub ourselves clean," he told her, pulling her gown from her shoulders. He led her to the bathroom, stripping her of her clothes.

"I was cleaned when I arrived," she said through a yawn but made no move to prevent him from undressing her.

"I must personally inspect that you have washed away any remnants of the day we have had," he told her, voice thick with tears as he tried to swallow them down. "Not a *trace* of that witch on our skin," he said as she was bared to him. She began to tug on his clothes, pulling his riding leathers and every layer he still had on.

"Get in," he told her as he turned on the water. He stepped in with her and washed her hair and body again before lathering himself, and rinsed them off thoroughly.

"I love you," he told her as the water dripped down their cheeks.

"I love you," she said as she kissed him gently.

They dried off and laid in the bed, hair still wet as Tandy brushed it out. They said nothing but kept close before tucking themselves under the covers. Pulling Tandy close, Davian curled behind her until they were wrapped together entirely. He kissed her cheek and breathed into her neck as their hair clung to his skin.

"Sleep well," she whispered as he began to drift off to sleep, completely exhausted.

***

Davian woke as the sun streamed into the room, catching his eyes. He rubbed his face and yawned, stretching to his full length. Tandy stirred next to him and matched his movements before turning towards him. He looked over at her and nearly gasped as her golden curls caught the morning light. She was so beautiful he could only stare at her, eyes traveling down her bare skin.

"When will the trials start?" She asked him, her words a stark contrast to his thoughts.

"As soon as the rest of the accused are transported back to the castle, along with their families," he told her, running his finger down her arm.

"How long will that take?" She persisted, edging herself closer to him.

"As long as it takes," he said. "I assure you, there is only one outcome from charging those criminals with their crimes. The cities will be cleaned out, Ligotus will be dead, Mariana will be recognized as a Tolzari after my crowning ceremony to assure no additional drama. Everything is going to be resolved properly, most likely by the end of the month. Sir Felton is leading these commands, and Bryson is handling everything until I join him later on." He continued, pulling her closer with each word.

"And what about --" Tandy started but he cut her off with a kiss.

"Anything else can be discussed *after* I've made love to you, Tandanea. Now stop talking and let me taste you," he kissed her gently, hands sliding down her back. She sighed into his kiss and wrapped her arms around him, locking her fingers in his hair.

Davian ran his lips over her cheek and down her neck before gently biting under her jaw where it met her throat, bringing a moan from her lips. Though he was desperate for her, he kept his pace slow. She pulled at his hair as she wordlessly urged him closer, slotting her leg over his hip. He ran his lips back to hers and grasped her ass tightly before sliding his knees between her own. He leaned over her and settled his hips into hers, their bodies still bare from the bath the night before. Her pussy was warm against his cock and he ground against her. She squirmed under him as she spread her legs further, urging him to where she wanted him to go. He trailed his fingers toward her pussy but she groaned and reached for his cock, guiding him to her entrance.

"Fuck, Tandy, let me take my time on you," he gasped as the tip of his cock entered her.

"No, I need you *now*," she begged him, stroking him further into her.

He rolled his hips until he was buried inside of her, bringing another moan from Tandy's lips. He lay still for a moment, kissing her deeply and urgently as she pulled at his hair and wrapped her legs around him. She tried to move her hips as he laid atop her, but he didn't budge. She whimpered and gasped as he covered her with kisses and bites around her collarbone.

"Please, Davian," she gasped, pulling his hair harder. He groaned at her desperation as she trembled beneath him, begging for his cock. Without pulling his hips from hers, he brought one of his knees closer to her ass and leaned further into her. She keened with the change in depth, back arching. He pulled his other knee under her and raised her ass with his hand, wrapping his other hand into the hair at the nape of her neck, forcing her to arch her body. He kissed her neck and rolled his hips, teasing her with the pressure.

"Oh my *fuck*, Davian I swear I *need* you to move," she begged.

"Hmm," he said, pretending to be unaffected by the pleasure he felt as she pleaded beneath him. "I think I could make you come just like this," he rolled his hips in a small circle, his cock pressing inside her insistently. Her eyes rolled as he moved, barely a sound from her lips as the pleasure hit her. Her legs shook with need, but he maintained the gentle motions despite her gasps.

"You should have let me taste your pussy, Tandy, but you were in *such* a rush to have me inside of you," he breathed into her ear. She moaned, scratching at his back.

"Need you," she cried, tears forming in the corner of her eyes. His hand was still locked in her hair, preventing her from turning her head. He licked a trail from her jaw to her chest before returning to her lips for a kiss. He ran his tongue along hers, biting her lip. He released his grip in her hair and wiped her eyes. She looked up at him with rosy cheeks and his cock throbbed at the sight of her. She looked well fucked, beautiful beyond words. He kissed her hard once more and finally gave her what she wanted.

"*Yes,*" she cried as he pumped his cock deep into her pussy. He pulled away slowly before plunging back into her, a stream of pleas falling from her lips. She wrapped her thighs around his waist and met his thrusts urgently, running her hands over every inch of him.

"I love you," he told her as he fucked her slowly, running his thumb along her cheek.

"I love you," she breathed as he reached the spot that brought a moan to her lips. She kissed him fervently, her grip on his shoulders near painful. Davian pumped his cock into her with increasing desperation.

"Oh fuck, Dav," Tandy cried out before her pussy tightened around his cock as she orgasmed hard. She moaned until her legs trembled, and gasped at the oversensitivity.

"You'll take what I give you, baby," he growled into her ear as he continued fucking her, not changing his pace. She groaned, back arching as her pussy continued to throb around his cock. His breath hitched as she massaged him inside of her, but he continued despite the desperate urge to come as fast as he could.

He kissed her hard one final time before raising his body until he kneeled with her ass propped against his thighs. Tandy cried out as his cock pounded into her as he continued his brutally slow pace. He ran his hands over her waist, the curve of her hips. He trailed his thumb over her pussy and felt the space where their bodies met, sending more pleas from Tandy's lips.

"Oh *please, please, please,*" she begged, scratching at his arms. He finally gave her the mercy she pleaded for. His hips sped up as he pounded into her hard, drawing her feet over his shoulders. He felt his orgasm nearing as he rolled his hips into her. He ran his thumb over her clit, wanting to bring her over the edge with him once again.

Suddenly, Davian dropped her legs and laid her back into the bed, spreading her knees apart as she gasped and trembled. He fell back into her with a grunt, bodies flush together as he fucked her. He wanted to be close to her face, to see her as he came. He wanted to make love to her, to bring stars to her eyes. She moaned into his lips as she ran her hands over his shoulders before tangling in his hair. With each pump of his cock, she cried out and continued to match his thrusts.

Finally, blissfully, Davian gasped and pounded into her before he came hard, filling her with his seed. As he rolled his hips into her, he felt her tensing against him with a desperate look on her face, and reached between their bellies to rub her clit while he rode out the aftershocks still rolling through his body. She came with a cry, kissing him fiercely as they rolled their hips together one last time.

He kissed her throat, resting his body over hers before rolling to his side. They laced their fingers together, facing one another as they caught their breath. They listened to the birds beyond the balcony doors as the sun rose higher into the sky, saying nothing for a long while.

"I think we shall finish our honeymoon this week, and let Sir Felton and Sir Bryson handle everything in between as far as the trials go," Davian murmured finally, twirling a strand of Tandy's hair in his fingers as lust swelled in him once again.

"We can have breakfast with them in the lounge and let them know," Tandy offered.

"I have a better idea," Davian said, pulling her closer to rest her head on his chest. "I will write a note with my Royal seal for each of them stating my desire, and we will continue our honeymoon *properly* this time. I will not be letting you go for quite some time," he said, palming her ass as his cock began to throb with need.

"Whatever pleases you, Your Highness," she said playfully, leaning into his touch.

"Good girl," he breathed into her ear. "Now lie on your belly," he said as he rolled her from his chest. He placed his knees between her thighs and settled behind her, squeezing her ass. He leaned over her and pressed a trail of kisses into her skin.

"I love you," he groaned as he sank into her. Silently, he thanked the gods for their hand in giving him everything he ever wanted. He didn't want to waste another second of his time in this life. Leaning down, he kissed his wife's cheek. Tandy smiled softly and sighed.

"I love you, too."

Twenty Nine

Seven Years Later

Tandy had read through the Queen's journal many times over the years. She wasn't sure what she would find in her delicate script, but as the days passed it was somehow a comfort to Tandy. She knew she should put these memories behind her, but the pull to the now dull ink was hard to fight. Despite the harrowing tales in the book, the lessons within its pages were evident. The Queen had not suffered needlessly, and justice was eventually served.

Tandy placed the worn leather bound book onto the table and picked up her own journal that had long been in disuse. She flicked through the pages and frowned at the early entries as the names of victims and their experiences filled the pages. The Ligotus name had been corrupted through its roots, and many had been executed for what they had committed against the crown and its people.

Martina had coerced, manipulated, blackmailed, drugged, abused and prostituted anyone that came into her path. Along with the men she had assisted in kidnapping young girls to be their wives, the trial was resolved within days. Each of the accused had their crimes listed for the judgment of the soon to be King, with the addition to the witnesses' testimonies. Essentially, the trials were over before they started. Martina and all of the others facing similar crimes plead their guilt and begged for mercy. They were executed publicly and Tandy still felt a sick sense of satisfaction when she remembered that day.

Lethe had been a plague to the Royal Circle and to the kingdom as a whole. With the majority of the loyal subjects affected by the side effects of the elixir, the birth rates were dangerously low along with a rise in civil unrest and violence throughout the realm. Despite the overall state of health, wealth, and prosperity the kingdom enjoyed after Lethe's eradication, the efforts were slow and the birth rate had not improved. As months passed without significant improvement, a relative of Sir Felton proved to be the help they needed to restore their community.

"I may know a healer that will be able to help us," Sir Felton had suggested one day during a meeting with Bryson and Davian. "My son was just married to a woman with healing expertise, and I would call upon them if you give me permission, Your Highness."

They had nothing to lose, and so a letter was sent with haste to the Fairwood Estate with a plea for their assistance in a matter that was beyond their own abilities to fix. All they could do was hope, and in only a few weeks they received a response. Instead of a letter, they were met by Arden and Willow Fairwood who had traveled their way upon receiving their plea. Immediately, the young woman gathered as much information as she could about the elixir and began to brew a cure for those still affected by Lethe.

"I will have more of this made for your kingdom when I am home, and will have it delivered to you," Will had told them as she offered the cure to them. "This is for you, Your Highness," she had told Davian as she handed him a jar of the strange liquid. Though he narrowed his eyes at it, he took it from Will without a word before glancing between Bryson and Felton. Felton's son, nearly identical to his father, only smiled at his hesitation. Willow laughed and assured him it was the same drink that would cure his mother, but suggested another victim be cured first to ease Davian's concern for his safety.

"We can try to cure your mother first," Tandy had whispered to him that day. They had lost hope in her ever returning to normal, and were out of options. She was certain to be bedridden for the remainder of her life as she continued to deteriorate before their eyes. Davian had sighed but agreed, and only hours after his mother sipped the drink, she was able to feed herself and engage in real conversation once again. The relief in her eyes as she gazed at Davian and the hug she pulled him into when she realized her efforts to protect him had been successful had brought tears to Tandy's eyes.

From then on, it was obvious that Will *was* able to restore the minds of those unable to regain cognitive abilities, the ones still trapped in the oblivion the elixir had caused leaving everyone stunned at the turn it would mean for the kingdom. Tandy encouraged Davian to take the healing potion despite his lingering paranoia over being drugged so they could begin distributing the cure within the following days. The change in him was small and almost unnoticeable, but his demeanor was more relaxed following those days and she was forever grateful for it.

"You do not need to take this, but I offer it as it is my nature to do so," Willow told them as she and Arden made their goodbyes. Will offered them a small potion in her outstretched hand. "This is a healing agent for fertility," she said quietly, out of earshot of those around them. Tandy was grateful for her discretion, and Davian took the potion with a curious look on his face. "I offer it as a friendly gesture, it is up to you if you want to use it or not. It has a very stable shelf life, as well, if you want to hold onto it for a few years." She smiled and stepped away, linking her hand with her husband's. With kind words and a sweet farewell, the Fairwoods left them with enough supplies to begin the process of healing the individuals nearest the Royal Circle.

Mrs Fairwood had made enough of the healing potion to distribute throughout the kingdom and though it wasn't enough to cure everyone at once, it was the start they needed and they were grateful for her swift efforts. Along with the cure, the Fairwoods also left a plethora of other medications for the Royal stores. Everyone within the castle walls slept a little easier after the kind young woman had marched through the halls.

The days after Davian's mother had been healed, the kingdom seemed to flourish. With only a few weeks with Lorraine's guidance, Tandy felt stronger in her role as soon to be Queen. They began to settle into a new routine and implemented many structural policies that would protect the kingdom from any other plague that tried to creep into their midst.

Davian soaked in the attention his mother gave him with an open heart, still as much his mother's baby boy as he'd been the day he was born. Despite how happy she was for Davian and his mother, Tandy couldn't help but feel a twinge of jealousy that her family was still completely absent. Whenever she saw Lorraine's love for her son, it left a bittersweet feeling in her heart. Until one day when the Queen called for her to join her in the drawing room and the last of the secrets in the kingdom were finally revealed.

"Tandy," her mother cried when she entered the room, pulling her into a tight hug. Tandy was shocked as Lorraine smiled encouragingly behind Simone. Tandy's hands trembled as she returned her mother's embrace, confused, angry and relieved all at the same time. Behind Simone was her father, and all of her siblings. Blonde with grey eyes and all very tall, her brothers and sisters were nearly identical between them.

"Forgive me, my love," Simone told her. After a long hug from her mother and father, Tandy was guided to the table where they began to explain where they had been for the last several years.

"We saw the elixir's power when we were pregnant," Lorraine explained.

"First, when Lorraine gave birth to Davian, and then when I gave birth to you. Abstaining from the parties and the wine of the Royal Circle due to pregnancy, the elixir's effects were clear to us when *we* were clear of it," Simone said.

"We decided the only way to protect you was to begin our own coup to prevent the one that was rooting in the Circle," Lorraine added.

"By binding you in a long, *long*, engagement, we hoped that you and Davian would be able to marry no matter what happened in the Royal family," Simone stroked Tandy's hand. "We prayed that you would fall in love and overcome the effects of the elixir, and see through the web that was being weaved before the potion completely wiped out our own minds."

"On the night of your betrothal ball, we realized the elixir was too strong to overcome. We saw how it made its way through the ball room before you were even announced into the hall," Lorraine continued. "We saw it grip Davian, and we feared what would happen if it got to you, too. We couldn't risk it."

"We sent you away to the Reform school, though it pained me greatly to do," Simone told her with tears in her eyes. "Of all the places to go, no one would follow you there. The rules would be too harsh and it would be seen as a punishment. We let Martina believe it was because of the rumor she started that night in order to keep you from her clutches."

"The reform school was our idea, our last attempt at giving you freedom and education where no one would look for you. Simone left with your father and hid away in a far reach of the Realm, hiding their location along with limited correspondence to be completely untraceable," Lorraine sighed heavily.

"After a few years, I was suddenly blessed with the ability to bear children again. It hurt me to stay away from you as your siblings grew, but it was the only thing we could do to keep you untouched from the potion," Simone said sadly.

Tandy wasn't sure how to feel about their admittance at first, but as they continued to explain themselves she only felt relieved. To finally know the truth, to finally see her family after all those years, she was grateful. Despite the years she suffered in the reform school, it had been worth it in the end. She and Davian had managed to heal the kingdom through their betrothal despite the efforts Martina had made to end their connection. They had released their subjects of the plague that haunted them all, and their families were restored. Her mother's apology and the Queen's truths had been all that Tandy needed to begin her own healing.

With all of Tandy's new siblings, Davian made sure to officially add Mariana to the Royal records once he was crowned King. With the new title of Crown Princess, her personality blossomed. Finally allowed to explore herself, she grew stronger and braver in the social settings she once found frightening. She had been unable to make friends over the years aside from Tandy or Davian and she found luncheons and garden parties to be her favorite.

With her newfound sense of self and inner growth, Mariana was changed. Her confidence made her even more beautiful than before, setting her eyes aglow with purpose and a desire to be in the world. Bryson was hopelessly in love with her and finally asked her to marry him when he felt she had enough time to recover from her unfortunate past. Mariana was thrilled and so ensued a very short engagement, followed by a long honeymoon. With Willow's potion, they were able to welcome their first child the following year, with another three children born over the next several years. They were happy, and their children were loved and spoiled by their Auntie Tandy along with the rest of the family they had made for themselves.

The girls in the reform school were released back to their families, and the families that had been aware of the true nature of the school were punished as well. Though the girls would never return to their original selves, Tandy had hope they would find solace in their freedom. The girls unfortunate enough to not have a close relative to be sent to, were relocated to the castle with the offer of temporary housing until their distant relatives were able to be contacted. The horrors faced at that school were documented and the Headmistress along with her Guards were dutifully punished with manual labor on the farms. The working conditions were much as the girls experienced under their control, and Tandy felt her meals were all the more sweeter knowing the hands that supplied it.

Much like the girls from the reform school, the young ladies that were coerced into marriages made under duress were annulled on the basis that the marriages had been made with deceit and lacked proper documentation and parental approval before the girls were all but kidnapped from their homes. Because of the fertility issue caused by Lethe within the men and women, the young women were blessed to be free of the marriages without any children born of the unions. They were absolved of the marital union and returned to their families, with compensations for the troubled years they were away. When they were given the medicine supplied by Mrs. Fairwood, the girls were able to find suitable husbands and start families of their own.

The young maid that had been coerced by Ligotus remained a part of their lives in the castle. Her mother admitted to an affair with the King during a summer in which her husband had taken a mistress and her paternity was confirmed when her smile neatly matched both Davian and Mariana's, down to their lovely brown eyes. They were unsure how the Lethe hadn't prevented the pregnancy considering the infertility it caused at first, but the Queen had offered the theory that it had been the year she had attempted to limit contact with Martina in an effort to distance Davian from the chaos. By traveling from province to province without a proper itinerary to label their presence, she had attempted to keep the King from imbibing Lethe. Though Lethe had been limited, his premarital affairs had not been. Tandy had even asked Mrs Fairwood her opinion, but all she could say was that sometimes a life was meant to be and there was no real reason for it.

"She must be here for a reason," she had written in her letter to Tandy. "Find the reason."

It hadn't taken long to find Leesa's calling, and nearly at every ball, the youngest Tolzari sister could be found singing at the harp. Her musicality was angelic and Mariana's children hovered around her whenever she sang nursery rhymes. Tandy's favorite evenings ended with one of her nieces or nephews snoring softly on her lap as the sound of Leesa's airy voice filled the room in a tranquil glow.

Despite trying for years, Tandy and Davian had not borne any children. His mother had had difficulty conceiving, as well, so they knew that Lethe had not been the sole cause of their issues. The fertility medication that was offered to them stayed exactly where it was on the stationary table, always in eyesight as though just its image could provide them with an heir. Tandy felt that she still had plenty more years left to bear children, despite having just turned thirty. Her face still had a youthlike appearance, but

Mariana teased her that it was from the lack of movement her facial muscles experienced in Tandy's life. She was probably right, as Davian had grown a crease between his brow over the years that Tandy had grown quite fond of.

Nevertheless, Tandy was not concerned about the time that had passed without a successful pregnancy. She and Davian had work to do as King and Queen to help the kingdom prosper and grow into the land it used to be before Lethe, and she knew a child would impact their ability to react swiftly to their subjects. Their lack of heirs was a blessing in her eyes but she knew Davian didn't feel the same. She did not need to bear Davian's children in order to feel fulfilled and was in fact happy with their life so far. She knew that if they never had children she would be okay with it, but she also knew that Davian would be heartbroken. Though she did not want to put Davian through another loss like the one she had experienced a few years prior ever again, she could only remain hopeful that they would welcome a baby one day in the future.

Davian was most worried that the throne would fall into the wrong hands and that the next surviving heir in the Tolzari bloodline would risk their lives yet again needlessly. Her reminder was that their nephews and nieces were next in line for the throne, and their kind and loving hearts would be perfect for their kingdom. Though it eased some of his worry, his stress over the topic consumed him despite his refusal to use the fertility drugs that Will had left for him.

"I will provide you with my children the way the gods desire me to," he told her, fighting back the tears in his eyes. She had prayed over that very statement every day at the shrine, asking every god for the right answer. He was troubled more than a newly crowned King should be and wanted to make it right no matter what she had to do.

Until one day, she woke up from a dream where she had placed the medicine into Davian's coffee and watched him swallow it with a smile. She had been disturbed that she would dream of drugging Davian after the past they had experienced, but it was impossible to remove from her mind.

She glanced at the small jar still sitting on the stationary table as she wrote a letter to Willow, asking for clarity on the perplexing dream and what she should do about Davian and their lack of successful pregnancies. Mrs Fairwood always seemed to have answers for everything, and Tandy knew she would have an answer for this, too.

As she handed the completed letter to the Knight at her door, Tandy realized what she had to do even without Willow's input. She called for a large breakfast to be brought to their bedroom as Davian snored behind her, still tired from Mariana's birthday ball the night before.

When Davian awoke, she would give him breakfast in bed with a large mug of coffee, just the way he liked it. She would pick up the fertility vial that she had placed on the breakfast tray and pour some into a small glass of juice. She would take a big gulp and drink it down quickly, placing the remainder of the vial on the tray. She would say nothing, and let Davian decide if he would meet her in the middle or not. She would leave his juice next to the vial, and sip her coffee patiently. It would not be his fertility or hers, it was *theirs*. And after he made his choice and they ate their breakfast, she would make love to him like her very life depended on it.

The sunrise was breathtaking as she leaned against the balcony door, hopeful for the future and anything that may come.

Instagram: @brittanyleannecarr.author
Tiktok: @brittanylcarr.author
Facebook: Brittany Leanne Carr; Author

www.ingramcontent.com/pod-product-compliance
Lightning Source LLC
Chambersburg PA
CBHW051132300726
48978CB00011B/251